IN THE DREAMING HOUR

A Contemporary Romantic Work of Fiction

By Kathryn Le Veque

Copyright © 2016 by Kathryn Le Veque
Print Edition
All rights reserved. No part of this book may be used or reproduced in any manner whatsoever without written permission, except in the case of brief quotations embodied in critical articles or reviews.

Printed by Kathryn Le Veque Novels in the United States of America

Text copyright 2016 by Kathryn Le Veque
Cover copyright 2016 by Kathryn Le Veque

Kathryn Le Veque Novels

Medieval Romance:

The de Russe Legacy:
The White Lord of Wellesbourne
The Dark One: Dark Knight
Beast
Lord of War: Black Angel
The Falls of Erith
The Iron Knight

The de Lohr Dynasty:
While Angels Slept (Lords of East Anglia)
Rise of the Defender
Steelheart
Spectre of the Sword
Archangel
Unending Love
Shadowmoor
Silversword

Great Lords of le Bec:
Great Protector
To the Lady Born (House of de Royans)
Lord of Winter (Lords of de Royans)

Lords of Eire:
The Darkland (Master Knights of Connaught)
Black Sword
Echoes of Ancient Dreams (time travel)

De Wolfe Pack Series:
The Wolfe
Serpent
Scorpion (Saxon Lords of Hage – Also related to The Questing)
Walls of Babylon
The Lion of the North
Dark Destroyer

Ancient Kings of Anglecynn:
The Whispering Night
Netherworld

Battle Lords of de Velt:
The Dark Lord
Devil's Dominion

Reign of the House of de Winter:
Lespada
Swords and Shields (also related to The Questing, While Angels Slept)

De Reyne Domination:
Guardian of Darkness
The Fallen One (part of Dragonblade Series)

Unrelated characters or family groups:
The Gorgon (Also related to Lords of Thunder)
The Warrior Poet (St. John and de Gare)
Tender is the Knight (House of d'Vant)
Lord of Light
The Questing (related to The Dark Lord, Scorpion)
The Legend (House of Summerlin)

**The Dragonblade Series: (Great

Marcher Lords of de Lara)
Dragonblade
Island of Glass (House of St. Hever)
The Savage Curtain (Lords of Pembury)
The Fallen One (De Reyne Domination)
Fragments of Grace (House of St. Hever)
Lord of the Shadows
Queen of Lost Stars (House of St. Hever)

Lords of Thunder: The de Shera Brotherhood Trilogy
The Thunder Lord
The Thunder Warrior
The Thunder Knight

Highland Warriors of Munro
The Red Lion

Time Travel Romance: (Saxon Lords of Hage)
The Crusader
Kingdom Come

Contemporary Romance:

Kathlyn Trent/Marcus Burton Series:
Valley of the Shadow
The Eden Factor
Canyon of the Sphinx

The American Heroes Series:
The Lucius Robe
Fires of Autumn
Evenshade
Sea of Dreams
Purgatory

Other Contemporary Romance:
Lady of Heaven
Darkling, I Listen

Multi-author Collections/Anthologies:
With Dreams Only of You (USA Today bestseller)
Sirens of the Northern Seas (Viking romance)
Ever My Love (sequel to With Dreams Only Of You) July 2016

Note: All Kathryn's novels are designed to be read as stand-alones, although many have cross-over characters or cross-over family groups. Novels that are grouped together have related characters or family groups.

Series are clearly marked. All series contain the same characters or family groups except the American Heroes Series, which is an anthology with unrelated characters.

There is NO particular chronological order for any of the novels because they can all be read as stand-alones, even the series.

For more information, find it in **A Reader's Guide to the Medieval World of Le Veque.**

Author's Note

This is a book I wrote for my mother....

My mother is a quiet, dignified woman born in the great state of Mississippi. For years, she's been asking me to "write a Mississippi book" and I wanted to oblige her, but none of the outlines I could come up with really satisfied me. I didn't just want to throw something together for her. I wanted it to be something she could be proud of.

So, before I start any of this, I will preface this story by saying this is *not* about my family. It's not about anyone in our family or anyone I know. This is purely a concoction of my imagination. So for any family members who might read this novel, I don't want them thinking I took a segment of our family's history and changed the names to protect the innocent. This is a complete work of fiction.

Back to the subject of the novel – it deals with the matter of race and racism, of love and loss, and of people caught up in the culture of the times. This novel is not meant to have a message other than love conquers all and it is not meant to glorify the negative in any race or culture. There is some brutality in it and there are some shocking moments, but the theme of the story is simple – that the Human Race has an uncanny ability to evolve and adapt, to love and to hate, and to justify that which, at times, is not justifiable. But if you have trigger issues with racism from the past, then know that this novel deals with such things. It deals with it honestly and tactfully, but consider yourself forewarned.

The story centers around rural Mississippi in the 1930s as well as in present day. As with each state in the union, the state of

Mississippi has a definable culture that is unique to that state. The language, the customs, the families, and the nuances that make it what it is. Good or bad, male or female, black or white, the history of the state, or of any state for that matter, can't be denied. History can't be erased.

In the pages of this book, you'll find the unforgivable as well as the forgivable, all of it stemming from a hope that all things come to pass and, in that, things that come full circle reach that state because the darkness of the past opens new doors to the future.

In no way is this book attempting to glorify or explain that darkness… it's simply the culture of the time, as sensitively explored as possible. But in that exploration, one thing is clear – love, in all of its forms, will find a way no matter what the distance or culture or obstacles. This book is a romance, but not in the traditional way. It's a subtle undercurrent throughout the story but it's also the roaring river that sweeps you away at the end.

Above all, this book is about hope and I believe you'll find it well worth the read. Most of all, I hope it makes my mama proud. Finally, she has her "Mississippi" book.

Love,
Kathryn

Contents

Prologue 1
Chapter One 10
Chapter Two 26
Chapter Three 29
Chapter Four 41
Chapter Five 44
Chapter Six 61
Chapter Seven 64
Chapter Eight 75
Chapter Nine 80
Chapter Ten 91
Chapter Eleven 94
Chapter Twelve 105
Chapter Thirteen 109
Chapter Fourteen 119
Chapter Fifteen 122
Chapter Sixteen 130
Chapter Seventeen 134
Chapter Eighteen 144
Chapter Nineteen 150
Chapter Twenty 163
Chapter Twenty-One 170

Chapter Twenty-Two 176
Chapter Twenty-Three 179
Chapter Twenty-Four 191
Chapter Twenty-Five 196
Chapter Twenty-Six... 206
Chapter Twenty-Seven....................................... 209
Chapter Twenty-Eight 222
Chapter Twenty-Nine.. 228
Chapter Thirty.. 242
Chapter Thirty-One.. 245
Chapter Thirty-Two 264
About Kathryn Le Veque 285

PROLOGUE
Pea Ridge, Mississippi
June, 1933
~ And Hell Followed with Him ~

IT WAS A warm, moist evening in the deepest rural heart of Mississippi, with the smell of dirt and damp leaves heavy in the air. On the outskirts of town, near a bend on the Yalobusha River where the insects buzzed and fireflies sprang from the grass, an old and run-down house was situated in a shanty town of coloreds known as Rose Cove.

In the garden behind the house, two young men faced one another. With skin the color of chocolate, their white teeth could be seen flashing in the darkness. Something unexpected and horrific had been spilled into the air this night between them, something that would change their world forever.

"How can yo' tell me this, Lewis?" one man pleaded. "Lawd have mercy... do yo' know what yo've done?"

"It's not like that," Lewis insisted. "I love her. She loves me. What happened... it just *happened*, Aldridge. I will not be shamed by it. I *can't* be."

It was brother against brother this night as Aldridge and Lewis Ragsdale faced off against each other. While Aldridge spoke in an uneducated twang, Lewis had an articulate speech pattern indicating that he was highly educated and wise beyond his years. But the truth was that much like his brother, he'd had no formal education, at least not in the higher sense, but that fine-speaking voice wouldn't matter in the face of the crisis he'd gotten himself in to.

No one was going to listen to him when his crime was discovered.

"It *happened?*" Aldridge repeated, aghast. "Nothin' like this *happens*, Lewis. Yo' touched what yo' shouldn't 'a touched an' when Mr. Laveau finds out, he's gonna... oh, Lawdy, he's gonna find out what yo' did to his daughter and *kill* yo'!"

Lewis was trying not to look too terrified, trying to hold his ground. "He won't know," he insisted quietly. "We are going to leave this town and go somewhere we can be together. We're going to get married."

"Married?" Aldridge gasped at the new horror. "Yo' *can't!*"

"We can and we will."

Aldridge's expression was wrought with shock. "Lewis, listen to me. What yo' want – what yo' askin' for – yo' know it can never be. I don't know how yo' got mixed up in this, but yo' haveta stay away from her. Yo' know what will happen if the men – Mr. Laveau's men – find out what yo' did. Yo' know what they'll do to yo'."

Aldridge spoke with great pain. They both knew what happened when black men got mixed up with white women down here and Lewis' jaw ticked as he tried to think of an argument that would help his older brother see his point.

But Aldridge had always thought differently than Lewis; they were brothers but they were quite dissimilar. The problem was that Lewis didn't want to fit into the world the way that it was. He wanted to fit into his own world which, in Aldridge's opinion, was dangerous.

It was deadly.

"Love doesn't see the color of someone's skin," Lewis said as Aldridge fretted. "It's blind to my black hair and her white skin. Love sees the heart, Aldridge. It sees the joy and the sorrows of the soul. I can't help that I'm in love with her and she doesn't want to help that she's in love with me. Do you know what we do sometimes? We sit and look up at the stars and we talk about the home we'll have someday. We talk about the children we'll have, children that don't see that their mother is a white woman and their father is a colored man. They won't see it because I will raise them not to see it. I want them to see a man for *who* he is and not *what* he isn't."

Aldridge was listening with more sorrow now than terror. "What isn't he?"

Lewis lifted his eyebrows. "Colored," he replied simply, picking up his brother's arm to indicate the smooth, dark skin. "My children won't see his color. The light in his soul, maybe. But not his color. Do you understand what I am saying?"

He let go of Aldridge's arm, letting it fall back down at his brother's side. Now that the terror of Lewis' secret had sunk in, all that remained was a miasma of uncertainty and Aldridge shook his head to Lewis' question. He wouldn't let his brother draw him into a world where prejudices didn't exist.

"I don't want to understand," he said, sighing heavily as he struggled with his composure. "Those dreams is what's gotten yo' into this mess. Yo' don't live on the moon, Lewis. Yo' live in Mississippi where relations between a colored man and a white woman are against the law. Yo' committin' a crime, Lewis, and not with just any white woman, but Mr. Laveau's daughter. Do yo' understand that?"

"I do."

"Then yo' know yo' haveta run before they come for yo'."

Lewis shook his head firmly. "I'm not running," he said. "I'm going to take her away from here and we're going to go someplace where we can live as man and wife."

"Where?" Aldridge demanded. "Yo' can't go anywhere!"

Lewis wouldn't be discouraged. "I can go somewhere," Lewis said as he suddenly broke away from his brother and headed towards the house. "I can take her somewhere. I've heard we can go north to Illinois or Iowa. We can get married there."

Aldridge took off after his brother. "Have yo' lost yo' mind?" he asked. "Lewis, yo' can't do this!"

"I have to," Lewis said with determination. "I have to take her someplace safe."

Aldridge grabbed at his brother to slow his forward momentum. "There *is* no place safe," he insisted. "If yo' leave, it has to be alone! She can't go with yo'!"

Lewis kept smacking his brother's hand away as he moved through the dusk, heading to the house that was weakly lit by coal oil lamps. They could smell the collards cooking, that pungent smell that was so familiar to them.

But the comfort of familiarity this night was replaced by angst so strong that it was all that existed at the moment. Lewis stopped smacking at Aldridge's hand and came to a halt.

"I *am* taking her away tonight," he hissed. "I must. If she stays, her life will be in danger."

Aldridge wasn't entirely unsympathetic. "But yo' can't...."

Lewis cut Aldridge off as he grabbed his brother, roughly. "I can and I will," he stressed. "She's pregnant with my child, Aldridge. *Mine*. I can't wait around for her father to discover her child is half-colored. He'll kill her. I *have* to take her away."

Aldridge shook his head miserably. "But he'll kill *yo'* if he catches yo'. Don't yo' even care?"

A flash of pain crossed Lewis' smooth features. "I care," he muttered. "Of course I care. But I have to try. If I don't try, then I can't look myself in the face. I'd hate myself, Aldridge. And I'd hate you for trying to stop me."

Aldridge let go of his brother's arm, rocking back from the force of the statement. "I'm not gonna say I'm sorry," he said. "Yo' an' me, Lewis... it's always been yo' an' me. We are brothers but there's more to it. I'd do anythin' for yo', includin' tryin' to stop yo' from gettin' yo'self killed. If yo' haveta hate me for that, I can't stop yo'. But I won't say I'm sorry for doin' it."

Strains of a song suddenly drifted from the house, piercing the tension between them. Their grandmother, Ma'ama, was starting to put food on the table and she always started singing when it came time to eat. It was a haunting melody with words that seemed particularly poignant at the moment.

They're writing songs of love, but not for me,
A lucky star's above, but not for me,
With love to lead the way,
I found more clouds of grey....

Ma'ama should have been singing hymns given the fact that she went to church three nights a week, but the old gal liked the songs from the Nickelodeon movie houses that had popped up in a neighboring town of Scobey where the coloreds could watch talkies. Tonight, Ma'ama was singing the Gershwin brothers, or "those Jewish brothas", as she called them.

Lewis and Aldridge paused, listening to their tiny grandmother belt out a love song, before Aldridge finally turned to his brother.

"What yo' gonna do now?" he asked softly. "It's time to eat."

Lewis looked at his feet, hands shoved deep into his pockets. "I'll eat," he said, "and then I'm taking the money I've put away in my sock and I'm leaving. Victory is waiting for me. I told her I'd come tonight and she'll be waiting for me."

Aldridge was coming to see that his brother wouldn't be discouraged from what he felt he had to do. He could argue with him until the sun rose but it wouldn't change Lewis' mind. Once his mind was set, it was set, and Aldridge had known him long enough to realize there was no turning back at this point.

But Aldridge knew differently. Lewis was going to go off and get himself killed because the moment he put his foot on the property of Laveau Hembree, the dogs would find him if Mr. Laveau's men didn't. Miss Victory might be waiting for him, but already, Aldridge could see disaster. This would not be a clean operation, any of it.

He couldn't let his brother walk into his death.

"Will she come with me?" Aldridge asked softly.

Lewis looked at him strangely. "What do you mean?"

Aldridge hung his head a moment before answering, as if hesitant to elaborate. But he'd come this far. "Yo' don't know the Hembree house like I do," he said. "I work there. I know how to get in and out without much bein' seen. Even if someone sees me, it wouldn't be strange. But if they see yo', they'll set the dogs on yo'."

Lewis' brow furrowed with confusion. "Are you wanting to go instead of me?"

Aldridge was still looking at the ground. He kicked at it with his worn boots. "I ain't a-wantin' to go at 'tall," he said, "but yo're gonna go no matter what I say. I'm afraid if yo' do, yo' won't make it. They'll kill yo' before yo' can get to the house."

Lewis could see that his brother was trying to help him. Any tension the conversation had brought about was now evaporating.

"I know that," he said quietly. "I've already thought of that. Victory is going to meet me on the dock by the river. I've got money to pay the ferryman to cross the Yalobusha and then we'll go north from there."

Aldridge shook his head. "Yo' don't know how they watch that girl," he said. "I see how they treat her, like a child who needs to be tended every second. If she leaves the house, her pappy'll follow her. It's wide-open land between the house and the river. She'll be seen."

Lewis was starting to feel more apprehension for Victory than for himself. "She knows the house and the land," he said. "She'll know to stay out of sight."

Aldridge lifted his dark eyebrows. "And if she's caught?" he asked. "What then? What if they make her tell 'em where she was goin'?"

Lewis tried to explain. "Aldridge, she has obviously gone out before without being caught. We are going to have a child, after all."

Lewis shook his head, interrupted from his explanation when they heard Ma'ama call out to them from the house telling them that supper was on the table. Purely out of the habit of obeying Ma'ama's commands, they began moving for the house again, slowly.

"She won't tell them," Lewis said. "She won't say anything."

"Yo' trust her with yo' life?"

"I do."

Aldridge grunted, an unhappy sound. He put a hand on Lewis' arm again, stopping him for the last time.

"I'll go to the dock and see if she there," he said. "Yo' wait at the ferry crossin' down river. If she's there, I'll bring her to yo'. If she's not, then yo' need to take the ferry anyway and get away before they come for yo'. If she not there, it means they got her and she'll tell 'em what she knows, I swear she will."

Lewis' jaw ticked faintly. "Aldridge...."

The older brother cut him off. "They won't pay no never-mind if they see me," he insisted. "If they see yo' waitin' on the dock and Ms. Victory runnin' to yo', yo' know what they'll do. Lewis, yo' got to let me help yo'. Yo're walkin' into the belly of the beast and yo' don't even know it. Let *me* go!"

There was wisdom in Aldridge's words, as much as Lewis hated to admit it. He began to shift around, uncomfortably. "Maybe you're right."

"Yo' know I am."

"And you'll bring her to the ferry crossing?"

"I said I would."

Lewis' dark gaze lingered on his brother. "You wouldn't try and talk her out of it?"

Aldridge shook his head. "She's in this as much as yo' are."

Lewis couldn't deny that. "She is," he said quietly. "But I have faith that there's something better for Victory and me, somewhere that isn't this southern state that smells of compost and reeks of hate. We're going north. After supper, I'm going to the ferry landing and I'll wait for you to bring Victory to me there."

Aldridge sensed that this was all so final, as if there was no turning back, ever. Lewis had made up his mind and he was going with or without his brother's help. He was still frightened, still nearly panicked by the thought of what Laveau Hembree would do if he found out about his daughter and Lewis, but there was also a sense of determination now to help his brother. He had to.

He couldn't live with himself if he didn't.

"I will," Aldridge said. "I'll find her and bring her to yo'."

Lewis nodded, knowing there was nothing more to say about that. Still, there was something else he needed to tell his brother.

"I know you don't agree with this," he said, touching the man on the arm, "but this is something I must do. I love her, Aldridge. We are going to make a life together."

Aldridge bit off the argument on his lips. Lewis wouldn't listen, anyway. "If yo' do, yo'll write to me and tell me where yo' are?"

Lewis smiled faintly. "I won't put my name on the letter, but you'll know it's me."

"How?"

Lewis' smile grew. "Because the letter will be very simple," he said. "It will say 'In the Dreaming Hour....'. And then you'll know it came from me."

Aldridge wasn't sure what the significance was of those words, but he didn't ask. Lewis didn't make a lot of sense sometimes, so he let it go. He and his brother continued on to the house, sitting down to supper with the other members of the Ragsdale family.

It was a special meal for the brothers and, in particular, for Lewis. His last meal with his Ma'ama, his parents, Pearl and Ezekiel, and his aunts, uncles, and younger siblings. He felt so safe and happy here. He was going to miss his Ma'ama chewing, open-mouthed, on her pork rinds and he was going to miss his father taking out his upper denture plate and scaring the younger kids with it. He was going to miss his family terribly, but it couldn't be helped.

In fact, Lewis spent more time looking at his family than eating and when the meal was over, Aldridge slipped off into the night and Lewis grabbed his money sock and his meager belongings, heading to the ferry crossing on the banks of the Yalobusha where he and Victory would cross the river, head north, and finally find their own particular brand of happiness. He had nothing but hope that night, nothing but joy for the future.

But that joy was shattered when Aldridge failed to show up at the ferry and was never heard from again.

Lewis and Victory never made it to Illinois, after all.

CHAPTER ONE

Pea Ridge, Mississippi
Present Day

~ *The Ghosts of Mississippi Past* ~

THE FUNERAL WAS being held in an old antebellum home that had been converted into a funeral parlor back in the nineteen fifties. The house was big and rambling, with peach-colored walls and scenes from Greek mythology painted in the ceilings. It was meant to look opulent but the unfortunate truth was that it simply looked garish.

A well-dressed woman with auburn hair and green eyes stood by the front door, drinking in all of the visual cheesiness and inhaling the musty smell inherent to the old houses in the southern states. Something between dirt and rot. That wasn't exactly the smell she wanted filling her nose as she gazed down at her grandmother's corpse, that event being just moments away.

God, she just didn't want to be here.

Having just flown in from Los Angeles on a red-eye, Lucy Bondurant had made the two-hour drive from the Memphis airport in time to make it to the service of Victory Hembree Bondurant, a gracious but firm woman she simply knew as Mamaw. Childhood memories lingered in her mind as she forced herself to enter the funeral parlor where Victory lay in the next room – Lucy knew that because she could see the tail-end of a coffin and people milling around in there, including her parents. She could see them through the doorway, speaking to people she didn't recognize.

Taking a deep breath, she forced herself to head into that room filled with death and grief.

You can do this. Get your ass in there.

Lucy's mother, Mary, quickly caught sight of her only child. A slender woman with neat blonde hair, Mary hugged her daughter but Lucy's attention was mostly on her father. It was, after all, his mother who had passed away and he had been inordinately close to her. Lucy knew that Mamaw's death had hit him hard.

"Hey, Dad," she said softly, hugging her tall and handsome father. "How are you holding up?"

Bill Bondurant wiped at his nose, sniffling, trying to pretend he was doing just fine. "I'm okay," he said, brushing off her question for the most part. He didn't like it when the focus was on him. "How was your flight?"

"It was fine," she said, eyeing her father's pale face. "Is Pop going to be here?"

They were speaking of Victory's husband, Hardy, still alive and extremely old. Bill nodded to Lucy's question.

"Yes," he said. "In fact, the assisted living home is supposed to call me any minute. They're bringing him over in one of their special vans. Daddy isn't really mobile anymore, you know."

"I know," Lucy said. Then, she hesitated. "Have you been to see him yet? Does he know what's going on?"

Bill shook his head. "We went to see him last night, straight from the airport," he said. "He kept calling me Johnny and wanted to know where Willie was."

"He spoke? That's a surprise."

"It wasn't anything more than saying 'where's Willie', but he did speak. I haven't heard him put two words together in a year."

Lucy smiled. "Well, at least he recognized you as being part of the family. That's something."

Bill lifted his eyebrows ironically. "Maybe he did," he agreed, his gaze moving towards the coffin. "But he was asking for me as a kid. He was the only one who ever called me Willie when I was little. Mama always called me Bill."

Lucy wasn't really focused on what he was saying because she knew he was looking at his mother's coffin. The time had come for her to look at it, too, although she was dreading the moment. She had never been very good at funerals but she summoned the courage to look over. Catching sight of her grandmother's sunken face, she felt a distinct shock. A hiss escaped her lips.

"Oh... Dad," she muttered. "That doesn't even *look* like... oh, God, I'm sorry. I shouldn't have said that."

Bill's gaze was fixed on his mother. "I know," he said quietly. "Mama had been sick for a while, you know. She lost a lot of weight. When they prepped her body, they took out her dentures. That's why her face looks so caved in."

Lucy wasn't even sure she could get next to the casket with Mamaw looking like that. The funeral director had done a horrendous job on the woman. It didn't even look like Victory, a once-beautiful woman. It looked like some kind of wax dummy from a cheap Boris Karloff flick.

Rather than comment on it again, however, she just shut her mouth; she could tell that her father was already upset enough so mentioning the state of his mother's body wouldn't do him any good. He knew it looked shitty. Summoning her courage, Lucy took her father's hand.

"Go with me to say goodbye, okay?" she asked softly.

Bill simply nodded, holding his daughter's hand tightly as they went up to the solid mahogany coffin built in Batesville, Mississippi. Mamaw had always been very clear about what she wanted to be buried in and there was no question that it would be a Batesville casket. It was a beautiful casket as far as caskets went with sleek lines and white velvet interior.

Gazing down at the distorted face of Mamaw, Lucy could feel her eyes stinging with tears. It wasn't just the state of the body; it was the simple fact that she was *dead*. No more grandmotherly hugs, no more tomato gravy and biscuits. No more stories about Mississippi while she was growing up and no more chasing fireflies at sunset.

All of that was at an end.

"Her... her dress is very pretty," Lucy said, a lump in her throat. "Did you pick it out?"

"*She* did," he said, looking at his daughter, his eyes twinkling, albeit dully. "You know she planned out every inch of this funeral. She wanted it exactly a certain way. You know Mama has always been like that and I think that same determination kind of rubbed off on you. I see a lot of her in you, Lucy."

Lucy forced a smile, swallowing away the tears that threatened. "I am proud to be just like my grandmother," she declared softly. "I don't take any crap, either."

"That is the truth," Bill agreed, "but you know she was that way because of her father. You had to stand up to that old bastard or he'd step all over you."

Lucy knew about her great-grandfather. In fact, the town of Pea Ridge still knew about the man although the generation of people who had known him personally had mostly died off. It had been a long time ago, back in the nineteen twenties and nineteen thirties, but it was something people around here still knew about.

It was an evil that still lingered.

"I know," Lucy said, her gaze still on her grandmother. The subject of her great-grandfather was a touchy one but, having not grown up in Pea Ridge with that stigma hanging over her head, she was a little more immune to the shame of it. "Mamaw didn't talk much about him but I do remember hearing stories now and then. You remember him, don't you?"

Bill nodded. "He died back in the sixties when I was about ten years old, so I remember him very well. He was always great with me because I was the son he'd always wanted. He only had one child, my mother, and I believe he always resented the fact that she was a girl. I never saw him be particularly nice to her, not ever. It was animosity that ran deep because she put in her will that she didn't want to be buried next to him. We're burying her next to my grandmother."

Lucy thought of Mamaw, a genuine steel magnolia with Satan for a father. "She never talked fondly of him," she said. "He was her father but I never got the impression that she loved him."

"I don't think she did," Bill said. "Though she never talked a lot about her younger years, I always got the impression that he was really hard on her back when she was growing up. I've heard a few things about Laveau but I don't think this is the time to talk about it. Suffice it to say that my grandfather was a bad dude back in the day, even to his own daughter."

"But you've heard stories?"

"Like I said – we'll talk about it another time."

Lucy let the subject go and reached out to gently touch her Mamaw's hand. Maybe they'd talk about the stories at some point, maybe they wouldn't. Maybe it didn't even matter anymore because Laveau Hembree's time was long past. They couldn't ever put the past behind them if they continued to dredge it up.

Beneath her fingers, Mamaw's skin was like velvet but cold to the touch. Slightly creeped out, Lucy removed her hand.

"Sweet dreams, Mamaw," she whispered, tears stinging her eyes again. "I hope you are warm and safe and happy now, wherever you are."

Bill started to say something but activity near the entry caught his attention and both he and Lucy turned to see a man in a wheelchair roll in through the front door. There were two male attendants with him and also a woman who was possibly a nurse, as one of the tall African American attendants rolled the wheelchair forward into the foyer.

Lucy's eyes widened at the sight. "Oh, my God, Dad," she gasped. "It's Pop!"

Bill was already on the move, heading towards the front door as a very old man was being brought into the funeral home. He went straight to his father, his expression full of concern.

"Someone was supposed to call me when he arrived," he said to the man pushing the wheelchair. "Is he okay? Did he tolerate the trip over here well?"

The attendant nodded his head. "Mr. Hardy did just fine," he said. "We tried to call you but you didn't answer."

Frowning, Bill looked at his cell phone to see he had a missed call. He'd never heard it ring. With a shrug, he put the phone back into his pocket.

"Sorry about that," he said. "I guess I didn't hear it. Has Dad said anything since I left him last night? Does he know why you've brought him here?"

The female stepped forward. She was young, and Caucasian, and wore too much makeup. "I sat in the back of the van with him and told him why we were coming here," she said. "He didn't acknowledge me so I have no idea if he really grasps what's going on. I doubt it."

"Pop?" Lucy came up to her grandfather and crouched down in front of the chair. She looked into his face, smiling. "Hi, Pop. Do you know me? It's Lucy. It's so good to see you."

Hardy Fowler Bondurant was still a big man with big hands, a little on the thin side but still healthy. It was his mind that had been destroyed by disease even though the body had remained relatively the same. He wore thick glasses over brilliant blue eyes and still had a head of full gray hair.

When Lucy put her hand on his and squeezed it, he seemed to recoil but she didn't let go. She squeezed it again.

"I'm so happy to see you," she said again, trying not to break down in tears at the sight of her beloved grandfather and what dementia had done to him. "It's been such a long time. I think I saw you last about five years ago on the Fourth of July. Do you remember? We rented that cabin out by the lake and shot off Roman candles. Remember we launched one into Dad's rental car? We set the interior on fire."

She was giggling, squeezing his hand, and he wasn't recoiling so much now. He was actually looking at her and Lucy smiled at him, holding his leathered fingers with both hands. She thought maybe that him looking at her might have been a sign that he was coming to recognize her. He seemed to be focusing on her, at any rate.

"Dad had to pay a fortune for ruined car seats," she went on. "I think he's still mad at me. I told him you were the one who gave me the fire crackers so it's really your fault."

Lucy glanced up to see her father rolling his eyes at her. Bill put his hand on Hardy's shoulder. "Don't worry, Daddy," he said. "I made her pay for the ruined seats. She didn't get away with it."

As Bill and Lucy snorted at each other, Hardy suddenly shifted in his seat. "*Lucy,*" he whispered.

Lucy and Bill froze, looking at Hardy in shock. Joy filled Lucy's expression as she gave Hardy's hand another big squeeze. "Yes, Pop," she said excitedly. "It's Lucy! It's me!"

"*Sugar.*"

Tears were in Lucy's eyes again, now tears of joy. "Right, Pop," she said. "It's Sugar. God, I haven't heard that name in years."

Sugar had been Hardy's nickname for the squirrelly little girl with long red hair. It was something from his past, something deep in his memory that his damaged mind had pulled forth.

Of course he knew his only grandchild; he loved her more than all of the stars in the heavens. He'd told her that once, back before his mind had left him completely. But before Lucy could get too excited about the recognition, Bill got in his father's face.

"Daddy?" he said, hoping Hardy's recognition of Lucy meant

that he had some manner of cognitive ability, something they hadn't seen in him in months. "Do you know why you're here? I told you last night that Mama has passed away. We're here today for her funeral."

Hardy was still looking at Lucy; his focus hadn't wavered. Bill wasn't sure if his father had even heard him but, clearly, there was something going on in the cobwebs of his mind, something that centered around Lucy. He was fixated on her.

Bill finally stood up and motioned to the attendant pushing the wheelchair.

"Bring him in here," he said quietly. "His wife is in here."

Dutifully, the attendant wheeled the chair across the old, stained carpet of the entry and onto the hardwood floors of the room where Ms. Victory was laid out in her mahogany casket.

As Bill and Lucy went to the coffin, flanking it, the attendant pushed the wheelchair right up to the open casket so that Hardy was parallel with Victory's head. The attendants and the nurse stepped back respectfully as Bill leaned over his father.

"Daddy?" he murmured. "It's Mama. Can you see her? She passed away from cancer three days ago. She was comfortable when she passed and not in any pain. Do you remember what I told you last night? She'd been sick for about three years. She was one hundred years old and it was just her time to go, Daddy. She... she was sorry you weren't with her when she went."

Hardy wasn't looking at the casket. In fact, he was still looking at Lucy, who was standing by the end of the wooden chest. Bill could see where his father was looking still and he waved Lucy away. After she quickly moved out of Hardy's line of sight, there was nothing left to capture Hardy's attention so the man just stared out into space.

"Daddy?" Bill tried again. "Say goodbye to Mama. She'll be waiting for you on the other side when it's your time. She'll be right there when it's your time to go. Can you say goodbye to her?"

No response. Bill sighed faintly, turning to look at Lucy and his wife, who were now standing together a few feet away. Mary, having escaped a horde of chatty relatives, now stood with her daughter, watching as Bill tried to move Hardy's attention to the casket. Mary could see the distress on her husband's features.

"It's okay, Bill," she said quietly. "You've done all you can. He simply can't understand."

Bill sighed again, turning to look at his dad, seeing that the man was still staring off into space. Moving around the chair, he knelt down in front of his father and tried to capture his focus.

"Daddy," he said softly. "Maybe you can understand me, maybe you can't. You loved Mama and she loved you, and I know you want to say farewell to her. I'll just step aside so you can be alone with her for a few moments, okay? I'll be right over there with Lucy and Mary if you need me."

Hardy didn't react. Disheartened, Bill moved over to where his wife and daughter were standing. They all stood back with the nurse and the attendants, with cousins and relatives and the man from the funeral home, waiting and watching for some movement from Hardy that would indicate he was saying farewell to his wife of sixty years.

But the seconds ticked by, and finally the minutes, and there was no movement from Hardy. It was becoming increasingly evident that there wouldn't be. Resigned, Bill went over to the funeral director to tell the man to start moving guests into the chapel, which was a cheap add-on to the side of the house. He wasn't halfway through his request when he heard a collective gasp go up. Whirling around, he saw his father standing out of his chair.

Hardy was on his feet next to the casket, hunched over Victory's body. The man hadn't been on his feet in over a year so he wasn't particularly steady, but he was standing nonetheless. It was a pivotal moment and the buzz of conversation died down, people quieting as if afraid to break the spell that now hung over Hardy.

As an entire room watched, holding their breaths, Hardy stared down at his wife. It was possible that the lights of recognition were struggling to fire because he simply stood there and leaned on the casket, staring at the nearly unrecognizable body cushioned by the white velvet. Did he recognize her? Did he even have a clue?

... could he tell her goodbye?

Finally, he moved. Hardy lifted his hand and grasped Victory's cold, soft fingers. He didn't say a word, however. He simply stood there holding the woman's hand for the longest time as if reconciling himself to what he was seeing. The lights of recognition had ignited and, in that brief moment of awareness, Hardy finally saw his wife for the last time. In his damaged mind, something was registering, something deep and sorrowful.

A tear fell from his eye, hitting Victory on the cheek.

It was a gesture not missed by anyone in the room. Eyes grew moist and people began sniffling. In awe, but very aware of the man's privacy, Bill and Lucy moved up on either side of Hardy, hoping to offer what support they could. Just as they came up beside him, they heard a string of barely audible words.

"I hope you find him."

It was Hardy's voice, very faint. The man, mostly silenced by years of dementia, had found his voice when he needed it most. But just like that, the spell was broken and Hardy tottered backwards, plopping down into his chair.

Lucy and Bill had hold of him, making sure the chair didn't roll away or tip over, and the attendants hurried up to help. But the moment of awareness was over and Hardy's expression remained empty of emotion even though tears had so recently fallen.

Whatever light had gone on in his mind was out again and the vacant eyes, though misty, were vacant once more.

Lucy knew that because she was looking at him. Those eyes she knew so well were dim, the realization of his wife's death perhaps more than he could bear. Still, the words out of his mouth had been very odd. Curious, she knelt in front of her grandfather again as the attendants secured the old man in the chair.

"Pop?" she asked softly. "What did you mean? Who is 'him'?"

"Jesus," Bill said with quiet confidence. "I'm sure he meant Jesus."

It made sense but something told Lucy that wasn't the case. She didn't know why, or how, but she just wasn't convinced that's what Hardy had meant. Call it a hunch, but she didn't think her grandfather had meant that his wife should find the lord. She'd already found him, a long time ago.

This was something else.

"Is that who you meant, Pop?" she said, holding the man's hand again. "Did you mean that Mamaw should find Jesus?"

Hardy didn't reply. All strapped into his chair again, he was devoid of recognition, once again, as Bill directed the attendants to take his father into the chapel where people were starting to gather. Lucy stood up and walked next to her grandfather's chair, still holding his hand, still puzzled over what he'd said to his wife.

Just as they neared the chapel entrance, a small, elderly African American woman, who had been seated in a corner, suddenly stood up. Lucy recognized the woman as the lady who had faithfully tended Mamaw for the last few years of her life.

"Hello, Aunt Vivien," Lucy said. "I'm so glad you're here. I'm sorry I didn't see you when I came in."

The woman was dressed in her finest; a cheap but clean blue suit, a rather beaten blue hat, and an old white purse. She clutched the purse against her chest.

"That's okay," the old woman assured her. "You saw who you needed to see. Ms. Victory would have been angry if you'd come to talk to me before you saw her."

Lucy laughed softly, letting go of her grandfather's hand and letting him, and her parents, pass on into the chapel as she remained behind to talk to Vivien. "That's very true," she said, walking up to the old woman, looking her over. "How are you? It's been a while."

Vivien nodded. "It has," she agreed. "Ms. Victory said you done got a new job."

Lucy nodded. "I did," she said. "A big law firm in Los Angeles. It takes all my time."

"No new husband yet?"

Lucy grinned and shook her head. "Not yet."

"Ms. Victory wouldn't like to hear that."

"No, she wouldn't." Lucy noticed that her family was starting to sit down inside of the chapel. "Shall we go in? I know Mamaw would want us right where she can see us. If we're late, she might crawl out of that casket and try to beat us."

She meant it as a joke but she wasn't far off; both she and Vivien knew of Ms. Victory's penchant for spanking or pinching when she was angry. Tardiness was a major sin in her book. Vivien started to follow Lucy but she didn't get very far; abruptly, she came to a halt.

"Can I talk to you a minute before we go in, Ms. Lucy?" she asked. "All I need is a minute."

Lucy came to a halt beside her. "Sure," she said. "What's on your mind?"

Vivien looked rather uncertain, still clutching that old, white purse to her breast. There was a nervous edge to her manner now.

"Ms. Victory was one of the few great ladies left," she said sincerely. "She was good to me and we understood each other. But... but that's not what I wanted to talk to you about. You see, before your Mamaw passed away, she told me to tell you somethin'."

Lucy was instantly curious. "She did?" she said. "What?"

Bill, standing in the doorway of the chapel, called to Lucy and when she looked over at him, he waved his hand at her, indicating for her to join him. Lucy held up a hand to assure him she was on her way but she looked back to Vivien first.

"Dad wants us to sit down," she stated the obvious. "What did Mamaw want you to tell me?"

Vivien put a wrinkled old hand on Lucy's wrist, a powerful gesture in spite of the light touch. Looking into Vivien's hazel eyes, Lucy could see something quite serious within the liquid depths.

"Your Mamaw told me to tell you this," Vivien whispered. "There's a big ol' chifforobe in her bedroom and in the bottom drawer, your Mamaw done left you somethin'. She says to tell you to not let nobody see it, 'cause she wants you to have it. She says not to let your daddy see it. It's for you and only you."

Lucy's curiosity deepened. "What is it?"

Vivien dropped her hand from Lucy's wrist. "It's a note," she muttered. "I was there when she wrote you a note and put it in the bottom drawer of her chifforobe. Go get it and don't let nobody see it, Miss Lucy. Your Mamaw wants it that way."

"But why?"

"Don't ask no questions. Just do as your Mamaw says."

Lucy wasn't any less curious than she had been moments earlier. As Vivien slipped away into the chapel, Lucy followed, mulling over what the woman had just told her.

A note. Lucy could only imagine it was some kind goodbye note to her only grandchild but she wondered if she was strong enough to read it. Still, she was more than a little eager to get her hands on it.

The funeral was a somber occasion bordering on morose. The mood was sad, as it should be, but there was something more to it, something that spoke of... relief. Various cousins and relatives filled up about half of the chapel and the remaining seats were filled up with people from the community who had come to pay their respects to the last of a great but brutal dynasty, the last woman to be born with the name of Hembree.

Victory's death was the passing of an era, the preacher said when he eulogized Ms. Victory Jewel Hembree Bondurant. He didn't speak of her father's darkness or of sins of the past. It wasn't the time or place. A great lady from a great family, he had said. A few songs and then a brief eulogy by Bill followed.

Thirty-five minutes later, it was over and a hearse was positioned next to the chapel so Ms. Victory could be loaded up for her last ride to the cemetery.

It seemed odd that someone's entire life could be summarized in less than an hour. Lucy was thinking that very thought as she stood with the funeral guests, holding her grandfather's hand as her grandmother's casket was loaded into the hearse. To think this was the end of a woman she'd known her entire life didn't seem real.

Maybe she'd wake up and this would have all been a nightmare. All she wanted was one more chance to talk to her grandmother on the phone and listen to the woman bitch about the fact that Vivien made better biscuits than she did. Just one more time to laugh at the old woman from two thousand miles away. That was the only safe distance when laughing at Victory.

But the truth was that she would never wake up from this. Neither would anyone else in her family. When Mamaw's casket was finally secured in the hearse, the people from her grandfather's living facility came forward to put the man back into the van and return him. He couldn't make the burial in a wheelchair because of the location of the grave, so Bill kissed his father goodbye, as did Lucy, and they watched the attendants wheel him back over to the white van.

I hope you find him.

Those words came back to Lucy as she watched them put her grandfather onto a platform that gently lifted him back up into the van, wheelchair and all. She thought about them as she headed to her car, preparing to follow the hearse. Those words were going to drive her crazy but maybe they really *were* the ramblings of an old man who had no idea what he was saying. She was sure she'd never know the truth.

With her parents already in their rental car, Lucy scooted out to the street where she'd parked, noting that it was a bright day with a hint of humidity in the air. That was something she didn't miss about her summers visiting in Mississippi, that sticky moisture that clung to everything. She could already feel the sweat on her back.

Digging into her purse, she made her way down the walkway to the curb. As she went, she noticed a lanky, very old African American man standing on the sidewalk, looking at the funeral home.

She wouldn't have paid much attention to him except for the fact that she had to walk around him to get to the curb where her car was parked. As she passed by, she glanced into his leathery, long face, flashing one of those fake polite smiles that one does when acknowledging someone unfamiliar.

"Hello," she said.

The old man stepped back and tipped his equally old hat at her. He was nicely dressed, in clean clothes that were exquisitely old.

"Good morning," he said.

Lucy continued on to the car, hitting the remote to unlock it. Opening the driver's door, she tossed her purse in and was about to climb in after it when she realized that the old man was still standing there, still looking at the funeral home. Lucy thought he might have been lost and she would have felt bad not finding out, just leaving him standing on the sidewalk in confusion. He was pretty old, after all. Maybe he had just lost his way.

"Sir?" she said to him. "Are you looking for someone?"

The elderly man looked at her, startled by the question. "No, ma'am," he said. "I'm right where I need to be."

He had a strangely deep and steady voice, for all of his obvious old age. It occurred to Lucy what he might have meant. "The funeral, you mean?" she asked. "The funeral for Victory Bondurant? You just missed it."

The old man nodded his head. "I just came to say a prayer, ma'am."

A smile creased Lucy's lips. "Did you know Victory?" she asked. "She was my grandmother, by the way. I'm Lucy. Her son, Bill, is my dad."

The old man just seemed to stare at her, an odd sort of expression on his face. But he was distracted when the hearse came around from the back of the home, down the driveway with a line of cars already behind it. The movement of the cars had his attention now and he paused when he saw the hearse, his yellowed eyes fixed on it.

For a moment, he simply gazed at it. Riveted to it, really. Then, the hat came off, respectfully, and he held it across his heart, watching as the hearse slowly rolled past him. A weathered hand with long, gnarled fingers reached out to gently touch the car as it moved by. Although he didn't speak, there was something in his touch that bespoke of grief.

It was odd, really. As the hearse pulled out and began its trek north towards the town square, he continued to stand and watch. He didn't seem inclined to speak with Lucy any further, however, so she climbed into her car and fired it up, making a U-turn to follow the funeral procession.

In her rearview mirror, she could see the old man still standing on the sidewalk, hat still over his heart, but that vision was cut short when she had to make the turn to head west.

The old African American gentleman was quickly forgotten. Lucy's thoughts were turning to Mamaw's burial now and Vivien's mysterious message. There was something in the bottom drawer of that old chifforobe, something meant for her, and the more Lucy thought about it, the more curious she became.

There was to be a reception at Mamaw's house after the burial and Lucy was determined to slip up to Mamaw's bedroom and dig around in that bottom drawer. *What do you have to say to me, Mamaw?* she thought. *And why don't you want Dad to see it?*

It was going to drive her crazy until she read the contents.

CHAPTER TWO
~ All of Us, Dying ~

"*D*ADDY, HOW COULD you do it?" A young woman with short, wavy auburn hair wept bitterly. "You... you killed him! I know you did!"

A big man, tall, with a full head of dark hair and piercing dark eyes watched the woman as she sat on her bed, crying. It was deep into the night now, the soft breezes off of the river lifting the curtains in her bedroom, filling the air with a moist, heavy smell.

But the man didn't seem to notice any of it, including his daughter's tears. He gazed at her emotionlessly.

"You remember this night," he said, his jaw flexing. "You remember what happened here tonight the next time you even look at a colored man. Do you understand me? Next time, I won't be careful about it – I'll cut him to pieces right in front of you. Are you listening to me?"

"You murdered him!"

"He was punished."

The young woman threw herself down onto her bed, weeping bitterly. Sitting on the bed next to her was an older woman, also in tears. There wasn't a hair out of place on her carefully-waved hair but the expression on her face suggested she knew better than to speak out against the man. Lord, she knew better. She kept her hand on the young woman's back in a futile attempt to comfort her.

"Daddy knows what's best for you, Victory," the woman said as if trying to convince herself of such a thing. "You shouldn't ought to have even talked to the man. It's over now. It's all over and you know what you did wrong."

"Does she?" the man snapped, coming over to the bed and grabbing the young woman by the arm. He raised his hand to her, open-palmed. "I should have done this when the doctor told us of your condition, you shameful hussy. The day you fainted at school and Dr. Latling told us why, I shoulda found the man that day. I shoulda found him and I shoulda punished him. And now you're gonna have a half-colored bastard that tells everybody in town that you've spread your legs for the wrong kind of man? Lord have mercy. I should have beat that baby out of you when the doctor first told us about it!"

The woman on the bed put her hands up, preventing him from striking the young woman. "No!" she screamed. "Laveau, no! You can't do it! You can't strike her like that! I won't let you!"

Laveau hit the older woman instead, mussing her neat Marcel wave. He hit her right on the side of the face, leaving a nearly-perfect hand print. As the older woman wept with pain and shame, the man kicked the bed but stopped short of hitting the young girl. He turned away from the bed, fists clenched.

"Damn you," he hissed, moving to the window that overlooked the dark front garden of the house. "Damn him, the black bastard. Now he knows. Now he knows what he shouldn't ought to have touched."

There was an odd hint of satisfaction in his tone, as if he'd been perfectly justified in doing what he'd done. He'd punished the man for sins against him and his family, and that was exactly the way he looked at it. On the bed, the two women continued to weep, their painful strains filling the night air, as a soft knock echoed from the bedroom door. Someone stood outside the cracked panel, clearing his throat.

"Mr. Laveau?" a man said. "Can I come in?"

Laveau turned to the door, waving the caller in. A man in dark blue slacks, a white shirt, and a slender dark tie entered. He had a brown snap-brim hat in his hand and sweat beading on his forehead as he looked at Laveau Hembree, still standing by the window surveying his front garden. But there was no remorse in Laveau's eyes, no hint of regret of what he'd just done. It was a look the man with the hat had seen before.

"What 'cha want, Terhune?" Laveau asked impatiently.

Terhune Meade was clearly uneasy as he fiddled with his hat. He couldn't even look at the women on the bed, sobbing. "I'm going to be leaving now," he said, sounding as if he was asking permission. "I'll have some of my men take that boy back over to the family. Ragsdale, you said?"

Laveau nodded. Then, he shook his head. "Damn him," he muttered again, looking out of the window where a few men were on horseback. "I liked him. For a colored, he was a good man. He listened when I told him something. But the whole time he was lusting after my daughter. I should have known. I should have at least seen what was going on under my own roof."

Before Terhune could speak, the young woman on the bed lifted her head, her tear-stained face red with sorrow and rage. "What did he do to him?" she screamed at Terhune. "You're the sheriff! You should have stopped him! You know what his men did to him, don't you?"

"Shut your mouth, girl," Laveau growled. "Another word out of you and you won't leave this room for the rest of your life. Do you hear me?"

By that time, he had marched over to the bed and grabbed the girl by the wrist, twisting it until she screamed. Terhune, seeing Laveau in a mood he had no desire to deal with, quickly turned and left the room as the women were beat upon. As Terhune took the darkened stairs down to the front door of Glory, he could hear the women screaming on the floor above.

Turning a deaf ear to the sounds, he went out into the moonlit night. He'd rather deal with an innocent dead man this night than the anger of Laveau Hembree.

CHAPTER THREE

Present

THE LADIES FROM the Presbyterian Church set up a post-burial giant buffet on Mamaw's old dining room table, an antique big enough to sit twelve people comfortably. The massive table sat in the cavernous dining room of the house, dwarfed by the sheer size of the room itself.

The whole house dwarfed everything within it, a larger-than-life structure that had a history nearly as old as the state of Mississippi. Built a half-mile from the Yalobusha River, the house known as Glory had been in the Hembree family since it had been built one hundred and eighty-six years earlier.

The big house originally had fifteen hundred acres of land that was used to plant cotton, sweet potatoes, and sorghum, all of it harvested by slave labor and shipped down the Yalobusha to Greenwood, Mississippi for distribution.

Glory had been the flagship home for the surrounding area, a stately Greek Revival with big white columns that could be seen for miles. But over the decades, and through hardship and necessity, the size of Glory's acreage gradually shrank. A city popped up around it and, bit by bit, the land was sold off and homes were built.

Now, several city blocks and hundreds of homes stood between Glory and the river. It sat on its last remaining three acres in the middle of a neighborhood on the outskirts of Pea Ridge behind a massive brick wall with barbed wire strung up on the top of it. It looked more like the neighborhood haunted house than the stately manor it had once been. But the truth was that the house was dying, just like the family who owned it.

Victory Bondurant's death brought the house back to life in a sense. On the day of Ms. Victory's funeral, the house was full of people the way it had always been in the past. Lights were on, doors slammed as people walked in and out, and the smell of food filled the air. The grand old dame was living again, no longer lonely and vacant-looking, and the old iron gates were open with a multitude of cars in the driveway as people came to bring food and pay their respects.

Lucy hadn't seen the house since she had last visited about five years ago. Having dropped her parents' rental car off after the burial, her parents were in the car with her as she pulled into the gravel driveway that wound its way up to the house.

Once her gaze fell on the house, she couldn't help but flinch when she saw the state of it. The overgrown trees hung all around the property and vines had grown up over one side of the house, pulling at the peeling paint. There was a broken window upstairs that had been patched with what looked like cardboard.

Pulling the car around to the back where there were still the remains of the outdoor kitchen as well as two old slave cabins that served as storage sheds, Lucy came to a halt and put the car in park, still looking up at the old house. Massive columns loomed before her, imposing and silent in their gloom.

"Wow, Dad," she said softly. "This place looks like Hell."

Bill eyed the house as he opened the rear passenger door. "I know," he said. "Mama didn't want to spend any money on it with Daddy in the home. Any money they had left had to go for his care and her medical bills."

Lucy gazed up at the tall, proud walls. It hurt her heart to see this big, beautiful house looking so derelict.

"So what are you going to do with it?" she asked, opening her driver's door. "It belongs to you now. I'm guessing it needs a shitload of repairs."

Bill got out of the car, opening the other rear door for his wife. "Me, too," he said, resignation in his tone. "I don't know what I'm going to do. Your mom and I haven't really talked about it."

Lucy climbed out of the car and shut the door. "Will you sell it to me?"

Bill looked at her, surprised. "What are you going to do with it?"

Lucy shrugged, turning to look at the massive ghost of a house. "It's not like I've got anyone or anything to spend my money on," she said. "It might be fun to restore the house and turn it into a bed and breakfast. Besides, I hate seeing it like this. Glory deserves better. It looks so… unloved and abandoned."

Like her. *Unloved and abandoned.* The words had more of a meaning to her these days but she didn't bother to explain what her parents already knew – a husband who had up and left her six months ago for a variety of reasons, including two miscarriages in the past three years.

He wanted a family Lucy couldn't seem to provide for him. They'd met in college, they'd fallen in love, and they'd gotten married. Everything was fine until they tried to have children. That's when things began to fall apart and, after the last miscarriage, he decided he didn't want to be married to her anymore.

Now, Lucy was as vacant as this old house.

"Well," Bill said reluctantly, eyeing his daughter and knowing that she was trying to fill that hole in her heart that her husband had left. But he didn't want her trying to fill it up with a worthless project. "We'll talk about it later. Let's go inside and get some lunch. I can smell the food out here."

Lucy didn't push it. Her depression was growing, feeling a kinship with this old house that she didn't want to feel. She didn't want to feel forgotten and neglected, either.

Collecting her purse, Lucy followed her parents through the back door of the home. There was a slowness to her movements, like she wasn't emotionally ready to enter the house.

As she came in through the big screened door, she stepped into one end of a long, wide hall that bisected the house, a straight shot from the front door to the back door. Up towards the front of the house where the dining room was, people milled about.

Lucy's parents were already heading for the group of people and Lucy could hear voices being raised in greeting. At that moment, the pungent scent of food assaulted her nostrils and she was semi-interested in finding the source of the delicious smell until she caught sight of her creepy cousin up front, a middle-aged man who was a son of one of Mamaw's cousins.

At that point, no Presbyterian chicken smell in the world was going to lure her up into the dining room where Cousin Clyde was, so she took a detour. Quickly, she made her way up the back staircase, a big, wide thing that doubled back on itself as it led up to the dark and humid second floor.

As she emerged onto the second floor, the memories began to come fast and furious. The old flowered wallpaper and the smell of mothballs reminded her so much of Mamaw. She closed her eyes, inhaling the scent, feeling her eyes sting with tears. She felt closest to Mamaw here in this dim, mothball-smelling corridor, and the grief she felt for the woman was magnified. She thought she had been doing pretty well at keeping her sorrow in check until this moment. Now, her guard was down and the sorrow was rolling full-force.

Tears filled her eyes but she fought them, struggling to stay on an even keel. Other than getting away from Cousin Clyde, she'd come up here with another purpose in mind and she didn't want to be distracted from it.

There was an old chifforobe that had something that belonged

IN THE DREAMING HOUR

to her.

Quietly, she made her way past the three other bedrooms on this level. Those bedrooms hadn't been touched in fifty years. They all had the same old chintz wallpaper with matching curtains that, back in the sixties, had been the height of interior décor. Now, they just looked old and battered. Even the bathrooms were stuck in a time warp with their garish tile and ancient hardware.

As Lucy neared Mamaw's room, up at the front of the house overlooking the driveway, she kept an eye on the front stairwell, making sure no one saw her from down below. There was a beautiful self-supporting staircase in the front entry and she could see people moving about. She didn't want to have to explain why she was trying not to be seen. Given that a funeral in the south was a social occasion, she wasn't sure anyone would understand.

Mamaw's bedroom door was shut and she quickly opened it, slipping inside and closing the door softly behind her. Once inside, she paused, taking a moment just to look around, to absorb the last place her grandmother ever saw alive.

The room was neatly made up but the blinds were down, giving the room a hazy glow. Her gaze fell on Mamaw's massive, antique bed, a piece with a half-tester on the top of it, all of the rich mahogany posts carved in a pineapple and palm frond motif. The bedspread on it, however, was a cheap polyester cover from a dollar store, utterly out of place on the lovely furniture.

Lucy's attention moved away from the cheap spread, noticing that all around the bed, on the nightstands and even a small table against the wall, were remnants of the last days of Mamaw's life – prescription pills, aspirators, an oxygen tank, an I.V. stand, dusty fake flowers, and a bedside commode. There was a bathroom attached to the bedroom and a glance through the open door showed more medical equipment in the pink-tiled, run-down bathroom.

It was a lot to take in, the snapshot of the room in its current state. Lucy wasn't sure what she had expected but, somehow, this wasn't it. There was something so terribly disheartening about it. Mamaw had been born in this house, more than likely in this very room, and it was the same room that ushered her out of the land of the living. There was irony in that thought.

Saddened, Lucy went to the windows and raised the blinds. Light streamed in from the floor to ceiling windows, all four of them opening out onto the balcony beyond. In the heyday of Glory, Lucy could imagine the soft night breezes upon that balcony, filling the house with the scent of blossoms and greenery. As she pulled up the last blind and let the sun come in, she caught sight of a massive piece of furniture against the nearest wall.

The chifforobe!

It was an exquisite piece of furniture made from tiger oak, with five drawers and a small cabinet on one side and then a single long cabinet on the other. It had claw-and-ball feet in the front and ornate carvings on the cabinet doors. Lucy remembered hiding in that long single cabinet as a child, playing games with her younger cousins. The old chifforobe held fond memories for her.

Now, it held something else for her. Quickly, she went to the piece of furniture and dropped to a knee, opening the bottom drawer as Vivien had instructed. Inside, there was neatly folded lingerie of some kind, camisoles and slips, and a lavender sachet was tucked into the side of the drawer.

Lucy began removing the underwear, piece by piece, stacking it on the floor beside her after she ran her hands along the fabric, looking for the note that was supposed to be inside the drawer somewhere. She'd managed to pull out several pieces of lingerie, soon coming to the bottom of the drawer without having yet seen the note she'd been told about.

As the drawer emptied, she realized that she would be horribly disappointed if the note wasn't here and she scolded herself for getting her hopes up. That had been a stupid thing to do. But just as she pulled out the last slip, a piece of paper fluttered from it and fell onto the floor.

Startled, Lucy swooped on it.

Snatching it off the floor, it was, indeed, a small white envelope but it was thick, as if stuffed with more than one sheet of paper. There wasn't any name on the envelope but Lucy opened it anyway. Carefully, she pulled forth two sheets of college-ruled paper, noticing right away that there wasn't any writing on them but as she fully unfolded them, a small iron key fell out.

The key hit her on the foot. Curious, Lucy picked it up, looking between the key and the notebook paper as she tried to figure out what in the world the key was for. Curiosity turned into puzzlement, and puzzlement into frustration.

So… there was no great deathbed note, no literary masterpiece welcoming death and giving advice to those left behind. Lucy turned the papers in her hand over at least twice, wondering if there was some secret cypher she had to figure out for invisible ink. Surely Mamaw wouldn't have given her two pieces of blank paper as a parting gift but, truthfully, she wasn't sure. She didn't know the woman's mental state the last few weeks of her life so maybe she had lost her mind a bit. Maybe she thought she had written a note when she'd stuffed the paper into the envelope along with an old-fashioned key and, with that thought, reality hit her.

There *was* no note.

Oh, God… seriously…?

Disappointed, Lucy leaned back against the chifforobe, looking at the key in her hand. It was tiny and it was very old; that much she could see. It was fairly ornate as far as keys went, with an interesting motif on it. In fact, the closer she looked, the more she thought it looked like the carved motif on the chifforobe.

Could it be a key for one of the drawers?

Hope was back. Lucy looked up at the chifforobe, at all of the drawers, and each one had a key hole, but the keyholes were too big. Lucy was coming to think that maybe one of the cabinets held a little locked cubby that the tiny key was meant for and she rose to her knees, turning around to open up the big cabinet to see if there was anything inside that the small key might fit. As she moved, she happened to glance into the open bottom drawer where she'd found the envelope.

And then, she saw it.

On the bottom of the drawer near the junction where the horizontal bottom met with the vertical front of the drawer, there was a tiny hole, just small enough for the key she held in her hand.

Seized with the possibility, Lucy put the key into the little hole. She had to do it four times, from different angles, before it finally engaged. Carefully, she turned the old tumblers and the entire bottom of the drawer came up on a spring system, revealing a secret hiding place beneath.

"I'll be damned," Lucy breathed in awe, noticing that there was something inside the hole. "Of all the...."

She couldn't even finish as she pulled out what looked like an old book. She clutched it, very carefully, for it was obvious that it was quite ancient. Further inspection showed it to be a leather-bound journal with *Victory Jewel Hembree* embossed on the front.

Stunned, Lucy opened it up, very cautiously because the pages were quite yellowed and brittle, only to quickly realize that she was looking at a journal. There were dates she could see clearly written out as well as days of the week, all of it scribed in very careful cursive, a skill that all fine young ladies were taught back in the day. It made her heart race to realize what she had come upon.

A diary!

The inside of the flap had a note to Victory from her mother, Caroline, congratulating her daughter on becoming "of age". It was dated 1931, when Victory Hembree would have been fifteen years old. Something like this was priceless, a sentimental value beyond measure. It was way better than any death-bed note.

The more she looked at it, the more excited she became.

But as she gazed at it, she realized that it was also a sad discovery. A diary hidden away where no one could see it. Lucy wasn't particularly surprised that the journal had been stashed because southern women didn't speak of their feelings much. They were expected to quietly weather whatever tribulations God gave them, so a journal documenting those feelings and hopes and dreams would have been the only outlet.

Maybe that's why Victory's mother had given her daughter that journal, knowing what was expected of a good southern woman – *shut your mouth and put your feelings on paper*. Lucy wondered if her great-grandmother also had a journal, hidden somewhere inside this house. She was willing to bet that the wife of Laveau Hembree would have had some pretty explosive things to say.

It was an intriguing thought as Lucy skimmed through the journal, noting the dates on the entries. In all, the journal was probably one hundred pages or so, thick and well-made paper all bound up with hand-stitching. There was writing on both sides of the pages from what she could see and there were spots where the dark ink had bled through to the other side of the pages, creating big black splotches.

But it didn't matter; Lucy could still read the words and she sank back against the chifforobe once more, journal in hand, devouring the pages.

As people ate and drank and spoke softly of Ms. Victory's life in the dining room on the floor below, up in Ms. Victory's bedroom, an entirely different kind of recollection was taking place – these were Mamaw's thoughts and feelings, her reflections, written in practiced handwriting on the brittle yellow paper.

Lucy started on the very first page of the journal, in the year nineteen hundred and thirty-one, when Mamaw spoke of a girlfriend named Eulalie who was a schoolmate at the Pea Ridge Female Academy. Eulalie brought cakes to school, made from white sugar, and Mamaw lamented the fact that she couldn't do the same.

More entries followed, drawing Lucy into the year when the

Great Depression had been particularly bad for the rural folks in the poor southern towns. Staples were at a premium and meat was only for the wealthy. At this point, Glory was still a working plantation but the acreage had been so reduced that they were barely scraping by on what they could grow. Lucy already knew that much from family stories and Mamaw touched on her daddy's "difficulties" with the plantation, and how they had both white and black sharecroppers working the land.

But those mentions were very limited. For the most part, Mamaw seemed like a normal fifteen-year-old girl and wrote about clothing styles, hats, lip rouge, boys, and even movies. Lucy found a passage where Mamaw wanted to see a Norma Shearer movie that had come to town but her mother wouldn't let her on the grounds of indecency.

The entry made Lucy giggle, thinking of Mamaw wanting to see a pre-Hayes code movie with Norma Shearer slinking across the screen in a silk gown and no bra. It was sure to be scandalous in the conservative small town. Reading further on the same entry, Mamaw was evidently mortified because Caroline had gone to the owner of the movie house and protested the movie, resulting in it never being shown. It was drama in Pea Ridge with pre-code movies at the center of it and Lucy chuckled through the entire entry.

But even as she appreciated the hilarity of it, one thing was becoming clear – the yellowed, brittle pages told the tale of a young girl who was very interested in the world in general, not simply scandalous Hollywood movies or things in her immediate world. She was interested in fashion and makeup and even literature, yet spoke of her home with disdain.

Given what Lucy already knew about Mamaw's relationship with her father, she wasn't surprised. Caroline was greatly respected but Laveau was barely mentioned at all. And when she did mention him, it was really only in passing, as in "Mama and Daddy" together, going somewhere, or her daddy hiring a foreman. Overall,

IN THE DREAMING HOUR

Lucy got a sense of detachment from Mamaw to the man who had fathered her.

On the pages of the old journal, nineteen hundred and thirty-one turned into nineteen hundred and thirty-two and, finally, nineteen hundred and thirty-three. Nineteen hundred and thirty-two had very few entries, mostly about school and about having a pet cat, and nineteen hundred and thirty-three had even fewer entries.

The entries, in fact, abruptly ended about three-quarters of the way into the journal with the rest of the pages being blank. The last entry was something about meeting a friend at school to do some studying. Lucy flipped through the pages, looking to see if there was any more writing, when a white envelope towards the very end of the book suddenly dislodged and fell to the floor. Curious, she was just reaching for it when she heard someone call her name.

"*Lucy!*"

It was her father. Startled, Lucy didn't want him catching her with the journal in her hand. *Don't let your daddy see it!* Vivien had warned. Not that there was anything inside the man couldn't read, but Vivien had been specific. Mamaw hadn't wanted anyone else to see what she'd left for her granddaughter.

Quickly, Lucy picked up the white envelope that had just fallen from the journal, shoved it back inside, and slapped the cover shut. Then she tried to put it back into the secret hiding place in the drawer but the old hinges wouldn't close properly so, not wanting to break them, she simply slapped the drawer shut and shoved the journal underneath the chifforobe. Leaping to her feet, she rushed over to stand by one of the windows just about the time the door opened.

Bill was standing in the doorway, hand on the knob as he peered curiously into the sunlit room. "What are you doing up here?" he asked. "Come on downstairs."

Lucy hoped she didn't look as flustered as she felt. "I... I just wanted to be alone in this room for a minute," she said, looking at the old walls. "I haven't been in this room in years. I just needed to be here for a moment, Dad. I'll be down in a minute."

Bill nodded his head, dropping his hand from the doorknob. "Oh," he said simply, understanding now why his daughter had disappeared. "Well, come down when you're finished. Aunt Dell is asking about you. People want to see you."

"Is Clyde still down there?"

Bill lifted his eyebrows. "You saw him, did you?"

"I did."

"Yes, he's still down there."

"Then call me when he's gone."

Bill snorted. "Honey, you can't ignore everyone down there just because Clyde is here," he said. "I promise I'll keep him away from you, okay? I won't let him hug you or try to kiss you."

Lucy shook her head, disgusted. "I swear to God, Dad...."

"Just come on down when you're finished up here. Okay?"

"Okay."

"Promise?"

"*Yes*, Dad."

"You're not going to jump out the window to get away from Clyde, are you?"

Lucy started laughing. "Not yet."

Bill grinned and winked at her. "Then I'll see you downstairs."

Lucy watched him go, waiting until she could see, through the open door, that he was taking the curved front stairs down to the first floor. Quickly, she went to the door and shut it before heading back to the old chifforobe and pulling out the journal, shoving it carefully into her big Louis Vuitton purse. It wasn't a very big journal so she was even able to zip the bag. She had more reading to do tonight in the hotel. In fact, it was all she could think of. Better to be done with Cousin Clyde and the others now and then get the hell back to the hotel.

Whispering a farewell to Mamaw's bedroom, she followed her father's lead to the first floor.

CHAPTER FOUR
~ Speak of the Devil ~

"*I*T'S HOTTER'N FRESH MILK *today,*" *Laveau said, fanning himself with his Yeddo straw hat as he stood in the plantation office.* "By noon, everything is going come to a standstill. I can't get work out of the men when it's this hot."

He sat down at his cluttered desk, tossing the hat aside as he loosened his collar. He couldn't help but notice that the sheriff was still standing in the doorway, unable or unwilling to enter. He hadn't come in and he hadn't moved out; he just stood there. Maybe it was just too hot for him to come into the office, the Robbins & Myers fan on Laveau's desk just blowing hot air around.

But Laveau didn't have time for indecisiveness. He eyed the sheriff impatiently as he settled back in his chair, putting a hand down to pet the big bloodhound lying miserably on the floor by his desk. Guapo was the dog's name; Spanish for handsome. Laveau named the dog that because it was the ugliest damn dog he'd ever seen.

"What ya'll need today, Terhune?" Laveau asked. "I got things I have to do today, so come to the point."

Terhune, dressed in a crisp white shirt his wife had starched and ironed and the familiar snap-brimmed hat in his hand, waited until a pair of workers passed by the office and out towards the fields before speaking.

"One of my deputies told me this morning that Lane Haltom has been talking to the sheriff over in Charleston about the Ragsdale boy," he said quietly. "You know Lane Haltom?"

Laveau nodded his head slowly, pulling out his handkerchief to wipe the sweat on his forehead. "Lawyer," he said. "I heard he got one of them boys that robbed that white woman last spring– the Coffey boys – off on good behavior. I think the other one got sent to Tallahatchie Correctional for a few months. Not what they deserved, no sir. They should've been put away for good, both of 'em."

Terhune took a step into the searing office. "The Ragsdale family went to him," he said. "They told him what you did to their boy. Now Haltom is going to the papers about it. My deputy said he was approached by someone from the Charleston newspaper about it. Wanted to know what we're going to do about it."

By this time, Laveau seemed to be less impatient with Terhune and more serious about his reason for coming. He tucked his handkerchief back into his pocket. "He went to the papers, did he?"

"Seems so."

Laveau stared at him with those dark, soulless eyes. Terhune had seen that stare before and nothing good ever came out of it.

"Well," Laveau said after a moment, leaning forward in his chair and pretending to look at the paperwork on his desk. "Someone ought to tell Haltom that he's meddling in something that is none of his business and if he isn't careful, someone might just teach him a very harsh lesson. Does he have children?"

Terhune nodded. "I think so."

Laveau wasn't looking at him, instead, finding an invoice from a local livery more interesting. "I think we should find out, don't you?" he asked. "Find out if the man has any children. Then, when you talk to him, make sure he knows we'd be very sorry if something happened to one of his children."

Terhune stood there a moment, watching Laveau read the invoice, feeling sick in the pit of his stomach. He always felt this way when situations with Laveau leaned in this direction, like he wanted to stop the leaning but wasn't strong enough to do it. Laveau leaned any *direction he wanted to without resistance. Terhune never offered him much. Like everyone else in Pea Ridge, he simply leaned in whatever direction Laveau told him to.*

"I'll take care of it," he said, turning for the door. He found he couldn't breathe. "I was just telling you in case you caught wind from someone else."

Laveau glanced up from the paper he was looking at. "I won't hear about it from someone else because you're going to take care of it."

"I am."

Terhune walked away and Laveau didn't say anything more. He didn't have to.

They both knew what would happen if Terhune didn't take care of it.

CHAPTER FIVE

Present

O N THE CURB next to Glory, two men sat in a marked police cruiser. It was a custom Ford Explorer, with all the bells and whistles, because it belonged to the sheriff of Tallahatchie County.

Beau Meade sat in the driver's seat with his father, Tommie, in the passenger seat because Tommie had asked his son to drive him over to Glory so they could extend their condolences to the family of Ms. Victory Hembree. But Tommie simply sat there, evidently unwilling to get out.

Beau had turned the car off some time ago. Now, he was just waiting for his father to make his move.

"Well?" he asked. "Are you going to get out?"

Tommie was looking up at the overgrown house, the old columns sticking out from the growth like rib bones. "Yes," he said. "I was just thinking."

"About what?"

"About what to say to this family. The Meades and the Hembrees go way back."

"I know."

Tommie turned to look at his son. "Then you also know that Victory Hembree wanted nothing to do with our family."

Again, Beau nodded his head. "I am well aware of that," he said. "That's why I was surprised when you said you wanted to come over here. Why *do* you want to come?"

Tommie's gaze lingered on his son a moment; he was a big, strapping example of a man who had been one of the youngest elected sheriffs in the state when he'd been sworn in five years ago. Tommie was proud beyond words of his boy but, in a sense, they were from two different worlds.

Tommie had never really left Pea Ridge except to go to college locally, but Beau had been all over the world. He had a Ph.D. in Sociology and even did a year in England in the course of his schooling. Therefore, Beau had a broader sense of the world in general and things like old family stigmas and prejudices weren't something he had a lot of patience for, no matter how hard Tommie tried to pound them home.

"You just don't know, Beau," Tommie finally said, looking back to the house again. "You just don't know how things were. How bad they were."

Beau sighed heavily, glancing at his watch. "Dad, I don't have time for this," he said. "Either you go in or I'm taking you home. I need to get back to work."

Tommie reached for the door latch. He wasn't ready to go home yet but he wasn't entirely sure he wanted to go inside, either. He was all torn up inside and had been since he'd heard of Ms. Victory's passing. Even with his hand on the door, he didn't open it yet.

"I came because I feel like I need to apologize," he said.

Beau struggled not to roll his eyes. "For what?"

Tommie was growing agitated at his son's impatience. "My granddaddy and Ms. Victory's daddy were thick as thieves back in the day," he said. "You know that. Terhune and Laveau did some terrible things, Beau. Horrible things."

Beau knew all about his great-grandfather and how the man had done the bidding of Laveau Hembree. Hell, the entire town knew the stories – even though Terhune Meade was the sworn sheriff back in the nineteen thirties, it was Laveau who ran the town. If Laveau told Terhune to throw someone in jail, then he did. If he told Terhune to shoot someone, then Terhune would.

So much evil had been done between the two of them, something Beau didn't particularly think about like his father did. Although he knew that old prejudices were hard to break down here, he found that the older he got, the more he didn't have much tolerance for them. Hatreds and rumors and cultural stigmas would never go away if people kept dredging them up.

"It shouldn't follow you around," Beau said after a moment. "That's all in the past. If you keep looking back, you'll never get away from it. Now, are you going to go inside or am I going to take you home?"

Tommie opened the door but still didn't get out. "It's your history, too, son," he said. "You've heard the stories about it. I've told you about it and I'm pretty sure Granddaddy told you about it. It's part of you whether or not you want it to be."

Beau groaned softly. "Dad, I *really* don't have time for this," he said. "People around here want to live in fear and remember horrible things from eighty years ago, then that's their deal. It's not mine. I didn't do any of that stuff and I'm not going to let it affect me. I never have. Now, let's go in and get this over with. I need to get back to the station."

Tommie sighed faintly. Beau was too pragmatic for his own good sometimes. Not that he disagreed with his attitude – it was true that, four generations removed, deeds and prejudices had a way of fading. Beau's generation just didn't give a lot of credence to things like that, which was good in a sense. It meant that, eventually, they would all heal from the horrors of the past. But they wouldn't heal soon enough for Tommie's taste. Swinging his legs out of the car, he stepped out onto the curb.

Quickly, Beau climbed out as well, slamming the door and locking it when his father shut the passenger door. He didn't want the man trying to climb back into the car again. Together, the two of them headed through the open gates to where the cars were parked, making their way to the lawn that was thick and overgrown. Both Beau and Tommie were looking up at the house as they walked, drinking it all in.

The structure exuded a sense of foreboding, from the chipped foundation to the roof that needed repairing. It was as if a million silent words poured from the old walls, like a symphony, reminding them of terrible deeds of long past, of the horrors the old house had seen. It was a sense of apprehension that was difficult to ignore.

"I remember as a kid, I'd walk this way on my way home from school," Tommie said quietly, his eyes riveted to the peeling paint of the old walls. "The house was in better shape back then. Laveau was still alive but this place was really locked in on itself. Big dogs in the yard, people sitting on the porch with shotguns. No one came near it. We were terrified just walking past it. In fact, I've never been this close to it."

Beau was looking up at the second floor. He swore he saw the outline of a woman standing in the corner room, near the windows. It was a rather curvaceous outline. But it was quickly gone and he snorted, thinking that maybe he'd seen a ghost. Given the stories about this place, it wouldn't have surprised him.

"It was starting to look pretty run down when I was a kid," Beau said, foregoing a mention of the ghost. "This had to be, oh, thirty years ago. Laveau was dead at that point but there were still people on the front porch with shotguns."

Tommie snorted. "You couldn't get away with that these days," he said, peering at the porch and the door beyond. "I've never been inside it, but I think my daddy was at some point."

Beau nodded. "I remember him talking about it," he said. "I don't really remember much about what he said, but I seem to recall him saying that he came here for a birthday party when he was young. Maybe it was Ms. Victory's party."

Tommie shrugged. "Maybe," he said. "Ms. Victory and my

daddy were born around the same time, so it's possible."

"Did they go to school together?"

Tommie shook his head. "Not back then," he said. "Well-bred young ladies went to private all-girl schools if they could afford them. Pea Ridge had an academy out on the outskirts of town that serviced the entire county. Not much call for expensive private schools in this rural area."

Beau didn't say anything more. They were up on the porch now, greeting the people who were standing outside, eating and talking. Tommie reached out to open the ancient screen door, admitting him and his son to the cool, dank home.

People were congregated in small groups in the two front rooms. To the left was the dining room with a massive table, laden with food and crock pots, and to the right was a parlor. Tommie wasn't sure which direction to go, so he headed into the parlor where people were sitting on furniture that was probably forty years old – all of it was covered in plastic but in surprisingly good shape.

As Beau stood back, visually inspecting the layout of the old house, Tommie approached a couple he knew and extended his hand to the male half. He shook hands with the man and exchanged some small talk, finally asking for Ms. Victory's relatives or whoever was in charge. The couple pointed him into the dining room, specifically, to a man and woman who were in conversation with a very old woman with a walker.

When Tommie spied the pair, something about the man struck a chord in him. In fact, he felt a bit of a jolt because the man looked just like Laveau Hembree – tall, good-looking, and with a head of graying hair, the resemblance was uncanny. Tommie thanked his friends for their direction and, taking Beau with him, headed into the dining room.

The cavernous dining room smelled heavily of food, of chicken and greens and cornbread. It was enough to pull Beau to the table to inspect the offerings but Tommie headed straight to the man who looked like Laveau Hembree. He waited politely for the man to finish his conversation with the very old woman in the walker before introducing himself.

"Excuse me," Tommie said, watching the man turn to look at him. He extended his hand. "My name is Tommie Meade. My family has lived in Pea Ridge nearly as long as the Hembree family and I wanted to come today to tell you how sorry I am to hear of Ms. Victory's passing. She is one of the last of a dying breed around here."

The man who resembled Laveau took the hand offered to him and shook it. "Bill Bondurant," he said, a twinkle in his eye. "You don't remember me, do you?"

Tommie suddenly looked stricken. "Bill Bondurant?" he hissed. Then, he broke down into ironic laughter. "Billy! Is it really you?"

"It is."

"Good Lord, I didn't even recognize you!"

Bill laughed right along with him. "Seriously, Tommie?" he said, feigning insult. "You and me hung around together right up through high school and you didn't even *recognize* me?"

Tommie shook his head, embarrassed. "I haven't seen you in over forty years," he said. "People change. And my eyesight is terrible. I'm really ashamed."

Bill kept grinning. "I left Pea Ridge when I was eighteen and went off to college," he said. "Then I moved to California. I haven't seen you in all of the times I've been back to visit my mother, so I'm the one who should be ashamed. I should have looked you up sometime in the past forty years but I didn't. You and I were good friends, once."

Tommie thought back to those days when he and his group of friends, Bill included, prowled around Pea Ridge on their bikes and later in their cars. They had all gone to school locally, a public whites-only school back in the days of the "Separate but Equal" movement before Dr. Martin Luther King's movement began to gain steam.

Most of the boys Tommie had hung around with never left the area, content to stay in their own neck of the woods. But Bill had been one of the very few to actually leave and make something of himself outside of the small town culture that tended to suck down and smother everything and everybody it touched.

Deep down, Tommie had always envied Bill for having gotten out when he did.

"We were blood brothers from what I recall," he said. "I seemed to remember slitting my finger over yours, once."

Bill chuckled. "You sure did."

Tommie's gaze lingered on the man. "Then from one blood brother to another, you don't need to explain things to me," he said quietly. "I understand why things were the way they were. Your mama didn't want me around and I get that. But we're seeing each other now, aren't we?"

Bill's smile faded. "I'm glad we are," he said. "With Mama gone, there's no reason not to see each other again. But I have to tell you… I'm really surprised to see you here, given how my mother always reacted to you."

Tommie scratched his head, an almost nervous gesture. "Me, too," he admitted. "But it's like I told my son – I felt like I had to come. I feel like I have to apologize."

Bill's eyebrows flew up. "For *what*, for Christ's sake?"

Tommie shrugged, averting his gaze. "Things," he said quietly. "Past things."

Bill knew what he meant. He found it rather sad that the man felt as if he needed to apologize for the sins of their fathers and grandfathers. "Tommie, your family and my family have a history together that neither one of us should apologize for," he said in a subdued tone. "We didn't do any of those things that people talk about. There have never been any apologies between you and me and there never will be as far as I'm concerned."

Tommie felt much better. In fact, now he was glad he had come. Seeing his old friend today had crossed his mind but he hadn't seen the man in so many years, he wasn't sure how Bill would react to his appearance. Now, he knew. It was better than he could have hoped for.

"Well...," he said, touched by Bill's attitude, relieved by the situation in general. "That's good to know, Billy. I hope we'll be seeing something of you in the future. I'd like that."

Bill put a hand on his shoulder. "Me, too," he said. "Mama left us this big, old monstrosity of a house. You will definitely be seeing us in the future while we spend some time here cleaning it out. This is my wife, by the way. I don't think you've ever met Mary."

Tommie turned his attention on the elegant blonde woman at Bill's side. He shook her hand politely. "No, I haven't," he said. "Nice to meet you, Mary."

Mary smiled pleasantly. "Nice to meet you, also," she said.

Tommie caught movement out of the corner of his eye then, seeing that Beau was close by. He reached out and pulled the rather large man in a sheriff's uniform away from the table and over to their group.

"This is my son," he said to Bill and Mary. "Beau, this is my old friend, Billy Bondurant, and his wife, Mary. Billy is Ms. Victory's son."

Beau smiled pleasantly at the pair. "Hello," he said, shaking their hands in succession. "My condolences on the passing of your mother, Mr. Bondurant. She was definitely one of the more respected residents in town. In fact, when my dad and I were walking up to the house, we were reminiscing about our memories of it. It's definitely an icon around here."

Bill shook the hand of the big man with broad shoulders and a superhero-square jaw. "Meade," he muttered, looking at the uniform. "Didn't I see that name on some posters around here?"

Beau nodded modestly. "I'm up for re-election."

Bill's eyes widened. "*Sheriff* Meade," he said, making the connection. "Well, for Heaven's sake… Tommie, your son is *Sheriff* Meade?"

Tommie nodded proudly. "That would be him."

Bill laughed, doing a lite-version of a face palm. "I have no idea why I never made the connection," he said. "I've seen that name around for a few years now, at least when I've come to visit Mama. Tommie, didn't you work for the Tallahatchie County Sheriff's Department, too?"

Tommie nodded. "I did," he said. "I retired out as a lieutenant a few years ago, right after Beau was elected sheriff. Seems I couldn't take orders from my own son."

As Bill and Mary grinned, Beau simply shook his head. "He had been on twenty-eight years already and he'd been planning retirement long before I came on board. He just likes to tell people I chased him away. Needless to say, he is *not* my campaign manager."

Bill chuckled softly, looking between father and son. "Your daddy also served in the sheriff's department, as did your granddaddy," he said to Tommie. "Four generations in the same family is pretty impressive."

Tommie looked at his son, the warmth of pride still in his eyes. "Beau is smarter and better and more educated than the rest of us ever were," he said. "I wouldn't be surprised if he ran for State Police Commissioner or even governor someday. This boy is working his way up."

As Beau tried to downplay his political future, a new player entered the dining room. Lucy had just come down the treacherous stairs from the upper floor, looking for her parents in the front parlor before seeing Cousin Clyde and quickly changing course. Now, she darted into the dining room on the hunt for her parents and hoping to evade Clyde's radar.

But she hadn't been fast enough. Cousin Clyde saw her and,

much to her horror, he was coming out of the parlor, waving to catch her attention. Mortified, Lucy pretended not to see him and quickly made her way through the people milling about in the dining room until she came to her parents. In a move of self-defense, she pushed herself between her mother and father, hoping Clyde wouldn't have the balls to join them.

"Hi," she whispered to her dad, eyeing Clyde as he entered the room. "Please hide me. Clyde has seen me and he wants to talk to me."

Bill wasn't the only one to hear her plea; Mary and Tommie and Beau did, too. Four heads turned in Clyde's direction to see the man sauntering into the room, his attention in their direction. In his cheap suit and with his greasy hair and smarmy expression, Clyde didn't seem to realize that Lucy had run from him. He was still trying to wave at her. Tommie was the first one to hiss.

"Not *that* boy," he muttered. "I didn't even see him when we came in. Did you, Beau?"

Beau was eyeing Clyde. "No," he said. "I haven't seen him in a while."

Tommie snorted. "That's a good thing," he said. Then, he looked at Lucy. "Honey, is he after you? Do you want me to take care of him?"

Lucy looked at Tommie in surprise. She didn't even know the man and couldn't decide if his offer was chivalrous or simply vigilante-like. She didn't need to set off some good ol' boy down here and get her cousin bumped off. Standing right next to him was a younger, bigger, and much better looking version of the same man. In fact, she nearly did a double-take at the man in the sheriff's uniform; to say he was hot would have been an understatement. Before she could reply to Tommie's offer, however, Bill got involved.

"No, I'll do it," he mumbled unhappily. Quickly, he made introductions to the woman clinging on his arm. "Sheriff Meade,

Tommie, this is my daughter, Lucy. Lucy, Tommie is an old friend of mine and this is his son, Beau. Now, head into the kitchen and I'll go have a word with Cousin Clyde."

It suddenly turned into some kind of covert operation and everyone was on the move, determined to get Lucy clear of the prowling cousin. While Mary and Bill went to head off Clyde, Tommie grabbed Beau by the arm and pointed to Lucy.

"Get her out of here," he ordered his son quietly. "If Clyde slips past us, you'll be her last line of defense."

Beau knew who Clyde McKibben was and he furthermore knew the man's reputation, thanks to his mother who went to church with Clyde's mother. Not only could those church ladies cook, but they could gossip with the best of them, which sometimes told him more than he needed to know about people in the community. Knowing what he did about Clyde, he had no problem protecting the lady from what was widely known as a lecherous pervert.

Without a word, he followed Lucy out of the dining room, through the butler's pantry, and into the big kitchen that hadn't been remodeled since the nineteen fifties.

A mix of the very old and the very, very old, the kitchen had old wooden counters, a cast iron farm sink and sideboard, and a massive O'Keefe and Merritt Town and Country model stove that literally had everything built into it – burners, stoves, warmers, and all. It was in good shape for being as old as it was.

Huge open shelves lined one wall because, in the old days, there was no such thing as closed cabinetry for the most part, and even though there was an old General Electric refrigerator towards the rear of the kitchen, there was also the old icebox that no one had ever gotten rid of. As he came to a halt just inside the kitchen door, Lucy evidently hadn't been aware that he'd followed her and she started when she realized he was standing in close proximity.

"Seriously," she said, holding up her hands. "I'm sure it's not all that critical that I need a bodyguard against Clyde. I think I can handle him if he comes in here."

Beau's gaze moved over the woman with the long auburn hair, cut into one of those sexy layered styles. She had the biggest green eyes he'd ever seen. He'd never seen her around town before, which was a shame considering how lovely she was. He would have definitely remembered her.

"How do you know?" he asked, lifting his eyebrows. "I hear he can be pretty wily."

Lucy laughed softly. "You know him, then?"

"I know *of* him."

She continued to giggle. "Oh, brother," she said. "Don't tell me he's got a criminal record, too."

Beau was rather enjoying listening to her laugh. "Let's just say his reputation precedes, him," he said. "Besides… my mama goes to church with his mama, so I hear things about him all of the time."

Lucy was intrigued. Plus, she kind of liked this big cop with the deep voice. She liked the way his blue eyes glimmered.

"Like… what?" she said. "Like he's been married six times? I can't tell you how many times he has tried to make me wife number seven. It doesn't even matter to him that we're from the same family. Whenever I'd come to visit Mamaw, he always found a reason to come hang around. She'd have to chase him off with her cane."

Beau broke out into a grin. "I believe it," he said, scratching his head. "Like I said, his reputation precedes him."

"Can't talk about it?"

He wriggled his eyebrows, a smile playing on his lips. "I don't want to gossip like my mama."

"Facts aren't gossip."

He chuckled softly. "True enough," he said. "It's nothing earth-shattering. We've had a few calls on him, in various situations. Following women home from the market and things like that.

Never enough to throw him in jail on, but he's got a reputation."

"Creepy?"

"Stalker is more like it."

Lucy rolled her eyes. "Terrific," she said, irony in her voice. "This family just can't have nice, normal people in it, can it? Everyone has to be a freak to some degree."

"You seem pretty normal."

Lucy thought that might have sounded like a hint of a flirt. She raised her eyebrows at him. "How do you know?" she asked. "I could be the biggest freak of the whole bunch for all you know."

Beau snorted. "That's true," he said. "Well, I suppose we've all got skeletons in our closets."

"Some of us have an entire cemetery in ours."

"You?"

She gave him a coy expression, much exaggerated. "Wouldn't you like to know?"

It really wasn't a question, but more of a statement. Beau, swept up in the increasingly flirty conversation, almost answering that, yes, that he would like to know, but he didn't give in to the urge. He shut his mouth and simply grinned. He didn't want anything he said to come out as leading or inappropriate, no matter how cute he thought she was. It was better, at that point, to change the subject, so he did.

"So, you're Ms. Victory's granddaughter," he said. "I don't ever remember seeing you around town before. You said you've come to visit before?"

Lucy couldn't help but notice that he had clumsily changed the subject and she was fairly certain it was because he had been uncomfortable with her subtle flirting. Too bad, too. The guy was a hunk. Feeling moderately embarrassed for her failed attempt at batting her eyelashes, she rolled easily with the shift in focus.

"I've been here many times," she said, a bit less friendly and a little more pleasantly polite. "The last time I was here was about five years ago. It's been a while. I had no idea the place was looking so run-down. I'm trying to talk my parents into selling it to me so I can fix it up."

Beau tore his eyes away from her long enough to look around the kitchen. "You'd sure have your work cut out for you," he said. "I'm guessing this place needs a whole lot of work."

Lucy looked around, too, because he was. "Yes, it does," she said, somewhat sadly. "I was just upstairs. I don't think that the entire upstairs has been touched for fifty years. But what's the alternative? We just can't let the house fall apart."

He shrugged in agreement. "It's definitely a piece of Tallahatchie County's history. It would be a tragedy to see it go, although my dad seems to think that some people around here would be happy to see it torn down."

Lucy knew what he meant. "Destroying Laveau Hembree's memory, so to speak."

He nodded. "Among other things," he said, not wanting to offend the woman since they were speaking of her great-grandfather. "That's actually why my dad came over here today – to apologize for our family's involvement in the things Laveau Hembree did during his heyday. People around here still remember that stuff. I think my dad just needed to clear his conscience."

By this time, Lucy was looking at him seriously. "Well, I really don't know all of it, but if even half of the stories I have heard are true, I think my family should apologize to yours. So, for what it's worth, I'm sorry my great-grandfather was such a nasty bastard. But it seems to me that it's really sad that a family and a house that have been around this area for almost two hundred years are only defined by one man. That just doesn't seem fair."

Beau shook his head. "No, it really doesn't." One of the Presbyterian ladies offered Beau a cup of coffee, which he gratefully accepted before returning his attention to Lucy. "So, you're thinking about moving here and fixing the place up, then?"

"Maybe."

"What do you do for a living that you can sink money into this old place?"

Lucy accepted her own cup of coffee from one of the church ladies. Before answering, she gave him a big, fake grin to preface what was to come. There was irony in the gesture.

"I'm a partner in a criminal defense firm in Los Angeles," she said.

Beau didn't react for a moment, sipping his coffee. His reply was deadpan. "So you're my mortal enemy."

"Essentially."

He snorted into his coffee. She laughed softly into hers. But abruptly, the kitchen door that led out to the back porch suddenly opened and Clyde appeared. He'd evidently gone around the dining room completely, pushed out of it by Lucy's parents, and come into the kitchen through the back way. The man wasn't stupid. He'd seen where Lucy had gone. And he knew how to get there, one way or another.

Startled by Clyde's abrupt appearance, Lucy spilled her coffee in her haste to move away from him. Clyde's eyes tracked her as she headed for the sink.

"You've been avoiding me, you naughty girl," he scolded. "Cousin Bill and Cousin Mary said you weren't feeling well, but I think it's something else."

Lucy was over by the sink now, setting the coffee cup down and trying to wipe the liquid off of her dark suit jacket. She couldn't even bring herself to be pleasant to Clyde.

"No, they were right," she said. "I'm not feeling great. In fact, I'm just getting ready to head back to the hotel now."

Clyde was moving towards her. "I'd be happy to drive you over there."

He was coming close and Lucy moved away, heading for the waste basket to throw the coffee-stained paper towel away.

"I have my own car, thanks," she said steadily.

Clyde didn't seem to take the hint. "I'll call you later, then," he said. "Maybe we can have breakfast together."

Lucy was backed up against the kitchen trash because he'd cornered her. He was too damn close and, in frustration, she reached out and shoved him away by the chest.

"Jesus, Clyde," she hissed. "You need to stay out of my personal space."

Clyde looked at her as if he had no idea what she meant. "I was just going to hug you," he said innocently. "I haven't seen you in years."

Lucy was moving away from him and, in doing so, she moved in Beau's direction. "There's a reason for that," she said. "I have no desire to see you. In fact, you really need to stay away from me. My parents tried to be nice about it but you obviously don't get it, so I'm going to make it clear – leave me alone. Don't call me, don't try to hug me, don't even think about me. Just leave me alone. Do you understand?"

Clyde had at least stopped following her. He stood in the middle of the kitchen, his brow furrowed. "Have I done something to offend you?" he asked as if genuinely perplexed. "Lucy, I'm sorry if I have. I didn't mean to."

Lucy waved him off. She didn't have time to waste on the man. Turning to Beau, she forced a smile. "It has been a pleasure to meet you," she said, holding out her hand. "What I said earlier about my family apologizing to yours – I hope you accept it."

Beau, who had been watching the entire situation with Clyde very carefully, took her small hand in his big one and shook it firmly. "You don't have to ask twice," he said. "The matter is settled as far as I'm concerned. And it was really nice to meet you, too."

Lucy's smile turned genuine. "Thanks," she said. Then, she jerked her head in Clyde's direction. "Can you at least keep him here until I leave? I don't want him following me."

Beau's gaze moved to Clyde, still standing in the middle of the kitchen, looking confused. "You bet," he said quietly. "Consider it done."

"Thanks."

With that, Lucy slipped out of the kitchen, clutching her big Louis Vuitton purse to her side. When Clyde started to move after her, Beau called out to him.

"McKibben," he said. "Hold on a minute. I need to talk to you."

Clyde wasn't happy that his prey was getting away. He frowned at Beau. "What do you want?" he asked. "I ain't got nothing to say to you."

Beau's gaze was intense. "That may be, but I have a lot to say to you. We're going to start with your cousin there – she told you to stay away from her. If you don't do as she asks, I'm going to be showing up on your doorstep."

Clyde's features twisted angrily. "You can't threaten me."

"I didn't. All I said was that I was going to show up on your doorstep. Take it any way you want to, but you're going to stay away from her."

Clyde sighed heavily. "I can do what I want and you can't stop me."

"You want to bet on that?"

Clyde's answer was to try and follow where Lucy had gone. Beau's response was to grab the man by the neck and pull him back out into the dining room where Bill, Mary, and Tommie still were. Clyde was whining about police brutality until Bill got a hold of him and told him to shut his mouth. When Beau explained how Clyde had managed to disregard the request to leave Lucy alone, the gloves came off.

Bill had several words with Clyde at that point and none of them were pleasant.

CHAPTER SIX

~ In the Dreaming Hour ~

"IT'S ABOUT MY DAUGHTER, Dr. Latling," the woman with the neat Marcel wave spoke nervously, sitting in the doctor's office that was attached to his house. "She won't eat. She hardly sleeps. Is… is she well, Doctor? You've examined her so you must now. Her daddy wants to know if she's well."

A round, older man with thin gray hair and thick glasses gazed at the woman across the room. Seated at his desk, he leaned back, wiping the sweat from his brow. The day had been hot and, with his size, he always sweated profusely.

"You mean Laveau wants to know if she's going to lose that child?" he asked frankly.

The woman with the Marcel wave nodded, once, and it took all of her strength to do that. Clutching her purse to her bosom, she couldn't bring herself to look at the doctor.

"It's a sin," she hissed. "I know it's a sin, but he prays for it. He prays for it daily. Dr. Latling, I fear for my daughter's life. Her daddy… he's just so ashamed of the state she's in. He won't let her out of the house – did you know that? She's not allowed to go out at all. When people come to the house, he locks her in her bedroom. He keeps her caged like an animal. It's no wonder she won't sleep or eat!"

The doctor sighed heavily. "Ms. Caroline, the last time I saw the girl, she was healthy."

"But she had fainted! She's been doing a lot of that, you know.

That's how we first found out about the… child."

The doctor nodded. "I know it," he said. "Your daughter is pregnant and praying for her to lose the child just ain't right. You need to make her eat. She needs to take care of herself or she may just die right along with the baby. As much as I'm sure that would make Laveau happy, I'm sure you won't let that happen. You're the girl's mother, Ms. Caroline. You need to start acting like it."

Caroline Hembree stiffed. "What is that supposed to mean?"

The doctor pointed a finger at her. "It means that ya'll are letting your husband bully you around about that girl," he said. "She's your child, for God's sake. Take care of her. Don't let Laveau keep you from your motherly duties."

Caroline was flustered but she was also torn. She knew the doctor was right. He was probably the only man in Pea Ridge that didn't subscribe to fear of Laveau Hembree because he'd once pulled Laveau through an episode of appendicitis and Laveau treated the man as if he owed him something.

Therefore, Dr. Latling could speak more freely of Laveau than most and he did so, without reserve, when faced with stupidity caused by the man. And that included his terrified wife and a terrified town. Abruptly, Caroline stood up, heading for the door.

"Thank you for your time, Doctor," she said stiffly. "If… if you can come by sometime soon and see my daughter, I would be grateful."

The doctor stood up, too, taking his handkerchief from his back pocket and wiping his brow. "Ms. Caroline, I ain't coming if Laveau is going to ask me to get rid of that baby," he said frankly. "He asked me once before, when I first told him she was carrying. I won't do it."

The woman sighed, hand on the door latch. She was trying not to succumb to the common and moral sense that the doctor was making, but it was difficult.

"He may ask," she admitted. "I don't really know. I'm asking you to come to the house to make sure my daughter is well. That's all I'm asking."

The doctor didn't say anything and the woman continued out the door, out to the 1913 Maxwell Model-24 touring car that was waiting for her. Ms. Caroline's colored maid sat in the back seat, as a traveling companion, and one of her husband's men sat in the driver's seat, the same man who drove Ms. Caroline everywhere. She wasn't allowed to drive and she was only allowed out with her maid and one of her husband's men to keep an eye on her.

The doctor watched the woman hustle out to the car, climbing into the back seat because that was where she was allowed to sit. Still swabbing himself with his handkerchief, the doctor shut the door, wondering how on earth a girl like Victory Hembree got herself pregnant with a daddy who hovered over the women in the family the way he did.

Of course, the doctor knew the rumor that had led to a colored man's demise. Thanks to Terhune Meade, the whole town knew it had been a rape. Terhune had to say something to justify his complicity in the murder. But given the girl's reaction to that man's death on that sultry night, the doctor wasn't so sure it was really rape.

He suspected that was far from the truth.

Dr. Latling further suspected that when that child was born, he would be the only one willing to protect it.

CHAPTER SEVEN

Present

THE JOURNAL DIDN'T stay in her purse for long.

It was a ten-minute drive from Mamaw's house to the nicer chain hotel in town but in spite of all of the food at the house, Lucy hadn't eaten any of it and she was starving. So she swung through a fast food restaurant drive-thru before shutting herself up in her hotel room for the night. To the smell of burgers and fries, Mamaw's journal and the big white envelope were carefully pulled out of the safe haven of the purse and placed on the bed.

The lure of food wasn't stronger than the lure of what was in the second white envelope, so Lucy left the food on a side table as she inspected the envelope. The glue wasn't very good and the flap came open with little prompting. With a good deal of anticipation, Lucy pulled out the contents.

This envelope contained paper with a lot of writing on it; Lucy could see that immediately. Pulling the paper apart, she could see that there were two pieces of paper, just like the other envelope had contained, but there was careful writing on both sides of these papers. She recognized Mamaw's distinctive cursive immediately and her excitement was building as she realized that this was the letter she had been hoping to find, great and meaningful words of wisdom from Mamaw to her only granddaughter. She had been building it up so much in her mind that she sincerely hoped it was something sweet and very personal. Knowing Mamaw, however, it would probably be family recipes she didn't want to share with anyone else. That would have been typical of the woman.

Don't let Cousin Margaret have this recipe!

The thought made Lucy giggle. As she unfolded the letter, a small scrap of paper fell out and drifted down onto the bed. It was an old piece of paper, yellowed with age and brittle. She retrieved it, noting that there was writing on it that she didn't recognize. Turning on the bedside lamp to get a better look, she read the printing on the old scrap:

In the Dreaming Hour,
Where my heart is free
The song of nighttime comforts me
And brings me thoughts of thee.
On beams of silver moonlight,
Against the dark of night,
The world beholds no color,
No blackness and no white.
And in this world, void of color,
The heart and soul combines,
For in the Dreaming Hour,
My love unites with thine.

It was exquisite. Lucy smiled, reading it over three or four times, wondering who had written this beautiful poem. Perhaps it was an old beau or perhaps it had been someone trying to woo Mamaw. It had made enough of an impression on the woman for her to save it all of these years and it was little wonder. People simply didn't court like this any longer and it was a shame, for a poem like this bespoke of days gone by where more thought and effort might have gone into a courtship. Dating today was little more than clicking and swiping.

My love unites with thine....

As Lucy's heart melted at the loveliness of the poem, it was also squeezed, just a little. She remembered her husband when they'd first met in college and started dating, and how sweet he'd been to her. Little notes, little texts, that kind of thing. He didn't have the poetic aptitude that Mamaw's suitor had, but he'd been sweet, at least as sweet as he'd been capable of.

But times had changed.

She didn't like to think of that change. It hurt her heart still, badly, to think of how much her world had been altered. With a sigh, longing for a time in her life she'd never see again, she set the poem on the bed, carefully, and opened up Mamaw's letter. Adjusting the light on the bedside lamp, she began to read.

My Dearest Lucy —

If you're reading this letter, then it must be because I am gone. I knew Vivien would give you my message and that you would find the journal in its hiding place. That journal has been there for many years and I'm the only one who has read the words in it until now. Try not to laugh too much at the silly ramblings of a child. For I was very much a child back then. But I was a child who had experienced too much in life and I want you to know what has been heavy in my heart for eighty years. It's time to tell the story, but I do this with a purpose.

If you're reading this letter, then it must be because I am gone. I knew Vivien would give you my message and that you would find the journal in its hiding place. That journal has been there for many years and I'm the only one who has read the words in it until now. Try not to laugh too much at the silly ramblings of a child. For I was very much a child back then. But I was a child who had experienced too much in life and I want you to know what has been heavy in my heart for eighty years. It's time to tell the story, but I do this with a purpose.

I need your help.

His name was Lewis. No, that's not your Pop's name. It's the name of a man I knew, and loved, long before Pop came along. I met Lewis when I attended the Pea Ridge Female Academy under the tutelage of Mr. J. Duncan Franklin of the Hattiesburg Franklins. Mr. Franklin was a good Christian man who wanted to teach us to be fine ladies. But he also tutored coloreds and the coloreds from Rose Cove knew he would teach them to read and write, which he did after hours out in the barn behind the academy. Lewis was one of his pupils.

Lewis Ragsdale was a fine man, smart and eager to learn. He was a good student and Mr. Franklin liked Lewis enough to give him a job taking care of the grounds at school. He would mow lawns and prune trees by day, and Mr. Franklin would teach him Hawthorne and Poe and Eliot by night.

One day, I left my books in the classroom and Lewis picked the lock so I could retrieve them. He noticed I had a copy of the "Sonnets of the Portuguese" and he expressed a desire to read them someday. I saw no harm in loaning Lewis my book, which he took graciously and humbly. He returned it the next day, having stayed up all night to read it.

After that, Lewis and I spoke of our love of poetry and literature whenever we could. I told Mr. Franklin that I had loaned Lewis my books, as a good Christian would do, and he didn't seem troubled by it. In fact, he invited me to help tutor his class of coloreds, but I couldn't tell Mama or Daddy about it, so I told them I was tutoring other girls after school. They would let me stay so long as I was home by supper. It was nearly the only time during my days that Mama or Daddy weren't hanging over me. I felt free.

Maybe you see where this is leading. Lewis was unlike any

man I had ever met before. He was a gentle soul with a heart that was pure. I never knew men like that existed. I came from a family where Daddy ruled our world and viewed me with resentment, having been born a girl as I was. But Lewis thought every word out of my mouth was the voice of an angel. He gave me the love and respect that Daddy had denied me. I can't describe to you what Lewis meant to me, only that he meant everything. With him, I was loved.

Now, a white woman with a colored man back in my younger days just wasn't done. It wasn't fitting. Lewis and I made plans to run away together and get married. In 1933, it was illegal in Mississippi for a colored person to marry a white person, so we knew we had to leave the state. Lewis had heard that we could go to Illinois and be legally married, so we made plans. Those plans became more important than ever when I discovered I was pregnant.

Dr. Latling was the town's doctor and probably the only man who wasn't afraid of Daddy. He told Daddy that I was pregnant. Mama cried as Daddy beat me and demanded to know who the father was, but I wouldn't tell him. I knew what would happen to Lewis if Daddy knew and I couldn't see him die by Daddy's hand. I would want to die, too.

But I was weak, and I was afraid, and I told a horrible lie to Daddy when I could no longer stand his beatings. I told him that a man had raped me but I didn't know who it was because it had been dark when it happened. Daddy went to Sheriff Meade and they determined that a colored man had raped me. After all, good white men were incapable of such things, weren't they?

They interrogated me until I broke and screamed at them that, yes, a colored man had raped me. But I would have said anything for them to leave me alone. The night that Lewis and I planned to run away together, his brother, Aldridge, came for me. He was to take me to Lewis. But Daddy saw us together and immediately assumed that Aldridge, who worked for Daddy, was the man who had raped me. Daddy took poor Aldridge away that night and I never did see him alive again. The next I heard, his body ended up back on his family's front porch.

After that, I never saw Lewis again because Daddy kept me locked in the house until I delivered the baby. Dr. Latling delivered the child but I never did see her. He gave me ether for the birth and when I woke up, he was gone and so was the baby. No one would tell me what happened to her and Dr. Latling would never answer my questions, but something told me he knew what happened to her. He was a doctor and doctors aren't supposed to kill, so I have to have hope that she made it out of that room alive.

I know I've never spoken kindly of Daddy, so if you have ever wondered why, now you know. He never forgave me for bearing a half-colored bastard and I never forgave him, or myself, for the death of an innocent man.

Now we come to the help I need from you. In the top of my chifforobe is a small wooden box containing a gold locket. On the locket are inscribed these words – In The Dreaming Hour. Lucy, I want you to find that baby girl I gave birth to so long ago and I want you to give her that locket. If she's dead, then give it to her daughter, if she has one. I want her, or her children, to have it because it's the only thing Lewis ever gave me. He saved his money for a long time to buy it. And in this letter is a scrap of a poem he wrote for me with those same words. It's the most valuable thing I own, that old piece of paper. I couldn't ask to be buried with it, but I wanted to be.

But now I ask you – keep it safe with you. It is more valuable than anything I've ever owned, other than the poem. And the inscription on the locket – In The Dreaming Hour – is *what I'd like written on my headstone. No one but me, and now you, will know what it means, but I'm content with that. I need some part of Lewis with me and that is all I'll ever have.*

I love you, my darling Lucy. You are my pride and my joy. Now that you know my deepest secret, I hope you won't judge me too harshly. Love is never wrong, no matter of the color of your skin. I was lucky because I was loved more deeply than most.

Find my baby. I named her Ruby. Give her the locket and tell her, if she is still alive, how very much I loved her even though I never knew her.

Mamaw

Lucy was sobbing softly as she read the last passage.

Hand to her mouth, the tears poured from her eyes. All she could think of was the suffering Mamaw must have gone through, the sheer hell of a love that was never meant to be and the sheer hell of an innocent man dying at the hands of her father.

God, it was just horrific, all of it. But in that horror, there was the core of a love story so true, so ageless, that even now, Lucy could feel the impact.

A baby. A murder. A forbidden love.

Lucy read the letter again, twice. No wonder Mamaw didn't want Lucy's father to know about the letter; her only son, and her only child with Pop, born to her when she was nearly forty years of age. Lucy had always wondered why Pop and Mamaw had gotten married so late in life, but now she was starting to understand why. Maybe Mamaw simply couldn't bring herself to be with another man after what had happened.

Lucy didn't really know the circumstances of Pop and Mamaw's courtship, only that Pop had been a childless widower and Mamaw had married him after knowing him for a couple of years. William Bondurant, her father, had been born less than a year later, the only child they'd ever had.

But now, things were starting to make some sense.

All of it was such a startling revelation that had Lucy's head reeling, but on the heels of thoughts of Mamaw were also thoughts of her father – Mamaw had specifically asked that Bill not know about the letter, but Lucy knew her father well – she knew he wouldn't overreact to information like this. Hell, in this day and age, it wasn't that big of a deal, at least not where Lucy came from, although she wasn't sure that would be true in a small Mississippi town.

Maybe it would be a big deal, still. The bottom line was that Lucy thought her father might like to know that he had an older sister. She couldn't, in good conscience, keep something like that from him. Bill had a right to know he had a sister.

A love child from a shocking love story.

Lucy didn't even eat her fast food that night, the burger and fries stone-cold by morning. She sat up past midnight, reading the letter again and again, and then the poem, trying to understand the gist of the love story between Mamaw and a black man.

From the words upon the paper, it was clear that Lewis Ragsdale had loved Mamaw. But it was more than that; it was a deep and meaningful message from a man of color who had been beaten and suppressed in a world of whites, yet the beauty of his words didn't convey that oppression. He hinted at the world they lived in, but not the unfairness of it. He conveyed an understanding of the times and just how forbidden his love for Victory Hembree was. He knew it; Lucy had no doubt that Lewis knew the consequences should they be discovered, but he had been willing to take the risk.

Ultimately, however, it was his brother who paid the price.

And what of this brother, Aldridge? The poor man got caught up in something of his brother's doing and ended up dead because of it. But *how* was he killed? Shot? Beaten? Even lynched? Now, the rumors of Laveau's evil were starting to make a great deal of sense because the proof of his wickedness had been exposed in Mamaw's letter.

Until that moment, the rumors and the stories had been just that – rumors and stories. It was just gossip until evidence was presented. But the reality was that it was hearsay and Lucy was very cognizant of the fact. There wasn't a picture of Aldridge's dead body included in the letter.

Still, Lucy believed Mamaw implicitly and tears flooded her eyes when she thought of the woman, knowing an innocent man had been killed because of her lies and her father's evil. The man had been murdered by her father and there wasn't a damn thing she could do to save him.

God, how she and Lewis must have suffered, two people caught up in a situation completely out of their control.

With thoughts of a murder and a forbidden love on her mind, Lucy somehow fell asleep. Flitting visions of a red-haired woman, her pale hand enfolded within a black palm, and visions of a big white house and angry men with torches as they prepared to kill an innocent man.

But when chaotic dreams eased, thoughts of the plan Lucy needed to make in order to fulfill Mamaw's last wish began to fill her mind. She'd been given a mission in life, something far away from faithless husbands and an empty life.

Now, she had a purpose. She was a lawyer, after all, and a damn good one. She had to find justice for Aldridge and Victory and Lewis. Maybe everything in her life, everything she had been through, had led up to this very moment when it was finally her time to shine. She had to *do* something.

And she would.

Therefore, Lucy slept lightly, fitfully, waking up at dawn feeling as if she'd just run a marathon. She was exhausted to the bone, mentally and physically, but sleep had helped her in some way because she had a rudimentary plan formulated in her head. Lucy's mind had always worked quickly, and tirelessly, and she wasn't one to sit around and ponder things for days. She couldn't rest until she had a plan of attack formed.

Climbing out of bed, she booted up her laptop computer. Collecting the pad of paper on the desk with the hotel's logo on it, she began to write.

The child
Lewis Ragsdale
Aldridge Ragsdale
Sheriff Meade
Dr. Latling

Those were people she needed to research, but at the core of that search was one simple fact – the reality was that after all of these years, the chances of finding the child still alive were slim. Lucy knew that. But, on the other hand, Mamaw had lived past her one hundredth birthday, so there was longevity in her family. Therefore, there was that possibility that the baby, wherever she was, was still alive.

Then there was Dr. Latling – he took the child away so maybe he had family left that knew the story and could tell her where the child had gone. She was pretty sure there wouldn't be any record of the birth. As for Lewis and Aldridge, county records might tell her something. She knew that Pea Ridge had a large historical society, proud of their town as they were. Maybe they even had a record of Aldridge Ragsdale's murder, although that was bound to be a touchy subject. She didn't suppose they'd want to talk about that very much.

Hi, I'm researching a murder of an innocent black man that took place in your town....? No, she didn't think the historical society would appreciate that kind of question.

But as she looked at Mamaw's letter for the fiftieth time, something else caught her attention – *Sheriff Meade*. And then, it hit her – it was all starting to make sense now why Sheriff Meade, her bodyguard against Lounge Lizard Clyde, said he'd brought his father to the house so the man could apologize for his family's sins. Big, handsome Beau Meade was a lawman just like his ancestor. It *had* to be the same family. In towns like this, there were no coincidences.

Sheriff Meade and Laveau Hembree had been thick as thieves in the murder of Aldridge Ragsdale.

Was that what Tommie Meade had been apologizing for? Did he know of that murder? Or was it the association in general he had been apologizing for? It was a sad legacy for both of their families as Lucy's thoughts drifted to the hunky sheriff who had followed her into the kitchen.

Although she wasn't in the market for a boyfriend, and not particularly ready to get back into the dating game, Beau Meade had been some serious eye candy. He seemed nice enough, too. Since he had mentioned his father's intention to apologize for the family wrongs, she wondered if Sheriff Meade might be someone who could help her track down the Ragsdales or even Dr. Latling's descendants. If the guy had grown up in the area and his family was a fixture here just as her family had been, then maybe he'd be able to tell her something about the key players in Mamaw's mystery. Or maybe he'd tell her to get lost.

Either way, she supposed she really had nothing to lose. If she wanted to carry out Mamaw's last wish, then she knew what she had to do.

She had to find that baby.

CHAPTER EIGHT
~ The Locket ~

*S*HE'D SEEN THE HEART-SHAPED LOCKET *in the Spiegel Christmas catalog last year for thirteen dollars and ninety-eight cents. It was real gold with a flower design etched into the cover and it opened to frame two tiny pictures, but there were no pictures in this locket. She didn't have a picture of what she wanted to put in there.*

The locket was something she kept hidden between her mattresses, some place her mother and father would never look. It had been a gift from Lewis, who had spent four months' salary on the gift when he could ill afford it. But he'd wanted very much to give her something for her birthday.

The locket had come in a box with a piece of paper tucked up into it, a poem that he'd written for her, one of many such poems he'd written for her over the past several months. But this poem was special; it summed up everything they felt for one another and it was the title of that poem he'd had inscribed on the locket.

In The Dreaming Hour.

The locket and the poem spent most of their time in the box shoved in between the mattresses on her bed, only coming out when the world around her was safe. She would often take them out late at night and read the poem, over and over, while fingering the locket. Such a tiny piece of metal that meant so much to her. Since the murder, she hadn't seen him at all, so the locket was all she had of him now.

That, and the baby growing inside her.

The baby was very active now in the sixth month, rolling and kicking. Victory would lay on her back at night, staring at the ceiling with her hands on her belly, just feeling those little kicks and flutters. She wished Lewis could feel them, too. Every night, she shed tears for what they both were missing.

The baby... and each other.

A knock on the door distracted her from her thoughts and, in a panic, she shoved the locket under her pillow along with the box and the poem. It was right after supper and the sun had gone down, so she wasn't expecting any visitors. Laying back down and covering herself up, she timidly answered the knock.

"Come in," she said.

The door opened and her mother appeared, forcing a smile as she so often did. Her mother was caught between a rock and a hard place when it came to running interference between father and daughter, afraid of one and loving the other. She stepped into the darkened bedroom and turned on the light.

"Are you sleeping, Victory?" she asked.

Victory shook her head. "No, Mama."

Her mother kept that same fake smile plastered on her lips. "Dr. Latling has come to see you," she said, turning to the door that was partially open. "Dr. Latling?"

A round man with round glasses entered the room, his black leather bag in-hand. It was a sultry night but in spite of the humidity, he wore a suit and a tie. The jacket was damp and wrinkled, as were the pants. He set his bag down on the nearest chair as he visually inspected his patient.

"Miss Victory," he greeted. "Your Mama says you're not feeling well."

Victory shrugged, keeping the covers up around her bosom. "I... I'm okay," she said. "Just tired."

Dr. Latling stood at the end of the bed, one of his bushy eyebrows cocked as he looked at her. "Are you eating?"

She nodded. "I am," she said, looking at her mother's strained expression. "Well, I'm trying to."

Dr. Latling could see the hesitation in the young girl. He turned to the mother. "Ms. Caroline, if ya'll let me have a few minutes alone with your daughter, I would appreciate it. I need to examine her."

Caroline was hesitant. "I... I don't know...."

"Out, please," Dr. Latling said more firmly. "If I need you, I'll call you."

He all but pushed Caroline out of the bedroom, shutting the door behind her. Once she was out and the door was shut, he waddled his way back over to the bed.

"Now," he said quietly. "Your Mama's not here so you can tell me the truth. She says ya'll been fainting regularly. Is that true?"

Victory nodded. Then, her face crumpled. "I'm afraid to eat," she sobbed.

"Why?"

"I'm afraid Daddy will poison my food!"

Dr. Latling sighed heavily. "He's not going to do that, sugar," he assured her quietly. "You're his daughter. He wouldn't do that to you."

She was quickly growing hysterical. "I heard him tell my Mama that he hopes the baby dies," she said. "I'm afraid he'll make me eat something that will kill her."

"Her?"

"My baby. Ruby."

Dr. Latling nodded his head, unsure what more to say. It was clear the girl was terrified, which was taking a toll on her health. Given Laveau's tendencies, he really wouldn't put anything past the man. Maybe he would, indeed, poison his own daughter to kill off her bastard baby, so in that respect, he didn't blame the girl for her fears.

"Well," he said as he turned back to his black bag to collect his stethoscope, "I wouldn't worry about your daddy. He's upset, that's true, but he's not going to hurt you. You need to stop worrying about that and eat something. You'll do more damage to Ruby if you don't."

That thought evidently hadn't occurred to Victory. Her sobs lessened and she put her hand to her belly. "I just want her to be born, Dr. Latling," she said, sniffling. "I want her to be born healthy."

"Then you need to eat what your Mama makes for you. Okay?"

"Okay."

Silently, he pulled down the covers. She was wearing a thin nightgown, thin enough that he was able to put his stethoscope against her belly and hear the baby's heartbeat through the fabric, chugging along like a train underwater. Chuga, chuga, chuga… it was fast and steady. He removed the stethoscope and felt Victory's pulse before turning back to his bag to put his things away.

"Well?" Victory asked anxiously. "Can you hear the baby?"

He nodded. "Strong and steady," he said. "And I think if you eat regularly, you won't be fainting anymore."

Victory watched the man snap his bag shut. "Can… can I tell you something?"

"'Course."

She took a deep breath. "I… I'm afraid of what Daddy is going to do once the baby is born," she said. "I mean, having this baby isn't going to be the hard part. It's what comes after. Dr. Latling, what if Daddy tries to kill my baby when she's born?"

Dr. Latling shook his head. "That's nonsense, Miss Victory. You have to stop thinking such terrible things."

Victory shook her head; she was no longer weeping, now deadly serious as she looked at him. "He will," she insisted. "He killed an innocent colored man right in front of this house and that isn't the first time he's done something like that. You know it's true. I'm afraid he'll take my baby and bash her skull against a tree. Or he'll have Terhune do it."

Dr. Latling couldn't very well deny what they both knew to be entirely possible. He'd been thinking the same thing all along – that maybe he was the only one who would be in a position to protect that baby. Still, he couldn't give in to her fear.

"Miss Victory...."

She cut him off as someone knocked on her bedroom door. "Promise me," she hissed quickly. "Promise me that when the baby is born, you'll take her away. You won't let him have her!"

Dr. Latling was clearly reluctant as he went for the door. "I'm not sure I can...."

"Promise me!"

He held up his hands to keep her from getting agitated. "Okay," he said quickly. "Just calm down, Miss Victory. I promise. Everything will be okay."

"Don't tell Mama!"

He opened the door, his only reply, to see Caroline stand there, looking at him anxiously. "Is... is everything all right?" she asked.

Dr. Latling moved away from the door to collect his bag. "Everything is fine," he said. "She'll start eating now. I'm going to prescribe some iron pills, too. That should help."

Bag in hand, he shuffled out of the room without another word. He could hear Caroline cooing to Victory, saying something about a woman named Lillian bringing her some grits and cornbread. But the doctor didn't stick around to see if his patient would really eat anything; he just wanted to get out of that house.

His promise to Victory was something he tried not to think about.

CHAPTER NINE

Present

THE HOUSE STILL smelled like Presbyterian chicken. Coming in through the back door of Glory, the old screen door slammed behind Lucy as she inhaled the smells of the morning and headed into the kitchen where her parents were banging around. Bill was making coffee and Mary was still wrapping up cakes from the day before. They both looked over when they heard the footsteps, seeing that their child had finally made an appearance. Bill went back to the coffee.

"Good morning," he said, plugging in the old percolator. "How'd you sleep?"

Lucy almost laughed at the question. She really did. Given that last night had been a game changer in the course of her life, the simple question seemed ludicrous. Instead of snorting at her father's question, however, she simply set her big Vuitton on the counter and yawned.

"I never sleep well in hotels," she said. "You guys didn't stay here last night, did you?"

Bill nodded. "We did," he said. "I thought it was safer that way. Big funeral yesterday and everybody knows Mama is gone, so I didn't want anyone trying to loot the place. No alarm, no dogs around here. It makes a perfect target. I asked Tommie's son if he'd assign extra patrols around the house and he said he would."

Lucy scratched her head. "How long did the sheriff and his dad hang around after I left?"

Bill wiped his hands on a dish towel and went to hunt for some cups. "Not too much longer," he said. "They escorted Clyde to his car and waited until he drove away. Sheriff Meade told us what happened in the kitchen. That son-of-a-bitch crawfished and came back around into the back of the kitchen after we told him to leave ya'll alone."

Lucy grinned faintly; her dad never really got mad but when he did, the Southerner came out in him, including an angry twang to his accent. As a kid, she had feared it. But as an adult, it made her laugh.

"Well," she said. "I was pretty straight forward with him. I told him to leave me the hell alone so I hope he got the message. I don't want to keep looking over my shoulder the entire time I'm here."

Bill pulled the cups out of the cabinet. "How long are you planning on staying?"

Until I can track down a baby that was born in this house eighty years ago, she thought. But she didn't say anything to that regard, at least not yet. She was going to have to find the right time to dump the revelation on her father and the morning after he buried his mother was probably not the right time.

Therefore, she was casual in her answer as she headed over to help her mom put away the rest of the desserts left behind.

"I'm supposed to fly back on Monday," she said, unrolling cling wrap. "That gives me six days to do what I can around here. I figure there's one hundred and eighty years' worth of family history and junk all stored up in this house. I'm sure six days won't even make a dent in it so I can extend that if I need to."

"But you just got that job, honey," Mary said. "You don't want to jeopardize it."

Lucy shook her head. "I won't," she said. "Trust me on this one, Mom. They recruited me very heavily and they won't do anything to piss me off so I decide to quit. So if you need me to stay for a while to help out, I can do that. In fact, what are the plans for today?"

Mary looked at Bill, who was wiping out cups. His movements seemed to slow. "Well," he sighed heavily. "I suppose the first thing we need to do is call Mama's lawyer. She has a will but she may have updated it. I tried to get her to put everything into a trust but she wouldn't do it. Said she didn't need to. She didn't own a credit card and paid everything with checks or cash. I have a joint bank account with her so I could watch everything she did, but I have to tell you that there just isn't a lot of money left. She and Daddy have a checking account and a savings account, and they have some bonds, but that's about it. Mama didn't know this, but I started paying Daddy's care from my own pocket about a year ago. The way things were going, it was going to drain everything Mama had to keep Daddy where he needed to be. So I can tell you right now that there won't be much to go through. There just wasn't much left."

Lucy suspected as much but it was still depressing to hear it. "Where's the will?" she asked. "At least let me get a look at that. You said she spelled everything out?"

Bill nodded. "She did," he said. "My copy of the will is in my suitcase, up in the front guest bedroom. In fact, her lawyer is in town, near the square with the statue of Robert E. Lee in the middle of it. Mo Guinn is his name. Maybe you can give him a call today so we can start finalizing everything."

The lawyer's last name was pronounced "gun" and Lucy's eyebrows lifted at the unusual name. "'Mo Gun'?" she repeated. Then, she laughed. "That's, uh, quite a name."

Bill grinned. "I went to school with his kids, Jasper and Sue," he said. "Jasper was a good friend in high school but Sue was a little strange. She used to smuggle her mother's peach schnapps to school and drink it at lunch time. By the early afternoon, she was wasted. I know this because for a solid year, I had my last period class with her. She was three sheets to the wind by then."

Lucy snorted softly, shaking her head at the lawyer's wild daughter. "If you went to school with his kids, he must be as old as the hills by now."

Bill nodded. "Pretty old, but still sharp the last time I saw him."

"And still practicing?"

"As far as I know."

Lucy shrugged. "Then I'll give him a call," she said. "Let's eat first and then we'll get down to business. What's for breakfast?"

Mary looked at her as if she'd lost her mind. "What's *not* for breakfast?" she asked. "Take your pick – five different kinds of cake, pie, chicken cooked ten different ways, potatoes, corn casserole… shall I go on?"

With that extensive menu, breakfast became a feast of nontraditional breakfast foods. The old refrigerator was stuffed to the brim and the counters were half-covered with things that would keep unrefrigerated for a day or two. Having not eaten since lunch the previous day, Lucy was starving and tucked into some re-heated chicken and dumplings that were out of this world.

They ate, drank coffee, and talked about the old state of the kitchen including the turn-of-the-century icebox and the old ice card that was still in the window. In the old days, it would tell the ice man how much ice they needed. Somewhere, there was an antique dealer just crying for some of these old things, Lucy thought, but she wasn't sure her dad was ready to part with anything at this point. The icebox was going to stay in the kitchen where it had been for over one hundred years, at least for the time being.

In fact, the more Lucy sat and listened to her dad talk about his youth and days spent with his parents, the more she wondered if telling him about Mamaw's letter would be wise. Her dad was a strong guy but in listening to him on this morning, he seemed emotionally fragile. She didn't want to dump more on him.

Therefore, she quickly came to the conclusion that her quest for Mamaw would have to be her secret alone for the time being; at least until she felt her father was strong enough to handle the information.

But the time would come.

Stuffed full of chicken and dumplings and coconut cake, Lucy headed up to the front guest bedroom to find the will as her parents hung out down in the kitchen, finishing their coffee. She took the back stairs to the second floor, pausing to look into every bedroom again as she went, smelling the dust and oldness that conveyed the passing of days gone by.

The back bedroom next to Mamaw's bedroom was the one Lucy had slept in as a child. It had very old wallpaper with big, pink cabbage roses and pink chiffon curtains with velvet ribbons. It was a perfect girly bedroom but she knew it hadn't been Mamaw's room as a child. Mamaw had the honor of having a front bedroom which was now the guest room where Bill and Mary were sleeping.

After reading Mamaw's letter, that room now had special meaning to Lucy. *Daddy murdered poor Aldridge.* Even as she crossed the hall, making her way to the bedroom, she could feel the pricks of horror peppering her skin. It was the realization of looking at this bedroom now in an entirely different light, knowing what had occurred here. Knowing that, more than likely, an interracial baby was born here and swiftly taken away as the mother screamed in agony.

With those thoughts, Lucy had worked herself up so much that she actually felt nauseous by the time she entered the big bedroom. But the room was quiet, bucolic, with the massive four-poster bed, decorated in shades of gold and green. Nothing here suggested any horror from the past.

The room had four enormous floor-to-ceiling windows and Lucy made her way to the two windows that overlooked the front of the house, the big yard, and the street beyond.

Being June, the grass was heavy and green, and the overgrowth was thick with moisture. There were big trees in the yard, six of them, that she once remembered Pop telling her were cherrybark oaks. They were huge, with big trunks, and certainly big enough to be several decades old. There were smaller trees around, colorful ones, but she didn't pay much attention to them. She was more focused on the big oak tree directly in front of the bedroom.

The branches were big, old, and gnarled. This tree was undoubtedly here in the nineteen thirties. Did the old oak hold the secret of Aldridge Ragsdale's murder? Was it a witness to the death of an innocent man, weeping silent tears at an injustice that was so common in the south back then? Not knowing the details of Aldridge's murder, Lucy could only guess what happened but whatever it was and however it happened, it sickened her to think of it.

"Hey."

The voice from behind nearly startled Lucy out of her skin. She whirled around to see her father coming into the room, heading for his suitcase. As she stood by the window, trying to get her heart started again, Bill opened up the suitcase on the end of the bed.

"Did you find it?" Bill asked as he opened a zipper pocket. "Wait – here it is."

Lucy took a deep breath, trying to steady herself. "I didn't even look yet," she said. As Bill pulled out a manila folder, her gaze returned to the tree outside the window. "Hey... Dad?"

"Yes?"

"I was thinking," Lucy said hesitantly. "Remember yesterday at Mamaw's funeral when I asked you about the stories about Laveau? I meant specific stories about what he really did around here that has everyone so hush-hush."

"I know."

"Since Mamaw never really spoke of him, the only story I did hear was something from Aunt Dell on how he ran a bootlegging operation. Did you hear that one?"

Bill nodded, glancing into the folder. "Yes, I've heard that one," he said. "Aunt Dell likes to talk. She'd be the one to tell you all of the stories. She was Mama's first cousin on her father's side and she knows everything. If you really want to know the stories, ask her. She was here last night, you know. She asked for you."

Lucy nodded, her focus still riveted to the gnarled old tree. "I know she did," she said. "I was just wondering what more you'd heard. I feel like now that Mamaw is gone, we can talk about those things. Get them out in the open. I mean, Tommie Meade came yesterday to apologize for his family's involvement in Laveau's dirty deeds. What the hell was so bad that he felt he had to come and apologize?"

Bill closed the folder, looking at his daughter. "Is it that important for you to know?"

Lucy pondered the question. "Yes," she said after a moment, "I really think it is. I never really cared much before, but now I do. I need to know why, specifically, Laveau Hembree was such terrifying man. I don't know why I need to know, but I just do. Maybe I just want to understand my family history a little better."

Bill scratched his chin, thinking on what he would tell her. She was certainly mature enough to handle the truth but he'd spent so many years either ignoring her questions about it or changing the subject that it was hard to know where to start. As a member of the Hembree family, he supposed she had a right to know the legacy behind the family name, good or bad. It wasn't unusual that these questions should come up now after his mother died since no one ever talked about it when she was alive.

"Laveau was a bastard from the time he was pretty young, so I understand," Bill finally said. "He was a thief and a gambler in school and it grew into bootlegging. He didn't have any formal education past the eighth grade but that wasn't unusual down here, especially in more rural areas. Aunt Dell told me once that Laveau also was a loan shark of sorts and beat people up when they didn't pay on time. Pretty nasty stories about what he'd do to men's families and homes if they didn't pay him back."

Lucy turned to look at him. "Seriously?" she said, incredulous. "That makes it sound like he was a gangster."

"He was."

"But he lived in Mississippi!"

Bill shook his head. "He had connections in New Orleans," he said. "Organized crime, evidently. At least, that's what Aunt Dell told me. Look, if you want to hear more, ask her. I really don't know much more than that."

Lucy wouldn't let him get off so easily. "So this man, who owns a plantation and acres of land, ends up being a loan shark with connections to organized crime?"

Bill shrugged. "Times were tough back then," he said simply. "I guess he couldn't depend on the sharecroppers to keep this place supplied with cash."

It made some sense; the economics of the early part of the last century hit the people in the country the hardest. Lucy thought on her gangster great-grandfather, her focus turning once more to the tree outside the window.

"Do you think he committed murder?" she asked.

Bill found himself looking out of the window, too, just because something out there had Lucy's attention. "I do," he said quietly. "There are rumors of instances where he killed people related to his loan shark business, but when he was really in power – oh, back in the 1930s – he and the town sheriff were in cahoots. My daddy told me that Laveau had the sheriff on his payroll. I'm sure Laveau did a lot of things we don't ever want to know about."

Lucy already knew the part about Terhune Meade thanks to Mamaw's letter, but the mention of the loan sharking was new. She hadn't heard that one before.

"Do think he might have even lynched people?" she asked. "I

mean, that kind of thing happened with a fair amount of frequency down here. There are dozens of documented cases."

Now Bill was looking at the tree outside of the window, too. It seemed that's where Lucy's attention was.

"Are you asking if I think he lynched people here on the property?" he asked, watching her nod. Reluctantly, he sighed. "It wouldn't surprise me one bit."

"But you haven't heard any stories about it?"

"No, thank God."

Lucy left it at that. Even if her dad didn't know of any lynchings here on the property, that didn't mean there hadn't been any. Aldridge could have very easily met his end that way. But she knew of two places that might know – the historical society and the sheriff's department. As she'd already determined, she wasn't sure she could get away with asking the historical society about a murder. But the sheriff's department – well, crime was their business. It might be the better place to start. Besides, she didn't know anyone at the historical society, but as of last night, she knew someone at the sheriff's department.

The plan for the day was starting to shape up.

"Well," she said casually, turning away from the window, "maybe I should talk to Aunt Dell at some point before I leave, just to hear what more she has to say. You don't think she's making shit up, do you?"

Bill grinned. "It's always possible with her," he said. "That woman tells some pretty tall tales. But she's also been around a long time, so it's difficult to know where her tales stop and the truths begin."

Lucy reached over to take the will from her father. "Maybe so," she said. "But she has some good qualities, too. The woman makes some killer coconut cake."

"True enough."

"Let me go call More Guns now and see if I can get in to see him today."

"That's Mo Guinn."

Lucy just giggled, heading out of the bedroom as her father followed. But as she reached the big central hall outside of the bedroom, she came to a halt as Bill continued to the stairs. Lucy's attention moved to Mamaw's bedroom door across the landing, her thoughts once again turning to the woman's letter.

In the top of my chifforobe is a small wooden box containing a gold locket. Lucy wanted to have a look at that old locket. Making sure her dad went all the way down the stairs, she hurried on into Mamaw's bedroom.

Someone had pulled the blinds down last night and the room was dim as sunlight seeped in between the edges of the blinds and the windows. Lucy went to the windows and raised the blinds again, allowing the morning to enter as she turned around to look at the old bed and chifforobe.

Somehow, the daylight didn't seem to make this room any more cheerful. It was still a sickroom of an old woman. Quickly, she went to the chifforobe and pulled open the top drawer that was made for jewelry storage.

Lined with green velvet, there were several cheap pieces of jewelry neatly arranged in the drawer. Plastic pearls and other costume jewelry lined the velvet and Lucy carefully fingered through them, looking for the small wooden box that Mamaw's letter had described.

At the back of the drawer were a few small boxes lined up and Lucy pulled the first two out, looking inside to find a cameo in one and a ring in the other. The third box was a little bigger, and made from wood, and when she popped open the sticky top, she was immediately met by a dark gold locket.

The moment her gaze fell on the jewelry, she felt a sense of awe wash over her. There was also an odd sense of validation, too, as if what her grandmother had been telling her was really the truth.

That bittersweet love story that had kept her up all night came flooding back to her as she carefully picked the locket up and inspected the etched gold flowers on the front before turning it over and seeing tiny words inscribed on the back.

In The Dreaming Hour.

Lucy stared at those words a moment. It was difficult to describe what she was feeling beyond the awe and the sense of truth. A man who had worked for months to save the money it took to buy this piece of jewelry had been a man who, his entire life, had probably known only degradation and hardship. But in his words, and in this little piece of jewelry, were such dignity and hope. The strength of the human spirit was strong with him.

Lucy didn't know Lewis and she never would, but she felt as if through Mamaw she had learned something about this extraordinary man. It was enough to bring tears to her eyes.

"Hello, Lewis," she whispered. "It's very nice to meet you."

It was like a secret she shared now, a secret with her and her grandmother and the man who wrote that beautiful poetry. Eighty years later, the secret had been divulged and although some might have seen it as a huge burden, Lucy didn't. She saw it as an honor.

And she had a job to do.

After a moment, she gently kissed the locket and quickly put it back into the box. That box ended up back in the drawer for safe keeping. Telling her parents she was heading out to see Mamaw's lawyer, she really headed in the opposite direction towards the Tallahatchie County Sheriff's Office.

CHAPTER TEN

~ Another Night, Another Death ~

"*D*ID YA'LL SEE THE *headlines?*"
The question came from Laveau as he walked into Terhune's office in the small, brick building in Charleston that served as the sheriff's office. It was another hot day in a long line of them, the General Electric fans blowing furiously in a vain attempt to stave off the heat. Terhune, bent over his desk as he went over a police report, glanced up when Laveau entered. It didn't take a genius to figure out what he'd meant by that question.

Quietly, Terhune set his pencil down, got up, and went to close the door to his office. It was too hot to close the door but he had to. For what he had to say, he didn't want anyone hearing.

"I saw," he said as he made his way back to his desk.

Laveau watched the man as he sat back down and picked up his pencil. He planted himself in a chair, a smile licking at his lips.

"Ya'll don't seem too pleased," he said.

Terhune wouldn't look at him. "It was an unfortunate accident," he said. "My deputies found that the brakes on the car were bad. That's what caused the accident."

Laveau nodded his head, pleased. "That's too bad for Haltom," he said. "Lost his wife and a son. A shame."

Terhune sighed heavily but he still wouldn't look at Laveau. "I'm sure he'll be much more careful from now on."

"You sure?"

"I'm sure."

Laveau's smile broke through and he stood up, pulling a handkerchief out to mop the sweat off his forehead. "That's good," *he said.* "Thank you for taking care of the problem, Terhune. Now, some of the boys are going over to the Ragsdales tonight. Thought we needed to have a chat with them folks. They got to know that they can't go spreading rumors like the ones they were telling Haltom. That kind of thing just gets people in trouble."

Terhune knew exactly what he meant. Most of those men were on Laveau's payroll, anyway, men who worked at Glory or just acted as Laveau's muscle. He looked at Laveau for the first time since the man entered the room.

"I don't want no trouble," he said, trying to sound firm. "Haltom won't make any more trouble and I don't need you going over to that shanty town and creating more trouble. Just let things lie, Mr. Hembree. There's no need for anything more."

Laveau was still smiling as he put his handkerchief back into his pocket. "There won't be no more trouble," *he said.* "We just gonna have a talk with old 'Zeke Ragsdale. He's the one starting trouble, not me."

Terhune stood up. "I'm telling you not to do that," *he said in the closest display of insubordination against Laveau he'd ever shown.* "Look, the situation is finished. Haltom won't talk. But if you go out and do something to 'Zeke Ragsdale, it's going to get around. People are going to talk and word is going to spread. And if they come up from the state capital to investigate something, I'm not sure I can keep you out of it. No need to stir up the hornets once they've all been put back in the nest, Mr. Hembree. Do you get my meaning?"

Laveau stood next to the door, his hand on the latch. The smile on his lips had turned into something of a grimace. He didn't like what Terhune was saying.

"I can take care of them boys," he said quietly.

Terhune lifted his eyebrows. "Can you take care of the whole state?" *he shot back quietly.* "Because that's what's going to happen if you don't *let this lie. The law is going to catch up with you at some point and I won't be able to stop it."*

Laveau's smile was completely gone by that point. With a lingering glare at Terhune, he jerked open the office door and stormed out, leaving the door to slam back on its hinges. Terhune could see him from where he sat, watching as Laveau left the building completely. Only when the door was shut did Terhune let out a pent-up sigh, sinking back in his chair as if his entire body had deflated.

He just knew there was going to be trouble.

CHAPTER ELEVEN

Present

The Tallahatchie County Sheriff's Office was located in the small town of Charleston, a town, like most southern towns, that was built up around a central square with a Confederate statue in the middle of it. It was a cute little town, with its Five-and-Dime store, an old-fashioned soda fountain, and a variety of other small stores that surrounded the well-kept square.

The sheriff's office was off the square on a side street. The headquarters was a one-story brick building that took up a good portion of the block. It was quite old, but as Lucy noticed when she parked her car next to it, it was in seemingly good repair with a secured yard and quite a few surveillance cameras all around. There was some money invested in it, unlike the rest of the shabby county.

Climbing out of her rental car, Lucy pulled her big Louis Vuitton bag out with her. The journal was still in there, as was Mamaw's letter. She was never going to let those two things out of her sight, ever, and she made her way up the sidewalk towards the front entrance of the station with that big bag hiked up on her shoulder.

All the while, she was fighting down a serious case of nerves, hoping that she was doing the right thing by going to Beau Meade. He'd seemed sympathetic enough the night before, but who knew what he really thought about the whole Hembree-Meade relationship. It was just possible he'd apologized for it only because his dad had been around, but Lucy didn't think so. She was really hoping to find some help from him for what she needed to do because the truth was that she didn't have many other alternatives.

So, she wandered into the vanilla-looking lobby of the station; pleather chairs, vinyl tile, and little else. On one wall, there was a window covered with bulletproof glass and a talk box with a clerk on the other side of it. Lucy walked up to the window and focused on the clerk inside, working. The woman didn't notice her. She took a business card out of the side pocket of her purse and cleared her throat politely.

"Hi," she said, watching the pretty African American woman look up at her. "I don't have an appointment but I was hoping to see Sheriff Meade. My name is Lucy Bondurant."

She put her business card up against the glass so the clerk could see it. It was an impressive card that usually opened doors, but Lucy wasn't sure that would work down here. They didn't care if she was a lawyer from Los Angeles who made three times what the police chief made. The clerk peered at it.

"Does the sheriff know you, ma'am?" the clerk asked.

Lucy nodded. "He does," she said. "I won't take much of his time, but this is a personal matter. I'm sorry, but I can't disclose the nature of it."

The clerk's gaze lingered on the card, then on Lucy for a moment, before picking up the phone. She turned her head away as she spoke into the receiver and Lucy took her card down, stepping back from the glass. She figured she had a fifty-fifty chance of getting in to see Sheriff Meade so she turned away from the glass after a moment, pretending to look at the décor of the room as she waited for the clerk to finish her call. It didn't take too long, in fact. Soon enough, the clerk was hailing her through the talk box.

"The sheriff went out this morning and hasn't come back yet," she said. "Do you want to wait?"

Lucy pondered the question. "Do you know when he'll be back?"

The clerk shook her head. "He had to go to Tutwiler, ma'am," she said. "His secretary isn't sure when he'll return."

Lucy didn't want to hang around the station all day. Her time was limited. "That's okay," she said, going to the glass again. "Can I leave my card for him?"

The clerk opened up a fortified drawer beneath the window, like the ones used by banks, and Lucy slipped her card into it. Thanking the clerk, she headed back outside.

It was a bright day, more humid than the day before, and she was coming to regret wearing jeans. Cute jeans, nonetheless, but too heavy for the weather. She was thinking about going back to her hotel and changing before she headed over to see Mo Guinn when she caught sight of a black unmarked Ford Edge heading back to the yard. She just caught it out of her periphery, not paying any attention to it, until someone yelled at her.

"Hey!"

She turned to see that Beau had pulled up alongside her. He was in the middle of the street, looking over at her with both pleasure and surprise. Lucy definitely saw the pleasure part and her heart leaped, just a bit. She was pleased to see him, too.

"Hey yourself," she said with a grin, coming off the curb and walking out into the street where he'd stopped his car. "What a coincidence – I was just coming to see you."

He flashed a smile. "Really?" he said, suddenly looking at his reflection in the rear view mirror. "Damn. I wish I'd combed my hair."

She laughed softly. "You look fine."

"I should have brushed my teeth, too."

"That's just gross."

He laughed because she did. "I'm kidding," he said, his gaze moving over her but trying to pretend like it wasn't. "What can I do for you that you'd drive all the way over here?"

Lucy's smile faded. "Well," she said, "it's kind of complicated. I need help and I didn't know who to turn to, so I thought I'd ask you."

He nodded his head. "Have you eaten breakfast yet?"

"No," she lied.

He motioned to her. "Get in."

She did, and off they went.

✧ ✧ ✧

"I DON'T EVEN know where to begin with this."

Lucy sat opposite Beau in the front window of a diner at the edge of town. They'd just ordered two massive breakfasts and she had no idea how she was going to eat any more food, but it didn't matter. She had Beau's attention and she actually felt quite emotional about what she was about to say to him. She'd been planning her speech all the way over to Charleston but now that the moment was here, her courage wavered – was she doing the right thing? Second thoughts pulled at her.

"Start at the beginning," Beau said as the waitress brought them two big cups of strong coffee. "Tell me what brings you all the way over to Charleston."

Lucy waited until the waitress wandered away. "It's funny," she said, puffing out her cheeks in a gesture of determination. "I had it all laid out, what I wanted to say, and now it's just not coming to me. I'm usually much more articulate than this."

He cocked an eyebrow. "Don't kid yourself," he said. "You're one of the most articulate people I've ever seen. You must be hell in a courtroom."

She grinned. "How would you know that?"

He poured sugar into his coffee. "It's my job to be a trained observer," he said. "You and I had a good conversation last night. I can tell that you're a woman who says what she means."

That statement bolstered her courage. "That's true," she said. Then, she took a deep breath. "Okay, so here goes – our families have a history together, as we figured out last night. I think that really links you and me more than if I'd just met a cousin I never knew about. There's some kind of weird bond between the Hembree and Meade families that defies explanation. Do you get that sense, too?"

He sipped at his coffee. "Yes," he said. "I've always gotten that sense."

"Like our families are partners in crime."

"That's exactly what it's like."

She watched him stir his coffee to cool it down. "I don't want to say we're family, but it's almost like that."

He nodded. "I never thought of it that way, but you're right. We share a lot of the same history."

More hesitation from Lucy. "Well, here goes," she finally said. "Up until last night, I didn't know you from Adam. But I have to find out a few things and that means I have to trust you. I have to swear you to secrecy on this, Sheriff. Will you do that for me?"

He nodded. "I will under one condition."

"What's that?"

"That you call me Beau."

She gave him a lopsided grin. "I can do that," she said, thinking he was trying to flirt with her but not wanting to read too much into it. Her smile faded. "This is something really heavy to lay on you and you're probably going to run screaming from this place and never talk to me again, but I need answers and I feel like you're the one who can help me find them. You've grown up here and you know this area and the legends about it, and I really don't feel as if I can turn to anyone else. I need to pick your brain."

"So pick."

Lucy chewed her lip in thought a moment. She was still clearly hesitant. Then, she opened up her purse. Carefully, she pulled forth

Victory's journal and set it on the table beside her. She put her hand on it as she spoke.

"Yesterday, at Mamaw's funeral, I was approached by the woman who took care of my grandmother in her last days," she said quietly. "The woman told me that my grandmother had written a letter to me and that I wasn't to let my dad see it. In fact, I'm probably not to let anyone see it but I'm going to show it to you because the answers I need result from this letter she left me. I can't tell you how much this letter means to me or how personal it is, so please... you never saw this, okay?"

Beau was looking at her seriously. "Of course."

Silently, Lucy opened the journal and removed the old envelope from the inside flap. Very carefully, she pulled out the letter, opened it, and handed it over to Beau. He took it with equal care, and maybe some confusion, as he pulled out a pair of readers from his uniform pocket and put them on.

Then, he began to read the letter. As Lucy watched with some apprehension, Beau read the entire letter without a reaction, all the way down to the very end, the end that'd had Lucy sobbing the first time she'd read it. Then, he clearly read it again, starting from the beginning. When he'd finished it a second time, he looked up at her from over the top of his readers.

"I don't even know what to say about this," he muttered. "This is... *wow*...."

Lucy nodded as she took the letter back. "I know," she said. "That was my reaction. *Wow*."

He lifted his eyebrows in agreement, slowing pulling his readers off. "Ragsdale," he said thoughtfully. "I know that name. In fact, we have a clerk at the station with that last name. It's not an uncommon name around here for African American families."

Lucy carefully folded up the letter. "I hardly slept at all last night after reading this," she admitted. "I mean... what a story. The daughter of the wickedest man in the county having a biracial baby?

And murdering the wrong man as a result? It sounds like a movie plot, doesn't it?"

Beau had to agree. "It does," he said. "That's an incredible story."

"And you've never heard anything about it?"

He shook his head firmly. "Not a thing," he said. "Not even a hint from my gossiping mama."

Lucy chuckled softly at the quirky way he'd accused his mother of being a gossip. "That's good, then," she said. "It means that there's nothing out there to shame my grandmother. But... but I feel compelled to carry out her last wish. She wants me to find the child she gave birth to."

Beau could feel the burden she'd been tasked with and it wasn't even his burden. He sat back against the seat, his expression pensive. "That might be difficult," he said. "From what I know of your great-granddad, the fact that his own daughter had a half-black child out of wedlock... honestly, I'm surprised she lived to a ripe old age. I'm surprised he didn't kill her when he found out."

Lucy nodded. "From what I know about him, I would agree with that," she said. "But that's part of the problem – my dad won't really talk about him so I don't even know who to ask. First off, would anyone even know about Mamaw's illicit pregnancy? And if anyone did, they're probably dead by now. But the baby... she says a Dr. Latling took it away, but I think that's an assumption. Do you think Laveau Hembree might have killed it? It would have solved the problem – it would have put an end to his shame and no one would ever know about the mulatto child. Maybe that's why you never heard about this – because that baby was killed from the start."

Beau was nodding, swept up in the speculation of that powerful letter. "Very true," he said. "Your grandmother mentions my great-grandfather, Sheriff Meade, as being part of the whole situation."

Lucy nodded. "I know," she said. "And that whole part about

the rape and the murder... God, I didn't even want to ask you if you think there'd be a record of such a thing."

Beau shook his head. "Not formally, no," he said. "A lot of those vigilante actions were never recorded in any fashion. They were just buried and forgotten. If you talked about it, then something similar might happen to you, so those kinds of things were kept hidden. We'll probably never know just how many murders took place back during the days of Laveau Hembree and Terhune Meade, and even before. That's part of the history down here that remains shameful to this day."

Lucy watched something flicker across his face, regret or disappointment or something. "Do a lot of people feel that way?"

He shrugged. "Old folks, probably not," he said. "They're still entrenched in the mindset from those days. But younger folks – there's a sense of outrage. You can see it all over the place. People look at cops like the enemy these days and for good reason. There were days past when men like my great-grandfather *were* the enemy."

"And you bear that name."

He looked at her, his pale eyes glimmering. "Much like you, I have a family name to clear."

That was very true, in more ways than one. Lucy was starting to feel a kinship to this man that she couldn't even begin to understand. All she knew was that she felt oddly close to a virtual stranger. She looked down at the letter as she put it back into the envelope.

"I never knew how much it needed clearing until the past couple of days," she said. "Ever since I read this letter, there's an entire world for me to clear up. Not just with that poor man who was murdered, but with the baby my grandmother had. That really seemed to be her entire purpose behind the letter – to find that child. But something tells me she isn't alive anymore. I'm really thinking that she never even made it out of that house. God, that makes my stomach hurt to think that."

Beau thought on that very grim possibility. "That could very well be true," he said, "but she does mentions Dr. Latling being at the delivery. As the attending physician, he'd have to fill out a birth certificate."

"Even on a baby no one wanted to admit existed?"

He shrugged. "It depends," he said. "Was he more afraid of Laveau or was he more loyal to his Hippocratic Oath and the laws of the state? I will admit that I'm inclined to believe that there's no record of that birth."

"Me, too," she said glumly. "Too bad we can't ask the good doctor."

"Maybe not directly, but there's a Latling family in Pea Ridge, a very old family."

Lucy perked up at that information. "Do you think they're part of the doctor's family?"

Beau shrugged. "It has to be," he said. "In small towns like this, there are no coincidences. But my grandmother might know. She wasn't born here but when she married my grandfather, she came to know people in the town. She knew Terhune and I would assume she knew Victory and Hardy to a certain extent, although I've never really asked. In fact… she might know something about this."

Lucy couldn't even dare to hope. "Do you think it would be too much to ask her?" she asked. "I don't want to impose, but I'm just trying to get to the bottom of this. Mamaw never really asked anything of me, but this letter… her request… it's a big one. I want to do what I can to see it through."

Beau nodded, thinking on that terribly poignant letter. "I don't blame you," he said. "I think the first place to start would be to talk to people who might have been around during that time, people like my grandmother. Do you have any relatives who were around at that time who are still alive?"

Lucy cocked her head thoughtfully. "In fact, I do," she said. "One of Mamaw's cousins is still alive, Aunt Dell. She tells a lot of stories and we don't know what's bullshit and what's truth, but she might know. But I'm afraid if I ask her, she might say something to my dad. I don't want him to know about this until I have some answers or at least know more about it. Dad took Mamaw's death hard and I just don't want to upset him with this right now."

Beau understood. "Then let's start with my grandmother," he said, sitting back as the waitress brought their food. "What are you doing for dinner tonight?"

Lucy's eyes widened at the hubcap-sized plate with all of the food piled on it. "Getting sick after eating all of this."

Beau snorted. "After you get sick, then."

Lucy picked up the salt. "Having dinner with my parents, I suppose. Why?"

Beau collected the hot sauce and dumped it all over his eggs. "How'd you like to have dinner with me and my grandmother?"

She looked up at him. "So we can get her liquored up and pump her for information?"

He laughed softly. "You're talking about a very old woman," he said. "We don't liquor her up. Well, at least not in public. Anyway, how about if I come pick you up at your hotel around six and we'll see what my Lovie has to say."

She looked at him strangely. "Your *Lovie*?"

He grinned, peppering his eggs heavily. "That's what we call my grandmother, Ms. Hollis Meade," he said. "Lovie. My kids call her that, too."

Kids. That meant marriage. Lucy's heart sank a little, suddenly feeling very stupid that she'd let herself feel giddy over the man. *Idiot!* "How many kids?" she asked with forced politeness.

"Three," he said. "Two boys and one girl. My sons, Gage and Ford, and my daughter, Georgia."

Lucy was feeling more foolish by the moment. "Nice," she said.

"How old?"

"Nine, seven, and three."

She looked down at her food at that point, unable to look at him. "That's awesome," she said, although she didn't mean it. "How long have you been married?"

He plowed into his eggs. "I'm not," he said. "She decided she didn't want to be part of the family right after Georgia was born and left. My folks have been helping me raise the kids."

Now, Lucy was feeling foolish for quite another reason, foolish because she was feeling hopeful again. She was glad his wife had left him. "That's too bad about their mother," she lied, "but it's great you have your parents to help out. I'm sure you're all doing a great job with them. But back to your grandmother – if you think it wouldn't be too hard on her, I'd love to meet her and see if we can casually get on to the subject of Victory Hembree and what she might have known of my grandmother from back in the day. Maybe she knows something."

Beau nodded, thinking he'd been rather clever about how he'd gotten her to go out on a date with him, using his Lovie as bait. Still, this was serious business. "Maybe," he said. "But I have to admit that I feel as if I need to help you with Ms. Victory's request considering my great-grandfather was evidently part of the problem. She said it right in that letter. Remember how we apologized to each other last night about our families and their mutual coercion?"

"Yes."

"Maybe… maybe I can help undo what he did in a small way."

She looked up at him. "Part of clearing the family name, eh?"

He nodded, meeting her eye over the steaming food. "You have your reasons," he said softly, "and I have mine."

That was good enough for Lucy. At six o'clock that evening, she was armed and ready.

CHAPTER TWELVE
~ Let the Dead Lie ~

"*V*ICKIE! LET ME IN!"

The hissed voice came from the east-facing window of Victory's bedroom, the side of the house that faced a grove of trees and beyond that, fields of sorghum. It was very late at night beneath a full moon as Victory sat up in bed, rubbing her eyes, thinking she might have imagined the voice. But there it came again, a female whisper, and tapping against the glass.

Victory leapt out of bed.

"Dell?" she said in disbelief as she wrenched open the window. "Girl, what are you doing here?"

Victory's cousin, Dell, slithered in through the window and ended up falling to the floor with a thud. Victory winced, fearful that someone would hear the sound as she pulled her cousin off of the floor.

"I had to come and see you," Dell said. A pale girl with curly red hair, she was the chatty and anxious sort. "Nobody's seen you in months! People are saying you're dead!"

Victory shook her head, glad to see her cousin but also torn about it. She didn't want her daddy to discover Dell in her bedroom.

"I'm not dead," Victory said. "But you'd better leave. I don't want Daddy to see you."

Dell wouldn't be pushed away. "What's wrong?" she demanded. "Why hasn't anybody seen you lately? What is Uncle Laveau punishing you for?"

Victory didn't want to tell her, mostly because she knew that Dell would run amok in the town, telling everyone what she knew. Dell was that way.

Dressed in a flowing, lightweight house coat, her six-month-pregnant belly wasn't terribly evident so she made sure that the fabric didn't bind up against her. She kept her arm in front of her as an extra measure of protection.

"Don't ask, Dell," *she said, turning to sit on the bed.* "Please don't ask. Go home, okay? I'm not sick and I'm not dead. Just… go home."

Dell was greatly concerned and greatly curious. "Why won't your daddy let you come out anymore?" *she asked again.* "The girls at school think you're a prisoner. Are you?"

Victory frowned; she didn't want to answer any questions. "Dell, please," *she said.* "I… I'm fine. You know how Daddy is – he gets something stuck in his mind and it's hard to change it. This is one of those times. You get out of here, ya hear? You don't want Daddy to catch you. He'll lock you up, too."

That was the truth. Dell knew that Laveau could do anything he wanted to do and she didn't want to be imprisoned like her cousin obviously was. Frustrated, she turned for the window.

"Are you sure you're okay?" *she asked her cousin.*

Victory nodded, refusing to look at her. "I am," *she said.* "Dell… wait a minute."

"What?"

Victory was hesitant. "How… how is everybody at school?"

Dell came back towards her. "We're all fine," *she said.* "We're just worried about you. Mr. Franklin won't talk about you. He says he don't know nothin', that your daddy pulled you out of school and didn't tell him why."

Victory's heart sank. "Daddy's mad at me," *was all she could bring herself to say.* "Just don't ask any more questions. He's mad at me and I'm not going to tell you why. How… how is Eulalie?"

Dell sat down on the bed beside her. "She's fine," *she said.* "She *cries about you all of the time. Does she know why you're here?"*

Victory shook her head. "No," she said. "How... how is Mr. Franklin? And Belle, the cook? And... and Lewis, the groundskeeper? Are they all okay?"

Dell continued to nod. "They're all fine," she said. "Except I don't see Lewis around anymore. I heard that Mr. Franklin discharged him."

It was like a knife to the heart and Victory tried not to weep over it. "Why?" she couldn't help but ask. "Mr. Franklin liked him."

Dell shrugged. "No one knows," she said. Then, she lowered her voice. "But we think it has something to do with his brother being killed. Is... is it true, Vickie? My daddy said that his brother was killed by Uncle Laveau."

Victory couldn't help the tears now, but she struggled against them. All she could do was nod, once, listening to Dell emit a ghastly hiss.

"He was?" she asked. "Sweet Jesus, Vickie, did... did you see it? Is that why your daddy has you locked up here? Because you saw him do it and he doesn't want you to tell anyone?"

That was as good a reason as any to force Dell from her bedroom. Maybe if Dell thought Laveau was trying to cover up a crime by keeping his daughter locked up, she'd go away and never come back. Swiftly, Victory nodded her head. "Get out of here," she said. "Don't you ever come back. And if you tell anyone about this, I'll tell Daddy that you came here and you're the one telling people he killed a man."

Dell's eyes widened in terror. She bolted up from the bed but as she did so, her arm came into contact with Victory's torso and landed across the young woman's swollen belly. In that instant, Dell saw the pregnancy and her hands flew to her mouth in shock.

"My God!" she cried, pointing to Victory's belly. "You... you...!"

Victory grabbed her cousin by the arms. "Keep your mouth shut," she hissed. "You didn't see anything here tonight. You don't know anything, ya hear? If you tell anyone about anything at all, Daddy will know about it and he'll come for you. Do you understand? Keep your mouth shut and don't ever come back!"

Dell was in a panic. She fled to the open window, trying to make her way down the climbing rose vine on the side of the house with all due haste. But in her rush, she got tangled up halfway down and fell, landing on her right arm and snapping the bones.

She never did tell her mother the truth about how she broke her arm.

CHAPTER THIRTEEN
Present

As Lucy found out, Beau really didn't know how old his grandmother was because women from her generation were so used to hiding their age that, he suspected, Ms. Hollis didn't even know how old she was. She didn't have a driver's license so he couldn't look her up in the Department of Motor Vehicles records and could, therefore, only really guess at how old she was.

Beau knew she had married Terhune Meade's son in nineteen hundred and forty-five, so he figured she was at least in her late eighties. Once Lucy met the woman at the New Orleans Bistro in downtown Pea Ridge, she had to agree. She was darn near ancient.

But the woman was a riot. She seemed to be quite sharp for her age and she dressed as one would have dressed in one's prime – in her case, from the nineteen fifties. She wore a powder blue suit, a wig, a hat, gloves, all the way down to the lip rouge and matching pocketbook.

With a grandmother's entitlement, she fawned over her grandson, much to his embarrassment, and after one Manhattan – surprising that she loved liquor living in a conservative southern town as she did – she was seemingly drunk and Beau cut her off at one drink. Lucy found it hysterical.

"Ms. Lucy," Lovie said from across the table after the dinner dishes were cleared. "I'm tired of talking about myself. Talk, talk, talk, all through dinner. You know all about me now. But I want to hear about you. My grandson doesn't date women, you know, so you must be very special. What do you do, my dear?"

She was waving her hands around as she spoke. Lucy looked at Beau, who was sitting next to Lovie and struggling not to appear too chagrinned at his grandmother's blunt nature. She fought off a grin.

"I'm a lawyer," she said, rather loudly because Lovie couldn't hear very well but refused to use a hearing aid. "Remember? When you and I first met, Beau told you I was a lawyer from California."

Lovie waved her off as if she didn't have time to remember things from an hour ago. "A pretty girl like you shouldn't have to work," Lovie said. "Can't you find a husband, honey? I'm not surprised, working as a lawyer. Men don't want a wife that works."

Lucy chuckled to herself. "I *was* married, once," she said. "It didn't last."

"Because you work!"

Lucy couldn't keep the giggles to herself anymore. "No, it wasn't because I worked," she said. "He was a lawyer, too."

She left the question of why she split with her husband hanging in the air, hoping it would be forgotten, but Lovie couldn't let it go.

"Then what happened?" Lovie asked, putting her hand on Lucy's. "I just don't understand the way young people look at marriage these days. Did you know that Beau's wife walked out on him? Left him with three babies to raise. She tried to come back last year but my Beau wouldn't take her back. I'm proud of him for doing that. What woman would leave her babies and then try to come back?"

Lucy wasn't particularly thrilled with the turn of the conversation. They had been quite happily talking about Lovie in her youth, hoping that would lead to the introduction of Laveau Hembree, but the subject had veered away from that. Now they were talking about marriages and spouses walking out, which was not something Lucy wanted to discuss. She wasn't laughing at the old woman's persistence anymore.

"I don't know," she said honestly. "I wouldn't have left my family, that's for sure, but I suppose I think differently. I believe you stick with your spouse, for better or for worse, but my ex-husband and Beau's ex-wife apparently don't believe in that. It's sad."

Lovie squeezed her hand. "It *is* sad," she agreed, letting her go. "Since Beau no longer has a wife and you no longer have a husband, maybe the two of you should get together."

Appalled, Lucy wasn't sure how to respond to that when Beau spoke up. "Lovie, that's enough," he said, firmly but gently. "You just met Ms. Lucy. You shouldn't push her like that. It's rude."

Lovie waved him off. "I'm honest," she said flatly. "That's not a crime. Miss Lucy, I know you're from California, but what are you doing in Pea Ridge? You got business here?"

They had swung back on to the exact subject Lucy had wanted to discuss from the beginning. The woman was jumping all over the place in her thoughts but with this new focus, Lucy was eager to take the lead. She was more than eager to be off the subject of broken marriages.

"In a sense," she said. "My grandmother's funeral was yesterday. My family is in Pea Ridge."

Lovie was interested. "Is that so?" she asked. "What's the name?"

"Hembree."

Lovie blinked as if surprised. She sat back in her seat. "Hembree?" she repeated. "You mean Victory Hembree?"

Lucy nodded. "Victory Hembree Bondurant was my grandmother," she said. "My father is her son."

Lovie seemed to lose her humor. She simply stared at Lucy for a minute, for a very long minute, before settling back in her chair even more. It was if is something had settled on her, or pushed her back, for she just sat there and stared at Lucy as she settled way back in her chair.

"Good Lord," she finally said. "You look like her. I didn't even realize that until now, but you look like her."

Lucy had heard that before. In fact, she'd seen pictures of Mamaw in her youth and she knew that she resembled her a great deal.

"Thank you," she said. "She was a beautiful woman so I'm flattered that you think so. Did you know her well?"

Odd how the loud-mouthed southern woman from moments before now suddenly seemed subdued. Her gaze never left Lucy.

"I knew her, though not well," she said. "She was older than I was by several years so we never traveled in the same circles, but I knew of her. I remember when she married Hardy. Her daddy forced her into that marriage, I seem to recall. She was quite old when they married."

"She was close to forty," Lucy said, thrilled that the woman was speaking on exactly what she wanted to hear. "My dad was born when she was forty years old, in fact. I… I always wondered why she was so old when she got married. You never heard rumor of a boyfriend or anything, did you?"

Lovie's expression seemed to tighten as if recalling things from the past, things that were unpleasant at best. The change in her demeanor was drastic; even Beau noticed it. He glanced at Lucy to see how she was reacting to it, but Lucy was completely focused on the old woman.

"No…," Lovie said after a moment. "I never heard of a boyfriend. I remember… I remember that her daddy didn't let her out of the house much. In fact, that whole family seemed to stay bottled up in Glory. He let her out to go to church with her mama, but that's the only time I really remember seeing her out and about, so I don't think she had a boyfriend at any time before marrying Hardy Bondurant."

It was information Lucy had never heard before. So Laveau

kept Victory a prisoner after the whole event with the child and Lewis and Aldridge? Seeing that Lovie was reluctant to speak on the subject, she sought to loosen the woman in the hopes of gaining more information.

"I have to tell you, it's really fascinating talking to someone who knew my grandmother when she was young," she said, smiling. "I know so little about her from that time in her life. In fact, I don't know a lot about my great-grandfather, either. She never talked much about him."

Lovie snorted. "She wouldn't," she said. "Beau, I want another Manhattan."

Beau was about to deny her but a pleading look from Lucy changed his mind. "Sure," he said. "I'll go get it."

As he got up, Lucy didn't give Lovie a chance to think over her statement. She went in for the kill. "Why would you say that, Ms. Lovie?" she asked. "I've heard that my great-grandfather wasn't a very nice man, but as I said, she never really talked about him. Didn't they get along?"

She was feigning ignorance, hoping the old woman who'd been a chatterbox all evening would keep it up. Lovie picked up her empty glass and tried to get a last drop out of it.

"Honey, no one got along with Laveau Hembree," she said. "I don't want to upset ya'll, but he was a mean son-of-a-bitch, and forgive my French for saying that. If ever there was a wicked man to walk the earth, it was Laveau Hembree."

Lucy continued to play ignorant. "Really?" she said. "Did you know him?"

Lovie wasn't looking at her; she was looking at her empty glass. "Everyone in town knew him," she said. "Or, at least, *of* him. He's gone now so I suppose it doesn't matter if I talk about him, but there was a time when no one talked about him. If you did and he didn't like it, you'd find your dog strung up in your yard, gutted, or the brake lines on your car cut. No sirree... you didn't speak of the devil or he would come after you."

Lucy found it very interesting to hear about her great-grandfather from someone who had lived during his time. In fact, it was fascinating. "And no one stood up to him?"

Lovie snorted. "Who?" she asked. "Terhune? My husband's father was a coward. He just did what Laveau told him to do."

Lucy could sense her disgust. "That's shocking," she said, eyeing the old woman. "But… well, I can't help but wonder why he kept my grandmother so caged up. That's just so cruel. You never heard why?"

Lovie didn't reply for a moment. "There were rumors, of course," she finally said. "But we didn't really speak of them. No one wanted Laveau's men to show up on their doorstep."

"What rumors?"

Lovie shifted in her seat uncomfortably. "You're asking me about unpleasant things about your own family," she said, a rebuke in her tone. "I don't want to be the one to tell you things like that."

Lucy thought she might have lost her witness. "If you don't tell me, no one will," she said, pressing gently. "Everyone who knew my grandmother as a young woman is dead now. I… I guess I'm just curious to know more about her, that's all. I didn't mean to make you uncomfortable, though. I apologize if I did."

"Sometimes it's better to let the dead lie."

"Excuse me?"

Lovie seemed to realize she'd been mumbling to herself. She spoke louder. "It was just a rumor we'd heard," she said. "I overheard Terhune talking about something Ms. Victory had done, the reason Laveau kept her locked up."

Lucy couldn't even dare to hope. It was a struggle not to show her eagerness. "What was it?"

Lovie leaned forward and put her hand up to her mouth as if to whisper. "She tried to run away with a colored," she hissed, looking around to make sure no one heard her. "Laveau kept her locked up because she tried to run away with a colored man who worked for him."

Lucy nodded, her mind whirling. It was part of what had had happened in a sense, but not all of it. "Really?" she said, acting surprised. "That must have been really shocking, especially back then."

Lovie nodded, sitting back just about the time Beau returned to the table with her Manhattan. The old woman took it eagerly. "Some said that Laveau killed the man she wanted to run away with," she elaborated. "If he did, they'd never find that body. No, sirree."

Beau sat down next to his grandmother, having heard her last sentence. "Laveau killed somebody?"

Lovie nearly choked on her drink. "Shush," she said. "Don't say that so loud."

Beau grinned. "Why?" he asked. "Nobody cares, Lovie. It's not like the man is going to rise up out of his grave and come for you. Who did he kill?"

Lovie slurped down about half of her Manhattan. "A colored boy," she said, shushing him again when he opened his mouth to question her. "Just one of the many rumors surrounding that man. I was just telling your lady friend how terrified we all were of him and how he kept his daughter locked up for a long time until she married Hardy Bondurant."

Beau was glad that his grandmother had evidently spilled what she knew about the Hembrees. "Whatever Dad has said about him wasn't good," he said. "I don't ever remember granddad talking about him except in passing."

Lovie wiped at her smeared lipstick with a cocktail napkin. "He wasn't a man to speak about, ever."

Beau could sense his grandmother's nervousness. "You're still afraid of him?"

Lovie shrugged. "Mr. Hembree's evil goes beyond the grave,"

she said. "That kind of evil wasn't meant to die."

"Why?"

"Because of everything he did. That kind of evil just keeps going, in every family it touched. It's like... like the ripple of a pond. It just spreads. Someday, it'll die down and be forgotten, but not soon. Poor Ms. Victory... she was at the center of her daddy's evil. I feel for her."

With that, she drained her Manhattan like a shot, all of it gone in a gulp. Lucy looked at Beau and, together, they silently determined that Lovie was, perhaps, done for the day. It was a lot of excitement for an old woman and Lucy was completely willing to let the subject go for now.

Little did she know that Lovie wasn't.

"Well," Lucy said after a moment, "I appreciate you telling me something about my family history. It's truly been an honor, ma'am. I've enjoyed meeting you."

Lovie smiled at her, but it was forced. "Have you seen the ghosts yet?"

Lucy looked at her, puzzled. "What ghosts?"

"At Glory," Lovie clarified. She was most definitely feeling her alcohol, made worse by the second drink. "It's full of ghosts, you know. People have said that Mr. Hembree buried bodies all around the place, so if I were you, I'd dig up that yard and see what's there."

It was horrific thought. "I haven't seen any ghosts," she said hesitantly. "People have really said there are bodies buried on the grounds?"

Lovie nodded. "Since I first married Beau's grandfather," she said. "People have talked about the men Mr. Hembree killed. He buried some of them on his property so they couldn't be dug up. No sane man is going to come onto Laveau Hembree's land, you know. That's what they say, anyway. People around here think that Glory is cursed. You know that colored man that Ms. Victory was supposed to run away with? I heard that Mr. Hembree killed him. He's probably buried around the house, too."

Lucy stared at the woman in shock. What had started out as an evening of trying to manipulate an old woman into telling what she knew of the younger years of Victory Hembree turned into more than Lucy had bargained for.

"You heard about that?" she asked, aghast.

Lovie nodded. "That's what they say," she said, starting to slur her words. "You want to know something else? I wasn't going to tell you, but if you want to know about your family's history, you may as well know – people said that Mr. Hembree kept his daughter locked up because he got her pregnant. Got his own daughter pregnant! I'm sure that baby is one of those bodies buried around the place. He kept that poor girl locked up because he didn't want anyone to know the truth."

Beau stepped in at that point; he had to. The two Manhattans were causing his grandmother to run off at the mouth with horrible stuff, true or not. He didn't even know and he didn't even care. All he knew was that Lucy, sitting across the table from them, was pale with shock. He felt a good deal of pity for her.

"I think it's time for us to go," he said to his grandmother. "I think there's been enough talk of ghosts and rumors, don't you? Where do you come up with this stuff, Lovie?"

Lovie's gaze had been lingering on Lucy, undoubtedly looking for a reaction to what she'd been told, but now she turned to Beau. She smiled.

"Such a sweet boy," she crooned as he stood up from the booth, reaching out a hand to pull her out. As she reached out to take his hand, she continued to speak to Lucy. "Ask your daddy, dear. See if he knows about the relationship between his mama and her daddy. Maybe he's not really Hardy Bondurant's son at all – Hardy was married for years and never had children. He married Miss Victory and suddenly, she had a son. It may very well be that your daddy is really Mr. Hembree's boy. I wouldn't be surprised."

Now the conversation was turning venomous. It was disgusting what the old woman was suggesting. Although Lucy had ridden in the car with Beau and his grandmother to the restaurant, she wasn't going to ride home in the same car with that woman. The tides had turned against her in the conversation and she was about as offended as she could possibly be. This wasn't what she had bargained for at all.

As Beau escorted his grandmother out to the car, Lucy made the excuse of going to the restroom when, in fact, she went out another entrance to the restaurant. Her hotel wasn't too far off and, in the darkness of a Mississippi night, she nearly ran the mile back to the hotel and shut herself up in her room for the night.

When her room phone rang about an hour later, she ignored it.

CHAPTER FOURTEEN
~ *The Plot Thickens* ~

*I*T WAS NIGHT.

That was the only time Laveau would let her out of the house, at night, to walk around the property near the house, covered up in a shawl that draped over her entire body, walking the grounds with her mother by her side so she could get some exercise. Come any weather, she and her mother walked in circles for an hour or two.

The weather was mild tonight, fortunately. A placid moon hung high in the heavens, bathing everything in a silver glow as Victory and her mother trudged beneath the canopy of oaks. Victory was tired from the walking, made worse by the fact that the baby was growing bigger.

Dr. Latling figured she had about another month to go before the birth and, like an execution date, that was all Victory could think of. She knew her life was going to change in a month, the very moment her child was pulled from her body.

She was terrified.

"Mama?" she asked quietly.

"Yes?"

"What has Daddy said about the baby when it's born?" she asked. "I mean, has he said what's going to happen?"

Caroline remained stoic. "If you're thinking on keeping your child, honey, I'm afraid that's out of the question."

Victory's eyes welled with tears. "I didn't think Daddy would let me keep her," she said. "But... but it'll be Daddy's grandchild. What if it's a boy? He's always wanted a boy."

Caroline sighed faintly, a wispy breath like the sound of the gentle breeze through the dark leaves in the trees.

"Not this boy," she said softly. "You know how your daddy feels about this situation, Victory. You got yourself into it and you're just going to have to accept his decision in all things. He knows what's best."

Victory came to a halt, facing her mother in the moonlight. "Does he?" she wanted to know, her manner growing agitated. "He wants to kill her. That's all he's wanted to do since the beginning. He killed poor Aldridge Ragsdale because he thought he was the father. Now he wants to kill the baby, too. He's just waiting until she's born so he can get his hands on her and smash her head against a tree. But I won't let him do it, do you hear? I won't let him!"

She was becoming loud and Caroline shushed her. "Quiet down," she said, grabbing her daughter before the girl could bolt off. "Do you want him to hear you?"

Victory was sobbing. "Please, Mama," she wept. "Please don't let him kill my baby."

Caroline held fast to her girl. "Your daddy will do what's best," she repeated.

Victory shook her head. "I can't believe you would let him do this," she said. "You're my mother — you're supposed to protect me!"

Caroline's expression was devoid of emotion. "I'm his wife."

"And that's more important than saving your child's life? Saving the life of your grandbaby?"

"He'll do what's best."

It was the standard answer Caroline had been giving her since almost the day they'd learned of the pregnancy. It was an answer that was becoming increasingly frustrating to Victory. Her mother just didn't seem to get the urgency of the situation.

"If Daddy kills my baby, he'll go to Hell," she hissed. "He'll go to Hell and you'll go, too, for letting him do it. All of the praying in the world won't save your soul if you help him kill my baby."

Caroline closed her eyes briefly, tightly. She had been wrestling with that exact thought for months now. The woman chain smoked in private, where no one could see her, and then she'd drink liquor to mask the smell, liquor her maid got from a still out north of Tillatoba. With smoke and liquor on her breath, she usually tried to gargle it away and put on copious amounts of perfume, which upset Laveau because he didn't like the smell of her perfume.

He'd often walk away from her in disgust, but that was part of her plan — she wanted him away from her. She wanted him to go find another woman to lay his fat body on, some local tramp that his men would bring to him. Sometimes, she could hear the mattress squeaking on the bed in the plantation office and she thanked God for it. One less night her husband would want to impose himself on her.

One less night to pray for death.

Caroline Hembree was a tortured soul, too tortured to save her own child.

"He'll do what's best," *she murmured again.*

In silence, she dragged her weeping daughter along on their nightly walk, a forced march in the darkness.

CHAPTER FIFTEEN

Present

The child
Lewis Ragsdale
Aldridge Ragsdale
~~Sheriff Meade~~
Dr. Latling

LUCY SAT AT her desk, looking at the list she'd made yesterday. She crossed out Sheriff Meade's name because she was pretty certain she was at a dead end with Beau, his help, and his family.

She'd spent another sleepless night thinking on Lovie Meade and the old bird's insulting remarks. But as morning came, Lucy came to the conclusion that she probably deserved everything she got. She'd pressed the woman, after all, and just because the old lady told her some unsavory things... well, she had no right to be offended by it. She'd wanted to know what the old women knew and by the end of the evening, she certainly had.

But that didn't make hearing it any easier.

So she rose early and took a long shower, planting herself in front of the desk with her hair wet as she looked at her list and pondered what she needed to do for the day. She'd failed to see Mo Guinn the day before because the man hadn't been in the office, but she'd made an appointment with him for later this afternoon, so that was one thing she needed to do on behalf of Mamaw's estate.

A quick call to her parents led her to believe that they were already starting to inventory the house, something she promised to help them with after her visit to Mo. But she couldn't take too much time with that. She remembered Beau saying that there was a Latling family in town and she intended to track them down.

Truth was, she was a little gun shy about pressing people for information after what happened with Lovie Meade but it couldn't be helped. She needed answers and her time was growing shorter by the day. She wondered how long she could brush her parents off until they figured out she had her own agenda.

As the morning progressed, she dried her hair and dressed comfortably, in jeans and a cute top with her hair pulled back. She thought a visit to the historical society might be in order to see if they had anything at all about Glory or the Hembrees, or even the Ragsdale family. She might even drop in on Aunt Dell to see if she, too, had insulting things to say about Laveau and Victory. God only knew what Aunt Dell would have to say, but Lucy was coming to think that the woman might be the motherlode. Gossip or not, she'd been around a long time. She might know a few things.

Glancing at her watch, Lucy saw that it was nearing the time when the hotel complimentary breakfast was cut off and she was hungry. So she put the journal and the letter back in her purse, collected her phone and iPad, and headed downstairs. The hotel was newer, with modern décor, and she headed to the area where they set out the breakfast to see that they were just starting to put things away.

Quickly, she grabbed a foam plate and helped herself to the remainder of the eggs and some cold bacon. There were grits, of course, and she piled them on the plate as well. This breakfast was nothing like the breakfast she and Beau had shared the day before, and thoughts of that meal brought on thoughts of Beau she had been trying very hard to avoid.

That big, handsome hunk had turned her head. She could admit that to herself but not to her parents. They would tell her she was rebounding, which wasn't true. Well, not entirely. Three months of therapy had helped her get over the hump of losing Kevin but she still wasn't out of the woods yet.

Still, Beau Meade was making her life a little brighter without even knowing it. Or, at least he *had*. After last night, she was certain there was nothing left of that and she struggled not to feel disappointed about it.

Sitting at one of the hotel's tables near the front lobby, she wolfed down her eggs as she pulled out her iPad, running a search for the historical society's address and hours. She found their website and saw that they weren't even open today, so her plans shifted to Aunt Dell for the day. She knew where the woman lived, or at least she thought she remembered, so she planned on making a call that morning after she'd finished eating. Just as she shut down her iPad, she caught a glimpse of someone approaching her table.

"I knew I'd find you!"

It was Clyde. Lucy nearly choked on her coffee when she saw the man. "What in the hell are you doing here?" she demanded.

Clyde had that usual smarmy look about him. "I've been looking at every hotel parking lot in town," he said proudly. "I drove around yesterday at the Comfort Inn, the Holiday Inn, and the Econo Inn hoping I'd see your car and I was lucky enough to see you last night when you pulled in here. When I want to find something, I don't give up."

"That's being a stalker," she said, anger in her tone. "There are laws against stalkers, Clyde. In fact, I'm going to the police station right now to file a stalking report against you and I also intend to file a restraining order."

His face fell. "Why?" he was genuinely bewildered. "I just wanted to see you before you went home, Lucy. Why are you so angry about it?"

Lucy stood up and collected her things. "I'm not sure how much plainer I can be with you," she said. "I don't want to see you. I don't want you following me or even thinking about me. The next time I see you, I'm not even going to say a word – I'm going to take the can of pepper spray I always carry and shoot you in the face with it. Is that what it's going to take for you to leave me the hell alone? Because that's what's going to happen if you come near me again."

Clyde had swiftly gone from bewildered to defensive. "You're not a nice girl, Lucy," he said flatly. "I'm just trying to be friendly with you and you're just not nice at all."

"Good," Lucy said as if in full agreement. "I'm glad you think so. Now, go away. I don't want to see you."

"It's a free country."

"Not when she asks you to leave, it's not."

Both Lucy and Clyde turned to see Beau standing a few feet away, dressed in his service uniform. He'd come in through the side entrance to the hotel and snuck up behind them both.

Now, Clyde was left to shuffle back, infuriated by the sheriff's appearance and humiliated by Lucy's treatment of him. He pointed at Beau.

"I haven't done anything," he pointed out. "This is public property and you can't arrest me."

Beau simply shook his head. "Do we really have to go through this again?" he asked. "You're going to walk out that door and never come back here. If you do, I will arrest you for harassment and I'm sure Miss Bondurant will be happy to press charges. This is the second time I've had to tell you to leave her alone so if you don't listen, you're going to find yourself in jail. Do you understand me?"

Clyde was angry and ashamed. Quickly, he turned and walked away, leaving through the front door of the hotel as Beau followed behind him at a distance. When he was sure that Clyde wasn't going to double back, he meandered over to the front desk and said something to the clerk, who in turn summoned her manager. Soon, it was the three of them up at the front desk as Beau evidently said something about Clyde because he kept pointing to the front door and the security monitors.

Lucy stood there, watching it all go down, more thrilled than she cared to admit that Beau had made an appearance. She was also embarrassed, having run out on him and his grandmother the previous night, so she thought to slip away while he was occupied. She was a coward, she knew, not wanting to face him. Just as she headed for the side entrance, she heard him call after her.

"Lucy," he said. "Wait a minute."

Begrudgingly, she stopped, waiting as he finished up his conversation with the hotel employees and headed in her direction. She was having a hard time looking at him as he joined her.

"Are you okay?" he asked. "Clyde didn't do anything, did he?"

She shook her head. "No," she replied. "But he said he'd been out all day yesterday looking for me. Now that he knows I'm staying here, I'm going to go somewhere else. I really don't want to be here if he knows I'm here."

Beau nodded. "I don't blame you," he said. "Where are you going to go?"

She shrugged. "I can always go stay at Glory," she said. "Or there are other hotels around here. I'm not really sure."

His gaze lingered on her a moment. "Why not just go back to Glory?"

She shrugged, somewhat sheepishly. "Would you go back there given everything you heard about the place yesterday?" she asked. "Honestly, I don't even know what to think about it anymore. It's always been something of a home for me because I stayed there so often throughout my life, but now…."

He understood what she meant or at least he thought he did. "Look," he said, lowering his voice. "I'm really sorry about dinner last night. I don't know what possessed Lovie to go off on your family like she did, but I am really sorry about it. I thought she might be able to help you get to the bottom of Ms. Victory's request, but I think all she did is freak you out."

Lucy was shaking her head even as he continued to apologize. "You know what?" she asked honestly. "I deserved it. I deserved everything she said. Here I was, using my interrogation skills on what I thought was a helpless old lady and she turned right around and bit me. I will admit, I was upset about it and I'm sorry that I ditched you at the restaurant. But I was so upset at that moment, I didn't trust myself to sit in the same car with her. If she started up again about my great-grandfather actually being my grandfather, I would have had to jump out the window."

He grinned, shaking his head at the ridiculousness of what Lovie had said. "I know," he said. "I am *really* sorry for that. No more Manhattans for her."

"Did she say anything more after I left?"

"She wanted to know why I chased you off."

Lucy laughed it away. There was, truthfully, nothing more she could do. The situation was almost comical as well as deeply serious and there wasn't a great divide between the two. After a moment, she extended her hand to him.

"Friends?"

His smile turned warm as he reached out and shook her hand. "Friends."

He didn't let her go. He kept holding on to her, looking at her and smiling. Lucy had to chuckle as she practically wrenched her hand from his grip.

"I'm off to see Aunt Dell this morning," she said, turning for the side door as he followed. "I figure I might as well know what she has to say about it. I have a feeling she knows a whole lot more than your Lovie did."

He nodded, opening the door for her as they stepped out into the parking lot. "I'm sure she does," he said. "But I actually have some more news about some things in that letter. Last night, I couldn't sleep, so I did some digging around, too."

Lucy put her sunglasses on, looking at him. "After I walked out on you?"

"I felt responsible for what happened. And you asked for my help, so I was helping."

"Even after all that?"

"Even after all that."

She laughed softly. "Okay," she conceded. "So what did you find?"

He put on his Ray-Bans. "Latling," he said. "I went back to the office and looked back through some police records of that time, records that we have buried in the basement storage. My great-granddad was sheriff in Tallahatchie County from nineteen hundred and thirty through nineteen hundred and forty-seven, when he had a heart attack that virtually crippled him. That's seventeen years of Terhune Meade and Laveau Hembree, if you get my drift. Seventeen years of police reports and such, and not one thing I came across ever mentioned Laveau Hembree. Not one."

That was a disheartening statement but not surprising. "Jesus," she breathed. "With everything that man did, you would have thought there would be some record of it. But surely you didn't go through everything last night."

He cocked his head. "Near abouts," he said. "Once I started, it was hard to stop. Once I realized that there wasn't a record of Laveau Hembree anywhere in official records, it became an obsession to find something. But there wasn't a thing. I did, however, find a few mentions of a Dr. S. S. Latling."

Lucy was very interested. "What did they say?"

Beau thought back on the reports. "It seems that Dr. Latling was the county coroner, too," he said. "Several mentions of him in death reports. There were some homicide reports that mentioned him, too, including a pretty nasty report about an old woman that was murdered in a house down the street from Glory. Seems that she was hacked to death with a machete of some kind. Anyway, Dr.

Latling was in the reports quite a bit and the address given on those reports is, in fact, the same address of the current Latling family. It's a big house in an older part of town. So I stopped by the house this morning before I came over to your hotel."

Lucy was on pins and needles. "And?"

"And the current owner, Stephen Latling, is the son of Dr. S.S Latling," he replied. "He's retired and was golfing. But I spoke with his wife and she said you could come by around lunchtime and talk to her husband."

Lucy was stunned. "Wow," she said. "I don't even know what to say. Thank you doesn't seem like enough, but thank you. From the bottom of my heart, thank you."

"You're welcome," he said, eyes glimmering at her. "So we're off to Aunt Dell's now?"

She gave him a quirky grin. "Don't you have to work?"

He snorted. "This *is* work," he said. "There was a crime committed somewhere along the line here, according to your grandmother's letter, and it's my job to get to the bottom of it."

She was touched by his enthusiasm. "Talk about cold cases," she said. "I think the statute of limitations has run out."

He shook his head. "For something like this, that statute never runs out. We're missing a baby and I aim to find her."

It was a very sweet thing to say. Lucy struggled not to become swept up in his chivalry, but it was good to have the attention and comfort of a man, even one she would have to leave in five days. But she supposed, until then, that whatever was stirring between them couldn't hurt. Selfishly, she needed it.

"Okay," she said. "We can be like Starsky and Hutch."

"I was thinking more Benson and Stabler."

"I like that better."

Once again, Lucy found herself in his custom Ford Edge police cruiser, now heading to the north side of town where Ms. Dell Alexander lived.

CHAPTER SIXTEEN
~ You Might Not Like What You Find ~

"Mr. Hembree, I just didn't want you to think I had anything to do with that article, sir. I had to come and tell you myself."

A tall, gaunt man in a sweat-stained suit stood in the front parlor of Glory, speaking to Laveau, Terhune, and a few of Laveau's men. They were spread out over the room, a few of them fanning themselves lazily in the warm night. The man in the stained suit held his snap-brim hat in-hand, but it was quivering, just like the rest of him.

Laveau could see the tremors. He liked it when men cowered before him. It made him feel powerful. He took a sip of his coffee without having offered any to his guests.

"Mr. Haltom, I haven't even seen the article," he said, sounding benevolent. "But you were right to come to me. Who printed it, did you say?"

"The Vicksburg Post, sir."

"Who is the editor?"

"Mr. John Surratt."

Laveau pondered that for a moment. "And what, exactly, did it say?"

Haltom cleared his throat nervously. "I have a copy in my car, sir...."

"Just tell me."

Haltom did. "The article talks about corruption in the State of

Mississippi as a whole," he said. "It speaks of pockets of crime. It goes on to say that there's some corruption in the state so thick that no one can touch it, not even at the ballot boxes, and that includes corruption in Pea Ridge. The reporter who ran the story tried to speak to me a few weeks ago about what I think on corruption in the state but I sent him away. I never spoke to him and he makes mention of the fact."

Laveau listened seriously. "Does he mention you by name?"

Haltom nodded, pulling at the collar of his shirt. "He does," he said. "He mentions you, too. He wanted to know my opinion of you, sir, but I didn't say a word. In his article, he states that I was a lawyer who used to fight for the people, but now...."

"Now... what?"

Haltom sighed heavily, averting his gaze. "Now I'm your slave," he muttered. "He went on to say that modern-day slavery isn't dead so long as corruption rules."

Laveau looked over at Terhune. "He said that, did he?" he asked rhetorically, watching Terhune nod. "Well, it seems as if that reporter is trying to make a name for himself by dragging me through the mud. I don't appreciate that he mentioned me by name. No sir, I don't."

That was probably a calm way of putting it. Terhune was watching him, as were the rest of his men, as Laveau finally stood up and paced his way across the front parlor, pushing the curtains aside to look at the night beyond. He was gazing into a blackness as dark as his very soul.

"What's the reporter's name?" he asked.

"Griffey," Haltom replied. "Terrence Griffey."

Laveau continued to ponder the situation. "Well," he said, turning away from the window. "You did right to come and tell me. I appreciate loyalty."

Haltom turned to go but he hesitated. "Do you want me to contact the reporter and tell him something for you?" he asked. "I... I'd be happy to. I'm not pleased at 'tall with the man mentioning my name as a slave and was planning on telling him so."

Laveau shook his head. "No," he said. "I'll have my own men contact him. You go on home, now. I need to talk this over with the boys."

Haltom didn't hesitate this time. He headed out of the house, bursting free of it and inhaling deeply of the clean night air. Something about that house was stifling and every time he visited, he felt as if he couldn't breathe. Laveau hung over that house like some great, wretched ghost, suffocating everything inside of it. At least, that's how Haltom felt.

The man was everywhere.

He was anxious to leave. His car was parked around the side of the house and as he made his way to it, he heard movement in the darkness over near the house. As he looked up, he saw a young woman emerge from the bushes. Startled, he just stared at her as she approached.

"Mr. Haltom?" she said hesitantly.

He nodded haltingly. "Yes."

She came closer. "You don't recognize me, do you?" she asked. When he shook his head, she continued. "You came to the Pea Ridge Female Academy last year and talked to us about the government and the laws of our country. Mr. Franklin said you were a big lawyer in Charleston."

He peered at her in the darkness. "I'm sorry, I don't remember you," he said. "What's your name?"

"Victory Hembree."

His eyes widened and he yanked his car door open. "It's nice to see you, Ms. Victory," he said quickly, throwing his hat into the car and following it inside. "Have a nice evening."

He couldn't get away from her fast enough and she ran towards him, holding out a hand. "Wait, please," she begged. "Please don't go. I need your help."

He slammed the door and tried to start the car. "Any help you need, go see your daddy," he told her. "I can't help you."

She was in tears now. "Please don't go," she pleaded. "My daddy is *planning a murder and I need your help!"*

He looked at her, pale, even in the moonlight. "Miss, I can't help you," he said flatly. "I won't help you. Now, get back in the house before your daddy sees us both."

He kept trying to start the car, which wouldn't turn over. "Please," she said, running to the car and putting her hands on the door. "I need you to contact the police in Jackson and send them here. My daddy has committed murder and he's going to commit more unless he's stopped. Sheriff Meade won't do anything. Will you please contact the Jackson police and tell them I need help? Please?"

Haltom was trying frantically to start the car, which finally turned over. He rolled up his window so the young woman couldn't talk to him anymore, but not before he saw her swollen midsection. She's pregnant! He thought in a panic. The girl couldn't be more than sixteen or seventeen years of age.

Lord, he didn't want to see any of this. He couldn't. Whatever help she wanted, it wasn't going to come from him. He'd already lost his wife and a son to Laveau Hembree and he wasn't about to risk the rest of his family. Throwing the car in reverse, he jerked away from Victory, driving off the Hembree property as if the Devil himself was after him.

It was three days later that Haltom heard that reporter from Vicksburg had died in a house fire.

CHAPTER SEVENTEEN

Present

DELL ALEXANDER LIVED in an old white house with clapboard sides on the northern outskirts of Pea Ridge. It was the same house she had lived in all of her life. Her mother, Laveau's only sister, had married a man named Alexander and they'd settled in the old farmhouse and raised their family. Two boys and one girl were born to them and both boys died young, leaving Dell as the only surviving child. She had never married.

The first thing Lucy noticed about the house was that it leaned. The floors leaned, the walls leaned – everything seemed to lean. Aunt Dell, incredibly old but still mobile, was thrilled to see her when she knocked on the woman's door. Both Lucy and Beau were invited into a house that was as neat as a pin.

They were directed to sit and asked if they'd like some Sanka, which Lucy didn't even know was made anymore. But, evidently, it was Aunt Dell's general term for coffee, which she produced quickly as she chatted up a storm.

Seated on the dated, plastic-covered furniture, Lucy took her coffee in a pretty tea cup as did Beau. She thought the delicate cup looked very out of place in his big hand and struggled to keep from grinning about it. He made a face at her when Aunt Dell wasn't looking.

"I didn't get a chance to see you after the funeral, Lucy," Aunt Dell said as she sat down opposite them in a gold-flower patterned easy chair. "I spent a good deal of time with Victory before she died, you know. I wanted to tell you that she asked for you quite often."

Lucy took a sip of the very strong coffee. "Did she?" she said. "I didn't know."

Dell nodded as she collected her own pretty cup filled with coffee. "She loved you so much," she said, somewhat wistfully. "She was very proud of you."

Lucy smiled weakly. "I wish I could have seen her before she died," she said. "I talked to her about every week or at least I tried to. She'd keep me on the phone for an hour telling me about things that happened last year, the year before, or five years ago. She had a lot of stories."

Dell smiled. "Yes, she did," she said. "Did she talk about Cousin Ruth and her Heimers?"

Lucy bit off a laugh. "You mean her Alzheimer's?"

"Yes, that."

"She talked about her quite a bit. She told me that Cousin Ruth used to hide vodka in shampoo bottles."

Dell shook her head reproachfully. "I grew up with Ruth," she said. "She started drinking a long time ago, sneaking her mother's brandy. If you ask me, it was the vodka that gave her the Heimers."

Lucy chewed on her lip to keep from laughing out loud, mostly because Dell was serious. The woman was a massive gossip so Lucy knew talk about Cousin Ruth was just the warm up. The good stuff was yet to come. But before Dell could go on, she turned to Beau, sitting silently next to Lucy.

"And I haven't seen you for a long time, either, Sheriff Meade," she said. "How proud your parents must be of you. Did pretty well for yourself, didn't you?"

Beau set the dainty coffee cup down, feeling somehow emasculated by the blue flowers. "Yes, ma'am."

"And your brother? Where is he these days?"

"Washington D.C., ma'am. He works for the FBI."

Dell crowed. "Of course he does," she said. "I'd forgotten all about that. Jefferson Meade left for school before you did, I believe."

Beau nodded. "Jeff is a year older than I am."

Dell sipped at her coffee. "So here you are," she said. "We are mighty lucky to have you around, Beau. And how do you know our Lucy?"

Beau turned to look at Lucy, who was verging on laughter. He could see it in her eyes. "I'm her bodyguard, ma'am," he said seriously. "I'm sorry, I can't elaborate on it, but suffice it to say that Ms. Lucy needs protection right now."

Dell grew gravely serious. "Is that so?" she said. Then, she slapped her thigh. "I knew that lawyer job would get you into trouble, Lucy! Victory told me that you defended criminals and now it's coming back to haunt you, isn't it?"

Lucy put a hand over her mouth so Dell wouldn't see how comical she found the entire conversation. "No, it's nothing like that," she said. "He was just kidding. Actually, he came with me because we wanted to ask you a few things. It seems that the Hembree and Meade families are tied together in this town and since you know everything about everyone, I have some questions that I think only you can answer."

Dell puffed up proudly. "I'll try," she said. "You know, I'll be ninety-eight years old in two weeks but I still remember everything. My mind hasn't left me at 'tall."

"No, ma'am, it hasn't," Lucy said. "I can see how sharp you are."

The flattery worked. Dell sipped at her coffee again. "So what do you want to know?"

Lucy had been very careful with Lovie Meade but she saw no reason to hold back from Aunt Dell. The woman knew the family secrets and then some. Still, she felt some apprehension as the reason for their visit came to the forefront. It was still a delicate subject.

"It's about Mamaw," she said. "I will admit that I've been hearing some very disturbing stories about Laveau and my dad said I should ask you about him. What you know about him and all."

The twinkle in Dell's eyes seemed to dim. "What do you want to know?"

Lucy shrugged. "Everything," she said. "I've never really been interested in the family history until now. I think I deserve to know what our family history is like, the good and the bad of it. Dad said you told him that Laveau was a gangster back in the day and that he had a loan shark business. Is that true?"

Dell set her coffee cup down. "It is," she said, her demeanor obviously subdued. "He did a lot of things he shouldn't have done."

"Did he ever kill a man?"

Dell stared at her, the old eyes scrutinizing her closely. Her bird-like hands gripped the arms of the chair. "Did someone tell you that?"

Lucy nodded. "Yes."

"Who?"

"Mamaw."

Dell's eyes widened. "She... she *told* you?"

Again, Lucy nodded. "Is it true?"

Dell's mouth popped open. "She *really* told you that?"

Lucy could see the woman's shock. "Aunt Dell, I'm just trying to figure out a few things," she said. "I'm not trying to upset you, but I really need to know – did Laveau Hembree kill a black man on the grounds of Glory?"

Dell stiffened; they could both see it. Suddenly, she was on her feet, heading for the door. "Ya'll need to leave now," she said crisply. "I'm not going to talk about this."

Beau stood up but Lucy didn't. She remained seated on the

couch, watching Aunt Dell flip out over the question. She had a suspicion as to why. Given the reputation of Laveau Hembree, still, she was fairly certain what had Aunt Dell so rattled.

"What are you afraid of?" Lucy asked gently. "He can't hurt you anymore, you know. He's long dead. And if you know something, tell me. Help me find some justice for the people he committed crimes against, Mamaw included."

Dell stood by the door, now half-open. Her thin hands were trembling as she took a deep breath or two. "Lucy, I don't want to talk about this."

Lucy wouldn't let go. "Why?" she asked. "If you don't tell me, when you die, all hope for justice for the people Laveau sinned against will be gone. No one will remember their names or what happened. They'll just fade away into history and we'll never know. Won't you please help me find some peace for them? I know he did terrible things to Mamaw. Are you really going to let him get away with it by keeping it all a secret, even after all of these years?"

Dell was shaken. She couldn't bring herself to voice what she'd spent all of her life keeping buried. After a moment, she moved away from the door but she didn't sit down again. She remained on her feet, over by the door to the kitchen. She kept her gaze averted, as if pondering Lucy's request and what, exactly, it entailed.

"You just don't know," she finally said. "You just don't know what you're asking."

"Then tell me." Lucy stood up, her voice soft but urgent. "Please, Aunt Dell; tell me what you know. I swear I won't tell anyone that you told me, but for my own peace of mind, I need to know."

Dell didn't move. She simply stood there, weaving a bit, her legs unsteady with age. When she finally spoke, it was in a whisper.

"Uncle Laveau was a very bad man, Lucy," she said. "Are you sure you know what you're asking for?"

"I won't know until you tell me."

Dell fell silent again. But the words came out, eventually. "Everybody was afraid of him," she said. "You didn't speak poorly of him or he'd send his men to burn your house down. He had poor Aunt Caroline beat down so much that when the woman died, my mama said Caroline thanked God for death. My mama thinks that Caroline took her own life, in fact, but if she did, we'll never know. Laveau had her buried quickly so no one could find out. Is that what you wanted to hear?"

Lucy felt a good deal of pity for her great-grandmother, but still, there was more she wanted to know. She braced herself.

"Yes," she said. "What else? What happened with the murdered man?"

Dell's shoulders seemed to slump. "I didn't see anything, but my daddy did," she said. "It was all rumor why Laveau done it. Some said that Victory wanted to run away with the man. Maybe that's true, but Laveau didn't really need a reason. He did as he pleased and Sheriff Meade let him. He just covered it up."

Lucy latched on to the mention of Aldridge Ragsdale. "Did you know the man who was murdered?"

Dell shook her head. "I didn't know him but I heard my daddy talking about him," she said. "He worked for Uncle Laveau and had been lusting after Victory. She must have been lusting after him, too, if they were planning on running away."

"Who was the family?"

"Ragsdale, I believe. The dead man's brother worked at my school as a janitor." She sighed heavily, lost in the terrible recollection. "After the killing, I remember Sheriff Meade coming out to the school to speak with the brother but by that time, he'd been discharged. I never saw him again. I don't know if Sheriff Meade ever caught up to him but I wouldn't have been surprised. He probably killed that boy, too."

Lucy was greatly distressed by the thought. What irony would it have been had Beau's great-grandfather killed Lewis Aldridge? She looked at Beau, who had been listening to the conversation intently. It was clear by his expression that he had the same thought as she did.

"I know what my great-granddad did," he said to Dell. "My dad has told me quite a bit but you... you were actually living here when all of that happened."

Dell nodded. "I was young," she said. "I was a few years younger than Victory. Your great-granddaddy was a man without power, Beau. They called him 'The Puppet' around here. He did what Uncle Laveau told him to do. But it wasn't his fault; he did it to keep his family safe. I can't say I blame him."

Lucy's attention lingered on Beau for a moment, seeing the resignation in his face, before returning her focus to Dell.

"So the two of them were in cahoots with each other," she said.

"They were."

Lucy felt like she was gaining a better picture of Laveau and his scope of evil. "Since you were close to Mamaw, I need to ask you about something else," she said. "There was a time when Laveau kept her locked up and away from the world for quite some time. It was some time around nineteen thirty-three. Do you remember that?"

Dell's head swiveled in her direction. "How would you know about that?"

"The same way I know about the murder."

"Victory *told* you?"

Lucy nodded. "Do you know why she was kept locked away?"

Dell was looking at her warily. "If Victory told you she'd been locked away, then maybe she told you why. It's not my place to...."

"She was pregnant, wasn't she?"

She cut off the old woman with those five words, words that sent Dell grasping for the nearest chair. Lucy and Beau ran forward to steady the woman, lowering her onto a plastic dining room chair. Dell waved them off as she struggled to catch her breath.

"She... she told you that?" she gasped.

Lucy nodded. "Did you know?"

Dell looked at her fearfully for a moment before nodding. "I... I did."

It was the confirmation that Lucy had been seeking. She didn't know why she divulged the pregnancy to the old gossip, only that she was hoping beyond hope that Dell already knew about it. If she was close to Mamaw, maybe she did. Maybe she knew more about it than Mamaw's letter let on. She was willing to take the chance.

Swallowing hard, she took one of Dell's fragile hands into her own.

"I know about the baby," she whispered. "You don't have to be afraid anymore, Aunt Dell. I know the secret. But I'm the only one; you kept that secret well, so well that no one else has a clue about it. But Mamaw herself told me. What she didn't tell me is what happened to the baby. Do you know?"

Dell shook her head, tears welling in the old eyes. "I don't," she murmured. "I don't know, Lucy. I don't even know how she became pregnant or who the father was. I found out by accident and Victory told me that if I told anyone, Uncle Laveau would come for me. Fear has kept me quiet for eight-three years. I've never told a soul."

Lucy squeezed the woman's hand, feeling her pain, her fear. It was such a terrible ache. "It's okay," she assured her. "Like I said, no one knows but me. My parents don't even know. But I'm trying to find out what happened to the baby. Mamaw asked me to. But you don't know anything about it?"

Dell wiped at her eyes. "No," she said. "Victory and I never spoke of it, not in all the years since. The only person who would know is Uncle Laveau. But... but maybe Dr. Latling would have known. He probably delivered the baby but I can't be sure. He was the town's doctor and I know that Uncle Laveau was his patient, so I'm sure he would have been there for the delivery."

Lucy knew, by Mamaw's letter, that Dr. Latling had been at the delivery. She turned to look at Beau, who was gazing down at the two women with sorrow in his expression. When Lucy turned to look at him, he spoke quietly.

"We're going to Dr. Latling's house this afternoon," he said. "I thought maybe his son might help us. Maybe Dr. Latling kept a birth record somewhere."

Dell kept wiping at her eyes. "I wouldn't know about that," she said. "Lucy, even though I don't know who the father was, I want you to know that your Mamaw wasn't one of *those* girls. Something terrible must have happen to her."

Lucy thought about the words of Mamaw's letter, about the rape she'd lied about to throw her father off of Lewis' scent. Quite honestly, if Mamaw hadn't told Dell who the father was, then she wouldn't, either. Maybe some secrets were meant to stay buried.

"Maybe," Lucy said as she squeezed Dell's hand. "Or maybe she was in love with someone you didn't know about."

Dell shook her head firmly. "Victory and I had no secrets from each other," she said firmly. "Well, not many, anyway. I would have known if she had a suitor."

Lucy didn't comment on that. It was obvious that Mamaw had at least one secret from Dell. Kissing the old woman's cheek as she stood up, she turned to Beau.

"Maybe we'd better go," she said quietly. "I think Aunt Dell has had enough conversation for one day."

Beau had to agree. They'd gotten the woman worked up enough. As Lucy went to collect her purse, he remained a few feet away from Dell, watching the woman sniffle.

"Ms. Dell," he said quietly, "for what it's worth, I'm sorry if my great-granddaddy put you through anything. I know he was Laveau's henchman, but like you said, I'm pretty sure he did it to protect his family. He knew what Laveau was capable of. I'm not making excuses for him, because he had a choice, but I do understand in a way."

Dell looked up at the man. "I see some of him in you," she said. "You have his eyes. I never had much dealings with him but my daddy did. He and Terhune were friends."

Beau simply nodded; he didn't have anything more to add. Lucy walked up to stand next to him at that point, digging in her purse for her sunglasses.

"One more thing, Aunt Dell," Lucy said. "While we're on the subject. Sorry if this is another upsetting question, but someone told me that there were bodies buried all around Glory from the people that Laveau killed. Do you think that's just an urban legend or do you think there's some truth to it?"

Dell nodded emphatically. "Oh, Lucy," she sighed. "Your daddy needs to have that entire yard tilled. Rumors like that have been going on for years. You might even find the baby you're looking for because I can't imagine Uncle Laveau would have let it live. He was just that way."

It was a gruesome thought. Now, two older folks who had been living during the time of Laveau Hembree had both told Lucy about the bodies all around the yard. The more she thought about it, the more sickened she became. Troubled, Lucy bent over to hug the old woman.

"I'm sorry if I upset you," she whispered. "I really am. But I'm trying to do something for Mamaw and I need all of the information I can have. Please forgive me if I've upset you, okay?"

Dell nodded, her old arms around Lucy. "You have Hembree blood in you," she said. "I suppose you have the right to know everything. If it will keep our family from repeating the sins of the past, I'm happy to pass our history along. But… Lucy?"

"Yes?"

"Be careful. You might not like what you find."

CHAPTER EIGHTEEN
~ No Blackness and No White ~

*T*HE BABY WAS SO *big now that she wasn't moving much.*
Up until a couple of weeks ago, the baby had been very active and Victory had taken delight in feeling the child kick and roll. At night, she'd lay on her back with her hands on her stomach, feeling the movement and wishing Lewis could feel it, too.

The past several months without him had been hell. There was no other way to describe it. She missed him more than a body had a right to miss someone, feeling that longing down to her bones. She missed his soothing voice, his laugh, and the way he looked at her, like there was no woman in the world but her. She missed his touch, his soft lips against hers, his smooth, dark skin against her white flesh.

The baby she carried had resulted from the one and only time they'd come together as a man and woman should, a child conceived in the back seat of Mr. Franklin's roadster one day last winter when the headmaster had been teaching class and Victory was supposed to be helping one of the ladies in the school's office.

It had been a quick encounter, but one that had clearly changed her life. Whenever Victory was feeling particularly sad or lonely, she'd go back to that time, a time she'd felt more love and attention than she'd ever felt in her life.

That moment had been her Dreaming Hour.

Now, in the days leading up to the birth, Lewis had been very heavy on her mind. Since Aldridge's death, she'd stayed far away from

Lewis, on the few occasions Laveau let her out of the house, fearful her daddy might catch on to who the real father was. She hadn't tried to contact him in any way, purely to protect him. But as the birth drew near, her resolve to stay clear of him weakened.

Victory soon came to the conclusion that she needed to send Lewis a message, to let him know that she was well and that the child was well. She was sure that the birth was going to kill her and she didn't want to die without having made an attempt to reach out to him one last time. But there was some trick to that — she knew that the only way she could get him a message would be to use a messenger that her father wouldn't pay attention to.

Certainly, she couldn't leave the house, but her mother's maid, Lillian, lived in the Rose Cove shanty town at the bend of the Yalobusha River a couple of miles away. Lillian had been with the family for a few years and she was trusted. Every night, she gathered her things and walked about a half mile down the road where her husband would pick her up and take her home. Victory knew that Lewis lived in Rose Cove, too, and with that realization, a plan came to mind.

The night she decided to write the note, Victory had slept fitfully, rising several times to compose her note to Lewis. She didn't use his name for fear her father might discover what she'd done, so everything she said in the letter was vague. The final version wasn't exactly as she had wanted, but it was good enough. She wasn't the poet that Lewis was, but in the end, she was proud of it. She hoped it conveyed exactly what she wanted it to.

My dearest Dreamer,
So long, I've spent away from you.
My heart aches for you.
I still hope for a time for us,
Maybe not in this lifetime, but in another.
I am reminded daily of the love we shared,
The joy of a life we two created.

Though my days are dark, you are the light in the darkness for me.
Never forget what you have meant to me.
I hold you close to me still, even though we are not together.
Someday, in the Dreaming Hour, we will be.
I have faith.
No blackness and no white.
V

Victory knew that if her daddy found the letter, he'd kill her. She had little doubt. So she kept it close to her, tucked inside her nightgown, and waited for the right moment to give it to Lillian.

The following day went by just like any other. Her mother came to see how she was feeling, bringing her breakfast with Lillian following behind her carrying the tray. Caroline wanted to speak of trivial things, like a local marriage and the church bazaar to raise money for the less fortunate. The white less fortunate, of course, but Caroline liked to feel she was somehow making up for the sins her husband committed on a daily basis. It was such a contrast, the two of them, and Victory listened with disinterest to her mother's chatter until the woman grew weary of being ignored and left the bedroom.

But that wasn't the end of Caroline's visits; they followed a pattern throughout the day. She'd come to her daughter every couple of hours with tea or magazines or talk, and Victory ignored her mother for the most part. She didn't have anything to say to a woman who wouldn't help her own child and grandchild. Dinner would come just after twelve noon and supper would come around six o'clock in the evening.

By dinnertime, Caroline was usually seeing to Laveau's meal. The man had a finicky stomach and she made sure to oversee his meals personally, directing the sweating cook as if the woman had never cooked a meal in her life. That was usually the time when Lillian would come up with a tray, alone, delivering dinner to the prisoner.

Tonight, Victory waited for that moment she knew Lillian would come. It was the moment she had been waiting for. Nervous, she paced around her room, rubbing her swollen belly and hearing the sounds of the house down below. She could hear voices and plates clinking as the dining table was set.

Victory wasn't allowed at the dining table these days because the very sight of her upset her father's digestion. He'd start drinking his favorite, bourbon, and talking about black bastards, which brought Victory to tears. No, it was safer if she simply remained in her room these days and out of his sight. It was better not to rile the man.

Lingering over by the windows that looked over the front of the house, she was startled when her bedroom door abruptly opened and Lillian entered bearing a tray of food. The smell of pork filled the room immediately. The scent was something Victory wasn't fond of these days. The smell made her gag. But she fought off the dry heaves as Lillian set the tray down on the table beside her bed.

"Your mama says that you must eat everythin' on the tray," Lillian said. "She says she'll be a-lookin'!"

Victory ignored the command. She rushed to Lillian, a woman about her age with skin the color of coal. She grasped her by the arm.

"Forget about the food," she hissed. "Lillian, I need your help."

The smile on Lillian's face weakened. "What help, Miss Victory?"

Victory eased her grip, the expression on her face softening. "I need you to take a message to someone," she said. "Mama mustn't know and neither must Daddy. When you go home tonight, I want you to take a message with you."

Lillian was torn between puzzlement and fear. "What message, Miss Victory?" she asked. "Who I gonna give it to?"

Already, Victory could see that the woman was vastly reluctant. Not that she blamed her. "Please, Lillian," she said. "If you love me, you'll do this for me. Please?"

Lillian's was wrought with alarm. "You knows I loves you, Miss Victory, but who am I givin' this message to?"

Victory had to tell her. How else could she get the message there? She took a deep breath before answering.

"*You have to promise me you won't tell a soul. Will you do that?*"

Lillian nodded fearfully. "*I promise,*" she said. "*But who's it for?*"

Victory pulled the message out of her bodice, a little piece of paper sealed up in a small envelope. Before answering, she looked at it as if pondering the contents. "*Do… do you know your neighbors where you live, Lillian?*"

The woman nodded. "*Of course I does,*" she said. "*The Nixons, the Pickles, the Ragsdales, the….*"

"*Ragsdale,*" Victory interrupted her. "*You know that family?*"

Lillian nodded reluctantly. "*I knows of them,*" she said. The distress on her features grew. "*I knows what your pappy did… that poor Ragsdale boy….*"

Victory knew what she meant and she quickly silenced her. "*Shush,*" she muttered. "*I know. Don't say it. We've never talked about it and we never will, Lillian, but today I need to mention it because I need you to take this message to Lewis Ragsdale. Do you know him?*"

Lillian's distress reverted back to confusion. "*Lewis?*" she repeated. "*Is he one of the older boys?*"

Victory nodded. "*Yes,*" she said, putting the small note in Lillian's hand. "*This is for Lewis. Please give it to him, Lillian. I'll give you everything I own if you'll do this for me.*"

Lillian looked at the envelope, having no idea what to say. "*I don't know the boy, Miss Victory,*" she said. "*But I'm sure my husband does. Can I have him give it to Lewis?*"

Victory nodded sharply. "*Yes, please,*" she said. "*So long as he gets it. Please, Lillian… you know what's happened around here since that… that killing. You know how Mama and Daddy keep me locked up here. It's not right. It's horrible. But they don't care; they don't care anything about me. Please do me this one favor and I'll never ask for another.*"

Lillian, indeed, knew how they treated their only daughter, a child who had shamed the family something terrible. Lillian also knew that not only did the white folks whisper about it, but the black folks did, too. They all whispered about poor Victory Hembree, shut up by her daddy like a prisoner, and there were all kinds of rumors as to why — she was crazy, she was a drug addict, she was a prostitute and her daddy found out. But only Laveau and Caroline and a few others, including Lillian, knew the truth. The truth of a young girl who had badly shamed her family.

"I'll have my husband give it to him, Miss Victory," she said hesitantly. "But... but why you be sendin' him a note?"

Victory stared at the woman for a moment, fearful to tell her the truth. What Lillian didn't know, she couldn't tell if she was cornered. Victory wasn't entirely certain the woman wouldn't talk if she was confronted by Laveau.

"I... I want to tell him I'm sorry about what happened to his brother," she finally said. "It was terrible what happened. I want him to know I'm sorry."

Lillian believed her. She had no reason not to. With a nod, she slipped the note down into her bosom, keeping it tucked safely away just as Victory had done.

After that, Victory ate most of her supper except for the pork, suffering through two more of her mother's visits before she finally went to bed and Lillian left for the night.

Bundled up against the cold, Lillian made her way down to the corner where her husband was waiting for her. He took her back to their neat little home in Rose Cove. Once they were home, Lillian pulled out the note from her bodice and explained to her husband what it was for.

Terrified that Laveau Hembree would somehow find out about it, Lillian's husband snatched the note from his wife and threw it into the fire.

CHAPTER NINETEEN

Present

THE LATLING LAKE house was a Victorian Gothic built in eighteen hundred and seventy, one of the most recognizable homes in all of Pea Ridge. It sat in an older section of town that was dotted with these big grand dames, Victorian homes built back at the turn of the last century, all of them perched on a rise above the town like crown jewels on a tiara. This particular house sat on a quarter of an acre on a corner of two small streets, the yard vast and the garden well-tended.

In fact, it was a beautiful home. Painted the original white color with massive amounts of gingerbread around the windows, roofline, and porch, Lucy was very interested in the home as they pulled up to the curb and saw the thing looming before them. It was clear that the family that lived there loved it a great deal and, in that knowledge, she felt some sadness for her own family's pathetic home.

"Wow," she said softly. "That's quite a house."

Beau peered from the windshield as he put the car in park. "It sure is," he agreed. "It's pretty famous in these parts for its garden. It's been in several books about the State of Mississippi."

Lucy opened her door. "For good reason," she said. "I'd always hoped that Glory would look like this house, loved and well-tended. Now it just looks like the house where The Munsters live."

Beau grinned as he climbed out of the car, adjusting his Sam

Browne belt as he shut the door. "Maybe you'll fix all that when you buy it from your folks and fix it up."

"Maybe."

"I've got a nine-year-old and a seven-year-old you can put to good use pulling out weeds and stuff."

She laughed softly. "Will they work for sour gummies and M & M's?"

"And grape soda."

"Sold."

Grinning at each other, they made their way up to the sidewalk and onto the great stone steps that led up from the street. The front yard was enormous and an old stone walkway led up to the great front porch.

As they walked, Lucy admired the beautiful gardens and the fountain, but as she was admiring that, Beau was admiring her. He'd put off several radio calls this morning because of her and he wasn't sorry about it in the least. He finally told dispatch he was on some personal business and not to bother him unless it was an emergency.

Right now, he was just where he wanted to be, entrenched in something that had brought some excitement and purpose back into his life. Odd as it sounded, he felt like this was one of the most important things he'd ever done but that was, in part, due to the fact that he wanted to impress Lucy.

There; he'd admitted it. He wanted her to be grateful to him for his help and a grateful woman might be willing to show her gratitude in many ways....

So he watched Lucy as they walked up to the front porch, his attention moving between the house and her as she bent over rose bushes or peered at flower vines to see what species they were. They were just nearing the porch when the front door flew open and a man appeared.

The man was older, maybe in his seventies, with white hair and bushy white eyebrows. He walked right out of the door, down the front steps, and held out a hand to them both.

"Stop right there," he said. "I'm Stephen Latling. My wife told me you two wanted to talk to me."

He sounded unwelcoming. Lucy came to a halt, as did Beau. "I'm Beau Meade," he introduced himself calmly. "I've lived in and around this town most of my life and I can't say that you and I have ever really crossed paths. That's strange, considering the size of this town, so I wanted to introduce myself."

Latling shook his head. "I know who you are," he said, disdain in his voice as his gaze lingered on him. "There's a good reason we haven't met. I wanted to make sure we never met, just like I've made sure to stay away from your daddy. Oh, I know who he is but he's a lot younger than me. I made sure our paths never crossed."

Beau had to admit he was a bit taken aback by the hostility. "Oh," he said, unsure how to proceed at that point. "My dad has never mentioned you, either. If there's some animosity between you two, I didn't know about it. I apologize."

Latling's bushy eyebrows lifted. "Animosity?" he repeated. "You're a Meade. That's all I need to hear. And you…"

He was looking at Lucy, who, at this point, had a cool but professional expression on her face. "I'm Lucy Bondurant," she said steadily. "My grandmother was Victory Bondurant. My father, Bill, is…."

"I know who Billy Bondurant is," Latling spat. "Good Lord, a Hembree standing right in front of me. I'd hoped your family had all died out by now. I saw in the paper that Victory died recently and I was glad to hear it. The last of that horrible family finally dead."

It was a harsh insult to Lucy but she didn't rise to it. "Mr. Latling, I understand where you're coming from," she said. "I know what the Hembree name means around here. But I was born in California and I personally had nothing to do with whatever happened in the past. I've come here today to find some answers about some things that happened years ago, things your father was involved in. I'm hoping that might bring some peace to both of us, sir."

Latling shook his head. "I already have peace," he said. "Whatever answers you're looking for, look elsewhere. I won't help you."

He sounded final. As he turned to walk away, Lucy called after him. "If you have peace, it's a lie," she said. Now, she was starting to sound nasty, spurred on by Latling's hostility. "If you think for one moment your father wasn't wrapped up with whatever the Hembrees or the Meades were doing, think again. He was just as dirty as the rest of them and I think you know it or you wouldn't be so upset about it. I've come here today to help us all find closure to sins of the past but if you want to keep ignoring everything that happened, then you don't deserve any peace."

She was harsh about it. Latling came to a halt and turned to her, his features contorted. "Who the hell are you to come to my home and talk to me like that?" he demanded. "I don't know you. In fact, if you don't get off my property, I'm going to tell Sheriff Meade here to remove you. And then he can get the hell off my property, too."

Lucy wouldn't be pushed around, not when she was determined to seek the truth for Mamaw above all else. Even in the face of a man who obviously knew the histories of the families, she was going to stand her ground.

"Your father delivered an illegitimate child back in nineteen thirty-three," she fired back. "Our guess is that the child was killed and, if it was, your father was in on it. That makes him a murderer. Now, do you still want to walk away from me and pretend that all of the Hembree-Meade ills weren't something your family contributed to?"

Latling's jaw dropped. "You bitch," he hissed. "That's slander! I'll sue you for slander!"

Lucy remained cool. "I have proof," she said. "You can't sue me if it's true."

Latling stood with one foot on the steps to his porch, his entire body twitching with rage. After a moment, he backed away from the porch and moved in her direction.

"What in the hell do you want from me?" he asked, perplexed. "I've spent my entire life ignoring the Hembrees and the Meades, and now you're both on my doorstep making threats. Are you trying to coerce me into something?"

"You never even asked why we were here," Lucy pointed out. "You came out throwing hate and accusations at us. Whatever you're pissed off about, I didn't do anything to cause it and neither did Sheriff Meade. Like you, we're descendants of families in this town who have lived here a very long time. Instead of being rude, you simply could have asked us our business. I have a couple of questions and it won't take very long."

Latling's jaw flexed dangerously. "I really have nothing to say to you."

Lucy took a step towards the man, her gaze imploring. "But I have something to say to *you*," she said quietly. "I am sorry for whatever my great-grandfather did to your family. I truly am. But I didn't perpetrate anything and neither did Sheriff Meade. You and I and the sheriff are from the generation that's dealing with the fallout. I know my great-grandfather was an evil bastard and I'm just trying to right some of those wrongs. If you still don't want to help me, then that's your business. I'll go away. But I'd like to think there's some humanity in you that wants to see justice served for the shit Laveau Hembree put people through in this town, your family included."

Latling's jaw was still ticking. By this time, his wife and the housekeeper had come out of the house, hearing the agitated voices. The elderly African American housekeeper stood back by the front door while the wife stood on the porch steps, listening to everything that was being said.

"Steve," the wife pleaded softly. "Please...."

Latling didn't look at his wife but he certainly heard her. Something in his expression changed and, after a moment, he simply shook his head. "Your great-granddaddy was purely evil."

"I know."

"What do you want to ask me?"

He said it as if he didn't mean it but Lucy didn't care. At least she had his attention. "The baby I just mentioned, the one born in nineteen thirty-three," she said. "I don't know how old you are but I'm guessing you weren't alive back then."

Latling shook his head. "I was born eight years later."

"I'm assuming your dad kept records from that time, but do you still have them? Specifically, I'm looking for any mention of that baby."

Latling sighed sharply, trying to recall over the frustration he was feeling. "Daddy kept records back then, of course, and we have boxes of stuff up in the attic," he said. "I don't know if there'd be any mention of a baby but I'm sure there must be if he delivered it. But you said he killed it. Did he or didn't he?"

Lucy nodded faintly. "I think he helped," she said. "But I'm really not sure. I'd like to find the records of that child to see if we can exonerate your father."

"Did you look at the county birth records yet?"

Lucy shook her head. "Not yet," she said. She hesitated a moment before continuing. "We don't think there would be any public record of the birth. The child was born out of wedlock and Laveau Hembree would have most certainly covered it up."

Latling was calming, thankfully. He seemed less agitated now, more thoughtful. "Whose baby was it?"

Lucy glanced at Beau, looking for some kind of support. Should she tell Latling? Should she keep quiet? Already, she'd mentioned the baby to Aunt Dell. Now she'd be telling a second person. If she wanted to keep the child secret, she wasn't doing a very good job of it. She didn't want it to get back to her parents before she had a chance to tell them.

"It was a biracial baby," she said, avoiding the question. "Suffice it to say it was born under Laveau's roof. Look, I'm a defense attorney. If you let me take a look at your father's records from that time, I swear I'll keep them in the strictest confidence. I just really need to see if your father had any record of the birth."

Latling looked at her a moment before his gaze shifted to Beau. He was considering the request but, after a few seconds, he simply shook his head.

"I... I don't know," he said. "They're all up in the attic in boxes. I'd have to go look for them because I don't want you pawing around in my daddy's private records. Let me... let me think about it. Come back tomorrow and we'll see."

Lucy was disappointed at his answer but at least he hadn't run them off altogether. She assumed that was as good as it was going to get at the moment so she didn't push.

"Okay," she said. "Thank you for the consideration. I promise I'll be very careful with the records and I'll keep them completely confidential, but I just want you to know how important this is, to so many people. I wouldn't be here if it wasn't."

Latling simply nodded his head and turned for the house. The wife was still standing on the stairs, looking worried, but the housekeeper had disappeared back inside. When her husband drew near, the wife reached out and put an arm around him, obviously very concerned for his mental state.

Lucy and Beau watched Latling and his wife disappear through the front door and the panel shut softly. When it was just the two of them again, they turned to each other.

"Wow," Lucy said with some disbelief. "That is one pissed-off man."

Beau nodded, turning for the car. "That's how a lot of people around here react to the name Hembree," he said. "If you spend any time here at all, that won't be the first time you run into that."

Lucy followed him as they headed to the cruiser. "Do you still get that? With the name Meade, I mean?"

He shrugged. "Sometimes," he said. "Not too much, though. There's really only a handful of people left who really remember my granddaddy and later generations just don't care too much. But Hembree… that's a name that most people know."

"And hate."

"Exactly."

They took the stairs down to the sidewalk and eventually to the curb, where Beau opened up the passenger door for her.

"Latling made it sound like it all happened yesterday," she said.

Beau glanced back up at the big, rambling Victorian. "It was his daddy who was involved in it," he said. "He's an old man. Old prejudices die hard with that generation. But you handled yourself admirably, counselor. I don't imagine many people get the best of you."

"Not many. No one, actually."

"I would believe that."

Lucy smiled weakly as he shut her door. He went around other side of the car, climbed in, and fired it up. He was just pulling around the side of the house, a smaller street that would take them to a major boulevard, when they saw someone on the driveway behind Latling's house.

It was the old African American housekeeper, the same woman they'd seen standing in the front door. She was waving a hand at them, flagging them down as she stood in the driveway. Curious, Beau pulled up to the driveway and lowered the passenger side window.

"Yes, ma'am?" he said. "Can I help you?"

The woman was very old and very agitated. "There's not much time," she said. "Ms. Priscilla has taken Dr. Latling up to his bedroom to rest, so there's not much time. I heard yous talkin' about a baby."

Lucy eyed the woman with some uncertainty. "Yes, we were talking about a baby," she said. "But we'll be back tomorrow. Why do you ask?"

The old woman shook her head. "Because," she said, "I... I think I have somethin' ya'll might want to know. My mama was the housekeeper for the first Dr. Latling back in the day. I used to come to work with her when I was little and I helped her around the house a bit, doin' what I could. You say this baby was born in nineteen hundred and thirty-three?"

Lucy didn't know why, but her heart suddenly began to beat faster. Something was stirring in her, something excitable. "Yes," she said. "Why?"

The housekeeper put her old hands on the car. "I was six years old in nineteen hundred and thirty-three, and this may not have nothin' to do with the baby yous lookin' fo', but Dr. Latling brought home a baby one night in October or November of that year. I knows it was autumn because the colors of the trees were changin'. I heards him and his wife talkin' about the baby and I heards it cryin'. I remember that Ms. Latling was cryin', too. I heard Dr. Latling said he done brought the baby over from Mr. Laveau's house and that Mr. Laveau wanted to kill it. He told Ms. Latling to hide the baby."

Lucy felt the car sway; it wasn't even moving but she felt it sway. Seized with the woman's astonishing tale, she grasped the side of the door for support.

"A... baby from Laveau Hembree's house?" she repeated. "My God... that's the baby we're looking for!"

The old woman looked behind her, nervously, just to make sure no one was watching her from the house. She was about to open her mouth again when a door slammed loudly somewhere in the house and they could all hear a woman's voice, high-pitched, calling for someone.

Cora!

The housekeeper shuffled away from the car. "I gots to go," she said fearfully, waving her hand at the car. "Go on, now – get! Don't let Ms. Priscilla see you here!"

She struggled up the driveway as fast as her little legs would carry her and Beau, not wanting to aggravate the confusing situation, put his foot on the gas and tore away from the curb.

But Lucy wasn't ready to let it go yet; she turned around in her seat, watching the rear of the Latling house fade away, watching the old housekeeper until she disappeared from view.

"Shit!" she hissed, facing forward again, her eyes wide with shock. "Holy Shit… did you hear that?"

Beau took a left turn at the intersection right in front of them. "I heard it."

"She knows about the baby!"

Beau straightened out the car and continued north on the main boulevard. "She knows about some baby," he said. "Don't get your hopes up, now. She could be mistaken. You don't know yet until you hear the whole thing."

Lucy knew that. God help her, she did. But her heart was pounding and her mind was racing. "Oh, my God," she breathed, struggling to calm down. "What if it's as easy as all that? What if an eye-witness really saw that baby and knows what happened to it?"

Beau reached over and patted her knee, a gesture of comfort and nothing more, but to Lucy, it was the touch of a man. She hadn't felt that in such a long time. Now her heart was racing for another reason entirely.

"Like I said," Beau said calmly. "Don't get your hopes up. She's a very old woman and there's no telling how she remembers things. Just keep that in perspective."

"But you heard what she said," she insisted. "A baby from Laveau Hembree's house? It *has* to be Mamaw's."

Beau was trying to stay even about the situation. "Possibly," he said. "But the old lady could have been mistaken. You shouldn't get too excited about it until you hear everything. What we want are all of the facts."

She couldn't believe he couldn't see the obvious. "But she said a baby in nineteen thirty-three from Laveau Hembree's house!"

He nodded. "I know."

"There couldn't be *two* babies from that year, that place."

"All I'm saying is that if it's not the baby we're looking for, it's going to crush you. We don't want that."

He was sounding chivalrous. After that pat on the knee, Lucy might have taken his chivalry for something more than just polite concern. She eyed him a moment before facing forward, looking out of the window.

"You're probably right," she sighed. "But it sure sounded to me like it was exactly what we're looking for."

"It did to me, too."

"And what about that Latling guy? He was seriously hostile to both of us."

Beau nodded as they came to a stop at a red light. "We're probably lucky he didn't come at us with a shotgun," he said. "People tend to still do that down here."

She grinned. "Great," she muttered. "I've spent my whole life in Los Angeles around criminals and I've never had my life threatened. It would be ironic that I'd come back to Mississippi and have a gun shoved into my face by some hillbilly."

"A hillbilly with a sweet house."

"True."

They laughed about that as the light turned green and he continued on to the main drag that would take them back to her hotel. The conversation died at that point but the silence wasn't uncomfortable. In fact, there was a warmth to it that hadn't been there before. Lucy tried not to read too much into it. Up ahead, her hotel came into view.

"Well," she said, "I guess that's it for today. Thanks for the ride, Sheriff."

He pulled into the driveway of the hotel. "Anytime," he said. "I suppose I should get back to work and do what the people of this county actually pay me to do."

She smiled as she gathered her things. "Are you usually busy?"

"Never a dull moment."

"Then I'll let you get back to work," she said as he pulled up in front of the hotel. She didn't get out right away; she turned to look at him. "I can't tell you how grateful I am for your help in all of this. I won't ever forget your kindness."

"It's been a pleasure, ma'am."

"Do you want to go with me back to Latling's tomorrow?"

He nodded. "I think I'd better," he said. "It might diffuse some of his prejudice off of you."

"I appreciate it. What time?"

"Same time as today, I'd think."

"Good. I'll see you tomorrow."

With that, she opened up the door and climbed out. She was half-hoping he'd mention something about having dinner together but he didn't. Maybe it was better that way because it would be easy to become accustomed to having him around. With a wave, he pulled out and she turned for the hotel lobby.

It was an effort to force herself away from thoughts of Beau Meade and on to Mo Guinn, the lawyer she had an appointment with in about an hour. She wanted to change her clothes to look more businesslike, especially when meeting with another lawyer, so she headed up to her room and took a quick shower before changing into a business pantsuit, the only one she'd brought with her.

When she should have been preparing for the meeting with Guinn, she found her thoughts going back to the Latlings' old housekeeper and what the woman had said. She wasn't sure if she could wait until tomorrow to question the old lady, but she'd have to. She had a feeling if she returned to the Latling house before tomorrow, it would jeopardize her chances of seeing any of Dr. Latling's old records. But if what the housekeeper said was true, and she had information about Mamaw's baby, then maybe she wouldn't need the records, after all.

It was that thought that plagued her as she brushed her hair back into a sleek ponytail and put on some lipstick. Her expensive jewelry went on and she made sure to collect her briefcase. She intended to swing by Glory and pick up her father's copy of the will before heading over to More Guns. Purse over her shoulder and stilettos on her feet, she headed out to the parking lot of the hotel looking every inch the Los Angeles lawyer.

The day was mild, a breeze kicking up and scattering puffy clouds overhead. Lucy glanced up at the sky, thinking she could get used to living in a place with no smog. It was nice to actually see the blue of the sky. Her car was over in a corner of the lot, towards the back, and her pristine heels made sharp clacking noises against the pavement as she went.

Pulling out her keys, thoughts of a bucolic life in Mississippi were abruptly cut short when someone came up behind her and wrapped her up in a big bear hug.

After that, the fight was on.

CHAPTER TWENTY
~ A Time for All Things ~

THE LABOR HAD BEEN going on most of the night. Victory had first felt the pangs of childbirth late the previous night and as the night progressed into morning, the pains were getting worse.

She was terrified to tell her mama, hoping she could deliver the child without anyone in attendance and then somehow take her to safety. So much fear was in her heart as the night went on and the pain worsened. It wasn't simply in her belly but down her legs as well, causing them to shake. There was a bloody discharge on her sheets but nothing more than that, no burst of waters as Lillian had once told her there would be.

The little maid was her only friend these days. She told Victory that she'd delivered her message to Lewis, or at least her husband had, so that gave Victory a tremendous amount of comfort. She had no idea it was all a lie. But that little lie gave her great comfort to know that Lewis knew she was thinking about him and that she was doing all she could to keep their child safe from harm.

And that meant not telling anyone she was in labor.

The pains hurt but they weren't terrible. She was sure she could deliver the baby herself and keep her hidden, at least until she could get her to safety. Maybe she could even run for Rose Cove, where Lewis was, and they could go to safety together. Since Lillian lived in Rose Cove, she was hoping the maid could help her run away. The risk *would be as great on Lillian as it would be on her, but she felt certain that Lillian would help her.*

At least, those were her thoughts until the sun rose and the pains grew worse. Lillian and her mother showed up just after sunrise with breakfast and Victory did her best to pretend that she wasn't in any pain. That wasn't easy, however, because the pains were increasing.

Victory managed to hold off her mother and Lillian again at noon, but by suppertime she was quickly succumbing to the misery of childbearing and there was no way to hide it. Gone were thoughts of running away to Lewis to protect their child; the swamp of misery had closed in over her and she was drowning in it. One big pain in front of her mother and Lillian and the news was out.

Caroline panicked when she realized her daughter was close to giving birth. Someone ran off to drive to Dr. Latling's house. In the parlor down below Victory's bedroom, Laveau was working himself up into a state.

It was as if the man had forgotten about his daughter's pregnancy for the last few months, as she was kept from his sight, but now that rage had returned again. He was yelling something about black bastards and cursing the mess his daughter had gotten herself in to. The bourbon came out and the more he drank, the more he yelled.

Victory could hear him up in her room. She began to pray for death, swallowed up by the horrific pain of childbirth and terrified of her father's anger. She was sure if one didn't kill her, the other would, so either way she was heading down that dark alley towards the afterlife. Her biggest concern was that her child remain safe if she didn't make it.

"Mama," she said after a particularly hard contraction. "Mama, promise me you won't let Daddy kill the baby if I die. I asked you once before but you didn't answer me. Promise me now that you won't let him hurt her!"

Caroline wasn't very good with people in pain. She squeezed her daughter's hand as Lillian put a cold cloth on her head. "He won't kill the baby," she assured her daughter. "He'll do what's best."

"Stop saying that!" Victory shouted. "You always say that Daddy will do what's best, but he won't do what's best for my child! If you let him kill her, I swear I'll haunt you from the grave! Do you hear me? I will haunt you forever!"

Caroline shushed her. "Don't get yourself worked up, sugar," she said softly. It was rare when she called her daughter by a term of endearment, but the moment called for it. "Everything will be all right. You just concentrate on bringing that baby into the world and everything will be all right."

Victory shook her head, miserable. She could feel her belly muscles tightening up again and she raised her knees because that seemed to give her some relief.

"Mama, please," she begged, her voice softer now. "You can't let him kill her. You have to promise me you won't. I can't have this baby without knowing she'll be safe if something happens to me."

Caroline looked across the bed at Lillian, who was clearly distraught. They both knew what would likely happen to the child once it was born, Lillian from a black perspective and Caroline from a white one. Either way, the child was doomed because Caroline couldn't, and wouldn't, fight against her husband. Laveau wanted that shameful baby taken care of and that was exactly what was going to happen.

The child had no chance at all.

"Don't trouble yourself, sugar," Caroline said again, softly. "God's will be done."

Another rarity with Caroline speaking of God. Because he was trying to keep a scandal quiet, Laveau didn't let her go to church these days and it was rare she spoke of the Lord, but tonight she did. Maybe she was seeking strength for what was to come, praying in her own way. But to Victory, it was all gibberish. Her mother would let Laveau do whatever he wanted to do and everyone knew it.

"I hate you for this," Victory hissed, turning her head away from her mother as a strong contraction rolled over her. "I'll hate you until I *die!"*

Increasingly distressed, Caroline was trying to comfort her daughter when the bedroom door opened and Dr. Latling entered.

A huge amount of relief settled over the room at his appearance. Carrying his black leather medical bag, the doctor was dressed in a wool suit because the weather had turned colder and there was a chill outside. Eyeing Victory writhing on the bed, he popped open his bag and pulled forth his stethoscope.

"Well, now," he said. "Looks like this baby is about to make an appearance. How long has she been in labor, Ms. Caroline?"

Caroline stepped back nervously so Dr. Latling could get to Victory. "I came in to bring her supper and found her like this," she said. "It's been going on for a while, I think."

Dr. Latling was listening to Victory's rock-hard belly. "Miss Victory?" he asked. "How long you been feeling pains?"

Victory was biting off the pain on her hand, leaving red teeth marks. "Last night," she said quietly. "Since last night."

Dr. Latling listened for another moment to her belly before pulling the stethoscope away and returning to his bag.

"Last night?" he asked. "When last night? Dinnertime? Midnight?"

"Probably around midnight."

"And you didn't tell your mama before now?"

"No."

It was an angry answer and Caroline stood there, wringing her hands, distraught over the situation. "What can we do?" she asked the doctor. "She's going to be okay, isn't she?"

Dr. Latling nodded patiently. "She's going to be fine," he said. Then, he turned to Lillian. "I want you to bring me all of the towels and sheets you can find, ya hear? Clean ones, too. And bring me a box."

Lillian was nodding eagerly until he asked for a box. "A box?" she repeated, confused. "What kind of box?"

Dr. Latling waved an impatient hand at her. "Anything," he said. "Got some old Coca-Cola crates around here? That'll do just fine. Bring *one up to me."*

Lillian fled. When she was gone, Caroline paced around nervously. "What do you want me to do, Doctor?" she asked. "How can I help?"

"You can't," Latling said flatly. "Your presence is upsetting my patient, so I want ya'll to go back downstairs with Laveau and keep him quiet. I could hear the man yelling all the way down the street. For the sake of your daughter, keep him quiet until this is over."

Caroline was shocked. "I can't leave you with... with her alone."

Dr. Latling was pulling a white rag of some kind out of his bag followed by a small, brown glass bottle. "You can and you will," he said. "I don't want you up here for what I have to do."

Caroline blanched. "What's that?"

Dr. Latling looked at her over the top of his glasses. "Laveau wanted this baby taken care of," he said. "I'm going to do that but I don't want you here when I do. I want you to get out and tell Laveau I'll take care of his problem."

Astonished and terrified, Caroline fled the room.

Meanwhile, Victory had heard everything. By the time Dr. Latling turned to her, he could see tears streaming down her temples. Her lower lip was trembling as she looked at him.

"Don't," she begged. "Please... don't hurt her."

Dr. Latling went to her, sitting down beside her and putting both the cloth and the brown glass bottle on the table beside her bed. In a surprising show of compassion, he took Victory's hand in his and squeezed it.

"Don't worry," he whispered. "I promised you I'd take the baby away when she was born and I'm going to do just that. But I need to do it my own way."

Lucy burst into soft tears. "You won't kill her?"

"I won't kill her."

"Promise?"

"I promise. Ruby, wasn't it?"

"Yes."

Dr. Latling gave her a forced smile and let go of her hand. Then, he unscrewed the top of the brown glass bottle to reveal a dropper attached it.

"I've brought a lot of babies into this world, Miss Victory," he said quietly. "I would never harm one of them, not even yours. I've spent my entire life saving people and I'm not about to kill one, no matter what your daddy says. So trust me… and never ask me about it, not ever. Your daddy or mama might hear and if they do, they'll be all kinds of trouble. You understand?"

Victory nodded, utter faith in her red-rimmed eyes. "I do," she murmured. "Thank you."

Dr. Latling didn't reply. He put a few drops of liquid from the brown bottle on the cloth and then put it over Victory's face, telling her to breathe deeply. She did and, within a few seconds, passed out cold from the ether. Carefully, Dr. Latling bottled the ether back up, tucked everything away, and went to work delivering a baby that was demanding to be born.

Lillian returned shortly with sheets and towels and the Coca-Cola crate, and Dr. Latling had the maid line the box with some of the clean towels. It wasn't a few minutes later that a fat baby girl was brought into the world, mewling and squirming.

And she was very much alive. With the dreaded baby now born and evidently healthy, Dr. Latling didn't have any time to waste. Ever since Victory had begged him to protect the baby, he'd been prepared to do just that. He had a plan. He had Lillian pull down the top of Victory's nightgown and hold the baby against her breast to suckle while he delivered the placenta and cleaned Victory up a little. She had weathered the birth well and he didn't foresee any complications.

Retrieving the now-quieting baby from Lillian, he swaddled the child tightly, put her in the Coca-Cola box, and draped a couple of the bloody towels over her. He also put the placenta in with her to make it look particularly distasteful. He figured Laveau and Caroline would think twice about looking into the box if they saw all of the blood. Then, he looked the maid in the eye.

"The baby died," he hissed at her. "You will go to your grave saying that this baby died. If you don't, I'll make sure Mr. Laveau knows you been stealing from his wife. Understand?"

Lillian's features flushed with fear. "But I didn't steal nothin'!"

"He won't believe you," Dr. Latling cut her off. "I'm taking the baby now to dispose of it and that's all you know. The baby died and that's all there is to it."

With that, he picked up the box with its bloody towels, his medical bag, and made his way downstairs where Caroline was waiting anxiously and Laveau was nearly drunk out of his mind.

Upon informing the family that the baby had been born dead, he flashed the placenta and dirty towels at them to discourage them from wanting to see the baby and it thankfully worked. No one wanted to view what was clearly a bloody mess. Caroline burst into tears and turned away as Laveau simply sat there with a confused look on his face.

Dr. Latling didn't wait around for the confusion to clear up or for someone decided to press him further. Mumbling something about taking care of the body, he shuffled out through the back door of Glory, praying that the baby wouldn't suddenly wake up and start crying. He prayed hard all the way out to his car, beseeching God to let the baby remain quiet just a little longer, just long enough to get it away from the house. One small cry and he'd have the whole house down around him.

Lord only knew what Laveau would do to him.

But God was listening to him that night. With the precious cargo in the back of the car, Dr. Latling drove away from Glory feeling as if he'd just committed a terrible crime. But the truth was that he'd just prevented a terrible crime, a crime against humanity and against a fragile baby whose birth had been so reviled. He had no idea what he was going to do with the child, only that he had to get it away from Glory. His wife would know what to do, he was sure. She was a patron to an orphanage up in Oxford and she would know what to do with a mulatto baby.

At least, he hoped so. It wasn't like he could give it back.

CHAPTER TWENTY-ONE

Present

"Are you sure you're okay, ma'am?" the paramedic asked Lucy. "You should probably go to the hospital and have that bump on your head checked out."

"No, I'm fine. It's not a big deal."

"It's a big bump, ma'am."

"Really – I'm okay."

Lucy had an icepack up against the side of her head, on the spot where she'd hit her head on the curb in the process of fighting off the man who'd grabbed her from behind.

But it wasn't just any man – Clyde had come up behind her and put his arms around her, and even now he was handcuffed in the back an ambulance, trying to explain to the arresting officer that Lucy was his cousin and he was only trying to give her a hug.

That very poor judgment call on his part had resulted in a split lip, a missing tooth, a few cracked ribs, and pepper spray to the face once Lucy had been able to get her canister out of her purse. That had been after she'd lost her balance in the course of fighting him and hit her head on the pavement, but once she regained her balance, she'd kicked the crap out of him with her pointy shoes. No part of Clyde's body had been left unassaulted and the paramedics on scene had determined he needed to go to the hospital.

They wanted Lucy to go, too, but she wasn't going to ride in the same ambulance as Clyde. She could hear him in the ambulance, whining and crying, as the sheriff's deputy stood next to her and took down the details of the assault. And make no mistake; it was an assault no matter what Clyde said. When he'd grabbed her from behind, one hand had managed to squeeze a breast. That, by definition, was sexual assault.

That asshole was going to pay.

"Ol' Clyde has been known to follow women home and otherwise annoy them, but this is the first time I've ever heard of him attacking anyone," the middle-aged deputy was saying. "I'm sorry this had to happen to you, ma'am, but if you press charges against him, it'll make this town safer for the women. That boy is a nuisance."

Lucy, seated on the curb, looked up at the deputy. "You're damn right I'm pressing charges," she said. "I told you what happened – he came up behind me, threw his arms around me, and managed to cop a feel on my left breast before I rammed an elbow back into his face."

"And that's when you fell?"

"I lost my balance, yes. Not only is it an assault charge, but sexual battery as well."

The deputy was writing. "How long ago would you say this happened?"

"At least twenty minutes now," she said. Then, she looked around at all of the units that had rolled on her; two deputy units, an ambulance, and an entire fire station. "Look, I don't mean to be rude, but I have an appointment in about fifteen minutes that I need to keep. I was just heading there when all of this happened. Can we please wrap this up?"

The deputy nodded. "Almost finished," he told her. Then, he looked up from his notepad. "You really should go get checked out at the hospital. Just to make sure that bump isn't something more."

Lucy wasn't stupid. She knew they were right but she was just hoping it was nothing more than a normal bump. She didn't have time for a head injury. Infuriated, she caught sight of Clyde as paramedics put a bandage over the lip she'd split.

"Damn that little prick," she growled. "You put him in jail and keep him there. I'm going to have him charged with everything I can think of."

Unsteadily, she stood up from the curb, growling because her suit pants were now dirty and one of the hems at the bottom had torn loose. Her expensive Jimmy Choo pumps were scuffed and that, more than anything, infuriated her.

As she handed the icepack back to the paramedic and lamented her scratched shoes, she failed to see the black unmarked sheriff's unit pull in to the parking lot, the very same car she'd been riding in not an hour before. Brushing off her pants and brushing off the concerns of the paramedics, she was startled to hear Beau's voice.

"Are you okay?" he asked.

Lucy's head snapped up, face to face with him. "I'm fine," she said, realizing she was very glad to see him. "Who told you?"

He shook his head. Somehow, his hands made it on her shoulders as if to see for himself that she was okay. There was reassurance in that touch. "I heard the call go out," he said. "When dispatch mentioned this hotel, I just had this feeling. Call it a hunch. What in the hell happened?"

Lucy pursed her lips irritably and pointed to the ambulance where Clyde was being forced into a supine position by the paramedics. "He came up behind me and grabbed me," she said. "He lifted me up off of my feet and tried to walk me over to the trees right here next to the parking lot. I managed to get him off of me and pepper spray the shit out of him, but he's going down now. I'm going to have him charged with everything I can."

Beau's jaw ticked as he turned to look at Clyde, being strapped down to the gurney now. He shook his head faintly, obvious displeasure in his expression. He turned to the deputy who had been interviewing Lucy.

"Who's going in with the suspect?" he asked.

The deputy threw a thumb in the direction of another deputy who was interviewing one of the hotel staff several feet away. "Whitaker," he said. "But I can go if you want me to."

Beau nodded. "Go," he said. "Don't let that boy out of your sight. Have the doctors check him out and when he's clear, get him over to the jail and keep him there. I'll be over to the station later on and have a talk with him."

The deputy nodded his head and, passing a glance between Beau and Lucy, headed over to the ambulance. Lucy watched the deputy walk away but Beau had already returned his attention to her, seeing the golf ball-sized lump on the right side of her head near her temple.

"You need to get that looked at," he said softly.

Lucy's fingers flitted up to her head, gingerly touching the lump. "I can't," she said. "I've got that appointment with Mamaw's lawyer in a few minutes."

"Can it wait an hour?"

She made a face, knowing he was probably going to pester her until she went to the hospital. That being the case, she was resigned to the fact that she was about to give in to his concern. It felt good to have a man be concerned over her again.

"I can call him," she said.

"Do it."

Begrudgingly, Lucy pulled her cell phone out of her purse, which still contained the journal and Mamaw's letter. The purse had flown off her shoulder at the beginning of the fight and was therefore relatively unscathed.

As Lucy called Mo Guinn's office to push her appointment back an hour, Beau walked over to the deputy who had been taking Lucy's information. Taking the notebook out of the man's hand, he read over the notes regarding the assault, shaking his head when he came to the conclusion. He could hardly believe Clyde McKibben had been stupid enough to try and assault his cousin. The creepy stalker had now gone too far. He handed the notebook back to the deputy.

"I'm going to take the victim over to the hospital," he said. "She's agreed to go."

The deputy nodded. "Good," he said. "She's got a knot on her head that needs to be looked at."

"It will be."

"Do you know her, then?"

Beau nodded. "A little," he said. "She's a defense attorney from Los Angeles. She's working on a… a case out here. Information gathering and all that. I've been helping her."

The deputy looked over at Lucy, now on her cell phone. "Oh," he said. Then, he snorted. "I knew she wasn't from around here before I ever saw her identification."

"Why?"

The deputy looked over at Clyde, lying on the gurney. "Because she beat the snot out of that boy," he said. "At first, he tried to make it look like she was the one who assaulted him, but a couple of maids from the hotel saw the assault through a window and came to tell us what they saw. They said he walked up behind her and grabbed her, just like she said."

Beau frowned. "He really tried to say *she* assaulted him?"

The deputy nodded. "Yup," he said. "I don't expect he's going to be going after another woman any time soon after this. He's really beat up."

Beau was disgusted by the entire thing but impressed by Lucy's strength. As he'd said to her before, he couldn't imagine anyone ever getting the better of her. She was a strong woman.

"Get him over to the hospital, then," he said. "I'm going to hang around here and see if she needs anything. I'll see you at the station later on."

The deputy nodded and headed off to climb into the back of

the ambulance while Beau went back over to Lucy. She was just hanging up the phone when he reached her.

"He can see me in an hour and half," she said. "Are you really going to make me go to the hospital now?"

"I am," he said firmly. "Come on."

"I can go by myself."

"No, you can't. I'm not letting you out of my sight again. You might get into trouble."

"I can take care of myself."

"So I've heard."

"Then you know you don't have to go with me."

"I know I don't have to."

"Then why –?"

"You talk too much."

He had her by the arm, pulling her away from the scene as the deputies wound up their investigation and the ambulance drove away. Putting Lucy in the passenger seat, he shut the door and rounded the car, climbing in and firing up the engine. In little time, they were heading to Pea Ridge Medical Center and it began to occur to Lucy why he was taking her.

No, he didn't have to. But he evidently *wanted* to.

The realization made her grin.

CHAPTER TWENTY-TWO
~ *We Don't Talk About It Anymore* ~

"Stop carrying on, Caroline," Laveau said. "What happened was God's justice. It's nothin' to be upset over."

Caroline sat in one of her fine chairs in the parlor on a bright autumn morning, the day after the birth of her first grandchild. Odd how everything looked so bright and cheery outside, when everything inside of Glory was cold and dank. So much sadness and misery. She held a handkerchief to her nose, sniffling into it.

"You speak of God when it's convenient for you," she said. "All you've done this whole time is curse Him for what happened with Victory. And now you think He's carried out justice for you?"

Laveau had been heading out to the plantation office when he caught his wife in the parlor, sobbing over the dead baby. He'd paused on his way out to offer some comfort, a rare gesture for him, but now he was sorry he'd bothered. His wife was angry with him and he just didn't understand it.

"God took back what oughtn't to have happened in the first place," he said as if she were an idiot. "God knows when there's been a mistake. He was just makin' it right, that's all."

Caroline looked away from him. "Then you go tell your daughter that," she said. "You go tell her that God was just cleaning up after a mistake."

Laveau sighed unhappily. "She knows it was a mistake," he said. "She knows she made a terrible mistake by lettin' that... that boy touch her, and now the mistake has been righted. And I don't want to hear about it anymore, ya hear? Leave well enough alone around this house. There will be no more mistakes like that, not ever."

Caroline simply shook her head, wiping at her eyes. "It wasn't her fault that she was raped," she whispered. "She didn't do anything but you blame her all the same."

Laveau's mood was sinking fast. "I took care of the man who touched her," he fired back. "He's dead and Victory is lucky she lived through it all. She's lucky I didn't punish her, too!"

Caroline's head snapped to him. "You spent the last several months punishing her," she said angrily. "You kept her locked up like a prisoner. She didn't do anything but you were ashamed of her just the same. It wasn't fair, Laveau."

It was the most Caroline had ever talked back to him and Laveau was sincerely trying not to let her ruin his day. He could have easily slapped her for what she'd just said but he didn't. He refrained, instead, moving towards the front door.

"It's over with now," he said, taking his hat from the rack by the door and putting it on his head. "She's going to want to go back to school and see her friends again, but I'm going to have a long talk with her before she does about how things are going to be from now on."

"And how's that?"

"No more parties, no more things outside of this house," he said. "If I even decide to let her go back to school, she's to go there and then come right back home again. That's all she's going to do. I don't want her giving any more colored boys ideas about her."

Caroline was stricken by his heartlessness. "Is that what you think?" she asked, aghast. "You think that she gave some colored boy an idea about her and that's why all this happened?"

Laveau opened the front door. "She'll talk to anybody," he said with disapproval. "She's got to learn not to be so friendly. She got herself into trouble with it but that trouble is over now. And we don't talk about it anymore. You got that?"

Caroline simply looked away from him, sniffing into her handkerchief, once again. She heard the front door slam and her husband's shoes as he stomped cross the porch and down the steps. After that, she didn't hear him anymore and she was glad. She'd never really loved him but she'd only come to hate him recently. A black, thick hate as heavy as delta mud. She couldn't stand the sight of him.

Overhead, her daughter was still asleep from the anesthesia Dr. Latling had given her the night before. She'd remained unconscious all night and the doctor had come back around dawn to check on his patient. She was still unconscious but he informed Caroline that her daughter was simply sleeping. Exhaustion had caused her to be sensitive to the ether. But that lengthy unconsciousness also meant that Victory had no idea she'd given birth to a dead baby and it was Caroline's job to tell her daughter that when she finally awoke.

When Lillian finally came to tell Caroline that Victory was awake, it was with a heavy heart that Caroline made the trek up to her daughter's room to tell her what had happened.

Caroline would remember Victory's screams of grief until the day she died.

CHAPTER TWENTY-THREE
Present

"Well," Bill said. "Your meeting with Mo went pretty much as I expected. He didn't tell you anything we didn't already know. Essentially, this whole estate belongs to me, such as it is. The only thing I'm happy about is that there aren't any serious debts. Mama made sure she paid everything off with the funds she had. The only thing we're looking at right now is the hospice care bill, but considering how long she'd been ill, I consider that a small price to pay. Anyway, I don't want to talk about that right now. Let's talk about what Clyde did to you, Lucy. Honest to Pete, I'm so mad right now I could kill that guy."

Bill, Mary, Lucy, and Beau were standing around the old kitchen of Glory because Bill and Mary had been finishing up an early dinner when Lucy and Beau came in through the back door bearing two distinct stories – one of Lucy's meeting with Mo Guinn and then – in a passing mention – the reason behind the massive lump on her temple.

Lucy hadn't wanted to upset her parents with tales of Clyde's assault but those hopes were for naught – they were upset and angry. As Lucy tried to soothe her mother, Beau found himself in the role of trying to keep Bill Bondurant calm.

"He's going to be in jail for a while," Beau assured the angry father. "In fact, I need to head back over to the station to follow up on the case. Trust me when I say he's going to pay for what he did.

In fact, he already paid for it a little when your daughter walloped the tar out of him. McKibben has been known to us for a while as a nuisance more than anything, but he's never been so bold about going after women. He'll think twice before doing anything like this again, I'm betting."

Mary was inspecting the bandage on Lucy's head as Bill, his gaze on his daughter, shook his head in disgust.

"Tommie and I told him to stay away from Lucy in no uncertain terms the other night," he said. "Obviously, he didn't listen. Does his mother know what he's done?"

Beau shrugged. "By now, she probably does," he said. "How is he related to ya'll, anyway?"

Bill's gaze was still on his daughter. "His mother's mother was a cousin to my mother," he said. "He's a distant cousin, but down here, there are no distant cousins. Everybody thinks they're all part of the close family no matter how removed their relations are and Clyde likes to think he's right down in Lucy's back pocket. He never leaves her alone."

Beau scratched his chin. "That's not surprising," he said. "I think he's a few bricks short of a load, quite honestly."

"He's a psychopath."

"That, too."

Bill grunted unhappily, displeased with the entire situation. "Well," he said. "I suppose ya'll are handling it the best way you can. I appreciate that."

"You're welcome."

The situation was settled, for the most part, but Bill still seemed frustrated by it. He sighed heavily and went over to the sink, pouring out a half-full cup of coffee that had been sitting on the counter. He was clearly trying to move away from the subject of Clyde, trying to busy himself with other things.

"We dropped by Aunt Dell's today just after lunch, Lucy," he said after a few moments. "She said you and the sheriff went to visit her today."

Lucy, who was standing over next to her mother, was caught off-guard by the statement. "We did," she said quickly; maybe *too* quickly. "Uh… did she say why?"

Bill didn't seem to notice her swift reply. "Not really," he said. "But she did seem upset. Was she like that when you were there?"

Lucy nodded. "A little bit, I think," she said, wanting to throw her parents off the scent of why they were really at Aunt Dell's. "She seemed tired and upset but she didn't tell me why. We just chatted with her a bit and left."

Bill accepted the explanation. "What did you talk about?"

Lucy glanced at Beau before answering, just to make sure he went along with whatever she said. "Family," she said. "You told me that Aunt Dell would be the one to ask about Laveau Hembree, so I did. She basically said everything you did."

Bill bent over his wife's shoulder to look at the bump on Lucy's head. "Hmmm," he said, peering at the bump for a moment longer before standing straight and moving away. "I'm curious why *you* were there, Beau. Are you following my daughter around now? Should I be worried?"

Beau grinned. "I'll tell you when you need to be worried," he teased. In no way did he want Bill to know that his attention towards Lucy went beyond polite courtesy. In fact, he didn't even want Lucy to know but he was coming to suspect she did, anyway. "Truthfully, the night of Ms. Victory's funeral, when Lucy was trying to get away from Clyde, she and I had a nice talk back here in the kitchen. She… well, she mentioned wanting to ask her Aunt Dell about some family history and I asked if I could tag along. Someone like Dell Alexander would know a lot about my family history, too. I just wanted to hear what she had to say."

It wasn't exactly the truth. They hadn't spoken about Aunt Dell the night they'd met but they had spoken about her the next day at breakfast, but Beau wasn't so sure he should mention he'd had breakfast with Lucy. Bill might really think something was up then. Still, he tried to sound convincing, as if the whole thing was quite casual. It must have worked because Bill seemed to buy it.

"Did she tell you anything you didn't know?" he asked.

Beau shook his head. "Most everything she spoke of was about Laveau Hembree," he said. It was the truth. "She mentioned my great-granddaddy a couple of times. She said everyone around here used to call him The Puppet. I hadn't heard that one."

Bill nodded to the revealed fact. "Me, either," he said. "That's a new one."

"Dad, what do you know about a guy named Stephen Latling?" Lucy suddenly asked.

Both Bill and Beau looked at her in surprise – Bill because he hadn't heard the name in a while and Beau because she brought it up at all.

"Stephen Latling?" Bill repeated. "I know of him but I don't know personally him. Why?"

Lucy wondered how long she was going to burn in purgatory for telling her parents such half-truths. "I ran into him today," she said. "He didn't seem too friendly. He seems to be one of those people in town who have a hatred for anything Hembree or Meade."

Bill's expression grew pensive. "Stephen Latling," he muttered again, more to himself. "His daddy was the town doctor many years ago. He tended my mother on more than one occasion and he was the doctor who took my tonsils out back when I was about five. He was very old then. How'd you come across him?"

"In town," Lucy said. Well, that one wasn't *quite* a lie. "I just wanted to know if you knew of him."

Bill shook his head. "No," he said. "I don't know him but I think that his daddy was all part of the Hembree – Meade corruption back in the day. It seems to me that he and my granddaddy were friends."

Lucy lifted her eyebrows. "Well, whatever they were, Stephen Latling has a lot of hatred for our family," she said. "He got all worked up when he found out who I was."

Bill shrugged it off. "That's too bad," he said. "But we're going to run into people like that around here. The older generation, especially."

"Did you run into it a lot as a kid? That kind of prejudice, I mean."

Bill shook his head. "No," he said. "Remember that Laveau was still alive until I was about ten years of age. Nobody in their right mind would speak against him, not even when he was a very old man. After that, I think people just wanted to forget about him, so nobody ever really said much to me about him. There were a few, of course, but not many." He looked at Beau. "Has Tommie talked about running into people who hate your family?"

Beau lifted his big shoulders. "There are always going to be those who remember the old prejudices," he said. "It's difficult to change a culture sometimes and that's what we're dealing with down here – a culture that will stay rooted in old hatreds and fears for as long as we'll let it. In fact, I was just saying that to my father the other day – if we keep bringing up the past, people will never get over it. I...."

He was cut off when his radio crackled, a call that was evidently directed at him. He excused himself to go outside and talk to dispatch, leaving Lucy and her parents inside the kitchen. Once he was gone, Mary piped up.

"What's going on with him, Lucy?" she asked. "Why is he driving you around? Where's your car?"

Lucy could see her mother was nearly bursting to pump her for information on the sheriff. The woman held it together as much as she could, waiting for the right moment to jump down her daughter's throat. Lucy grinned.

"He came to the call at the hotel after Clyde bushwhacked me," she said. "Clyde took the only ambulance and I wasn't about to ride with him, so the sheriff took me to the hospital in his car. Then I had the appointment with Mo right afterwards so he just took me over there. Now we're here. Very simple."

Mary gave her daughter a long look. "He's a handsome, successful man."

"So?"

"He's just your type."

"Mary, lay off," Bill said quietly. "It's her life. Leave her alone."

Mary sighed heavily, unhappy that her husband had intervened. She knew how miserable Lucy had been since Kevin had left and if her daughter was finding attraction in Tommie Meade's son, then she wanted to know. As she turned away, flustered, Lucy turned to her father, sorry her mother was upset but grateful for her father's intervention.

"Seriously, Dad," she said, changing the subject away from Beau Meade. "Something has to be done about Clyde. What I didn't tell you was that when he first grabbed me, he was trying to drag me off into some trees. The man fits all of the signs of being a predator and it's only a matter of time before he really hurts somebody, so I don't care what his mother says or what anyone in the family says – I'm pressing all of the charges I can against him so that he gets the message. He can't get away with shit like this."

Bill was nodding firmly to what she was saying. "I'm behind you one hundred percent," he said. "I still can't believe he did that, though. I always thought he was a pest, but to attack you in broad daylight? The man is an idiot."

Lucy was in full agreement. She started to reply but Beau suddenly came in through the back door, his focus right on her. He had a rather strange look in his eyes, something that Lucy found unnerving. He seemed... edgy.

"What's up?" she asked him.

He crooked a finger at her. "Can I see you a minute?"

Concerned, Lucy followed him outside. Beau waited until they were over by his car, far enough away from the house and parental eavesdroppers, before speaking.

"That was dispatch," he said quietly. "Apparently, Stephen Latling has called the station a couple of times looking for me. He finally spoke to my secretary and told her to tell me to get over to his house as soon as I can."

Lucy's eyes widened. "Oh, my God," she breathed. "Do you think he's found something about the baby? Maybe he went looking after we left and…."

Beau held up a hand, cutting her off before she could continue. "My thoughts exactly," he said. "Go tell your parents that I have to take you to the station to make a statement about Clyde. I'll wait for you in the car."

Lucy bolted off, rushing into the old kitchen to tell her parents exactly what Beau had told her to. When Bill wanted to come, she waved the man off and gave him a few excuses as to why he couldn't come that probably made it look like she was rambling. If her parents didn't think something was up with her and the sheriff before, they probably did now. But she couldn't worry about that; collecting her purse and the briefcase, Lucy dashed out to the waiting police cruiser.

Beau hadn't meant to burn rubber on the gravel, but that's exactly what he did, spraying the side of Glory with a rooster tail of rocks and dirt.

The sense of urgency was palpable.

THE SECOND TIME around at Stephen Latling's house, he was slightly more friendly. Not entirely, but a little. At least he hadn't come charging out at them. He actually opened the door politely and invited them into his home.

Inside, it smelled like dust. The furnishings had probably only been freshened or moderately updated since the house was built because everything in it was exquisitely vintage. Antiques were everywhere. The carpet was thick wool, a very specific burgundy color with cream-colored roses strewn through it, a typically Victorian pattern.

In all, it looked like a time capsule and Lucy tried not to appear too interested in her surroundings, even though she was. But she kept her gaze on Latling, who seemed to be somewhat subdued.

It was strange, really, from a man who had been so all-fired up with hatred only hours earlier to the quiet man standing before them at that minute. Things were a bit awkward. In fact, so much so that Beau finally said something because Latling couldn't seem to say anything at all.

"Thank you for inviting us back," he said. "Your message said it was urgent."

Latling nodded his head, eyeing both Beau and Lucy. "It may be, to you," he said. "My wife told me to call you."

He trailed off. Beau and Lucy were expecting a little more out of him but he just stood there, looking very uncomfortable. Lucy cast Beau a curious glance before speaking.

"Your gardens are really lovely," she said. "I was noticing them earlier. And your house is positively exquisite. We have very few grand old dames like this out in California so it's really a privilege to see inside one of these. Thank you for inviting us over."

Latling looked up at the ceiling, around the walls, as if just noticing what she was talking about. "My great-granddaddy built the house," he said. "Septimus Stephen Latling the First. My daddy was the third Septimus Stephen and I'm the fourth. The first S.S. Latling built this house with his wife, Nannie. It was Nannie who designed it and had all of the gingerbread outside commissioned."

"It's stunning," Lucy said sincerely. Latling simply nodded without elaborating and Lucy was at a loss as to why he'd called them back. It certainly seemed strange. "You wanted to talk to us about something, Mr. Latling?"

Latling scratched his head. "It's Dr. Latling," he said, "and my wife wants to talk to you."

No sooner did he mention the woman than they heard her voice, back over beyond the dining room. She was calling the man by name and he looked over his shoulder, calling back to her.

"They're here," he told her. "Where do you want me to take them?"

"In here!"

Latling motioned them to follow. Passing curious and even wary glances between them, Beau and Lucy followed the man through the dining room, through a butler's pantry, and into a kitchen that was in need of being updated.

It was a big kitchen with black and white flooring and fifty-year-old fixtures. On the far end they could see what looked like a breakfast nook. Mrs. Latling was sitting there along with the old housekeeper. Mrs. Latling stood up when she saw them, waving them all over.

"Hello," she said, extending her hand to Lucy. "I'm Priscilla Latling."

Lucy took the woman's hand. "Hello," she said. "It's so nice to meet you. I was just telling your husband how beautiful this house is. What an amazing piece of history you live in."

Priscilla nodded. An attractive woman with short blonde hair, she didn't seem nearly as awkward as her husband did. "It really is," she said. "I grew up around here and I remember walking to school every day past this house. Little did I know I'd end up marrying a Latling."

Lucy smiled. "Lucky for you."

Priscilla grinned in return. "Definitely," she said. Then, she quickly sobered and indicated the housekeeper, sitting at the table. "This is Cora Ransom. She's been with the family longer than my husband has been alive. Her mother was a housekeeper here, too, for many years with the first Dr. Latling's family. Cora tells me that she spoke to you two."

Upon closer inspection, it looked as if the old woman had been crying and Lucy was instantly alarmed. The old woman had seemed terrified earlier, trying to contact them without the Latlings seeing her, so she wondered if they'd gotten the woman in some kind of trouble. She really hoped not.

"It was very brief," Lucy said, trying to ease whatever anger the Latlings might have about it. "In fact, I didn't even know her name."

Priscilla's gaze lingered on the housekeeper. "I know," she said. "She told me everything. I called you two back here because Cora has something she wants to tell you. You came to the house earlier for a reason and we all heard it. Cora has some information that may be helpful. Go ahead, Cora. Tell them what you told me. It's okay."

The old housekeeper fidgeted with the tissue in her hands, looking between Lucy and Beau. She seemed hesitant until Priscilla put her hand on her bony shoulder in a comforting gesture.

"You come askin' about a baby," Cora finally said.

Lucy's heart began to race again, just as it did the first time Cora had spoken of the child. "Yes," she said, trying not to sound too anxious. "You said you knew about a baby born that year, a baby that Dr. Latling had brought home from Glory, but you didn't tell me anymore than that."

Cora sniffled; it was clear that she was upset, emotional over memories of the past. She wiped at her eyes before speaking.

"If that's the baby you want to know about, Ms. Latling gave it to my mama and told her to take it home," she said. "My mama brought it back to our house but she was a-feared to keep it, bein' that Laveau Hembree wanted the baby dead, so my mama gave it over to her sister to raise."

Lucy could hardly believe what she was hearing. Her knees went weak and she found herself sinking into the chair next to the old woman. "The baby was biracial," she breathed. "Her mother was white, her father black. Are we talking about the same baby?"

"Yes'm. A little girl."

Lucy's heart leapt right up into her throat. "Then the baby lived?" she breathed. "Laveau never got his hands on her?"

The old woman shook her head. "No, ma'am," she said. "That baby was raised by my Aunt Florence. That's what I wanted to tell you, ma'am."

That was what Lucy had been hoping to hear, those sweet words that meant everything to her. A confirmation that had been eighty-three years in the making. A hand flew to her mouth but not before a gasp escaped, something like glee, excitement, joy all rolled into one. She tried to speak but she got all choked up, emotion rendering her unable to say a word.

Beau, standing behind her, could see how emotional she was. He, too, was shocked to hear what the old housekeeper had to say but he had more composure than Lucy did.

He crouched down beside Lucy, bringing himself down to Cora's level. He was much less intimidating that way and now that the old woman was talking, he wanted to know everything. He'd been with Lucy since the beginning of this hunt two days ago and whether or not he liked it, he was nearly as emotionally entrenched in it as she was.

He had to know, too.

"So the baby lived," he said, a sense of satisfaction in his voice. "Did she grow up to adulthood?"

The old housekeeper nodded. "She did, sir," she said. "My aunt raised her with her own children. There were seven of them and she was somewhere in the middle."

"And no one ever asked where she came from?"

The old woman shrugged. "They knew she done come from Dr. Latling," she said, "but my aunt loved her like she was her very own. I think she was her favorite."

Beau smiled faintly. "What became of her?"

"*Became* of her, sir?"

He nodded. "Did she have children of her own?" he asked. "Are they still alive?"

The old housekeeper cocked her head as if puzzled by the question. "She never had no children," she said. "And Miss Ruby Ransom is still alive."

CHAPTER TWENTY-FOUR
~ The Bonds of Family ~

CAROLINE HAD THE VAPORS *again. Or, at least, that's what she called them, a term she got from her mama, something that meant she felt faint and weak. Dr. Latling just called it nerves.*

Caroline was a nervous woman in the best of times but since the circumstances involving her daughter, she'd become more nervous than usual over the past several months. It wasn't her fault entirely, the way Laveau treated her. Even the strongest woman would have broken under that kind of strain, as was evidenced by Victory herself. The strong, vivacious daughter of Laveau and Caroline was a pale wraith these days. It was truly sad to see.

As a misty evening enveloped the land, Dr. Latling had come to Glory to see to Caroline. Her maid said she'd had a fainting spell for no reason at all but then let it slip that Mr. Laveau had yelled at her prior to her spell, so Dr. Latling was coming to think that the woman was just overwrought. Once he examined her, he was sure there was nothing physically wrong with her. Ms. Caroline's problem was all in her mind.

So he prescribed Dr. Greene's Brain and Nerve tonic, something he often prescribed for women who were convinced they had something wrong with them. He used a big word to diagnose their troubles – neurasthenia – and wrote out the prescription for the tonic, which was really nothing more than alcohol and bitters. He knew that, as did most physicians, but when the situation called for a hypochondriac to have a diagnosis, that's what he usually prescribed. Often times, it was enough to do the trick.

So he assured Caroline she'd be fine if she took her tonic twice a day and rested, and she was very grateful for his visit. He checked on Victory while he was there, finding the young woman sitting in her bedroom where she spent so much time, reading a book on poetry. In fact, Dr. Latling had noticed she had a lot of poetry books. For a vital young woman who spent so much time alone, those books were her door to the world outside.

He had stopped by to see Victory about once a week since the child had been born, just to check up on her health and make sure she was recovering. Her smile would light up when she saw him and he could tell, every time he came to see her, that she wanted to press him about the baby. He knew she had so many things on her mind but, to her credit, she never asked. She must have remembered his request for her to never ask about it in case someone overheard, so she stayed true to his request. She never questioned him. But he knew it must have killed her not to.

After visiting with Victory for a few minutes and telling her she needed to eat more red meat to build up her blood, he closed up his medical bag and headed downstairs with Lillian right behind him. She was his escort through the house since he'd come to see the woman. Just as he was heading to the front door of Glory, he heard Laveau call to him from the front parlor.

"Latling," he said. "Come on over here."

Dr. Latling turned to see Laveau sitting in the parlor surrounded by his usual henchmen, including Terhune. Meade was there and so was Lane Haltom, who had become a henchman as of late.

Ever since Laveau arranged the death of the man's wife and son, Haltom had been more than willing to do Laveau's bidding in order to protect his other three children. It was probably the same reason that Terhune stuck with him, or at least that's what Dr. Latling suspected. Terhune had four children and wanted to see them grow up. As Dr. Latling entered the parlor, Laveau gestured to him.

"Have a drink, Doc," he said. "I've got the finest bourbon north of New Orleans."

Dr. Latling shook his head. "No, thanks," he said. "I got to be getting home. Besides, Mrs. Latling doesn't tolerate drinking."

Laveau grunted. "A member of the Temperance League, eh?"

"Definitely."

Laveau stood up. "Women," he grunted unhappily. "They don't let us have no fun at 'tall. Speaking of women, how's my wife?"

Dr. Latling nodded. "She's going to be fine," he said. "She'd be better if things weren't so stressful around here. She needs rest."

Laveau came towards him, his brow furrowed. "Things ain't stressful around here," he insisted. "She doesn't have a lot of work to do. Why does she need rest?"

Dr. Latling almost spit it out — because you smother everything you touch, you nasty bastard! But he kept his mouth shut, instead, trying to tactfully couch his meaning.

"She's a tired woman," he said. "Some women just aren't strong, Laveau. They need to be treated a little more gently than others. That's all there is to it."

Laveau came to within a couple of feet of him, nodding his head as if he understood what he was being told. "You mean she's worthless," he grumbled, shaking his head with disgust. "A silly, worthless woman. Sometimes I wish… well, that don't matter. But she's going to be okay?"

"She's going to be fine."

"What about my daughter? Did you look in on her, too?"

Dr. Latling couldn't help but notice that he couldn't bring himself to mention Victory by name. In fact, Latling couldn't remember if he'd ever heard the man mention his daughter by name. It was always "she", or "her", or "my daughter". Never Victory, the only legitimate child he had. Maybe he just didn't think she was worth mentioning since her troubles began.

"I did," the doctor replied. "She seems to be recovering well."

Laveau's gaze lingered on the doctor for a moment and he put his hand on the man's shoulder, escorting him to the front door and away from the men in the living room. When it was just the two of them, Laveau spoke softly.

"I been meaning to ask you," he said. "The night that bastard was brought into the world, I never did know if it was a boy or a girl. I wasn't in my right mind that night, Doc. You understand."

Unfortunately, Dr. Latling understood all too well. "It was a boy," he lied. He'd been prepared for this moment, prepared to throw Laveau off the scent of that baby just as far as he could. "It… it was born dead, Laveau. And it wasn't well formed. You didn't want to see it, trust me. That's why I took it away, why I didn't let Ms. Caroline see it. It would have only given ya'll nightmares for the rest of your life."

Laveau seemed to recoil at the thought. "It… it was deformed?"

Dr. Latling averted his gaze, trying to pretend he was disgusted by the child, too, when the truth was that he didn't want to look the man in the eye because he was afraid he might let it slip what a low-lying scum he thought he really was.

"Like I said," he muttered, "it would have given ya'll nightmares had you seen it. I took it home and burned it in the incinerator. It's gone."

"No trace?"

"Nothing."

Laveau still had his hand on the doctor's shoulder. He squeezed, but it wasn't a comforting or a polite one. It was an intimidating one.

"That's good," he said. "I just wanted to make sure there's no trace of it. Or that no one talks about it."

Dr. Latling knew that was a threat if he'd ever heard one. He looked Laveau in the eye. "Laveau, you and I have had an understanding for a while now," he said. "I don't talk about my patients and I especially don't talk about you, so if that's worrying you, I think you know me better than that."

Laveau's dark eyes glittered for a moment, as if the evil inside of *him was rolling and flickering back in his brain. There was so much darkness in the man that those eyes were the first place it became apparent. But he suddenly grinned, slapping Dr. Latling on the shoulder before dropping his hand.*

"You are the last person I worry about, Doc," he said. "I just wanted to make sure we understood each other."

"We do."

"Good."

Dr. Latling had to admit, he was a little shaken after that. He put his hand on the door and opened it. "Your wife has a prescription for some tonic," he said. "You might want to send one of your boys out to get it for her."

Laveau was still smiling. "I'll do that."

Dr. Latling stepped through the door, shutting it quietly behind him. Involuntarily, he shuddered almost immediately and it wasn't because of the cold outside. It was because his encounters with Laveau always made him feel as if he'd just met the Devil face-to-face and lived to tell the tale.

And Glory was the closest he would ever come to stepping into Hell.

CHAPTER TWENTY-FIVE

Present

"R UBY!" LUCY BURST into tears, her hands covering her face. "Oh, my God, her name *was* Ruby! It's really her!"

Beau put his big arm around her shoulders, giving her a squeeze of comfort. He didn't know what else to do as the shocking news settled – Victory Hembree's baby had not only been kept safe all these years, but she was still alive.

Lucy was rattled and had every right to be. Her sobs were so pitiful that Priscilla quickly moved to comfort her, too, feeling very badly that the news of Ruby Ransom evidently was something quite terrible or quite wonderful. She couldn't tell which from the way Lucy was carrying on.

Startled, Cora jumped up from her seat and rushed to the stove, putting on the tea kettle as a sort of reflex reaction. Tea or coffee always cured all white folk's ills, didn't it? Once the kettle was on, and Priscilla and Beau, and even Stephen to a certain extent, were trying to calm Lucy down, Cora made her way back over to the weeping woman.

"I'm sorry, ma'am," she said, lowering herself back into a chair across the table. "I didn't mean to make you cry. But that's what happened to the baby. She came with the name Ruby. Dr. Latling told my mama that her name was Ruby."

Lucy was trying so hard to stop her tears. She wiped at her face furiously. "I know," she said, seeing how upset the little housekeeper was. "Oh, my God, I'm so sorry to react like this. But this is just such an important thing for me to hear. You have no idea how important it is for me to hear that Ruby is alive."

Priscilla, who was sitting down next to Lucy with her hands on the woman's forearms, was looking at her with great concern. "Why?" she asked. "Can you tell me why it's so important to you and why you came here asking about that particular baby?"

Lucy nodded, gratefully accepting a box of tissue from Stephen. "Yes, I can," she said, blowing her nose. "But if you don't mind... please don't repeat it. This is really a private family matter but you all have provided a major piece of the puzzle so you deserve to hear the truth. You see, the baby in question – the biracial baby born in nineteen hundred and thirty-three, the one Dr. Latling brought home because Laveau Hembree was going to kill it – is Victory Hembree's child. She fell in love with a black man and became pregnant. When Laveau found out, he beat her so badly that she lied and told him she'd been raped by a black man. Laveau ended up killing an innocent man because of it and when the baby was born, Dr. Latling must have snuck it out of the house and brought it home. I have no idea how he got it past Laveau, but what he did... it was incredibly risky and incredibly heroic. Dr. Latling, your father is a hero. He's *my* hero. He saved that baby."

By the time she finished her story, Stephen and Priscilla and even Cora were looking at her with varied degrees of horror and shock. In fact, Stephen had to sit down. He planted his butt on the nearest chair as the reality of Lucy's words sank in.

"My God," he finally said, rubbing his chin. "Do you mean to tell me that Victory Hembree had a mulatto baby and my daddy spirited that child away right under Laveau Hembree's nose?"

"He did," Lucy said, wiping away the last of her tears. "That's exactly what he did. Think what you want of my family, Dr. Latling, but your family... I will sing your praises until the day I die. From the bottom of my heart and on behalf of Victory

Hembree, I thank your father for what he did. He literally risked his life to do it."

Stephen looked at her, a faint gleam coming to his eye. "I will admit, that was a pretty brave thing," he said. "I still can't believe it. And that's why you wanted to look at his records? To see if there was any record of the baby?"

"That's why."

Stephen's gaze lingered on her a moment. He was filled with disbelief but he was also filled with pride. Pride that his father had done the right thing under such harrowing circumstances against a man the entire state was afraid of. It was enough to make him misty-eyed.

"My daddy was older when I was born," he said after a moment. "I had three sisters who were much older than I was. By the time I came around, the only boy, my daddy was verging on becoming an old man. I spent a lot of time with him and came to know a warm man who was devoted to his family, but this bravery… you've told me something about my daddy that I didn't know and for that, I thank you. Maybe we did something for you today, but you sure did something for me, too."

Lucy smiled. "I'm glad," she said. "Without your father's bravery, I'm sure the story would have been much different."

Stephen couldn't disagree. "From what we've all known about Laveau, that's the truth," he said. "But I have to ask – how did you know about the baby? Who told you?"

"My Mamaw," Lucy said. "Victory Hembree, I mean. She left me a letter about it. In fact… I have it with me."

With that, she dug into her purse and carefully pulled out the journal, setting it on the breakfast table. As the others watched curiously, she opened the front cover and she pulled out the white envelope that contained the letter. Carefully unfolding it, she handed it to Stephen.

With Priscilla hanging over his shoulder, reading the letter right along with him, Stephen did what Beau had done – he read it slowly once and then went over it a second time. By the time he was finished, he was misty-eyed again and his wife was quietly weeping. She took a tissue from the box Lucy had on her lap, silently absorbing the tragic story as Stephen looked rather stricken by it all.

"My God," he finally breathed, clearing his throat because his voice was husky. "What the woman went through. What her daddy did to that man… that's one of the worst things I've ever heard of."

Lucy looked at the letter in his hands. "Now you know why I had to come and ask you about it."

Stephen nodded fervently. "Had I know about that letter, I never would have yelled at ya'll when you first came around," he said, grinning because Lucy and Beau were laughing softly. He sobered, his focus on Lucy. "I'm so sorry I called you a bitch earlier. I was mad. I shouldn't have done that."

Lucy laughed softly. "I've been called worse. No offense taken."

Stephen still had that sheepish look, now because his wife was looking at him as if she were ready to wash his mouth out with soap. He was feeling so much regret at his behavior that he didn't blame Priscilla in the least.

"Ms. Victory mentioned giving the baby a locket," he said. "Do you have it?"

Lucy nodded. "I found it in her chifforobe," she said. "It had the words 'In The Dreaming Hour' inscribed on the back, just like she said."

"That poem," Priscilla said, wiping at her nose. "Did you find it? The one Ms. Victory talks about?"

Lucy went back to the envelope that had contained the letter, pulling out a very small scrap of old paper. Just holding it brought the tears back, as she looked at it, and she knew she couldn't read it aloud. She handed it to Beau.

"Will you read this to them?" she asked, her throat tight.

Beau pulled his readers out of his pocket, putting them on as he focused on the faded ink. In his gentle baritone, sounding probably much the same way Lewis Ragsdale had once sounded, he read the words quietly. It was only appropriate that a man read the words aloud, considering a man had once written the poem to the woman he loved.

In the Dreaming Hour,
Where my heart is free
The song of nighttime comforts me
And brings me thoughts of thee.
On beams of silver moonlight,
Against the dark of night,
The world beholds no color,
No blackness and no white.
In this world, void of color,
The heart and soul combines,
For in the Dreaming Hour,
My love unites with thine.

When he was finished, he took off his glasses and looked up at the Latlings. Priscilla's eyes were closed and she held the tissue against her nose, while Stephen seemed to be frozen, staring at the scrap in Beau's hand. It was as if the poem had put him in a trance, those remarkable words filling his senses with the powerful story they represented.

"I have never heard anything quite so beautiful," he finally said, his gaze now moving between Lucy and Beau. "Thank you for sharing that. The man who wrote that... well, that's no ordinary man."

Lucy took the fragile piece of paper back from Beau, folding it up in the letter once more. "I can't even imagine what he went through, being born during that era and living in the kind of oppression that was taking place down here in the south during that time. And the fact that my mamaw fell in love with him just makes it all the more tragic."

Stephen nodded as Priscilla finally opened her eyes and went over to the stove where the kettle was starting to hiss. "Yes, it does," he said. "It really does."

Seeing that Priscilla was tending to the kettle, Cora stood up from her chair. She'd been completely silent through the reading of the letter and the poem, not uttering a sound. When she moved, Lucy looked over to the old woman as if completely forgetting she had been sitting there.

"Do you want to read it, too?" she asked. "I didn't mean to be rude and not offer."

But Cora shook her head, almost recoiling from the paper that Lucy was extending to her. "No, ma'am," she said. "Somethin' like that… it wasn't meant for nobody else to read it. It's only meant for one person."

Lucy smiled faintly as the housekeeper hustled over to help her employer. She looked at Beau. "There's something in what she says," she said. "It's so incredibly personal."

Beau nodded, pushing himself onto his feet, grunting because he'd gotten stiff kneeling down for so long. "I didn't realize you had the poem with you," he said. "That's the first time I've seen it. Something like that should have been buried with Ms. Victory."

Lucy carefully put the folded note and poem back into the envelope. "Had I know about it, I would have made sure it was," she said. "I only found out about it after she'd been put in the ground."

"But you can still have those words inscribed on her head stone," Stephen said. "That's what she said she wanted."

Lucy looked up at him as she put the journal back into her purse. "I intend to," she said. "But knowing Ruby is alive… I think

I'm going to give this poem and this journal to her, if she wants it. It's her father and mother, after all. She might want to have something from them."

Stephen looked over at Cora as the old woman brought tea cups to the table. "Where's Ruby living now?" he asked her. "Do you know?"

Cora nodded. "She lives over in Cleveland," she said. "She's a retired professor from Delta State."

Lucy looked at the woman in surprise. "She was a college professor?" she said. "My God… a woman of color born in that era getting a college education?"

Cora set the cups down. "My Aunt Florence insisted that all of her children be educated," she said. "She'd saved up the money, so Ruby and her sisters went to Spelman College in Georgia."

Stephen looked at Lucy. "Spelman is an all-Black woman's college," he said. "It's been around a long time."

Lucy already knew that about Spelman. She was hugely impressed that Ruby had grown up to become a teacher and there was a massive part of her that wanted to jump in the car and drive right over to Cleveland at that very moment. But at this juncture in the search for Mamaw's baby, she knew she couldn't do that.

Right now, she needed to let her family in on what she'd discovered. That was going to be a daunting task because she still wasn't entirely sure if her dad was ready for such an emotional burden. Still, she couldn't keep him out of it any longer. It was his right to know.

"Cora," she said. "Do you think you could give me Ruby's phone number? I'd like to call her and introduce myself. Do you know if she's ever expressed any interest in knowing about her roots? I'm assuming she knew she was adopted."

Cora gazed back at her, rather fearfully. "I don't know," she said. "I don't know if anyone ever told her where she really come from."

That threw a monkey wrench into things. If Ruby didn't know she wasn't a biological child of Florence, then that could complicate things a great deal. That thought had never occurred to Lucy, frankly, and her joy in the discovery of Ruby was dampened by that thought.

"Oh," she said, looking at Beau with something of a puzzled expression. "If she doesn't know she's adopted, do I tell an eighty-year-old woman what her roots really were? I'm not sure that's even right."

Beau was contemplating that very thought. "That's true, but you wanted to give her that locket."

"So I just give it to her and not tell her why?" Lucy asked, increasingly disappointed. "That doesn't make any sense. She's going to think the whole thing is crazy if some stranger gives her an antique locket."

"Then tell her," Stephen said. He'd been standing off to the side, listening to the chatter. When Lucy and Beau looked at him, he continued. "The woman is a teacher, after all. That means she's somewhat pragmatic, hopefully. So she's eighty years old? It's never too late to learn the truth, even about yourself. I know this isn't my family or my situation, but if it was me, I'd just tell her the truth."

Lucy thought he made some sense. "But how?" she asked. "Just show up on her doorstep?"

Stephen shook his head. "No," he shoved his hands in his pockets, his manner pensive. "Something like that needs to be handled delicately. Look, I'm a clinical psychiatrist by trade. I'm also Dr. Latling but I don't practice medicine like my daddy did. If you want my advice and my help, I'm willing to offer it. I feel as if I have an investment in this situation given that my daddy rescued Ruby from Laveau. I can have Cora bring her over to our house and you can be here, too. We'll call it a party or something. Then you can get to know her and decided when to tell her the truth."

Lucy liked that idea a great deal. "Would you really do that?"

she asked. "I don't even know how to thank you. That's twice the Latling family has helped my family."

Stephen modestly waved her off. He looked at Cora. "You usually go home on Sundays," he said. "When Priscilla and I drive you home, you can get in touch with Ruby and ask her to come out next week sometime. We'll say we're giving you a party or something. Tell her we want her to come."

"Wait," Lucy put up a hand. "I have to go back to Los Angeles next week. I'm not going to be out here for that long."

"Oh," Stephen said, re-thinking his strategy. "Well, then… Cora, call her tonight and tell her we're coming out tomorrow to pick her up and bring her back over here for a special dinner tomorrow night. The same celebratory excuse. Can you do that?"

Cora nodded, but it was clear she was uncertain about the whole thing. "Yessir," she said. "I'll call her tonight."

"Good," Stephen said, turning his attention back to Lucy and Beau. "Tomorrow night, then?"

Lucy was already feeling the pinpricks of anticipation. "That would be perfect," she said. "Can I bring my parents?"

Stephen nodded, clearing his throat as he suddenly looked embarrassed again. "Like I said, I've gone out of my way not to meet your daddy and…."

Lucy cut him off, grinning. "He won't care about that," she said, standing up from the chair. "He'll just be glad that things are mending between the Latlings and the Hembrees. Well, between the Latlings and the Bondurants, anyway. He'll be fine with it. And he'll be grateful for your help."

Stephen smiled, still somewhat embarrassed. "I'd like to meet him."

As Lucy collected her purse, signaling to Beau that their business was finished, Priscilla came over to the table with the kettle and tea bags.

"Where are you going?" she wanted to know. "Don't you want

some tea?"

Lucy didn't want any and neither did Beau, but to be polite, they sat back down and spent another hour shooting a variety of subjects around the table, sipping on the strong black tea that Priscilla had produced. They remained polite and cordial, because this kind of easy conversation with the Latlings had been hard-won, but the moment that hour was up, Lucy insisted that they really did need to leave.

With plans to meet Ruby Ransom for dinner the following night, Lucy left the Latling house feeling more fulfilled, more excited, than she'd felt in a very long time. Sure, there was still more to come and quite a bit could go wrong, but she had faith that, somehow, everything would work out as it should. At least, that was her prayer. But before tomorrow night occurred, she had one more thing to do.

She had to tell her father everything.

CHAPTER TWENTY-SIX
~ A Time for Truth ~

"*I*'M SO GLAD YOUR *daddy finally let you have visitors,*" Dell said. "*I've been asking for you, every time I come over.*"

Sitting in Victory's bedroom on a cloudy spring day, Victory sat on a chair over by the window while Dell rifled through the top drawer of her chifforobe, looking for anything that struck her fancy. There were ribbons and jewelry in that drawer. Dell would pull out ribbons and look at herself in the mirror as she wrapped them around her red head, imaging how they would look on her.

Legs tucked up underneath her, Victory watched her cousin primp. "*Daddy says I can go back to school when it starts again in the fall,*" *she said.* "*Has much changed? How is Eulalie?*"

"*Fine,*" *Dell said, disinterested. Then, she suddenly turned away from the mirror, her pale face alive with glee.* "*She has a boyfriend now. He goes to the boy's school in Tillatoba — you know the one. Anyway, they've been meeting in secret, or so Eulalie says. She's telling everyone she's going to marry the boy.*"

"*Who is it?*"

Dell burst out giggling. "*Peter Pickle!*" *she said.* "*You remember that family, don't you? Pauline, Penelope, Pamela, Peggy, and Pete! Their daddy has a dairy farm over near Oxberry. The girls don't even go to school; they just work on the farm. Pete goes to the boy's school and he met Eulalie at church. Can you imagine? Eulalie Pickle!*"

She was rambling, giggling, and Victory smiled weakly. "*I wish* she'd come to visit me," Victory said. "I've missed her. I want to hear about Pete."

Dell's smile faded. "I asked her to come with me but... but she won't," she said, turning back to the drawer filled with treasures. "Victory... there's something you should know. I don't believe any of it, of course, but the girls have been saying things about you on account you've been gone so long. That's why they won't come see you. Their parents won't let them."

Victory looked at her cousin. "What sorts of things are they saying?"

Dell sighed, pulling out a red ribbon with less enthusiasm. "About you," she said softly. "Uncle Laveau has kept you locked away for so long and no one has seen you. People say you've either gone crazy or you got in trouble somehow."

Victory didn't like the sound of that. "Trouble how?" she asked. "Tell me."

Dell wouldn't look at her. "Trouble," she muttered. "Some of the girls said your daddy don't want to let you out, if you know what I mean."

"No, I don't know what you mean."

Dell sighed sharply. "Because he wants you close to him. Do you understand me?"

"No."

Dell looked at her. "That your mama can't have no more babies so your daddy has done things... to you... he doesn't want people to know about."

Victory understood, then. Her jaw fell open. "Who has been saying such things, Dell?" she demanded, coming out of the chair. "Who has repeated that filth?"

Dell backed up against the chifforobe as Victory grabbed her by the wrist and squeezed. "Ouch!" she yelped. "It wasn't me! I never said those things!"

Victory was infuriated. "Yes, you did," she hissed. "You just said them to me. And I know you, Dell Alexander — you have a mouth that spills over like a waterfall. You can't ever keep anything to yourself. You said something, didn't you? About the last time you were here – you said something about me!"

Dell was terrified. "No, I didn't! I swear!"

Victory didn't believe her. She knew her cousin well enough to know that if any rumors got started, they would have come from her because Dell liked to make things up if she didn't know the truth. Letting go of Dell's wrist, she smacked her right across the face.

"Get out," she screamed. "Get out and don't you ever come back! You tell those girls that you lied to them about me, you hear? I'm going to tell my daddy what you told them!"

Dell was in tears, her hand over the left side of her face where Victory had slapped her. "Don't tell him!" she begged even as she backed out of the room. "Please don't, Victory! It's not true! I didn't say nothing!"

Victory shoved her towards the door, throwing it open. "Get out," she said through clenched teeth. "Don't you come back here until you've taken back all of the lies you told about me. I knew you were a gossipmonger, but you've never turned that against me. Now, you have, and I hate you for it. You'd better tell everyone you lied about me or I swear my daddy will show up at your house and punish you!"

Dell sobbed. "No, Victory, please!"

"Then you make it right!"

With that, Victory slammed the door in Dell's face, listening to her cousin sob as she headed down the hall, running from the house.

But Victory felt no remorse. She knew what her cousin was capable of and it sickened her. The better the rumor, the more satisfaction Dell got out of it. But now, there were rumors about Victory spreading through her friends, horrible rumors that Dell had encouraged. All of those girls that Victory thought were her friends were really not her friends at all; now, they were people who were whispering about her, sickening rumors about Laveau and his only daughter. Lies, all of it.

As if her life wasn't lonely enough already.

Victory sat down on her bed and wept.

CHAPTER TWENTY-SEVEN
Present

"ARE YOU REALLY going home next week?" Beau asked the question as they crossed the major boulevard from the Latling house, heading in the direction of Glory. It was just the two of them in the car, reflecting on a very eventful meeting with the Latlings. Head against the headrest, weary from what the day had brought her, Lucy watched the scenery go by.

"Yes," she said. "I'm scheduled to fly back on Monday."

"Oh," Beau said as they slowed as they approached a red light. "That's too bad."

"Why?"

"Just when we were learning to play well together."

Lucy grinned, looking over at him. "I'm sure you have more than enough playmates."

He shook his head, not looking at her. "No time," he said. "With three small children and a job like this, who has the time?"

"You have time to hang out with me."

He wriggled his eyebrows, an ironic gesture. "That was hard-fought time I had to carve out," he said. "Plus, this isn't really play. It's work. I kind of like being Stabler to your Benson."

Lucy laughed, feeling as if the conversation was going to take some kind of emotional turn. "Well," she said, watching the cars pass as the light turned green and they took off again. "I'm sure you'll find someone else to hang out with, someone who actually lives around here."

"I thought you said you were going to buy Glory and fix it up?"

"I might."

"When?"

She looked at him, then. "Sheriff, are you coming on to me?" she asked. "Because I'm sensing this is more than just a casual conversation."

He shook his head but she could tell he was fighting off a grin. "Just making conversation, ma'am."

"Liar."

"You can't prove that."

She chuckled, looking away from him, not at all displeased with the thought of having him to hang around with all of the time. But, right now, she wasn't sure she could emotionally handle anything more than the casual flirting that was going on even though that big hole that Kevin had left in her was healing remarkably well over the past couple of days. In fact, she hadn't even thought about him since the search for Ruby started and that was major progress in her book.

Maybe life really did get better, after all.

"Since you told me about your wife leaving you with three babies to raise, it's probably fair that you know a little something about my background, too," she said. "My husband left me a little more than six months ago. We'd been married since college but after two miscarriages in the past three years, he decided he just didn't want to be married to me anymore. He wanted a family that I can't seem to give him, so he bailed. I'm still picking up the pieces from that."

Beau grunted softly. "Wow," he said quietly. "I'm sorry to hear that. Seems you and I both got hooked up with people who couldn't weather out any storm. I'm sorry for you."

Lucy was studying the big, old houses they were passing, houses that told her they were getting close to Glory. "Don't be," she said. "I appreciate it, but don't be. I'd rather find out now that he couldn't handle a crisis than have him walk out on me with three little kids to raise. I suppose everything happens for a reason. I've just been trying to figure out what the reason might be."

Beau took the turn onto Glory's street. "When you find out, let me know," he said. "I've been trying to figure that one out myself."

She turned to look at him. "You want to hear something weird?" she asked. "At the risk of sounding philosophical, maybe that reason was to come to Mississippi without my husband for Mamaw's funeral and go on the hunt of a lifetime. I honestly couldn't have done this if Kevin was around. He was so impatient. He'd be demanding we fly back to Los Angeles yesterday. My family didn't matter a whole lot to him."

"And now?"

"I'm realizing just how much it means to *me*."

He gave her a half-grin, slowing down as he pulled up to the curb in front of Glory. He put the car in park and looked at her.

"This little hunt we've been on has opened my eyes a little, too," he said. "Talk about something weird… two days ago, I was sitting right in this spot with my dad in the car and we were talking about the history between the Meades and the Hembrees. My dad is really sensitive to things from the past and I was giving him a bad time about it. So… thank you for asking me to help you on this hunt for your Mamaw. It's helped me see a lot of things, not just from my perspective, but from other people's."

"How?"

He cocked his head thoughtfully. "Mostly, it's been through that letter," he said. "We all go around thinking our life is so hard, thinking that we've got it worse than anyone else, but long ago there was a young woman who got pregnant by her black lover during the worst possible time in history for that to happen, yet she came through it. She never lost that sense of faith for herself, for the future. She wouldn't have asked you to find her baby if she had lost it because she believed somehow, someway, that child survived. She had that faith. But it's more than that – she had a love that very few people experience. To love someone so deeply, and for so long, that you hold them close to your heart your entire life? I really envy her."

Lucy liked the way he'd put things into perspective. "Me, too," she said. "In a time when there was such a great racial divide, neither one of them saw that about each other."

"That's pretty amazing."

The conversation tapered off and Lucy picked up her purse and her briefcase. She was about to open the door but he stopped her.

"Are you doing anything for dinner tonight?"

She paused, her hand on the door. "No."

"Want to go get something to eat?"

"Are you asking me out on a date?"

He fought off a grin. "Maybe," he said. "I can bring my Lovie as a chaperone if it would make you feel better."

She burst into laughter and opened the door. "Only if I get to bring Aunt Dell."

"Hell, we'd never get any talking done. They'd overwhelm us both."

"Then maybe we should leave the old girls at home, eh?"

"Agreed." He watched her as she climbed out. "Are you going to tell your parents now about our adventures over the past couple of days?"

She stopped, leaning against the back of the door. "Yes," she said. "I have to. I don't know if my dad is emotionally ready to handle it, but I can't keep it from him any longer. Especially if we're going to meet Ruby tomorrow, he has to know."

Beau nodded, thinking on the task she had ahead of her. "Do you want me to go with you for moral support?"

She shook her head. "I think I can handle this on my own."

"If you need help, you just call. I'll be right over."

"I don't have your number."

He reached into his wallet and pulled out a business card. Taking a pen that was in the console, he turned the card over and wrote on the back of it. He passed the card over to her.

"That's my cell," he said. "Call me anytime."

With a grin, she reached into her purse and pulled out her fancy law business card, extending it to him. "I left a card for you at the station, but here's another one. My cell is at the bottom."

He looked at it the sleek card before tucking it into his shirt pocket where he kept his reading glasses. "When do you want me to pick you up for dinner?"

She glanced at her watch. "Give me at least an hour," she said. "I'll call you when I'm ready."

He nodded. "Until then."

Lucy shut the car door and stood back, giving him a wave as he drove off. She watched his car until he turned a corner and disappeared from view. Then, she turned to look at the big, run-down house in front of her.

Glory.

Thoughts of Beau faded as she pondered what was coming next. Everything she was about to tell her dad happened within the old walls in front of her. Now, Glory was about to experience another life-changing event as Lucy told her father that he had a sister he never knew about.

Summoning her courage, she began the trek towards the house, towards the moment that would change her father's family dynamics forever.

✧ ✧ ✧

"Hey," Bill said from the central hallway as Lucy came in through the front door. "Did everything work out okay?"

Lucy gave him a blank look as she shut the door. "Okay?"

"With Clyde."

She instantly remembered the lie she'd told him earlier. "Oh, right," she said. "Yes, everything is fine. Clyde won't go to prison for long, but he'll face some kind of incarceration. Maybe it'll be enough to scare him straight."

"Either that or he'll come back a hardened criminal."

"There's always that possibility."

Bill disappeared back into the kitchen as Lucy went into the dining room and set her purse and briefcase on the table. It was odd how she was looking at the house with new eyes now; she could look in the parlor and imagine Laveau and his henchmen sitting in there, or here in the dining room where a troubled family took their meals.

But it wasn't just Laveau and his family; it was the generations of Hembrees that had come before him, men and women who literally built this state. Laveau's father, Sat Hembree (short for Saturnius) had even run for governor back in the day. Beyond that, she didn't know much about her Hembree ancestors but she wanted to found out now, more than ever.

But before she could do that, she had something she had to do.

Digging into her purse, she pulled out Mamaw's journal. She eyed it a moment, running her fingers over it, her heart beginning to pound with what she was about to do. She really had no idea how her father was going to react but she couldn't worry about that. Taking deep breath, she headed into the kitchen.

Her mother was throwing out some of the food from Mamaw's wake and her father was at the kitchen table, reading something on his tablet. Lucy stood in the doorway and shook her head.

"Every time I come here, you two are in the kitchen," she teased. "This house has about ten other rooms. Don't you like any of them?"

Bill looked up at her over his glasses. "You're one to talk," he said. "You don't even stay here for more than five minutes at a time."

Lucy laughed, coming into the kitchen and heading over to the table where her dad was sitting. "That's because I've been busy," she said. "Actually, I need to talk to you about that, Dad. I've got something I need to share with you."

Bill still had the tablet in his hands but he was looking at her. "What's up? Christ, is this about Clyde?"

Lucy shook her head, chuckling. "It is not about Clyde," she said. "It's about Mamaw. I have something I need to tell you."

Bill laid the tablet down on the table. "Lay it on me."

He was being very relaxed about it, having no idea she was about to change his life. Lucy felt sorry for him and she tried to cushion the news as best she could.

"Okay, here goes," she said. "At Mamaw's funeral, Aunt Vivien told me something. Mom, can you come over here and sit down? I want you to hear this. Anyway, Aunt Vivian told me that Mamaw had left a note for me and that I wasn't to share it with my daddy. I wasn't to let anyone know. So, for what it's worth, I'm disobeying Mamaw to tell you this, but it's important. You need to know."

Bill still wasn't sensing the seriousness of what she was about to say. "What is it?"

Lucy cleared her throat softly, feeling her nerves. "You remember when I was up in her bedroom when we came back from the funeral?"

"Yes."

"I was looking for the note she left me."

A light went on in Bill's eyes. "Oh," he said, drawing out the word. "Now I get it. I thought it was kind of strange that you were hanging around in there."

Lucy nodded. "I know," she said. Then, she laid the journal down on the table, making sure her parents got a look at it. "Mamaw gave me the key to a secret drawer in her chifforobe and this was in it. It's her diary from when she was a teenager, from about nineteen hundred and thirty-one until nineteen hundred and thirty-three. It's just a couple of years' worth of entries, but they were really insightful into her as a young woman. It's really sweet."

Both Bill and Mary were looking over the journal with great curiosity. "I've never seen this," Bill said, reaching out to pull it over to him. "I didn't even know she...."

Lucy put her hand on it, preventing him from getting a better look at it. When he looked at her curiously, she shook her head and pulled it back against her.

"Not yet," she said. "This journal isn't what I need to tell you about. You know I haven't really been around for the past couple of days and there's a reason for that. Something that Mamaw asked me to do for her. You see, there was a letter in this journal she left for me, a letter that she didn't want me to show you, Dad. But I'm going to show it to you because it's something you need to read. In the letter, Mamaw asked me to track someone down for her. That's what I've been doing the past couple of days. That's why I went to see Aunt Dell. And remember I mentioned Stephen Latling? I didn't run into him in town – I tracked him down. He and his family are part of this, too. So I'm just going to let you read the letter. I think that will tell you exactly what I've been up to."

With that, she opened up the journal and pulled out the now-familiar white envelope. Carefully, she pulled out the letter, keeping the scrap with the poem still inside the envelope, and opened up the letter for her father. She placed it in Bill's hands.

Both Bill and Mary peered at the letter with great curiosity and began to read. As Lucy sat there and watched, she could see her father's cheeks turning shades of pale to pink and to a reddish color. Although he didn't say anything, his emotions were running the gamut and showing all over his face.

Mary was less subtle about it – her hand flew to her mouth about a minute after she began reading and the more she read, the more she gasped. Her eyes widened. By the time she got to the end, she had the same reaction that Lucy had and that Priscilla Latling had after reading it – there were tears in her eyes. She began to sniffle and wipe them away, finally turning her back on the letter and going to find a tissue.

While Lucy's mother sniffled over by the kitchen sink, Bill hadn't really reacted at all other than the color of his cheeks. Lucy was glued to her father's face as he finished the letter and, predictably, went to read it again. It seemed that anyone who read it had to do it a second time for maximum impact.

The third time through, he finally handed the letter back over to Lucy. She watched him closely for a reaction.

"You okay?" she asked gently, touching his hand.

He nodded. But he didn't look fine. "Oh… God," he finally said. "All of those questions you were asking me about our family. Is this why?"

Lucy nodded. "Exactly."

Bill stared at her a moment. "You asked me if I thought Laveau committed murder, too. Did you mean the murder in that letter?"

"Yes."

Bill sighed heavily, his gaze drawn back to the letter. He didn't speak for a moment, collecting his thoughts. "I… I can't even pretend to be calm and cool about this," he said. "I always knew my grandfather was a vile son-of-a-bitch, but this… this is confirmation of the worst he had to offer. Killing an innocent man? My God… that man's evil knew no limits."

Lucy could see that he was hurting, much as she had been hurting when she first read the letter.

"I know," she said quietly. "As much as I'd like to see justice for that poor man, I've had to deal with one issue at a time and my primary issue is that of finding the baby. You wondered why I've been hanging around with the sheriff? It's because I needed his help. He knows people and he knows this town. We've been all over town trying to find people who might have known about

Mamaw's baby."

Bill looked at her. "So he knows about this, too?"

"He does. His great-grandfather was in on it from the start. So in a sense, he's part of this as much as we are. He's been a huge help."

Bill didn't argue with her about letting someone outside of the family in on such a terrible secret; what she said made sense. The Meades were part of the Hembree web of evil back then. There was no disputing that, especially when Mamaw mentioned Terhune Meade by name in her letter.

"Did you find anything?" he asked, his voice dull with sorrow.

"We did," Lucy said, hoping her father was prepared for her answer. "It wasn't easy because it was a well-kept secret, but I wanted you to know that I've located the baby."

That drew a strong reaction from Bill. His eyes widened and he abruptly stood up, a hand flying to his face.

"Oh, no," he muttered. "Oh… God, did you really?"

Lucy nodded, thinking that he didn't sound too pleased about it, but given he'd just read a game-changing revelation from his own mother, she wasn't too surprised.

"Yes," she said steadily. "You'll notice that in the letter, Mamaw mentioned that Dr. Latling attended the birth so I went to his son, Stephen, and asked if I could see Dr. Latling's birth records. As it turned out, I didn't need to – their housekeeper heard my request and she is the daughter of the woman who tended Dr. Latling's house back when he delivered Mamaw's baby. It was Dr. Latling who took the baby out of Glory and kept it from Laveau. I don't know how he did it, but he took the baby home with him and turned her over to his housekeeper, who then turned the baby over to her sister to raise. Her name is Ruby Ransom and she just retired from Delta State. She's still alive and lives over in Cleveland."

Bill was standing in the middle of the kitchen, a hand over his mouth and his gaze on the journal. He just stood there a moment, struggling with what he'd been told.

"Hold on," he said, raising a hand as if to put everything to a stop. "Ruby *Ransom* is her name?"

Lucy nodded. "Yes," she said. "Mamaw named the baby Ruby and they evidently kept the name."

Bill was shaking his head. "Wait..," he mumbled. "Oh, God... just wait a minute. I can't believe I'm hearing this."

Lucy looked at her mother and the two of them passed sympathetic glances. "Dad, I know it's hard, but...."

Bill cut her off, almost sharply. "No, that's not what I mean," he said. "What I mean is... Jesus, I don't even know where to begin with this, but about five years ago, a woman showed up at Glory. Your mother and I were visiting Mamaw at the time but I remember distinctly that Mamaw wasn't feeling well. We'd just brought her back from Memphis where she'd had some bloodwork done, because that's when she was first diagnosed with cancer, so she was in bed when this woman showed up at the door. This woman and I got to talking and she proceeded to tell me that she was a Hembree bastard and she'd come to see her roots. Well, that upset the hell out of me so I told her to go away and not come back."

Lucy was on her feet, eyes wide with surprise. "Did she tell you her name?"

Bill nodded. Now, he was back to looking pale. "Ruby Ransom," he could barely spit out the words. "I didn't even make the connection until now, until you said her full name. I thought she meant she was *Laveau's* bastard because, God only knew, I've heard rumor of more than one of those around here and I was angry that she'd shown up at the house. I didn't want Mama finding out about her, so I never mentioned her, not ever. Now... now you're telling me that she was my *mother's* bastard?"

Lucy was astonished to the bone, feeling a stab of sorrow through her heart that she couldn't begin to comprehend. "Ruby

Ransom is Mamaw's missing baby," she breathed. "Oh, my God, Dad… you chased her away?"

Bill nodded, sickened. "I did," he said. "I wasn't nice about it, either. I didn't want my mother shamed or upset by it, so I practically threw the woman out."

Lucy didn't even know what to say. She sank back into the chair, looking at the note that was open and resting on the journal. Her eyes began to swim with tears, her heart torn up by the tragic reality of a terrible misunderstanding.

"She was here," she whispered, picking up the letter and looking at the writing on it. "She came back to where she was born."

Bill closed his eyes, overwhelmed with what had happened. "I didn't know," he said, his voice tight with emotion. "I had no idea who she really was. And it was me who sent her away when my mama had been looking for her all along. If only I had talked to her a little more and understood what she was telling me, but I didn't. I told her to go away. Oh, God… what have I done…."

He turned away, heading out into the house, wrought with sorrow he couldn't reconcile. Mary ran after him and she could hear her parents whispering out in the hall, her father's distraught voice and her mother's soothing one. Lucy would have liked to have given them both time to regain their composure but there wasn't time for that. Wearily, she stood up and went out into the corridor where they were standing.

"I'm sorry," she said. "I don't mean to intrude, but there's still more to this. Stephen Latling has invited Ruby over to dinner at his house tomorrow night and he wants us to come over and meet her. Dad, I had no idea what had happened with you and sending Ruby away. I'm going to go but I understand if you don't want to."

Bill was clearly edgy and distressed. "I doubt she's going to want to see me," he said. "But you should go, Lucy. Mama mentioned some kind of locket in her letter, something she wanted the baby to have – do you have that?"

"I do," Lucy said. "I found it yesterday."

"Then you need to go and give it to her. It's what Mama wanted."

"Are you sure?"

Bill nodded, removing his glasses and rubbing wearily at his eyes. "Yes," he said. "And make sure you tell her how sorry I am for sending her away. I just didn't understand who she was or what she meant to my mother. Now I have to live with the fact that my mother had a chance to meet her lost baby while she was still alive but because of me, she died not knowing what happened to her."

With that, he turned and walked away, heading down the corridor towards the front of the house. Mary trailed after him, leaving Lucy standing in the dimness of the hall, with just the kitchen light piercing the darkness.

Her heart was heavy as she watched her father walk away, knowing how horribly troubled he was by the situation. It was even more grief on top of having just lost his mother, but Lucy knew she'd done the right thing by telling him. It was just a burden Bill would have to come to grips with.

For his sake, she prayed he would find peace with it.

Wandering back into the kitchen where the letter and the journal still sat on the old Formica table, she pulled her cell phone out of her purse as well as Beau's business card. She wasn't particularly hungry and didn't want to go out to dinner, and she didn't want to return to the hotel that night. She wanted to stay close to her parents. When she explained everything to Beau, who picked up the phone on the second ring, he completely understood.

Tonight belonged to the Bondurants.

CHAPTER TWENTY-EIGHT
~ And Brings Me Thoughts of Thee ~

*I*T WAS A COLD DAY in early nineteen hundred and thirty-four. With spring on the approach, the frozen ground was trying to warm itself in the weak sun, struggling to bring forth the dormant greenery deep inside of her.

Even so, everything still looked winter-frozen beneath the fragile sun. There was no warmth to be had but the planting for the coming year had to begin, the cold earth tilled and turned so the seeds could be sewn.

Glory still had about two hundred acres to tend, far less than the original plot of land but enough to grow good crops of cotton and sorghum. It was that earth that needed to be tended and Laveau and his men had gone to the work camp on the edge of town, a place where sharecroppers gathered who were looking for work, and selected about sixty men to help till the land. Since most of the men who worked the land at Glory were sharecroppers or drifters, there was nearly a new group of men every year to work the dark soil.

On this day, Victory was sitting on the porch of Glory with her mother with a pot of coffee between them, watching the road in the distance as the old trucks began to bring the men to the plantation. It was chilly outside but the ladies were bundled up because being outside in the fresh air during the day was better than being inside in the stale air.

Moreover, the sun was out and Caroline thought that Victory was *looking a little pale. She'd been pale for the past five months, ever since she delivered her dead baby, and on the doctor's orders, Caroline was doing everything she could to try and bring some color back into her daughter's cheeks.*

Victory didn't care much about color these days. In fact, she didn't care much about anything. Laveau and his oppression had finally beaten her down. After the death of her baby, she didn't have the strength to fight him anymore but she certainly had the strength to hate him. That hatred grew stronger by the day.

"Look, Victory," Caroline said pleasantly. "There's Daddy and the men. Look at all of them! I talked to your daddy about extending our vegetable garden, so maybe we can use some of those men to do that."

Victory didn't care about vegetable gardens. She sighed restlessly, watching her father in is 1933 Ford Model 40, its top down and his henchmen shoved all into the front, back, and rumble seat.

"Has Daddy said when I can go back to school?" she asked her mother, completely off subject. "It's almost spring. If I don't go back soon, I'll have missed more than a year of school."

Caroline picked up her cup of coffee. "He hasn't said anything about it," she said. "I'll ask him again."

"And what about Dell?" Victory asked. "I saw her come to the house yesterday but she didn't come up and see me. Why not?"

Caroline sipped at her coffee. "She brought something over from her mama," she said. "She didn't come to visit."

Victory looked at her mother. "You mean Daddy wouldn't let her come to see me."

Caroline sighed faintly, feeling the mood between them grow sharp again. It was sharp so often these days. "Not yet, sugar," she said softly. "Daddy wants to make sure you're feeling better before you have any visitors."

Victory was hurt and furious, just as she'd been hurt and furious for months. She couldn't even remember when she hadn't been hurt and furious about her treatment, but she supposed that by now she should be used to it. She wasn't. She was still hurt, still missing her friends and her life that was.

She didn't think of Lewis much anymore, although he lingered in her mind occasionally, like a dream from another time. Eventually, she'd forced herself to stop thinking about something that was never meant to be. And with that decision, it was as if the life had been sucked right out of her.

Standing up from the lawn chair she'd been sitting on, she wandered to the edge of the porch, leaning against a big white column as her father pulled up in front of the house. The plantation office was off to the east, a white building several dozen yards from the house, and the trucks carrying the men headed in that direction. Victory could see the men, most of them colored, as the trucks came to a halt and the men began to climb out.

Laveau parked his car right in front of the house and climbed out, lumbering towards the porch. His men bailed out after him, carrying shotguns and other weaponry like they were expecting a small war. Some followed her father but some headed over to the trucks carrying the men. Victory watched all of the activity as Laveau came up on the steps.

"Got a good crop of men this time," he said to his wife. "We should get that north field dug up in no time."

Caroline pretended to be very interested in what he was saying. "Good," she said. "And what about our vegetable garden? Can we have a couple of men to expand it so we can plant carrots and cabbage? I might even like a fruit tree or two planted."

Laveau nodded, removing his hat and wiping at his brow with the back of his hand. "I don't see why not," he said. Then, his gaze moved to Victory, who was still looking over at the gangs of men that had arrived. "Hey. Don't you get no funny ideas, now."

Victory looked at him, puzzled by his comment. "What do you mean?"

He grunted, waving her off as if it wasn't worth the breath to repeat it. "Never you mind," he said, taking a step onto the porch and, seeing coffee on a table next to his wife, picked up a cup and sipped at it. "You stay to the house, Victory. I don't want you out and about with all of these men around. You hear me?"

Victory nodded, once again struck by the man's cruel words. "I hear you," she said. "I was just looking at how many of them there were. I haven't seen that many people in one place in a long time."

Laveau eyed his daughter. "And don't go talking to them," he said. "You're the friendly type. Don't talk to them at all."

"I won't."

Laveau gulped down what was left of his wife's coffee and went down off the porch, motioning to his henchmen as he went, that brigade of white men who always followed him around to do his bidding.

With her father off of the porch, Victory wandered back over to the pillar she had been standing by, now watching some of her father's men separate the sharecroppers into groups. She could see that they were grouping the older men and then the younger, stronger men together, and then lining them all up. The front of the line was up near the plantation office while the end of it was closer to the house.

The end of the line that was closer to the house had younger colored men; she could see them in line, speaking with Laveau's men who were keeping them in line like a string of prisoners. She was about to turn away from the sight when something caught her eye. Out of all of the men her father had brought home from the work camp, it seemed strange that one of them caught her eye but the more she looked at him, the more familiar he became. Like a vision from the past, she recognized one of those men as someone she had known very well, once.

It was Lewis.

Suddenly, the world rocked and Victory grasped the pillar to keep from falling. She could see Lewis near the very end of the line, standing long and tall and proud, his hands shoved into the pockets of his tattered overalls in a vain attempt to keep warm. He was poorly dressed against the weather and that was how she recognized him; he wasn't bundled up like some of them. He looked just the way she remembered; tall and lithe yet muscular. And his handsomeness was without dispute. Yes, it was definitely Lewis.

Victory's heart was pounding so forcefully that she could hear it in her ears. Oh, how she wanted to call out to him! She wanted to scream at him, to run to him and throw herself into his arms. The only man she had ever loved, the only man she ever would love, was standing a few dozen feet away. But she didn't dare call out to him. She didn't dare move. Yet she saw, very distinctly, when he turned in her direction.

Lewis wasn't a sharecropper; he was a janitor. Yet something must have told him to come to Glory, knowing that it would be his one and only chance to see her. Risking both his life and her life, still he had come. Now, their eyes locked and, for a moment, Victory was floating, floating in sea of astonishment where time and space had no meaning. She couldn't even breathe.

As she watched, a faint smile crept over Lewis' lips. Very faintly, his head dipped. Victory smiled in return, knowing how horribly dangerous it was to do so but unable to help herself. That one smile, just for Lewis, was an acknowledgement that the love she had for him, the joy and respect, was still there. It had never left, nor would it ever.

It was that smile that suddenly gave her the will to live again.

"Victory?" Caroline was suddenly beside her, putting her hands on her shoulders. "Are you okay?"

Victory quickly looked away from Lewis, terrified her mother would see the expressions between them.

"I... I'm tired," she said. "Will you help me inside, Mama? I don't feel very well."

Caroline put her arms around her daughter, bracing her up, and none the wiser to the fact that Victory was trying to get her off of the porch and into the house. She wanted her mother far away from Lewis just in case that simple southern woman could suddenly read minds.

"Shall I call Dr. Latling?" Caroline asked with concern as they *made their way to the front door.* "Maybe he needs to examine you."

Victory shook her head, opening up the front door as her mother practically carried her through it.

"No, Mama," she said. "I'll be fine. Just let me go to my room and lie down. I just need to rest."

It was a ploy, all of it. Caroline helped her daughter up to her room but when she offered to help her into bed, Victory insisted she was capable and chased her mother away. When the door to her bedroom shut and she was finally alone, she rushed to the front windows that overlooked the front of the yard. But her view also had the plantation office and the line of men that was still out on that lawn. Now, instead of the view bringing her horror, it brought her more peace than she could have ever imagined.

From the privacy of her bedroom, she watched Lewis until she could watch him no more, until he disappeared from her line of sight a short time later. But it didn't matter, because that moment, that blissful gift from God where she was able see Lewis one last time, was her Dreaming Hour.

She would hold that moment in her heart for the rest of her life.

CHAPTER TWENTY-NINE
Present

SLEEPING IN MAMAW'S bed hadn't been the creepy experience Lucy thought it might have been.

In fact, it had been very comforting to sleep in the bed that Mamaw had last slept in. She could imagine Mamaw laying there, singing hymns in her soft voice or scolding Aunt Vivien because she put too much baking soda in the biscuits. She felt closer to Mamaw than she ever had, lying in the bed in the dark, remembering the woman with great fondness. When the sun started coming up, she was awakened by streams of light coming in between the blinds and the wall.

Hair askew, she climbed out of bed and headed into Mamaw's ancient bathroom, which had a separate shower built in. There was an old showerhead and an even older bar of soap. Since all of her clothes were back at the hotel, Lucy had borrowed a pair of soft knit pants and a knee-length sweater from her mother until she could collect her clothing. She'd slept in her bra and panties.

After a shower with the old soap that smelled like pine, she put her mother's clothing on and opened up Mamaw's bathroom drawers until she came across a comb. Running it through her hair, she braided it and tied it off with a big rubber band she'd found in the drawers.

The house was quiet at this time of the morning. A glance at her phone showed it to be around seven-thirty. Her parents didn't seem to be up yet so she went downstairs to start the coffee. The kitchen wasn't loaded down with Presbyterian chicken anymore, most of it having either been eaten or thrown out, so she hunted around for something for breakfast. She had just found a half a loaf of white bread when she caught a glimpse of something out of the kitchen windows. The blinds were down but she could see something moving around outside. Raising one of the blinds, she saw Beau's black police unit parked next to the house.

A smile spread across her lips as she went to the back door, opening it just as Beau came up on the porch. He was dressed in street clothes today, in jeans and a collared shirt, and Lucy was pretty sure she'd never seen such a hot guy. Buying Glory and moving to Mississippi to restore it was looking better and better all the time.

"Good morning," he said, grinning. "You're up early."

Lucy unlatched the screen and pushed it open for him. "It's a good thing I am," she said. "You would have woken the entire house up if you'd knocked on the door. My parents are still in bed."

He came into the dark, cool house. "How's the bump on your head?"

She put her fingers to the bump, which had gone down considerably. "It's fine. I'll live."

"No nausea or anything?"

"No."

"That's good. How's your dad doing after everything that happened yesterday?"

Her smile faded with the shift in subject. "I don't really know," she said. "He didn't seem all that great last night when they went to bed. All he kept saying was that he turned away the baby that Mamaw had been searching for. He blames himself that Mamaw and Ruby never got to meet while Mamaw was still alive."

Beau shook his head sadly. "I can't even imagine his guilt," he said. "But that's actually why I've come. I got a call from Stephen Latling about a half hour ago."

Lucy was interested. "Oh?" she said. "What did he have to say?"

Beau sighed faintly. "It seems that Ruby is holding a grudge from that first meeting with your dad," he said. "She told Cora that she had no desire to see any of you, so she's not coming to dinner tonight."

Lucy's heart sank. "Shit," she cursed softly. "My dad said he was pretty rude to her the day he chased her away so I guess I don't blame her. Did you tell Stephen that part of the story?"

Beau nodded. "I did," he said. "He thought it would be best if your dad and Ruby hashed it out between them rather than go through intermediaries, so he's given me Ruby's address in Cleveland. Do you think your dad would be up to a trip over to her house?"

Lucy contemplated that action and quickly came to a conclusion. "No," she said. "He's really dealing with some heavy shit right now and getting verbally beaten up by a half-sister with a grudge isn't something I think he could take."

"I didn't think so."

"But I'm up to it."

He looked at her, a faint twinkle in his blue eyes. "Somehow, I had a feeling you were going to say that."

Lucy motioned him to follow her back into the kitchen. "I think I need to be the one to see if I can straighten this out," she said. "My dad made a genuine mistake sending her away those years ago so maybe I can help her understand that. I've got to try, anyway. Can you take me over to the hotel so I can change? I hate to ask you, but my car is still over there."

"Why do you think I came by so early?"

She chuckled. "Do you double as an Uber drive in that unit?"

He snorted. "Only on the special occasions," he said, "and this is definitely that."

Lucy pointed to the coffee pot, percolating away. "I just put the coffee on if you want some," she said. "I'll just be a minute. I need to grab my purse."

He waved her off and she dashed out of the kitchen, scooting up the big back staircase and making her way swiftly and silently to Mamaw's front bedroom. She still didn't hear anything stirring in her parents' bedroom so she quickly ducked into Mamaw's bedroom and collected her possessions – her clothing from the day before, her scuffed Jimmy Choos, her briefcase, and her purse.

She was just about to skip out when she realized she'd left something very important behind. Dropping her stuff back on the bed, she went over to the old chifforobe and opened the top drawer, pulling out the old wooden box that contained the locket. She even looked inside to make sure it was there. Dropping it into her purse, she picked up all of her things and was nearing the door when a vision struck her.

On the table next to Mamaw's bed were a few family photos, but one in particular was a picture of Mamaw when she had been young. It was one of those posed studio shots, probably some kind of graduation photo, but it was of a young Mamaw when her skin was like cream and her auburn hair stylishly curled. Something told her to take it, so Lucy grabbed that picture and quietly made her way back downstairs.

Beau was leaning against the counter, sipping at a mug of very hot coffee when she came back in. The moment he saw her, however, he set the coffee down.

"Ready?" he asked.

She nodded. "Ready."

Without another word, they headed out to his car and took off towards the hotel on the other side of town.

✧ ✧ ✧

HI. I'M LUCY BONDURANT. *My dad is the one who threw you off the property at Glory.*

Hi. My name is Lucy Bondurant. My grandmother is your birth mother. Wait, Ruby – don't you want to hear this before you bodily throw me off of your porch?

All of those crazy thoughts were rolling through Lucy's head, ways to introduce herself to a woman who had made it clear she didn't want anything to do with her biological family. Lucy sighed heavily.

"How do I even start this conversation?" she asked Beau. "The second Ruby sees me, she's probably going to figure out who I am. How can I get all of this out before she sets her dog on me?"

They were about ten minutes out of Cleveland, Mississippi. Beau had put the address of Ruby Ransom in his car's navigation and the car was talking to them every so often as they drew closer.

After returning to the hotel and quickly changing clothes and styling her hair so she didn't look like a crazy bag lady, Beau and Lucy had taken off for the Ransom house. It was early in the morning, early enough that they were hoping to catch Ruby at home before she started her day.

But Lucy was nervous. As she put on lipstick and mascara in the car, she was wracking her brain for the right thing to say to Ruby when she first saw her. She knew the woman didn't want to see her or her family, but this was something she had to do. This was what she'd been searching for, the moment she'd prayed would happen before she had to head back home to Los Angeles. It was odd; it had only been a matter of days but it felt as if she'd been looking for Ruby her entire life. This was such a pivotal time in her life. She was distressed that Ruby wouldn't feel the same way.

"I've been thinking about that, too," Beau said in answer to her question. "If you'd like me to talk to her first, I'll do that. I'll flash my badge and maybe that'll help."

Lucy looked at him. "Help what?" she asked. "You'll throw her in jail if she doesn't talk to me?"

"If you want me to."

Lucy giggled, turning back to the compact she had in her hand and putting the last of her lipstick on. "I don't think that would be good for your public relations," she said. "But if you're willing, I'm happy to stand behind you while you talk to her first. Maybe she won't knee-jerk react to my presence if you've had a chance to soften her. Thank you for offering."

He glanced at his in-car navigation to see that they were about to make a turn. "You're welcome," he said. "I've been trained in negotiation. That's what this is – a negotiation."

Lucy put the lipstick away and the compact back in her purse. "It is," she agreed. "I only hope I can say what I need to say before she throws something at me."

"She's not going to throw anything at you."

Lucy looked at him, hearing another one of those chivalrous declarations. This boy from the south was full of them, a southern gentleman like they didn't make them anymore. She smiled faintly.

"Thank you for taking your time to drive me over here," she said. "It just wouldn't have seemed right reaching out to Ruby without you."

He made a left turn, following the directions on the navigation. "I was off today. It wasn't any trouble."

"Where are your kids?"

"They spent the night at my parents' house. They're probably eating pancakes right now."

Lucy's gaze lingered on him a moment before facing forward, watching the residential streets come into view. "I wish I was," she muttered. "Will your mom make some for me, too, when this is all over?"

He grinned, lopsided. "She'd cook for you until you burst."

"Will she make them with a shot of bourbon? Because that's what I'm going to need when this is over."

"She'll make them with Xanax if you want her to."

Lucy laughed as she put her purse aside. "My kind of woman," she said, looking at the street signs. "What street are we looking for?"

"College," he said. "Then to Tenth Street. She's on Tenth."

College Street came, a residential street for the most part, and then a short while later, he made the turn onto Tenth. Now they were in a typical middle class neighborhood. Lucy found herself sitting further and further back in the seat, her stomach in knots as they found the house number and Beau pulled over to the curb.

The home was a neat brick house with a pretty glass door. The yard was nicely kept and there was a stone bench seat near some camellia bushes. Beau turned off the car and looked at her.

"Well," he said. "I'm going in."

Lucy could only nod, not up to the usual repartee that they seemed to have. She was vastly nervous, her palms sweating and her stomach twisting. She sat in the car, even going so far as to push the sat back so she couldn't be seen through the passenger window. She could, however, see from the back seat window, watching as Beau made his way up to the porch and rang the bell.

Lucy held her breath. After several seconds, no one answered the door so he rang it again and waited. He had to do it twice more and still no answer. He took to knocking on the glass door, but he received no answer.

Lucy's heart sank. As nervous as she was, she didn't want this to be a wasted trip. She very much wanted to see Ruby Ransom, to at least get a look at the woman. She knew the woman's entire life story, and the story of her conception, so in a sense, she was an almost surreal character. A woman who had been the result of an illicit love affair, a woman who very nearly didn't live to grow up. Lucy had been building her up so much in her mind that she realized she was very disappointed when no one answered the door.

Finally, after the fifth ring of the bell, it was clear no one was home and Lucy was resigned to the fact that she wouldn't be meeting Ruby any time soon. They'd driven an hour from Pea Ridge and she didn't want to give up so easily, so maybe she could talk Beau into taking her for breakfast somewhere nearby and then they'd come back to try again. Just as Beau was coming off the porch and heading for the car, a small white sedan pulled into the driveway.

Lucy perked up, straining to catch a glimpse of who was in the driver's seat. Beau politely stood on the walkway, not wanting to go near the car and possibly scare whoever was driving it, so he simply stood there as the sedan door opened.

A woman climbed out with a bag of groceries in her hand and Lucy took a very good look at her; she was elderly, thin and well dressed, and her white hair was cropped very close against her head. Lucy saw clearly when she spoke to Beau, although she couldn't hear what was being said, and Beau held out a business card to the woman so she would know he wasn't a masher. The woman took the card from him and read it.

As Lucy watched from the car, heart in her throat, she saw as Beau spoke to the woman. Mostly, she found herself watching the woman and realizing how much she looked like Mamaw. The high cheekbones, the long jaw... everything about the woman screamed of Victory Hembree and Lucy found herself getting very emotional. Her eyes filled with tears at the realization of who she was looking at – Ruby Ransom in the flesh.

The baby, finally, had been found.

Lucy found herself praying that Beau was at least able to convince Ruby to listen to what she had to say, but as she watched, Ruby began to shake her head, holding up her hand to Beau as if to silence him. Then she was moving away from him, towards her house, carrying her groceries and shaking her head.

No, no, no....

Before she even realized what she was doing, Lucy grabbed her grandmother's picture from her purse and yanked open the car door, rushing towards Ruby as the woman headed to her porch. Ruby was saying something to Beau that Lucy couldn't quite hear but she could tell simply from the body language that it wasn't good. Her composure left her as she rushed towards the woman, close enough to speak with her.

"Wait," she said quickly. "Wait, please. My name is Lucy Bondurant and it was my father who chased you away from Glory. Ruby, he's so sorry he did that. He regrets it terribly. But you have to understand that...."

Ruby, startled by the appearance of a young woman rushing at her, took a hasty step onto her porch. "Hold on, there," she said, holding out a hand to her. "Now, Miss Lucy Bondurant, you can get right back in that car and go back to Pea Ridge. I was very clear with Dr. Latling that I had no interest in speaking with you or your family. I already tried that a few years ago and got yelled at for my efforts, so you can just get on out of here."

Lucy shook her head, feeling desperate. "You don't understand," she said. "My dad told you to go away because he thought you were his grandfather's bastard. He had no idea you were...."

"A black bastard," Ruby said loudly. "I understand perfectly. No Hembree wants a black bastard as part of the family, so you just go back to your white folks and forget about me. I won't be bothering you again."

Lucy looked at Ruby as if the woman had physically struck her. "Is *that* what you think?" she said. "That he chased you away because you were black? That's not it at all. He had no idea you were his mother's daughter – he thought you were one of his grandfather's many bastards and he was just trying to protect his mother, who was ill at the time. It had nothing to do with black and white."

Ruby snorted; she wasn't buying it. "Honey, this is Mississippi," she said. "No old white family wants to acknowledge any black relations."

Lucy stared at the woman, seeing the walls of defense up, feeling her pain in a sense. It was enough to bring tears to her eyes again. But it also brought tremendous outrage.

"That's the most ignorant statement I've ever heard," she said hoarsely. "If you had any idea of the love between your biological parents, a black man and a white woman who happened to be my grandmother, you wouldn't say that. Look at this –" She held up the picture of Victory, taking a step or two towards Ruby as she extended it for the woman to see. "This is your birth mother, Miss Victory Jewel Hembree Bondurant. Take a good look at her because she risked everything for you."

Ruby stared at the picture of a woman she shared similar features with. She seemed to falter. "I don't need to see that," she said, averting her eyes as if beholding something horrendously painful. "I don't want to see that. You need to leave *now*."

Lucy was trembling with emotion. "I'll go," she said. "But you're going to hear me out first. Victory Hembree fell in love with a colored man in nineteen hundred and thirty-three, a man she loved with all her heart. This man wrote her poetry the likes of which you've never seen and she loved him until the day she died. They wanted to marry but biracial marriages were illegal in Mississippi back then, so her father kept her locked in her room until she delivered you and then a doctor risked his life to take you to safety. A *white* doctor, Ruby. You want to make this all about black and white? Then let's do that."

Ruby's eyes were closed, her hand on her front door knob. "*Stop!*"

Lucy wouldn't; it was all coming out now and she couldn't control it. "For God's sake, a black man was even murdered because of you," she said passionately. "A man who happened to be in the wrong place at the wrong time. He *died* because of you. You don't know the half of your story, Ruby Ransom, but I am telling you it has nothing to do with being black or white. It has everything to do with a love that has withstood the test of time. Damn you for walking away from this. You're not worthy of the people who risked their lives for you if you think this all boils down to race."

With that, the tears streamed down her face and she turned around, heading back to car. She was sobbing by the time she climbed back into the vehicle, slamming the door and weeping bitterly with Victory's picture clutched to her chest.

The silence she left behind between Ruby and Beau was palpable. It was full of grief and sorrow. Beau, his heart aching for Lucy and the dead end she'd come to, simply dipped his head at Ruby in a silent farewell and headed back to his car.

As he pulled away from the curb, the last he saw was of Ruby still standing on her front porch with her grocery bags in hand. But he didn't look any more than that. He was more concerned for Lucy at the moment. Gently, he put a hand on her lowered head.

Truthfully, he didn't know what to say. He simply stroked her lowered head, tenderly, knowing how heartbroken she was.

"I'm so sorry," he finally said. "I wish I could have done more."

Lucy grasped his hand, holding it tightly. "You've done so much already," she said, struggling to regain her composure. "I can't believe that everything Mamaw hoped for is at an end. She wanted to find her baby, she wanted the baby to have her locket, but I'll be damned if I give that bitter old woman that locket. She'd probably throw it in the trash."

He squeezed her hand. "You tried," he said. "You did everything you could, Lucy. You fulfilled what Ms. Victory asked of you. Don't beat yourself up over an angry old woman."

Lucy was huddled back against the seat, holding his hand tightly, still clutching Victory's picture against her chest. "She thinks this is really about race?" she said. "Honest to God, that never even occurred to me. Where I come from… we just don't see race like people do here. I went to school with African Americans and count several among my close friends, so this kind of attitude… I just don't get it. I don't like it."

He sighed faintly. "Old prejudices die hard," he said. "Especially down here. California is a little more liberal, but here in Mississippi, things are just different. In fact, when I went away to college, I met a girl who just lit me up. She was smart and beautiful and funny. She was also Japanese. We started dating and I brought her home for Thanksgiving my first year away and although my parents didn't say anything about her race, other family members did. She knew it, too. We didn't date for too much longer after that, needless to say. That was a truly heartbreaking moment for me."

Lucy was looking at him as he spoke. "I'm so sorry," she said, sniffling. "That just sucks."

"Yes, it does."

Lucy remained huddled against the car seat as the car sped along the highway back to Pea Ridge, still holding Beau's hand, her thoughts drifting back to Ruby Ransom and the sadness she felt at the animosity from the woman. But as she pondered their encounter, one thing became clear to her.

"You know what?" she finally said. "I'm glad this happened. I'm glad we found out what kind of woman Ruby Ransom really was. I don't want her being part of my family. We don't need or want that kind of intolerance. But I have to say that considering where she came from and the people who risked everything to make sure she came into the world, I am really disappointed for Mamaw and Lewis and Aldridge and Dr. Latling. Hell, Aldridge *died* because of that woman – is that fair to him that she behaves like that?"

Beau shook his head. "No," he said quietly. "But everything happens for a reason. Remember what we've been saying? Maybe we can't see that reason now and maybe we don't know why Ruby is as embittered as she is, but there's got to be a reason for it all."

"Even for the trip to Cleveland?"

"Even that," he said firmly. "Had you never come, you would have never known."

"That's true."

He glanced over at her, smiling encouragingly and squeezing her fingers. "So how about if I take you over to my folks' house and let my mom make you pancakes with bourbon and Xanax?"

She smiled weakly, knowing he was trying to cheer her up. "Maybe tomorrow," she said. "Right now, I'd really like to go back to the hotel and take a hot bath. I've got a lot of thinking to do."

He nodded. "Sure," he said. "I have a few things I could be doing, too, considering I've ignored my work for the past few days. I've got paperwork on my desk like you can't believe."

Lucy looked over at him, the smile still on her lips. "I can believe it," she said, "because that same paperwork is piling up on my desk back in Los Angeles."

He shrugged. "If you never go back, someone else will do it."

"Who says I'm never going back?"

"Me. You're buying Glory and restoring it, remember?"

Lucy laughed softly. Truth was, she didn't have the heart to refute him this time and she realized, as she looked at him, that she was finished resisting him. He was kind, and attentive, and all shades of sexy. Impulsively, she leaned over and she deposited a warm, gentle kiss on his right cheek, but it wasn't any kiss – she lingered on his skin a moment, her lips against his flesh, kissing him twice before moving to his jaw and kissing him there, too. It was as alluring as it could be, moist and lingering.

"Thank you," she whispered, her lips against his flesh. "For everything you've done for me, thank you."

Beau groaned. "Sweet Baby Jesus," he hissed. "That's just not fair. I'm driving and I can't reciprocate."

"Do you want to?" she asked breathlessly.

"If you let me pull the car over, I'll show you how much."

She laughed softly and pulled away from him, settling back in her seat. "I don't think it would look too good for the Sheriff of Tallahatchie County to be seen making out in his car," she said. "We can revisit this when you take me back to the hotel."

He looked at her, then. "Seriously?"

Lucy could see that he was all shook up, a glittering look to his eye that she hadn't seen before. Gone was any self-restraint she put on herself because the truth was that Beau Meade was hot as hell and she wanted a piece of him. She had since the first time they'd met, but he'd never been sexier than he was now when trying to comfort her about Ruby. That moment, in of itself, was enough to finally break her down.

She was ready for him.

"Seriously," she said, a twinkle in her eye. "You've flirted and charmed your way enough so that I've received your message loud and clear."

He grinned. "It's about time."

"I just didn't want you to think I was easy."

"I thought you were dumb and blind. Either that, or I'd lost my touch."

She shook her head, giggling. "You haven't lost your touch."

"Care to test that theory out?"

When they got back to the hotel, they did. All afternoon.

CHAPTER THIRTY
~ Evil Is as Evil Does ~

"**M**AMA? DADDY? I'D *like to ask you something.*"
It was suppertime at Glory on a fine evening in May when the air was starting to warm for the onslaught of summer. Victory was seated at the big dining table with her father on one end and her mother on the other. Laveau was well into his second bourbon while Caroline had hardly touched her stew that contained chicken, pork, and butterbeans. Laveau looked up from his bourbon when his daughter spoke.

"*What is it?*" he asked, none too eager to know.

Victory was nicely dressed for dinner in a soft white dress with her auburn hair pulled back. She had been genuinely trying to make an effort as of late because she wanted something from her parents. Therefore, she was putting on a show of being a good, obedient girl.

"I would like to go to the Gore Springs Girls Academy in the autumn," she said politely. "It might be better, you know… not returning to a school like Pea Ridge where all the girls are talking about me. It would be better to start at a school where I don't know anyone. I'd like to make new friends."

Caroline looked at her, puzzled. "But I thought you loved Pea Ridge and Mr. Franklin," she said. "In fact, I saw the man at the market last week and he asked to your health. I told him you were just fine and that you'd be going back to school in the fall."

Victory shook her head. "I don't want to go back there, Mama," she said, appealing to her father. "Daddy, Dell told me that they've said all kinds of terrible things about me there. I can't go back and face those horrible girls. Can I please go to Gore Springs?"

Laveau actually seemed interested in what she had to say, but considering the man was bothered by anybody who said anything about him or his family, it wasn't surprising.

"What are they saying?" he asked.

Victory thought that she needed to be truthful with him to emphasize her point. "Awful things," she said. "The girls over there are saying I'm crazy and that's why you won't allow me back at school. But some of them... Daddy, they're saying terrible things about you and why you like to keep me here at home, and if I go back to school, I'll just slap them all silly. Please let me go to Gore Springs. No one knows me there and it will be much better for me."

Laveau scratched his chin. "They're saying terrible things about me, are they?"

"Yes, Daddy."

"Dell told you that?"

"Yes, Daddy."

"But she didn't tell you what?"

Victory shook her head. "Not really," she said. "All I know was that they were not very nice things."

Laveau looked at his bourbon a moment. Then, he took another drink. "I must say that I'm disappointed to hear that Mr. Franklin is allowing that school to become a hotbed of gossip," he said. "I thought he had a better school than that."

"Then I don't have to go back?"

Laveau moved to pour himself more liquor. "Your mama will go see to the school in Gore Springs," he said. "If she likes it, then you can go there."

Victory smiled with relief. "Thank you, Daddy," she said. "I promise to work hard and get good grades. I'll make you proud."

Laveau didn't look at her as he lifted his glass to his lips again.

"That would be a first," he muttered. "But I don't like that those girls over at Pea Ridge are spreading gossip. That disturbs me."

Deeply hurt by his comment, Victory lowered her head and went back to her food. It wouldn't do to cry or cause a scene, not when she had what she wanted. New friends and no gossip. Girls who didn't know her or her family. Gore Springs was about an hour away, but it didn't matter. It would be a much better place for her to get an education. Her father was known to go back on his word, so she kept her mouth shut and finished her stew, relieved that she would be starting a new school in the fall.

"Don't bother yourself with those girls, Laveau," Caroline said from across the table. "They're just children. It doesn't matter what they say."

Laveau looked at her. "They have parents who may hear what they say," he said. "That just won't do. After supper, you get Dell over here. I want to hear what those girls have said."

Victory knew what that meant. Poor Dell would now have to face Laveau and tell him what she'd told Victory. Not that Victory felt too sorry for her gossiping cousin. Maybe it was time to put the fear of God into her a little bit so she'd learn to keep her mouth shut in the future.

Dell and her mother, Sedelia, came over about an hour later. Up in her bedroom, Victory could hear Dell crying as Laveau interrogated her. The questioning went on well into the night and Victory even heard slapping sounds, and Dell screaming, and she knew that Dell was being spanked. By Laveau or by her mother, she didn't know, but she was very glad she wasn't Dell Alexander that night.

But the night passed, Dell and her mother went home, and Laveau never said another word about the Pea Ridge Female Academy until four days later when she heard him mention that it was a tragedy that the school had burned down the night before. Everything had been lost, Laveau told Caroline, and it was truly a shame that so fine a school had been reduced to ashes.

Victory had a feeling she knew how Mr. J. Duncan Franklin's school was no more.

CHAPTER THIRTY-ONE

Present

Two Days Later

IN YOGA PANTS and a tank top, with her hair all wound up on top of her head, Lucy stood at the kitchen window, looking at the yard beyond. Her parents were out running errands and she was alone in the house on a gentle morning, enjoying the peace and quiet of it.

After her encounter with Ruby, she'd gathered her things from the hotel and returned to Glory to stay for the remainder of her trip. She didn't want to be away from the old house anymore. Something drew her back to it, the old homestead of her ancestors, and she didn't want to leave.

In fact, she didn't even want to go home to Los Angeles but she knew she had to, at least for a little while. But she'd made up her mind on that sex-filled afternoon with Beau two days ago that she was going to, indeed, buy Glory from her dad and restore it. Beau had promised he would help her and the thought of restoring an old home with him filled her with excitement beyond anything she could have ever imagined. The fairy tale she thought she'd lost when Kevin had walked out the door had returned, full-force, in the form of Beau Meade. Lucy never believed she could be so happy again.

So, she brought it up to her parents the day before, a solid offer to buy the home. Bill didn't seem too keen on the idea but when

Beau showed up later that night and sat around with Lucy and her parents, playing a card game with the three of them because there was no television in the house and no internet, he began to see why Lucy wanted to come back to Pea Ridge and take on the massive project of restoring the old house. There was something going on between Beau and Lucy, although it was very subtle, and Bill couldn't have been happier. So what if his daughter wanted to fill up her time with the restoration of an old house? Now, there was a better reason for her to do it.

A certain sheriff who seemed quite fond of her.

Staring out of the kitchen window with a mug of coffee in her hand, Lucy grinned when she thought of her mother and father bickering gently about Beau Meade and the event of some kind of romance. Lucy wouldn't confirm it but she wouldn't deny it, even though she was bursting to. She liked Beau a great deal but she didn't want her parents to know *how* much she liked him. They'd only known each other a few days and she didn't want her parents to think she was rushing into anything. Maybe she was, but that was too bad. She hadn't been this happy in a very long time.

A breeze was pushing the trees around outside the kitchen window and she could see the branches swaying in the wind. She thought she remembered someone talking about the fact that a storm was coming but, so far, the sky remained clear. She didn't have much for the day planned other than maybe helping her parents as they continued to clean out the house, although Beau had mentioned something about having lunch or dinner together. Knowing him, probably both. She didn't mind in the least.

With mug in hand, she wandered through the butler's pantry and into the front dining room with the big floor-to-ceiling windows that overlooked the front yard. She thought about everything that had happened since she came to Mississippi, a somber trip that had turned into so much more than she'd bargained for – a death, a new romance, and old family mysteries had come to light, including a new family member that didn't want anything to do with them.

In fact, Lucy didn't even tell her parents about her encounter with Ruby. Given how her dad felt about the entire thing, she didn't think he'd be able to take it, so she kept that incident tucked away, to be told to him at another time when he was stronger. More than that, it really didn't matter in the grand scheme of things – Bill knew what he needed to know, and that was that he had an older half-sister from his mother, and he knew of his mother's love affair with Ruby's father. He knew what his mother went through and he knew even more of the evils of his grandfather. At the moment, that was really all he needed to know. Lucy didn't see the point of burdening him further.

The wind was blowing a little harder now and, looking up at the sky, she could see clouds beginning to scatter across the horizon. As she walked into the entry, upstairs, she could hear her cell phone faintly ringing.

Taking the steep front stairs, she ended up in Mamaw's bedroom, where she'd been sleeping, in time to see that she'd missed a call from Beau. Hitting the redial, she called him back. He picked up on the second ring.

"Hey," she said. "It's Lucy. You called?"

"Hey, sugar," he said. Ever since their sizzling encounter in the hotel, he'd been calling by that pet name, which she thought was pretty dang cute. "Everything okay?"

"Yes," she said. "Why wouldn't it be?"

He grunted. "Well, I've got some not-so-good news," he said. "Your cousin, Clyde, made bail this morning. I just wanted to make sure he hasn't shown up at the house to cause trouble."

"No, he hasn't," she said, sounding disappointed. "I thought the district attorney was going to file sexual assault and battery against him?"

A pause on the other end of the phone. "You're not going to

like this. Because Clyde has no criminal background, the D.A. filed common assault. Clyde's out on bail and he'll probably only get community service for what he did."

"What the hell?" she said, outraged. "When did this happen?"

"Yesterday. I just found out about it this morning when the paperwork crossed my desk."

Now, she was getting fired up. "That's ridiculous. It's not common assault. I have the bump on my head to prove it."

Beau was clearly reluctant to tell her the all of it. "Well, based on the fact that you refused to go to the hospital right away and the fact that Clyde has no criminal record, the charges were reduced to common assault and Clyde was released on bail this morning," he said. "I'm sorry, Lucy. I know he did more than that but the district attorney and the judge didn't see it that way. Anyway, I'll have a patrol run by the house every hour or so, just to make sure he stays away. I can't imagine he's too happy about having been in jail for the past few days."

Lucy was disgusted as well as angry. "If he comes near me again, he'll be lucky if pepper spraying him is all I do. I can't believe they reduced the charges like that. Thanks a hell of a lot, Mississippi Justice System."

Without much to say to that, Beau changed the subject. "How about lunch today?" he asked, sounding like he was offering her a consolation prize. "I'll come a little early, around eleven?"

Lucy was still lingering on Clyde's release. "Sure," she said without much enthusiasm. "I'll see you in a bit."

"Okay."

She hung up the phone, standing there for a few moments with it in her hand as she pondered her creepy cousin and the failure of justice as she saw it.

"Well, that just *sucks*," she muttered to herself.

Tossing the phone on the bed, she headed back downstairs to refill her coffee cup. All the while, she was mulling over the fact that

Clyde was now out on bail. Would he stay away from her? Or would he try to contact her again, now blaming her for him having ended up in jail? Although she'd known him her whole life, she really didn't know him as a person. They'd never had an in-depth conversation and they'd never hung out for any length of time. He'd been creepy even as a child and wasn't someone her parents or Mamaw allowed her to really play with. The only reason she was ever around him was because his mama was a cousin and family gatherings brought them together.

Truthfully, she wasn't frightened of him and not at all worried that he would try to contact her again. She was fairly certain she could take care of him if he tried, the same way she'd beat the crap out of him when he'd grabbed her at the hotel. She hoped that would be enough deterrent for Clyde McKibben.

The back door of the house was open, with just the screen closed, letting some of that cool breeze into the house and helping blow away some of the old, musty smell of it. Lucy paused by the screen door, looking out over the back yard, which really wasn't much of a yard. Most of the property of Glory was the front and side yards, with the house backed up almost to the rear property line.

Moving back into the kitchen, she was starting to think of food along with the coffee and she opened up the old refrigerator to see what was left of Mamaw's funeral food. No more chicken at all but there were a couple of casseroles, tightly wrapped, on the bottom shelf.

Setting her coffee mug down, she bent over to pull out the casseroles and see what they were, peeling up the edge of the cling wrap and sticking her finger into them. One was pasta and the other one had a flavor like taco pie. Thinking that taco pie might be good for breakfast, she was just pulling it out when something heavy hit her across the back of the skull.

The taco pie dish clattered to the floor and Lucy along with it.

A few things fell out of the refrigerator as well, falling on the floor in a great racket as she hit the refrigerator on her way to the floor. Half-conscious, she struggled to come around, hardly realizing when someone grabbed her by the leg and pulled her away from the refrigerator and out into the middle of the kitchen floor. Then, someone was touching her thigh.

Lucy wasn't quite lucid but her sense of self-survival kicked in and she began to fight, kicking and swinging her arms, thrashing violently against what was a blurry figure at this point. Head swimming, sight blurred, the blackness of unconsciousness threatened but she fought against that, too, shaking her head, trying to right her vision. She couldn't even see what she was fighting against but she knew, instinctively, that she was in a good deal of trouble. Fear clutched at her.

"Stop, *stop!*" a male voice said as hands tried to touch her, grabbing at her arms and legs as she kicked about. "You don't need to fight, Lucy. Stop kicking!"

Oh, God… *she knew that voice*!

Feeling sick and dizzy, Lucy began to fight harder, knowing that somehow, someway, Clyde had come into the house. It was his voice she heard, echoing in her swimming head like a nightmare. Jesus, she'd been standing right by the back door and hadn't seen a thing outside. She hadn't heard anything at all, not a sound of footsteps or the creak of a door. Not a damn thing! In a panic, she struggled to roll away from him as he continued to try and touch her.

"Get the hell away from me!" she snarled. "Get the *fuck* away from me, you asshole! Don't you touch me!"

Clyde was standing there with the instrument he'd used to knock her over the head with, a copper sauce pan that had been hanging by the stove with several other hanging pans, right by the door that led to the back porch. Pots like that made perfect weapons and when he'd come into the house, he'd found one quickly. Mamaw's pot storage had made that all too easy for him.

"I don't want to hurt you," Clyde insisted, trying to grab her hand as she slapped him away. "I could have knocked you out, but I didn't. See? I don't want to hurt you but you need to listen to me. You never listen to me, Lucy, and now it's gotten us into all kinds of trouble. Why don't you ever want to be friendly to me?"

Lucy was coming around a bit now, at least well enough that her vision was starting to clear. She had a hand up against the back of her aching head and her ears were ringing as she ended up huddled against the cabinets, cowering from Clyde as he stood there with the pot in his hand.

"You son-of-a-bitch," she hissed. "I'm going to charge you with everything I can think of and you won't be getting out of jail after this. What in the hell is wrong with you? I told you I don't want to talk to you. I told you to stay the hell away from me. What part of that didn't you understand?"

Clyde still hadn't dropped the pot, which concerned Lucy. He could easily use it again. He looked at her as if he really had no idea what she meant.

"All I want to do is *talk* to you," he repeated.

"I don't want to talk to you!"

His brow furrowed. "Why not?" he asked, growing edgy. "I've never given you no reason to be mean to me! Why are you so mean to me?"

He was waving the pot around as he spoke and Lucy didn't want to be hit again because she was woozy enough. She was coming to think that it would be in her best interest to keep things calm, at least for a minute or two until she could shake off the effects of that saucepan against her head. But once she felt strong enough, she was going to beat the shit out of him. This time, he wouldn't walk away because she had a feeling, right now, he fully intended to do far worse to her than he'd done to her in the parking lot.

She could see it in his eyes.

God, this old house had seen so much evil in it. Laveau and his evil still clung to the house like a film, covering everything, embedded in the very walls. One more evil within these old walls would just add to that film, solidifying it, turning this place into a true house of horrors. Lucy thought too much of the house and all of the good memories there to let one more act of violence hurt it. It wasn't in her nature to surrender.

She had to fight.

"Fine," she said, her voice trembling with rage. "What do you want to talk about?"

Clyde looked rather surprised by her reaction. "I just wanted to talk to you."

"So talk."

He crouched down a few feet away from her, the pot still in hand. Lucy eyed it warily because he didn't seem inclined to put it down. Furthermore, she didn't seem to be feeling much better. The bump on her head a few days ago, now coupled with a fairly serious blow, and she felt hugely nauseous and unsteady. Even if she could fight him, she wasn't sure how well she could do it. For the first time, Lucy began to feel the pangs of panic.

"You're such a pretty woman," Clyde said, looking at her in a way that made her skin crawl. "Why wouldn't you talk to me on the night of Ms. Victory's funeral? You ran away from me."

Lucy was coming to think there was something seriously the matter with Clyde, like he had a screw loose. She'd heard Beau mention that once but she didn't give much thought to it until now. He was talking like a serial killer did, gently and kindly, before ramming a knife down his next victim's throat.

"I had just lost Mamaw," she said. "I wasn't feeling sociable."

Clyde reached out and touched her foot, which she quickly yanked back. He frowned. "You felt sociable enough to talk to Sheriff Meade," he pointed out. "Don't lie to me."

Lucy tried to move away from him as best she could, but the cabinets were behind her and next to them was the wall. She was, literally, cornered and trying not to give in to the terror that was slowly building in her chest.

"He happened to be here," she said. "I didn't go out of my way to talk to him. And I told you not to touch me."

Clyde stood up now. "You can't tell me what to do," he said, a rumble of hazard in his tone. "You did a lot of terrible things to me, being mean to me and then having me arrested. You had no right to do that."

Lucy tried to stand up but he swung that saucepan at her again, barely missing her head. She fell back to the floor and crawled away, trying to get some distance from him as he followed.

"Clyde, if you hit me with that pan again, I'm going to make sure you stay in jail forever," she threatened, although her voice was quivering. "You need to get out of here. My parents are going to be back any moment and if they find you here, my dad is going to hurt you. Do you understand me? Don't you even get that what you did to me was wrong?"

Clyde was stalking her; for every inch she moved away from him, he closed the gap. "It's your fault," he said. "If you didn't want me to talk to you, you wouldn't dress the way you do or look the way you do. Look at what you're wearing now; it's sexy."

Lucy was losing control of her fear because the look in his eye was seriously predatory. *I can't believe this. I'm going to get raped by this freak!* "I'm in my own home wearing pajamas," she said loudly. "I'm not out in public dressed like this! Get the hell out of here, Clyde. I'm not going to tell you again. I'm going to start screaming my head off and everybody is going to hear me."

Clyde shook his head. "No," he said frankly. "You won't do anything. I'm going to show you why you should talk to me, Lucy. Once you see what I can do, you won't be mean to me anymore."

Lucy was horrified. "Don't you even think it," she said. "I want you to get the hell out of here now. If you leave now, I won't tell my parents you were here but if you stay, if you try something, so help me I'll tell everybody and have your stupid ass thrown in jail!"

So much for trying to keep the situation calm. Without warning, Clyde came down on top of her and tried to hit her in the head with the saucepan again. Lucy held her hands up, trying to protect her head, and trying with all of her might to kick him in the groin.

A hell of a struggle went on as Clyde tried to brain her and she tried to land a foot in his crotch and, all the while, Lucy was getting pummeled pretty hard by that copper pot. It was heavy and it hurt. He lifted it at one point and tried to grab her hair, but she made contact with his belly with a hard kick.

Momentarily stunned, Clyde fell off of her and Lucy scrambled to her knees, struggling to her feet so she could make a run for it, but Clyde grabbed her by the foot again and pulled her back. She fell onto the floor, hard, and he climbed right up over her as she lay on her belly.

Now, she was in a position she definitely didn't want to be in as Clyde used his body weight to keep her down. He put a forearm across the back of her neck, pinning her, as a hand reached around her torso and squeezed her right breast.

"You'll like it," he said, saliva on his lips. "Don't fight me anymore because you'll like what I do. The women always do."

Lucy twisted and fought as much as she could, but he had her pinned good as he used his body weight on his arm to pin her head down. In fact, she was starting to black out because she couldn't breathe. There was too much weight on her neck. She began to scream and yell, at least as much as she was able, and Clyde tried to put his fist in her mouth. She bit him and he slapped her.

"Lucy, *stop*," he commanded, trying to hike her tank top up from behind. "I want you to like this, but you have to stop fighting."

There was too much pressure on her neck and Lucy knew she

was about to pass out. She couldn't breathe and the blood flow was being impeded. She couldn't even swallow the way he had her neck angled and spit dripped from her mouth to the floor.

"Clyde," she begged, voice raspy. "Get the hell off of me!"

Her hoarse voice had no impact on him. He continued to pull her tank top up from behind, reaching around again to touch the underside of her exposed breast. Just as Lucy began to slip into unconsciousness, a loud thumping echoed off of the kitchen walls.

Clyde instantly went limp.

Lucy was very nearly unconscious but she heard two more thumping sounds, like something hitting heavily against a hollow surface. An eternity of silence followed, or at least it seemed like an eternity. Lucy was trying to crawl away but she wasn't doing a very good job. Then, someone rolled her onto her back.

"Ms. Lucy?" It was a woman's anxious voice. "Oh, my God. Ms. Lucy, can you hear me?"

Lucy was struggling to breathe now that the pressure was off of her. She was only semi-coherent. "Help me," she muttered. "Please... help me."

"It's okay, honey," the woman said softly. "You're going to be okay. He's not going to hurt you again."

"He... he tried to kill me."

"I know, honey. I saw."

Lucy didn't say anything more after that. Blissful blackness closed in on her.

✧ ✧ ✧

THE CRACKLE OF police and fire radios were the next things Lucy was aware of.

Coming out of unconsciousness to the sound of soft chatter, Lucy flinched, a reflex reaction to the noise and light. Hands were on her, holding her steady.

"Easy," a soft, deep voice whispered steadily. "Take it easy, sugar. You're going to be okay."

A man's voice. The last thing Lucy remembered, she had been fighting for her life with a man, with Clyde, so she suddenly began kicking and swinging her arms. Many hands stilled her again, trying to keep her from moving around, and that deep voice was in her ear again.

"It's okay," Beau said gently but firmly. "Lucy, you're okay now. Nothing is going to hurt you. Stop fighting, okay? There's no need. I'm here."

Coming through the cobwebs of unconsciousness, Lucy's eyes opened to his anxious face looking down at her. It took her a moment to recognize him. Then, her first reaction was one of terror.

"Clyde!" she suddenly gasped, throwing her arms around his neck and nearly pulling him down on top of her. "He's here! He tried to kill me!"

Beau was in an awkward position the way she had him. In her fear, she was nearly strangling him. "I know," he said steadily, his big hands caressing her in a comforting gesture. "I promise, he won't hurt you again, okay? I won't let that happen. I've got him now and he's not getting away, not ever again. Do you understand me?"

Lucy still held on to him with a death grip and Beau let her hang on to him for a moment longer before one of the EMTs pulled her arms off of him and laid her gently back on the floor of the kitchen. Another EMT put an oxygen mask over her face.

"Breathe deeply, ma'am," he told her, looking her in the eye. "Just take a few deep breaths, okay? That's right."

A blood pressure cuff was on one arm and they were taking her vitals. Men were working all around her but Lucy's eyes were on Beau as if there was no one else in the room.

"He came here," she told him through the oxygen mask. "He came back. He tried to kill me. He hit me over the head with a pan and tried to suffocate me. He kept telling me that I was mean to him and that I need to let him show me... something. I don't even know. I kept telling him to leave and he wouldn't do it. He kept trying to knock me unconscious."

Beau listened to her breathy statement. He was usually a pretty cool character, even in the worst of times, but listening to Lucy tell him what had happened with Clyde had his blood boiling.

"I was afraid he'd do something stupid like that," he muttered, shaking his head. "He must have already been at the house when I called you."

"Why do you say that?"

"Because that was only a half-hour ago," he pointed out. He looked around the kitchen. "It looks like you gave him a hell of a fight, though."

Lucy was trying to think back to the struggle for her life. She was still groggy, but things were becoming clearer. "He kept trying to hit me with a pot," she said. "He'd already hit me once with it and caught me off guard. But he kept trying to smack me with it. I tried to get away from him but he jumped on top of me and tried to suffocate me. I thought I was a goner for sure but... but someone pulled him off of me or something. Some woman saved me. She said something to me but I don't even remember what it was."

Beau was looking up, at someone behind Lucy. "Some woman saved you, all right," he said quietly. "Ms. Ruby?"

Ruby Ransom suddenly appeared in Lucy's line of sight. Beau motioned for the EMTs to move away and they did, leaving a space for Ruby to kneel beside Lucy. The woman's expression was much different than it had been a couple of days before. There was great concern there... and great emotion.

"How are you feeling, honey?" she asked softly.

Lucy was stunned. "R... *Ruby*?" she finally said. "What on earth are you doing here?"

Ruby sighed softly, glancing at Beau hesitantly before she began speaking. "I came because I wanted to apologize," she said quietly. "I've spent the past two days thinking about what you said to me and… and something told me to come here today. It was as if God told me to get in my car and come over here, because early this morning I had such a need to see you, I can't even describe it. Something was pushing me over here, Miss Lucy. When I got here, I heard you screaming. I came in the back door and saw that man squirming on top of you, so I hit him over the head."

Lucy was staring at the woman. "You did *that?*" she asked, astonished. "Oh, my God… it was you?"

Ruby nodded, looking rather sickened by the whole thing. "I took the lamp out there in the corridor," she said. "It's that old brass lamp on the floor over there. I hit him with it as hard as I could, three times. That boy isn't going to walk away from what I did to him, but he was trying to kill you. I saw it."

Lucy could hardly believe what she was hearing. "Is he dead?" she asked, looking at Beau. "Did she kill him?"

Beau shook his head. "He's not dead," he said. "But I would be willing to believe he is seriously injured. He hasn't regained consciousness."

Lucy's attention moved back to Ruby. "You saved me," she said sincerely. "He was absolutely trying to kill me. If you hadn't come when you did, I probably wouldn't be talking to you right now. It doesn't seem like enough to say thank you, but thank you from the bottom of my heart."

Ruby averted her eyes, maybe modestly, maybe because the entire situation still freaked her out. She wasn't even sure. But she looked down the length of Lucy's body as the woman lay upon the floor before coming to rest on her left hand. After a moment, she picked it up and squeezed it.

"After you left my home, it occurred to me that I did the same thing to you that your daddy did to me," she said, her voice tight with emotion. "See, when I came to Glory five years ago, it was right after my mama had died. At least, she was the woman who raised me. She never told me I wasn't one of her own children, although I should have guessed because my brothers and sisters were all so much darker than I was. I'm very light skinned for an African American, but I never thought much about it until my mama told me the truth. She told me that I had been born at Glory and that my kinfolk still lived there. And that's when I came over to the house to see if I could talk to anyone. Well, your daddy chased me off and fast. He's a white man from an old family, so I naturally assumed it was because he was embarrassed over a black relation. But what you said to me two days ago... I haven't been able to get it out of my mind. You said that a man was killed because of me and that a white doctor risked his life for me."

Lucy squeezed the woman's hand. "Dr. Latling," she said softly. "The first Dr. Latling, I mean. If you want to know the whole story, I'll be happy to tell you."

Ruby nodded, looking at their two hands, bound together, holding each other. "I think I need to hear all of it," she said. "I want to understand where I've come from. Even at my age, that's important."

Lucy was looking at their hands, too, because Ruby was. "See the color of your skin against mine?" she asked. "It's the same color, Ruby. I don't see a difference. Do you?"

"Not really."

Lucy was still looking at their hands. "It reminds me of a poem that your father wrote for your mother. I have that poem, in fact. Your mother wanted you to have it. That poem talks about no blackness and no white. Maybe this is what he meant – our skin of the same color."

Ruby smiled, a sad smile, but it seemed to Lucy that it was one also filled with hope. "I'd like to think that," she said. "I'd like to hope that. But I grew up in rural Mississippi and I've seen prejudice. I've seen a lot of it. I suppose that's why I was so willing to believe that about your daddy."

Lucy shook her head, as much as she was able considering it was killing her to even move it.

"I can't pretend to say that I understand where you're coming from, because I don't," she said. "But I can promise you that I see that you have the same skin color as I do. And your mother was my Mamaw, who was a strong and amazing woman in her own right. If it took a hunch or a nudge from God to get you back over here, I'll take it. I'm just so glad you came."

Ruby just held her hand, squeezing it. When Lucy smiled at her, brightly, Ruby smiled back and giggled. It was a joyful moment and one that Lucy truly thought she'd never know. It might have taken a near-death experience for them to come to this point, but here they were, holding hands and smiling.

"Holy hell!"

Lucy heard the boom from the hallway, recognizing her dad's voice in an instant. Beau was already on his feet, moving through the deputies and the EMTs, meeting Bill and Mary just as they charged in through the back door, panic-stricken.

Beau went straight to Bill, grasping the man by the arm as he looked at all of the activity with a wild-eyed expression.

"Mr. Bondurant," Beau said calmly and steadily. "Lucy is going to be okay. I just want you to know that right off the bat. But there's been a little incident and that's why there are deputies and ambulances here."

Bill looked as if his eyes were about to pop out of his head. "Incident?" he repeated. "What in the hell is going on?"

Beau hated to tell the man the truth. "Clyde was released on bail this morning," he said. "It seems that he came back here to try to finish what he started with Lucy. Now, she's banged up a bit, but she's going to be fine. Luckily, Lucy had a guardian angel today."

Bill wanted to see his daughter. "What guardian angel?" he

demanded as he pushed past Beau and headed towards the kitchen. "And where in the hell is Clyde? I'm going to kill him!"

Beau was following, as was Mary. "Clyde is going to be in the hospital for a few days. He got it worse than Lucy did."

"Good!" Bill boomed. "That son-of-a-bitch better stay in that hospital because when I get finished with him, he's going to be a permanent resident!"

He was furious and terrified, entering the kitchen to see his daughter lying on the floor with EMTs around her. But there was also a woman kneeling next to her, thin and attractive, with close-cropped white hair. She was holding Lucy's hand. Bill came right up to his daughter but something about the woman caught his eye.

He found himself looking at the woman more than he was looking at his daughter. There was something familiar about her....

"Hello, there," the woman said. "Do you remember me?"

Bill was overcome with an odd sense of déjà vu. "I… I'm not sure," he said. "I think we've met."

"I'm Ruby Ransom."

Bill's eyes bugged for the second time in as many minutes. "Oh, my God…," he hissed. "*Now* I remember!"

Ruby nodded. "Yes," she said. "I was just coming to see ya'll this morning and came up to the house just as your daughter was in a bit of trouble."

"She saved me, Dad," Lucy said, tears in her eyes now that her mother and father were there. "If she hadn't whacked Clyde over the head, he would have killed me."

Bill turned ashen. As if his strength suddenly left him, he fell to his knees by his daughter's head, his gaze fixed on Ruby.

"Good Lord," he finally said, struggling to regain his composure. "I can hardly believe it. Ms. Ransom, I can't thank you enough for your help."

Ruby smiled, looking back at Lucy. "It was just a favor returned," she said. "Your daughter did me a favor a couple of days ago, so I owed her."

Bill wasn't following what Ruby meant since had no idea that Lucy had gone to see Ruby. He shook his head. "I don't understand."

The EMT was trying to put an I.V. line in Lucy's arm but she lifted it anyway, reaching for her father, who took her hand tightly.

"I went to tell her how sorry you were for chasing her away those years ago," she said. "I told her that you just didn't understand who she was."

Bill looked at Ruby, his eyes wide with sincerity. "No, I didn't. I had no idea who you really were. I'm so sorry I was rude, Ms. Ransom. I hope you'll forgive me."

Ruby nodded. "I know that now," she said. "I guess it was rather bold of me to just show up uninvited and expect ya'll to embrace me."

"Had I know who you really were, I would have. I'm just sorry my rush to judgement cost my mother a chance to meet you before she died. I am so, so sorry about that."

Ruby could see the remorse in his eyes. "Maybe it just wasn't meant to be," she said. "Maybe it just wasn't the right time. Who knows? I like to think God has a plan for everything and maybe right now, right here, is my plan. It was His plan for me to be here so that man couldn't hurt your daughter. He drove me over here as sure as He was behind the wheel of my car."

The EMT pulled Lucy's arm away from Bill so he could insert the line and Bill put a hand on Lucy's head. "I've never been one to believe in divine providence, but I have to admit, this did work out for a reason," he said. "I'm... I'm just really glad you're here. There's so much to talk about."

Lucy, lying on the ground looking up at Ruby and Bill, piped up. "Don't do anything before I come back from the hospital," she said. "I want to be part of this, too."

Bill and Ruby chuckled. Even Beau, standing back behind Bill with Mary, laughed softly. "You mean you're actually going to go to the hospital this time?" he asked.

Lucy made a face at him. "I hate hospitals," she said. "But I think, in this case, I really should go. I admit it."

When Lucy was finally loaded up into the ambulance, Beau took Bill, Mary, and Ruby with him in his police cruiser, following the ambulance to Pea Ridge Memorial Hospital and remaining with them the entire time as they waited for news of Lucy's injuries.

As he sat with Lucy's parents and her aunt in the waiting room, Beau couldn't help but think that hanging with the Bondurants and Hembrees was the most natural thing in the world to him. After all, the Meades and the Hembrees had always been intertwined one way or another, but in this case, there was no evil attached to it.

Time had passed and prejudices were passing. Beau thought of the poem Lewis had written to Victory, a poem that wished for a day when there would be no black and no white. A poem like that could have a thousand different meanings to a thousand different people, but at that moment, Beau could see the meaning translated into peace for two families who very badly needed it.

CHAPTER THIRTY-TWO
~ *Where My Heart Is Free* ~

Lucy had spent most of the day in the hospital getting checked out, finally coming home in the late afternoon. She had a concussion this time, her second good knock on the skull in just a few days, but there was no serious damage. The first thing she did upon returning home was to take Ruby up to Mamaw's bedroom to show her Mamaw's letter.

Nothing else in the world, at that moment, was as important as that, including her own battered state. Lucy wanted to make sure that Ruby knew how much she had been loved and the tragic circumstances surrounding her birth. That had been her promise to Mamaw. Therefore, this was the moment she'd been waiting for. With great anticipation, she handed Ruby the letter to read.

Ruby reacted the way everyone who had read Mamaw's letter had reacted – by the end of the note, she was in a flood of tears, only this time, the tears were different. She was reading about herself as an infant, her conception and birth, revealed in Mamaw's careful handwriting. Sitting on her mother's bed as she read it, surrounded by her newfound family, it was both traumatic and heartbreaking.

But it was also empowering.

Empowering in the sense that Laveau Hembree didn't triumph after all. The man who had breathed and bled evil hadn't been able to keep mother and daughter apart in the end. Love stronger than his hate had bridged that gap. Maybe it was a little too late, considering Victory's recent passing, but that didn't matter much.

Ruby was home where she belonged.

Lewis' poem seemed to affect Ruby even more. After reading it, she closed her eyes and held it against her chest as if clutching the man to her. Discovering the words of her father, in his own handwriting, had been a soul-transforming experience. She, too, saw the sensitive man trapped in a world of oppression, only allowed to free himself of that bond through his words.

It was the words of both parents that combined to tell the tragic story of a love that never died. Even though Lucy and Bill and Mary were in the room, no one said anything as Ruby digested everything. It wasn't their right to speak. This was Ruby's time, coming to grips with her biological parents' circumstances.

"I was raised in Cleveland," Ruby finally said, hoarsely. "I don't know the families around here, but I taught history at Delta State. I know a good deal about the cultures of this state and the history behind them. I'm not sure ya'll understand the impact of the relationship between Victory and Lewis. They were literally committing a crime, one of the worst possible crimes around here. Not only would Laveau Hembree have considered his daughter's relationship a horribly shameful thing, but she was quite literally a criminal in falling in love with a black man."

Lucy watched the woman as she looked over the poem again. "I've never experienced racism so I'm not even going to pretend I know how you feel," she said, "but the mere fact that Victory was kept from the man she loved… I *do* understand that. I understand it all too well."

She was thinking of the husband who had left her, the man whose absence in her heart had seen miraculous healing over the past several days. She realized that the event of Beau Meade had healed a lot of things.

"I think we can all understand what it's like to be kept apart from those we love," Ruby agreed. "But this… there was so much more to it. And to think I never knew about this… I'm just overcome, really. Lucy, I'm so glad you came to my house and said what you said to me. You can't even know how much richer you've made my life, just by coming here and knowing my roots. It means so much to me."

Lucy smiled faintly. She pointed to the open bedroom door, to the room across the hall. "That was Mamaw's bedroom as a child," she said. "I'm guessing that's the room you were born in."

Ruby turned to look at the room across the hall. She sighed. "It seems so peaceful now, doesn't it?" she asked. "To think of the horror that room has seen."

Lucy shuddered. "I can't even imagine," she said softly. "Honestly, I try not to think about it. But something good did happen in it if you were born there."

Ruby smiled at her as she stood up from the bed and made her way over to the windows that overlooked the front yard. A garden that was run down from neglect, much of it dying just as the house was. She imagined the family that had owned it, the proud Hembree family, now reduced to the memory of a single man and the evil he perpetrated. With a sigh, she turned away from the yard.

"I believe the memory of Laveau Hembree with fade in time," she said quietly. "This house won't be sad and desolate forever. New blood will come into it, filling it with better memories. The evils of the past will fade."

"Do you really think so?" Lucy asked.

"I do. People won't remember the killing of a young black man as the legacy of this house, but it's too bad we don't know what really happened to Aldridge. His is a memory I'd like to honor as a tribute to other young men of color who met their end unfairly."

Mary, who had been sitting on the other side of Mamaw's bed, spoke softly. "I wonder what happened to him?" she asked. "What would they have done with him once he was dead?"

Lucy lifted her eyebrows, as if she was about to say something unpleasant. "I hate to say it, but maybe he was buried here," she said. "I had lunch with Beau's grandmother, Lovie, and she told me that there was a rumor that there are bodies buried all over the place around here. She said Laveau buried the men he killed on his property so no one would dig them up. Then I asked Aunt Dell about it and she said the same thing. In fact, she even suggested that Mamaw's baby was buried here, but of course, we know now that it's not true. Still, she said that Dad should till up the entire yard to see who's buried around here."

Bill and Mary instinctively turned to look at the grass outside, Bill going so far as to rise from his chair and go stand by the window. He looked out over the expanse of green.

"That really wouldn't surprise me," he said, disgust in his tone. Then, he turned to Ruby. "You have to understand what a horrible man Laveau Hembree was. I don't know if you've heard anything about him other than what's in my mother's letter, but he was a mean son-of-a-bitch."

Ruby was still holding on to Lewis' poem, glancing over her shoulder to the yard again. "I've heard enough," she said. "Maybe someday I'll know more about him, but right now, I think what I've been told is enough. He was the man who changed the course of my life."

That was quite true and Bill nodded his head to acknowledge that. "I think he changed the course of a lot of people's lives and not for the better," he said. "But we can talk about him another time. I don't want to bring that evil into this room right now."

It was an understandable statement. For the first time in many decades, the house didn't have that dark feeling. It was difficult to describe but, somehow, it seemed that some of the sins of the past had been righted over the past few days. The darkness was being pushed out by the light. Laveau didn't have a grip over the house or the family as he'd had all of these years.

When Ruby entered the house, the tides seemed to change.

"Oh, my God," Lucy suddenly exclaimed. "With all of this talk about Mamaw's letter and Lewis' poem, I'd almost forgotten the most important piece of all."

She quickly went to the chifforobe and opened the top drawer, pulling out the wooden box that she'd put back after her visit to Ruby a couple of days ago. She had put the box in there thinking it would never go to the rightful person. But now she was excited about it, excited to see that lovely locket finally where it belonged. She opened the lid as she went over to Ruby, extending the small box to the woman.

"This is the locket Mamaw wanted you to have," she said. "It's the one she mentioned in her letter, the one that Lewis saved his money for."

Ruby stared at the jewelry, her eyes moist, before gently pulling it from the box. Carefully, she turned it over in her hands, reading the inscription on the back.

"In The Dreaming Hour," she murmured. "Lord… look how beautiful it is."

Lucy lifted her hands, silently offering to help her put it on, and Ruby handed her the necklace and turned around so Lucy could lay it on her neck and close the clasp. Ruby kept fingering it before going to look at her reflection in the mirror of the old chifforobe. There was magic in that moment.

"How many times did Victory look at herself in this mirror, looking at the same necklace I now wear?" she asked wistfully. "A young girl, full of hopes and dreams and love, standing here looking at her reflection."

Lucy felt a lump in her throat as she watched Ruby admire the necklace. "You look a lot like her," she said. "Everyone says I do, but I can really see her features in your face. I wish so much that she was here to see this. It would have made her so happy."

Ruby looked at her. "But she *is* here," she said. "Can't you feel her? This is the first time I can recall being in this house, but I was born here... somehow, it's part of me. I know that sounds odd, but that's the way I feel. And I can tell you that Victory is all over this house. I've never even met her, but I know her. I know that I feel her right now."

Lucy's eyes filled with tears and she went to take a tissue from the bedside. As she wiped at her eyes, Bill walked up behind Ruby, seeing his reflection over her shoulder.

"Look at us," he said, smiling when she made eye contact with him. "I think Mama would be very proud to see us together like this. I never had any siblings, so this is pretty special to me."

Ruby turned to look at him. "I hope so," she said sincerely. "I know we had a rough start, Bill, but I don't even think of that anymore. I hope that you and Mary and I can get to know each other well. I want to hear about this side of my family that I never knew about. But you know what else I'd like?"

"What?"

"I'd like to see where Lewis Ragsdale lived. Now that I've discovered Victory, I very much want to discover Lewis, too. There's something in me that just needs to know about him, this man who wrote such beautiful poetry."

Lucy was wiping at her nose. "I haven't had time to go look for him or his family," she said. "I was really only concerned with finding you. Mamaw mentioned a town called Rose Cove in her letter and from the way it sounded, I think that Lewis might have lived there."

Ruby nodded. "Yes, she did mention the coloreds from Rose Cove," she said. "There were a lot of shanty towns back in that era and that was probably one of them because I've never heard of an established town called Rose Cove."

Bill stepped away from the windows. "I've never heard of it, either," he said. "Lucy, maybe Beau knows of it. Isn't he coming back here tonight?"

Lucy could hear the hope in her father's voice, but not about Lewis. It was about Beau. *Please say this wonderful man is coming back and that you'll marry him someday!* She had to chuckle inwardly because she was sure that was exactly what her father and mother were thinking. In spite of everything that had happened that day, they still were concerned for their daughter's romantic life.

"He said he was," she said. "He had to go back to the station after he dropped us home to take care of some paperwork. Look, the man has hardly worked at all since I came to town. He's been driving me all over the place in the hunt for great family mysteries, so he should probably put some time in at his job."

Bill grinned at her. "I was just asking. No need to get defensive."

Lucy rolled her eyes. "He's a very nice man, I will admit. He's pretty great, in fact."

Mary was thrilled. "He seems to like you, too."

"How do you know that?" Lucy asked.

It was Ruby who answered. "You didn't see the way he looked at you earlier today like I did. After I knocked that man off of you and called the police, he was one of the first ones to come. You should have seen the way he looked at you when he came in the door. He likes you a great deal, honey."

Lucy turned away, blushing, as her parents laughed at her. Ruby, sensing that this budding romance was meeting with parental approval, put her hands on Lucy's shoulders.

"Leave it to me," she insisted. "I made sure that all of my nieces and nephews got married and I'll make sure you do, too. I won't let him get away from you, honey. Trust me."

Lucy laughed softly, unwilling to elaborate on anything. She didn't want her nosy parents and her newly-found aunt to know what she was feeling, or to know what really happened between her and Beau, so she simply grinned.

"I appreciate your concern, but I'm not ready to talk about my love life right now," she said. "So let's go back to the subject of Lewis Ragsdale. I'm more comfortable talking about him."

Everyone was grinning. "We've still got some leftovers downstairs," Mary said. "Why don't we talk about it over some supper?"

Lucy was very happy to have the distraction of food but she waved everyone on ahead of her so she could at least change out of the clothes she was wearing. Other than a jacket her parents had brought her at the hospital, she was still wearing the yoga pants and tank top that Clyde had touched. She needed to get them off.

As Bill and Mary and Ruby headed down to the kitchen to eat, Lucy quickly changed into something more appropriate to have dinner in. She was just brushing her hair into a ponytail when she heard a car pull up the driveway. Peering from the bathroom window, she caught a glimpse of a black Ford Explorer.

Grinning, she felt giddy, like she was a teenager waiting for her date to show up. She'd gotten used to Beau coming around. She was actually coming to expect it now, knowing that if he never came back again, she would have been horribly disappointed. But he seemed to be just as interested in her as she was in him, so that was a good thing. She was happy for a good thing or two in her life these days.

As she headed down the back stairs towards the kitchen, she could already hear Beau inside the house. She could hear her father talking to him, offering him some of the taco pie casserole, which made Lucy shudder just to think about it. Last time she was interested in that casserole, something terrible happened, so she was pretty certain she didn't have an appetite for it.

She entered the kitchen in time to see her mother hand Beau a plate of something steaming. Beau took the plate but his focus was on Lucy.

"Well," he said, looking her over in a way that made her heart leap. "You look better than you did the last time I saw you."

She batted her eyes at him obviously. "You sweet talker."

"I guess that did sound kind of bad," he said, chuckling. "How do you feel?"

"Okay," she said, meandering over to him. "My head hurts, but the doctor said it will for a couple of days. And it's sore to the touch where he hit me."

Beau's gaze was appreciative on her. "You really don't look bad. I didn't mean what I said."

"I know." She smiled, catching movement out of her the corner of her eye and noticing that her mother was handing her a plate of something, too. She took it gratefully. "So what's going on with Clyde? Is he still in the hospital?"

"The prisoner is still there," Beau said, reverting to a more formal manner. "Ms. Ruby did a number on him. She fractured his skull, so he's going to be there for a long while. When he gets out, he's facing a lot of serious charges."

Lucy's smile faded. "Good," she said, gingerly touching the back of her head. "Attempted murder ought to put him in jail for several years."

"Most definitely. His days of terrorizing women are over."

"You make sure you keep us posted about him," Bill said. "I want to keep tabs on that boy."

"Don't worry, I will," Beau said. "Lucy will have to testify at his trial, as will Ms. Ruby, so you'll definitely be in the loop about him."

"You sure I can't have five minutes alone with him in his hospital room?"

Beau grinned at the still-enraged father. "If you do, you'll have to get in line behind me and a few others who'd like to get their hands on him."

"I don't doubt that in the least."

A silence settled in the kitchen, but it wasn't uncomfortable. Mary was hustling around making sure everyone had something to eat, as Lucy spoke again.

"We've been talking about a place called Rose Cove," she said to Beau. "I don't know if you remember, but Mamaw mentioned it in her letter."

Beau spooned some cooled taco pie into his mouth. "I remember. What about it?"

"Have you ever heard of it?"

He looked thoughtful and Ruby spoke up. "We think it's a shanty town. There were a lot of those work camps back in Lewis' time and shanty towns sprang up around them. We think Lewis lived in Rose Cove."

He swallowed the bite in his mouth. "I think it's around here. I seemed to remember when I was a kid, my dad helped put down some sort of riot or protest or something in a local shanty town and I think the name was Rose Cove. That had to be back in the nineteen seventies. I was pretty young, but I remember my mother being scared for him. There was a series of riots there and it became a hotbed of crime, so I think the cops went in and dismantled it."

Lucy was interested. "Where is it? Do you remember?"

He put more food in his mouth, chewing as he thought. "As I recall, it's over on the west side of Martin Luther King Boulevard. That whole area over there was the poor side of town for a lot of years. In fact… hold on a minute…."

He pulled out his phone and started messing with it, clearly looking for something on the internet. Lucy looked over his shoulder curiously, seeing that he was looking at the maps feature. After a moment, he began to nod his head.

"I thought that name sounded familiar," he said. "There's street over in that area called Rose Cove. I'm guessing that's in the general vicinity of the shanty town the Ragsdales lived in."

"How far away is it?" Lucy asked.

"Not far. Maybe a couple of miles, as the crow flies."

Lucy looked at Ruby. "It's still light outside. Do you want to go for a drive over there?"

Ruby had a cup of coffee in her hand. "Yes, I do. I'd love to get a look at the area."

"It's not a very good area," Beau warned.

Lucy looked at him. "We'd be safe with a police escort."

"How did I know that was coming?"

Bill shook his head as he set his coffee cup down. He put a hand on Beau's shoulder. "You stepped into that one. You'll learn."

Beau wriggled his eyebrows. "I'm going to have to if I'm going to hang around with her much longer."

Mary started to open her mouth but Bill put a stop to it with a hand gesture. He just knew that look on his wife's face, that eager "my daughter is single" expression. So Mary reluctantly shut her mouth as Beau and Lucy continued that easy, funny repartee they seemed to have, something they'd had since the beginning. Now, others were starting to see it.

It did Bill and Mary's heart good. In fact, this trip to Mississippi, which had taken place under the most sorrowful of circumstances, was starting to become a positive experience. With new family members discovered and old secrets well on the way to healing for the most part, the icing on the cake would be if Lucy could come away with a renewed sense of hope and a healing heart.

Maybe this trip would have a silver lining, after all.

✧ ✧ ✧

ROSE COVE WAS still a shanty town.

That's what Lucy thought as they drove through the residential streets with poor to moderate housing. The houses were spaced fairly far apart and everybody had very big yards, most of them fenced, keeping in a variety of dogs and livestock.

The population was African American, concentrated in the northwestern part of Pea Ridge. The poverty was pretty shocking in some instances, with homes that had plywood doors or no glass for windows, people sitting out on their leaning porches in plastic lawn chairs.

Even so, there was still joy in the children of the neighborhood, riding their bikes or chasing each other around in their yards as the sun set behind a cloudy sky. Dogs barked, joining in the fun.

Beau was driving fairly slowly through the neighborhoods, getting a lot of attention as the police car rolled down the streets. From King Drive they headed on to Kennedy Street, and from there on to Garden Lane. He was looking at everything as a trained observer, a law enforcement official, while everyone else in the car was simply looking at the area curiously. But Ruby, sitting in the back seat behind Lucy, was looking at it a bit more clinically.

"Thirty-four percent of children in Mississippi live in poverty," Ruby said, watching a group of children play on an old slide in someone's front yard. "This isn't even the worst of it here, what you see. The children in the rural areas suffer the most."

Lucy was watching the kids play. "They seem so happy. Maybe they don't even know they're living in poverty, you know? To them, maybe this is just life and they make the best of it."

"I think we could all learn lessons from them."

The car turned onto Sunflower Drive. It wasn't a pretty street like the name suggested. It was dirty and run down, with older houses dotting the lots. A couple of the houses were particularly old, maybe even built before the Great Depression, looking sad and sagging. In fact, everything about the area was sad and sagging.

Suddenly, Beau came to a halt.

"Look at that street sign," he said.

Everyone looked to where he was pointing. *Rose Cove* was plain to see, the white letters against the dark green. Just for the hell of it, Beau turned down Rose Cove Street. There were only three houses on it and it was a dead end with the river beyond the edge of the cul-de-sac. Beau came to a halt, unable to drive any further, and parked the car by a large empty lot. Since it was sunset, they could see fireflies rising out of the moist earth.

Lucy opened the door and walked out onto the grass as the dots of light began to float about in the dusk. Ruby opened her door and followed, leaving Beau and Bill and Mary in the car.

"Should I go get them?" Bill asked.

Beau removed his sunglasses; he didn't need them any longer. His gaze was on Lucy as she grabbed at a few fireflies.

"No," he said. "I can keep an eye on them from here."

Several feet away on the grass, Lucy was catching the fireflies and letting them go. Ruby was standing next to her, looking at the green, muddy river in the distance.

"The Yalobusha has been that ugly color since I can remember," Ruby said. "It turns into the Yazoo River down where I live. Ugly, ugly river."

Lucy wandered off, chasing another firefly. "Where I come from in California, it's bone-dry all of the time. Wet grass like this and rivers like this, don't exist."

Ruby took her attention from the river to watch Lucy grasp a handful of fireflies midair. But beyond Lucy, she noticed a very old house with a leaning front porch. It looked as if it had been there forever. She could also see an old man sitting there, nearly hidden by the dim light, a pipe lit up because she could see the flare of the tobacco now and again.

Curious, she made her way towards the house, walking past Lucy as she went. Lucy saw the woman brush by her.

"Where are you going?" Lucy asked.

"That man on the porch up there," she said. "I'm going to ask him if he knows who the Ragsdales are. He looks old enough that he might just know something."

Lucy followed, still with the fireflies in her hand. Ruby made her way through the grass, coming onto a dirt driveway as she headed towards the sagging porch. She didn't see anyone else around as she lifted her hand to the old African American gentleman, sitting alone.

"Hello," she said. "May I ask you a question, sir? I'm looking for a family that may have lived around here a long time ago. Have you lived here your whole life?"

The old man was puffing on his pipe. He was evidently hard of hearing because he stood up and shuffled his way to the end of the porch, leaning against the wobbly banister.

"What's that?" he asked.

"I'm looking for a family that may have lived around here," Ruby repeated, loudly. She came closer. "Have you lived around here your whole life?"

"Yes, ma'am. My whole life."

"Then maybe you know the family. The name was Ragsdale."

At that point, Lucy came up behind Ruby, getting a good look at the elderly gentleman. Before he could reply to Ruby's question, Lucy spoke.

"Wait a minute," she said, peering at the elderly man curiously. "I think I've seen you before."

The tall, rail-thin man came off of the stairs. He walked somewhat unsteadily, his pipe in his hand. He was looking more at Lucy than at Ruby.

"Yes, ma'am, you have. I saw you in town," he said.

Lucy knew she recognized him but couldn't quite place him. Familiar but not familiar. Suddenly, it occurred to her. "You're the gentleman I saw outside of the funeral home the day we buried my grandmother. Now I remember – you were standing outside of the funeral home."

"Yes, ma'am."

Lucy grinned, looking at Ruby. "Small world," she told her. "He happened to be there just as the hearse was pulling out."

"Not happened, ma'am," he said.

Both Lucy and Ruby looked at him. "I'm sorry?" Lucy said, not understanding. "Not happened...?"

He took a step towards the woman. "I didn't *happen* to be

there, ma'am," he said. "It's where I needed to be."

Lucy eyed him a moment because those words sounded very familiar to her. She remembered asking him, at the time, if he was lost and she seemed to remember those very words from him.

"That's what you told me before," she said. "You told me that you were just where you needed to be."

"Yes, ma'am."

"At the funeral of Victory Bondurant?"

The man's yellowed eyes lingered on her for a moment before turning to Ruby. "You're looking for the Ragsdales, ma'am?"

He didn't seem inclined to answer Lucy's question, so Ruby replied to him. "I am. Do you know the family?"

"I *am* the family, ma'am."

That drew a reaction from both Lucy and Ruby. "You are?" Lucy gasped. "Oh, my God… that's amazing! Why didn't you tell me that when we met?"

"Because it didn't matter, ma'am. I'm nobody to you."

"That's not true," Ruby insisted. "My name is Ruby Ransom, by the way. I don't mean to be nosy, but are you related to a man named Lewis Ragsdale?"

The old man bobbed his head. "Yes, ma'am."

Ruby was starting to show her excitement. "I'm so glad to hear that. You see, I'm trying to find out something about him. How are you related to him?"

The old man's eyes glimmered, just a bit. "My name is Lewis."

Lucy was unable to contain her shock. "*You're* Lewis Ragsdale?"

"Yes, ma'am."

Lucy and Ruby looked at each other, their astonishment wide open. A thousand silent words of surprise and curiosity flew between them, each one of them thinking essentially the same thing –

A son!

A nephew!

"The Lewis Ragsdale we're looking for was born sometime in the early part of the last century," Lucy said. "He would have been maybe eighteen years old around nineteen hundred and thirty-three. Maybe he was a little older; I really don't know. Are you his son?"

The old man put his pipe in his mouth and gave it a puff. "I was born in nineteen hundred and fourteen," he said. "I *am* Lewis Ragsdale."

"No!"

"Yes, ma'am."

Lucy's hands flew to her mouth in shock. "Lewis... oh, my God... *the* Lewis Ragsdale?"

"Yes, ma'am."

"Your brother was Aldridge?"

That caused him to falter. "How do you know about my brother?"

There was suspicion there. Considering what had happened to Aldridge those years ago, Lucy didn't blame him in the least. Not wanting him to run them off the property, the only thing she could think of at that moment was the locket around Ruby's neck, the one Lewis had given Victory so long ago. It was hidden by Ruby's blouse and Lucy had her pull it out and hold it up in the fading sunlight, hoping the old man could see what it was.

"Do you see this?" Lucy whispered, pointing to the locket. "You gave this locket to my grandmother. Her name was Victory Hembree. There are words inscribed on the back. Do you remember giving this to her?"

His old, yellowed eyes stared at it and, after a moment, a faint smile crept across his ancient lips. His suspicion faded. Reaching out, he fingered the locket, looking at it as if every lovely memory he'd ever had was filling his mind at that very moment. He turned it over and saw some kind of etching, but his eyesight was too poor to make it out. Still, he knew the words there.

He'd put them there, eighty-four years ago.

"In The Dreaming Hour," he murmured. "Yes, ma'am, I remember putting those words there. You said Ms. Victory is your grandma?"

Lucy nodded, hardly believing that the man before her was the man that Mamaw had fallen in love with over eighty years ago. *Lewis Ragsdale, in the flesh*. Truthfully, she might not have believed it except for the fact that he'd known the words on the locket immediately. No hesitation at all. After a moment, she put her arm around Ruby's shoulders.

"Yes, she was my grandmother," she said, her voice so tight with emotion she could hardly speak. "And this is my Aunt Ruby – my grandmother gave birth to her in nineteen hundred and thirty-three. Ruby's biological father was a man named Lewis Ragsdale – *you*."

He stopped fingering the locket. Then, he looked at Ruby closely, maybe too closely because his eyesight was bad, but after a moment, he drew back and the yellow eyes were glistening with unshed tears. His mouth worked as if there was a great deal he wanted to say, but he couldn't seem to make the words come forth. All of that movement and no sound. Finally, he seemed to find his tongue.

"You have her eyes."

It was a simple statement, but one of great truth. The moment was as powerful and poignant as it could possibly be.

"Yes, I think I do," Ruby said, her eyes filling with tears. Then, she broke down. "I… I can't believe it's really you. We didn't expect to find you. We'd only hoped to find people who knew of you or, hopefully, even family members. I can't believe we really found *you*!"

Lewis sniffled, pulling an old handkerchief out of his pocked and wiping at his nose. "I've been here all the time," he said. "I never left."

The impact from those words was undeniable. *I never left.* So he'd been here all of this time? Lucy had so many questions she could hardly single out one. Living history was in front of her and she was overwhelmed. All she could think to say was the first thing that came to mind – answering his question about his brother.

"We know what happened to Aldridge," she said. "We know that Laveau Hembree killed him, thinking he was the father of Victory's baby. I also know that Mamaw loved you so much that she went to her grave loving you. She left a note when she died, telling the tale of Ruby's birth and she mentioned you by name. And that poem you wrote her – In the Dreaming Hour – she kept that all of these years, too. We've all read it. It's the most beautiful poem I've ever read."

Lewis had his head down, overwhelmed with this shocking encounter just as Lucy and Ruby were.

"That was all a very long time ago, ma'am. A very long time."

"Maybe so, but you never forgot about her," Lucy said gently. "You came to the funeral to pay your respects to her. Why didn't you just come in? You know she would have wanted you there. Lewis, do you have any idea what finding you means to our family? Never in my wildest dreams did I imagine we'd find you alive."

Lewis was wiping at his eyes. "My ma'ama lived until she was a hundred and six and so did my pappy. People in my family live a very long time, but I've lived too long. As for going to Victory's funeral… like I said, I was where I needed to be. I needed to see her off."

Lucy could sense great sorrow in that statement. "I'm sure she knew you were there," she said. "I'm glad you came. But what about your own children and grandchildren? You must have your own family around, right?"

He shook his head. "I never married."

That statement was like a dagger through Lucy's heart, a bittersweet realization that was painful to hear. "Why not?"

Lewis didn't look at her. "I gave my heart once. It wasn't mine to give again."

It sounded like his poetry. That little statement proved to her almost more than the identification of the locket that this polite old man was, indeed, Lewis Ragsdale. His deep voice, his distinct way of speaking... she could imagine him reading poetry to Mamaw those years ago, mesmerizing her with that voice. The whole story of Victory and Lewis' relationship came back to her in a rush and she could see it with blinding clarity – an isolated white girl and a gentle black man.

It was a love story for the ages.

But as Lucy stood there, something else occurred to her – she was intruding on an incredibly private moment between Ruby and the man who fathered her. Other than the fact that Victory was her grandmother, she really had no business being there.

Now, this moment was between Ruby and Lewis, two elderly people who, in the twilight of life, happened to find each other. It was the most unbelievable thing Lucy had ever witnessed much less heard of. Looking at the two of them, she knew she had to leave them alone together. The two people Victory loved most in the world.

The very people she'd risked her life for.

So Lucy stepped away, heading back to the police cruiser just as the mercury vapor streetlights started to come on. Night was falling, gentle and still. As she neared the cruiser, the door opened and Beau stepped out.

"Who is that man?" he asked. "Does Ruby know him?"

Lucy looked up at him, a man she'd known only a few days but a man, she decided, she was going to know very well for the rest of her life. Already, it seemed as if they'd lived a few lifetimes together, considering what all they'd been through. She came around the side of the car to where he was standing and looped her arm through his, her hand sliding easily into his palm. It was a sweet touch yet a powerful one. She squeezed his hand tightly.

"You could say that," she said. "You're not going to believe who that is."

"Who?"

"Lewis Ragsdale."

Beau's eyes widened. "What?" he said, astonished. "Who is he? A son of Lewis'?"

Lucy shook her head. "No," she said. "*The* Lewis Ragsdale. He was born in nineteen hundred and fourteen. That's the man Mamaw went to her grave loving."

Bill and Mary, still inside the car, had heard her. Bill threw open the rear passenger door, utter astonishment on his face as he stumbled out. "That's *him*?" he asked. "Oh, God... are you serious?"

Lucy turned to look at Ruby and Lewis, illuminated only by the distant street lights. "That's really him," she said. "I can hardly believe it even as I say it, but it is."

Bill leaned against the car, looking at the pair and not oblivious to the fact that they were holding hands. "Lewis was here all this time?" He shook his head in wonder. "He never reached out to her? Never tried to see her? I don't understand... he's been living two miles away from her the *whole time*?"

That fact baffled Lucy, too, but she figured maybe that was too personal a question to ask the old man. He had his reasons, she was sure, and given that his life had been threatened by his love for a white woman, maybe he just felt it was better to leave well enough alone. For both their sakes, it was a necessity.

"Maybe we're not meant to know that," she said. "I'm sure he had his reasons. Maybe it's all part of the old prejudices down here, the ones we keep hoping will fade away. He's still entrenched in them; he and everyone else of that generation. Dad... do you remember at Mamaw's funeral when Pop stood up next to her casket and said 'I hope you find him'?"

Bill nodded at the memory. "I do."

"I think I know what he meant."

Bill suddenly looked to Ruby and Lewis in the distance. "I think I do, too."

Lucy smiled at her father, and then at Beau, before returning her gaze to Ruby and Lewis as the pair began to head in their direction. Ruby had her arm looped in Lewis', a gesture that was deeply poignant. Father and daughter, together the way it was always meant to be. Together, the way Victory would have wanted.

Lucy's heart was so full at the moment that she could hardly describe it, but she knew it had to do with life coming full circle. Finally, everything had come full circle and hope was on the horizon again. Laying her cheek on Beau's big bicep, all she could see was a bright future.

The Dreaming Hour had come for them all.

The End

About Kathryn Le Veque
Medieval Just Got Real.

KATHRYN LE VEQUE is a USA TODAY Bestselling author, an Amazon All-Star author, and a #1 bestselling, award-winning, multi-published author in Medieval Historical Romance and Historical Fiction. She has been featured in the NEW YORK TIMES and on USA TODAY's HEA blog. In March 2015, Kathryn was the featured cover story for the March issue of InD'Tale Magazine, the premier Indie author magazine. She was also a quadruple nominee (a record!) for the prestigious RONE awards for 2015.

Kathryn's Medieval Romance novels have been called 'detailed', 'highly romantic', and 'character-rich'. She crafts great adventures of love, battles, passion, and romance in the High Middle Ages. More than that, she writes for both women AND men – an unusual crossover for a romance author – and Kathryn has many male readers who enjoy her stories because of the male perspective, the action, and the adventure.

On October 29, 2015, Amazon launched Kathryn's Kindle Worlds Fan Fiction site WORLD OF DE WOLFE PACK. Please visit Kindle Worlds for Kathryn Le Veque's World of de Wolfe Pack and find many action-packed adventures written by some of the top authors in their genre using Kathryn's characters from the de Wolfe Pack series. As Kindle World's FIRST Historical Romance fan fiction world, Kathryn Le Veque's World of de Wolfe Pack will contain all of the great story-telling you have come to expect.

Kathryn loves to hear from her readers. Please find Kathryn on Facebook at Kathryn Le Veque, Author, or join her on Twitter @kathrynleveque, and don't forget to visit her website at www.kathrynleveque.com.

Made in the USA
Middletown, DE
10 September 2017